Taking Shots

Toni Aleo

ISBN 978-1-105-11487-8

For my hockey player.

Because he makes me feel like the most beautiful woman in the world.

Michael

Eleanor, "Elli," Fisher didn't understand why she was so forgetful. She was convinced that if her ass wasn't attached to her, she would forget that too, but really? How in the world did she forget all the bulbs for her light stands! Elli stood in the entrance of the Luther Arena, waiting for Harper Allen, her assistant, to bring the bulbs back from her studio on the western side of Nashville, TN. This was one of the most important days of her career and she forgot the bulbs.

God, she was an idiot.

How did she manage this? She ran her hand through her unruly brown curly hair, sighing. She was having a bad hair day to top things off. As if forgetting the bulbs weren't enough. This was her first year with the Nashville Assassins, she couldn't blow it. Being chosen to be the photographer for a hockey team was huge, but when it was for the team that just won the Stanley Cup and had the prospect of winning again? Hello, it was HUGE.

When she saw Harper running into the arena with the bulbs in hand, she let out a breath. Damn that was fast.

"For Christ sakes! It's a mad house out there!" She complained in her thick southern accent, her hair was in spikes this week, and purple to top it off. Didn't she discuss with Harper how they needed to keep a professional image? Yes, purple was a team color, but still!

"I know, come on let's go put the bulbs in." She didn't have time to have it out with Harper right now; she had to get to the ice. They all but ran towards the entrance to the ice, once there, she was greeted by the Assassins' PR.

"Ms. Fisher, how do you do! Are you ready?"

Melody Yates was intense, that was the only way Elli could explain her. She was from Jersey, converted into a southerner, which made no damn sense to her, but whatever, this was her boss, so she grinned extra hard, turning on her southern charm.

"Yes ma'am, let my assistant put these bulbs in and we can get started."

"Good, the boys will be out soon, then we'll go downstairs for the other shots we need."

"Yes ma'am."

Harper ran ahead and started setting everything up. Elli took in a deep breath, she had been doing weddings almost her whole adult life, and now she was moving to sports, something she has been wanting to do all along since she had such a love for hockey but never could get the opportunity, but thanks to being related to the new owner of the Assassins, here she was.

Here was her chance.

Harper handed Elli her camera, with a big smile. Harper knew how important this day was, and also how nervous Elli was.

"Go on over there, and let me test shoot, Harp." Harper started towards the goal, and turned with a stick in her hand, making a stern face. It brought a smile to Elli's face, Harper was a dork, but God, Elli loved her. After fixing the aperture on her camera, she called Harper over as the guys started coming on the ice.

"Good golly Miss. Molly, look at them! Good Lord! They are gorgeous!" Harper whispered as all the guys came out, and sat on the bench. Elli took her time looking the guys over too. They were gorgeous but she already knew that since she never missed a home game. Sometimes she thought it was the uniforms; bright purple and black, with a masked man on the front as the emblem that brought out their good looks, but nope, even with the helmets off these men were just plain gorgeous.

Getting back in the zone, she called for the coaches first. Trying to bottle her nerves, she got started. After shooting the coaches, it was on to the team. Each guy came out in front of the goal, taking their pose. Elli zoomed in, taking shots of their heads, then they held a stick, after taking that picture, they lined up for a action shot, which consisted of them skating towards her, shooting a puck. During all this, Harper gave commentary.

"For the love of God, El, that dude is hot!" Elli rolled her eyes, taking the shots she needed.

"Hush, Harp."

"No really, like please can I hit on one of them, just one?"

"No."

"You're no fun."

Elli laughed it off; she was starting to get comfortable just as the alternate captains and the captain came off the bench.

"Oh, the hell with what you say, number two is mine after this." Elli gave her a pointed look as Jakob Titov, the Assassins leading scoring forward, skated in front of the goal. Jakob was extremely good looking, hard lines to his face, bright green eyes, and blonde hair; he was a looker but not Elli's type. He reminded her too much of Justin, her ex.

"Hush, Harper!" Elli said as she took the shots she needed, what she didn't need was Jakob making eyes at her assistant, because of course Harper returned them. She didn't know why it always bothered her so much that Harper always flirted with the clients, it didn't matter how old they were or what they looked like, or even if they were the groom, she always found something in them she liked; probably the fact that they all had a penis.

Elli loved Harper, but she was a little promiscuous, and she didn't care who knew. Guys had no worth to her unless they were naked and inside her, as she always says. Elli always wondered what made Harper that way since it made no sense. There had never been a guy that hurt her or anything in the twenty two years they had been friends, her parents were good people, so Elli really didn't understand where it came from. And of course guys liked her; she was wild, beautiful, skinny, amazing.

Everything Elli wasn't.

Jakob lined up, giving her his action shot, after she got it, instead of him skating towards his teammates, he came towards them.

"Nice hair, beautiful," he said in his thick Russian accent, Harper just smiled widely, as Elli flushed deep red. She didn't know why she was embarrassed but she was. She didn't want attention on Harper right now, not with how important this job was.

"Nice stick," Harper said, looking down at where he was holding his stick. Jakob gave her a devilish smile, and skated towards the bench.

"You are impossible Harper Allen," Elli said, flustered. After getting it together, next came Alex Welch, Alex was easy to shoot, he had good lines, so the pictures came out fabulous. Next was the captain, Shea Adler.

Elli blushed as she got to the close up of Shea; she had always thought the defenseman was gorgeous. With his almost black hair that fell in the brightest, bluest eyes she had ever seen, and with his crooked nose, that had been broken two years ago during a game with the Red Wings, she had to admit, she had a little bit of a crush on him. He smiled and her heart melted. Yeah, his teeth were probably fake, but damn he had a pretty mouth.

"Why's he blinking so much?" Harper asked. Elli was too busy looking at his mouth to notice.

"Harp, shut up," she whispered, but then she noticed too that the captain was blinking a little too much.

"Is he hitting on you?"

"Oh my God!" Elli's whole face blushed deep red as she looked down at the picture viewer of her camera. In all the pictures, the captain's eyes were shut. Elli looked up, and Shea was rubbing his eyes. "Mr. Adler," she said as she started walking towards him, he looked over at her. "I'm sorry, but I need you to stop blinking, your eyes are closed in every picture I have taken."

"I'm sorry." Oh God, his voice was butter. Thick with a Boston accent, Elli swore she came at the sound of it. "I got new contacts, and they are bugging the hell out of me."

"Someone get Adler another pair!" Someone yelled as he pinched the little lenses out of his eyes, throwing them down on the ice.

"We can do this without them right?" Elli just nodded, gosh, he was gorgeous as he tried to make eye contact with her, and it was obvious it was hard for him to see. "I won't be able to see your beautiful face for a little bit, but I'll have a new pair soon, then I can stare some more." Elli just stood there blinking, was he flirting with her? Did he just call her beautiful?

She turned without a word, and went back to work. When it came time for Shea Adler to skate off, he ran into the goal, then the wall before making it to the bench. Everyone was in a fit of laughter except her, she was still in shock.

Shea Adler had called her beautiful.

After the shoot downstairs, which consisted of the guys in sexy suits, Harper and Elli started cleaning up and tearing down. Elli didn't hire big crews, didn't like them. All she needed was Harper and two other assistants and she was good. The day had gone good, all the shots had come out great, and once she edited them, they would be golden. The guys were amazing and sweet, not really as cocky as the sports reporters make them sound, they were good guys.

Elli was packing up her camera when she saw Jakob Titvo coming towards her; he gave her a grin before going to where Harper was standing. She watched as he flirted, hard, with Harper, she of course was playing hard to get, something she has perfected. Jakob pulled his phone out as she pulled hers out, they were exchanging numbers. He asked her something and Harper just giggled, and then leaned forward, giving him a kiss on his cheek.

Jakob put his hand on his heart before stepping backwards, a dazed look on his face causing Harper to laugh. He shot her a wave as he left with his bag over his shoulder. Harper smiled and looked over at Elli.

"He'll call when he gets in the car," she said as she walked towards Elli with the rods from the light stands.

"How do you know? He said that?"

"Nope, but I know his type, needy."

The sad thing was Harper was probably right. Elli looked down at her camera, taking care to put it away. As she zipped the zipper to her purple and black bag (yes, team colors) she cursed herself for being shy and stupid with guys. When Shea said she was beautiful, she should have said something clever, that's what Harper would do, but nope she just stood there blinking, looking downright stupid.

Elli knew the problem, it was her confidence issue. She didn't think she was good enough for male attention. She wouldn't say she was plus sized, but she was thick. She wasn't a size two anymore, nope good ole ten now. The sad thing was; she hadn't even had any kids yet. Yes, she did have a thyroid problem, but still that was seven years ago, and she still wasn't able to get the weight off. It didn't matter if she had great fashion sense, guys didn't hit on her the way they did when she was a size two. It was depressing, because Elli was lonely.

She would never admit it to anyone, but she wanted that happily ever after. She always put on this front that she liked being alone, didn't need a man, but it was such a lie. She wished she could be like her sister Victoria, Victoria loved being single, loved sleeping with different men. Elli just couldn't do it. It was so private, and with the way she felt about her body, no one was getting her undressed until she knew she loved them, and they loved her.

After packing everything on the carts, they started pushing them down the hall towards the car. After three trips they had everything packed, so they started walking towards their cars when Harper's phone rang, Elli didn't even stay back to listen, she kept walking with a wave to Harper as she cooed into the phone.

Once in her F-150 (Hey, Trucks aren't just for boys), she drove off towards the west end of Nashville to get on the interstate. She'd planned to ask Harper if she could stay the night with her since she was stupid tired and didn't want to drive for forty five minutes, but since it looked like Harper was gonna be busy, she decided to go home. Elli hit the interstate preparing herself for the drive. It was probably good she was going home; she had forgotten to call Ally, her neighbor, to let her dog out.

When Elli had bought the old country home outside of Nashville five years ago, it had seemed like a great idea. The studio had been open for two years, it was thriving, and she wanted a home, not some apartment or condo. So she bought it, didn't even look at anything else, this was the house for her. After five years, it wasn't the old country home she had bought, it was a masterpiece. Everything was redone, the décor classic and beautiful. Whenever Elli's dad came to visit he would always say; it was like he's standing in sunshine, because it was so bright. She smiled just thinking of her home. She was proud of both her studio and house. They showed she was doing something with her life. That she didn't need her family's money, she was successful after losing her stint on Broadway, and that she could live without Justin.

She pulled into her round driveway, grabbing all her bags. Even before getting to the door she heard her pug running down the hall, and then the barking started.

"I know, Adler, I'm home darling, hold on." Elli opened the door, and her forty pound pug attacked her, well, tried to anyways. She laughed as she threw her keys in the basket by the door, before bending down to her puppy, who was struggling to breathe.

"Oh my goodness, Adler, honey, breathe, darling." Elli petted him till he calmed down, kissed the top of his head, and then locked the door as her house phone rang. She didn't answer it since it would be her mother, and Elli was not in the mood to talk to her. After the machine picked it up, and her mother's voice rang over the machine, telling her to call her, she pushed delete before going to the kitchen for some dinner. She decided on a frozen dinner, since she didn't feel like cooking, and went to get her laptop while it heated up.

Elli walked through her bright yellow living room; she always loved the décor in here. The yellow accenting the black wrap around couches that had yellow throw pillows that matched the walls; her extremely large TV - a gift from her father because she loved watching the away games in HD - hung above her mantel that held pictures of her nieces and nephews. She smiled as she passed them to get her laptop. She loved her nieces and nephews and couldn't wait to take them to the park next weekend for their monthly visit.

After getting her laptop and returning to the bar, she loaded the pictures from her camera as she got a fork and napkin. She sat down at the bar, food and laptop in front of her. She had taken over three thousand shots of the Assassins, good amount, lots of work ahead of her. She inhaled her frozen pasta meal, realizing she was hungrier than she thought as she looked over the pictures. They were good shots, real good. Only a few were crappy but with Photoshop, she could fix them with no problem.

As she went from picture to picture, Elli stopped at Shea Adler's pictures. Gosh, he was so stinking gorgeous. He had the most amazing eyes she'd ever seen. They were such a gorgeous shade of blue, so bright, and so happy. He probably had a beautiful girlfriend at home, with a dog, and a 9 bedroom house with all the fixings. He just looked like he was happy. When she came to the pictures of him in the suit, it was breathtaking really. The suit was black with a purple vest underneath and the hockey stick that he held was so slick looking. But you really didn't look at the stick or the suit, you looked at his eyes.

Good golly, they were mesmerizing.

Not that Elli would admit this to anyone, but while she worked that night, she always came back to the pictures of Shea. Looking at his beautiful eyes, his hard body, wishing that she was the girlfriend at his house waiting for him to get home so they could sit on the couch cuddling as they watched highlights from the games that night, while Adler lay beside them along with Shea's dog. Elli smiled just at the thought, and then rolled her eyes.

As if that would ever happen.

"Not only did I run into the goal, but the wall too!"

Shea Adler sat with the side of his face in his hand, his glasses were crooked but he didn't care. He was beyond embarrassed about what happened that day at the photo shoot the Assassins' had.

"I can't stand it when I get new contacts, they eff my eyes all to hell. God, it was so embarrassing, Grace, so embarrassing."

His twin sister laughed on the other end as Shea rolled his eyes, dropping his hand from his face to get up for a drink of water.

"I don't know why you're so embarrassed Shea, it was only the guys."

"And the staff!"

"Okay, and the staff, so what?"

"And the photo people!"

"So? You're never embarrassed about anything, what aren't you telling me?"

Shea didn't say anything, he wasn't telling Grace about the beautiful brunette with the biggest and brightest green eyes he had ever seen. The kind of eyes that when he looked into them, he lost his breath, something that had never happened to him.

"Who is she?" Grace asked with a knowing voice, "Hopefully not some dumb blonde bimbo that will suck you dry."

"Hey, no one has sucked me dry!" Shea said defensively.

"They tried."

"Now you know that's not true. I won't even let them close enough to suck me dry."

"Whatever, the last chick, Marie, you bought her a diamond necklace!"

"Because I cheated on her with her sister and she threatened to kill herself because she loved me so much!"

"Oh yeah, well anyways, who is she?"

"How do you know it's a woman?"

"Because like I said, you don't get embarrassed, so shut up and tell me."

"I don't know who she is, she was the photographer today."

"Okay, and?"

"And she was beautiful."

"Did you ask her out?"

"No, she is kind of different."

"What the hell Shea, you're not making sense. Who am I talking too?" she said teasingly, "This isn't my brother, big scary captain Adler, because my brother's motto is 'I came, I saw, I conquered.'"

Shea let out a booming laugh, which caused her to laugh.

"I don't know, she wouldn't look me in the eye, she was shy, cute."

"Hmm, sounds like a winner in my book," Grace cooed.

"Maybe."

"So anyways, the party for this weekend is almost done, planning wise."

"Sounds good."

"I'm excited, the guys are gonna have a ball."

"That's why I hire the best party planner in Nashville."

Grace giggled, and went on with details as Shea stood in his stainless steel kitchen. Grace had decorated the whole condo for him when they came to Nashville, 4 years ago. He had just gotten signed with the Assassins from the Flyers, and couldn't be happier to be moved to a team that was gonna pay a hell of lot more than the Flyers ever did. Plus Grace had hated Philadelphia probably as much as Shea did. Luckily they both loved Nashville, since Grace would never go anywhere without Shea, as he wouldn't without her.

The joy of being twins!

Grace had helped pick out the condo and even lived with him for a while to get it looking perfect before looking for her own. Then she met James Justice and after only being together for a couple of months, got pregnant. Now Grace lived ten minutes from Shea in a beautiful 1.2 million dollar house, blissfully married, with two of the greatest kids in the world, Ryan and Amelia, while running the biggest party planning business in Nashville. Shea couldn't be happier for her, but he always got nervous with the thought that one day he would be leaving her, if he got traded or anything.

"Does that sound okay?" Grace asked, bringing him back to the conversation.

"Of course, do you have a photographer?" Shea found himself asking, Grace starting laughing.

"No, you never said you wanted one."

"Well, maybe it would be a good idea. With all the new players and their families, don't you think?"

"Yeah, you have a certain photographer in mind, Shea?"

"Oh hush, and get her."

"Who is she!?"

"I don't know, but find her and get her, offer her a price she can't refuse."

"You have no idea what her name is?"

"I think I heard Elli, but I'm not sure, call Melody, she would know."

"Fine, I've got three days to find this chick, jeez Shea."

"I love you Gracey," he cooed, she laughed.

"I love you too, bye."

"Bye."

He hung up his phone, tucking it into his pocket with a grin on his face. He went to his fridge, smiling at his niece and nephew's pictures before opening it to get a beer. He popped the top as he walked to the dimly lit living room. He sat down on his leather coach, turning on the TV to catch some of the highlights before turning in. He had an early practice in the morning, plus he was volunteering at the hospital with the team tomorrow over at Vanderbilt.

As he drank his beer, he found himself grinning. If Grace came through, he would be seeing the beautiful photographer by this weekend, and this time, he would conquer.

Chapter 2

Elli was dragging ass when she came into the studio the next morning. The tall mocha from Starbucks, she had stopped to get, was not doing the job. She was exhausted. She had stayed up till two in the morning editing pictures and got up at six to let Adler out and to get ready for work. She had two newborn shoots, a senior, and then two families, all before three o'clock.

Today was gonna be long.

As Elli unlocked the big glass doors to the studio, she read the writing on the doors, something she did every morning.

Time Standing Still

Owner: Eleanor Fisher

Established: 2004

She smiled to herself as she shut the door behind her, turning the lights on as she walked to the back, where her office was. She laid her coffee down before slipping off her heels, and picking up her phone to listen to her messages since she wasn't there all day yesterday. Usually Harper would do all this, but she wasn't coming in today. Elli had given all the assistants the day off, since yesterday was such a biggie.

She had forty messages, so she sat down, and listened to every one of them. Writing phone number's down and putting stars beside her past clients because she would call them last. She took a drink as the answering machine lady said "Message Forty, September 13rd, 2010, 10:30pm"

"Wow, they are calling late," she muttered as she listened.

"Hello, my name is Grace Justice, and I am calling on behalf of Shea Adler."

And with just the mention of his name, Elli knocked her coffee cup all over her desk.

"Shit!" she yelled as she flew up, wiping off the front of her skirt.

"If you would like to listen to the message again, press five."

"Shit!" Elli yelled again, pushing five on the number pad.

"Hello, my name is Grace Justice, and I am calling on behalf of Shea Adler. I am planning his team party that he is having this weekend and we need a photographer. The one I had canceled on me, so I am in a spot. Melody recommended me to you after Mr. Adler had mentioned meeting you yesterday. He asked me to tell you that whatever the price is to get you here for the party is the price he'll pay. Please give me a call at -"

Elli wrote the number quickly, and then listened to the message again, just to make sure she wasn't imagining what was happening. Shea Adler had mentioned meeting her? He said he would pay anything for her to be at the party?

This had to be a prank.

Elli glanced at the clock, than dialed the number that Mrs. Justice had left, the phone rang twice before a thick Boston accent came over the line.

"Planning Your Moment, Grace Justice speaking, how can I help you?"

"Yes, this is Eleanor Fisher, with Time Standing Still; I just got your message and was returning your call."

"Yes! Hello! How are you?"

"Fine, thank you, and yourself?"

"Oh girl, I'm dragging this morning, my daughter kept me up all night, you would think at the age of fifteen months she would be sleeping through the night!"

"I hate to tell you this, but my youngest niece didn't sleep through the night till she was three."

"Oh good God, please don't tell me that!"

"Sorry!" Elli said with a laugh.

"I just don't understand, my son, perfect angel, my daughter, a demon!" That had both women in a fit of giggles. "So anyways, sorry to get off subject and bother you with my problems."

"Don't you pay it any mind, I love talking about kids."

"Okay, good, I'm hoping you can help me this weekend, Ms. Fisher."

"Call me, Elli. When is the party?"

"Saturday at one o'clock until everyone leaves."

"Okay, just a second."

Elli pulled up her schedule. She had a wedding that day, but Harper could do it with Alice as her assistant. They would be fine, but then that left the studio business, Ryan could handle it probably; maybe she could call Alice's brother, Jack, to back Ryan up. It could work.

"Okay, I might be able to, when do you need an answer?"

"When can you give me one?"

"By lunch?"

"Sounds good to me, I'll be waiting for your call, Elli."

"Okay, talk to you soon." Elli hung up the phone and just sat there staring into space. Was this really happening? She couldn't do the party, she was booked that day. She picked up the phone, dialing Harper's number but it went to voicemail but that didn't stop Elli from continuing to call her. Harper finally picked up after the ninth time.

"I mean Jesus, El, if I don't answer, obviously, I don't want to talk to you!"

"Shea Adler's party planner called me to do his team party this Saturday."

"Really?"

"Yeah!"

"Okay, well we have the Baker/Poke wedding this weekend, so Alice and me will cover it, while Ryan runs the studio, and we'll have Jack come in to back him up."

"That's what I was thinking."

"Of course it was! But you told the party planner you'll call her back because you're too chicken shit to do it, so call the girl back and tell her yes, and then don't call me back until a decent hour."

The line went dead.

Elli didn't pick it back up though; she just stared at the phone, telling herself to pick it up at call Mrs. Justice.

But she couldn't.

The day went on, the party for Shea Adler heavy on Elli's mind. Why couldn't she just call Mrs. Justice back, tell her yes, she had the coverage. What was the problem?

Seeing Shea again.

Her crush had gotten stronger since she spent most of the night staring at his pictures, and she didn't know if she could face him again, let alone work for him. After her senior shoot, Elli was sitting at her desk when her phone rang. Elli picked up, with her regular greeting, only to hear the same Boston accent from earlier.

"Alright now, Ms. Fisher, you have not called me back, does that mean no?"

"Oh, I'm so sorry, I've had clients all day, and lost track of time," Elli lied.

"I'm just teasing you; will you be able to do the party?"

Just say yes, say it! Elli bit down hard on her lip.

"Yes, Ma'am, I can. I'll be there at 12:30. I just need the address and your email to send you the invoice."

"Wonderful! You're a life saver Elli!" Grace gave her the email and the address to a well known subdivision, before thanking her again, then hanging up. After staring at the wall for what seemed like forever, she dialed Harper's number.

"I said yes," Elli said when Harper answered.

"Good, I knew you would."

"How did you know? I didn't even know I would!"

"Because you want to see Adler again, you won't admit it, but I saw the way you looked at him yesterday, you're smitten," Harper said

"I am not!"

"Yes you are."

"I'm hanging up."

"Go ahead, but listen, make sure you wear the white tube top dress with the blue flowers, and your bright blue Manolo heels to the party. You're smoking in that dress."

"I will not! I'm wearing jeans and a studio tee."

"Whatever you say, Elli."

The line went dead again, and Elli threw the phone down. She sat down behind her desk and looked up to look at the Assassins' team picture from last year. She needed to print one out of this year's team, since there were new players, and some of the guys looked a little different. She looked at her favorite spot, row four, eight guys in from the left, to where Shea Adler stood in his jersey with a C on his chest and a big grin on his face.

She took a deep breath and shook her head as she said "Damn it. I'm gonna wear the damn dress."

"Her name is Eleanor Fisher, Elli for short."

"Excuse me guys, it's my sister," Shea said as he stood up, leaving his fellow teammates in the living room as he walked to the kitchen to talk to Grace in private.

"Elli, I like it."

"She's so sweet, shy like you said, but sweet. She said yes, after making me wait most of the day, she said she got extremely busy, which was probably true. Her studio is extremely hot right now. Not only is her wedding photography beautiful but her in studio stuff is amazing. You should look it up online; I'll send you the link with the invoice for her services."

"Okay sounds good, how much is she charging me?"

"Not enough in my opinion, five hundred."

"Add a thousand to it and send it in, don't forward me anything, I'll just lose it."

"It's an email, Shea."

"I lose everything."

"True, so fifteen hundred?"

"Yeah, she's really coming?"

"Yes, Shea."

"You're awesome, Grace. I owe you."

"It's my job, I'm glad I've made you happy."

"You've made my day babe, thanks, listen I got Jakob and Alex over, see you Saturday?"

"I'll talk to you tomorrow."

"Yep, love you."

"Love you too."

Shea hung up the phone, tucking it into his pocket, a huge grin on his face.

Eleanor Fisher. Elli.

The name fit her. He couldn't believe Grace had come through. When he came into the living room Jakob looked up at him and shook his head.

"What's up with the grin bro?"

"Grace came through for me. You didn't finish the story did you?" Shea said changing the subject. Jakob had gone out last night with some girl he had met, and was telling the guys about it.

"No, so after going at it all night, then a good part of the morning, we wake up, and she rolls over and tells me to leave! I couldn't believe it! No woman has ever done that!"

"Maybe you weren't good," Alex said with laugh, Jakob threw him a glare.

"Fuck off Welch, I was amazing, she was amazing. I don't know what happened."

"Crazy dude," Shea said as he leaned back on the couch, a beer in hand.

"Damn right it was, she was heaven, damn it."

"What she won't talk to you?" Alex asked.

"Hell no, she won't answer any of my calls or texts."

"Maybe she used you."

"Maybe," he said with a shake of his head. Jakob was one of those guys that were looking for true love; not that Shea wasn't looking for *the one*, but not right now like Jakob was. Alex had found his true love years ago; he was married to his beautiful wife and had five girls, something Jakob was extremely jealous of.

Shea hated seeing his best friend so upset over a girl, but luckily he thought with a smile, that would never happen to him.

Shea never planned on what to wear, he usually just threw on a pair of ripped up jeans and a tee, but he would be seeing Elli today, and he wanted to look good. So he spent a good thirty minutes trying to pick something out, he even made the mistake of calling Grace. After being cussed out, he went back to trying to pick something out on his own. He decided a nice white button up shirt, and a pair of cargo shorts. After fixing his hair, he threw his black Billabong hat on and slid his black canvas shoes on.

He was nervous, something he never felt. Not even during game seven of the playoffs was he nervous, he was always ready.

Shea was basically bouncing in his seat as he drove his chromed out Range Rover over to Grace's house, where the party was being held. Grace had way more room than he did, plus she loved having parties on his expense. When he pulled up into her driveway, he noticed a huge black F-150 sitting on the side of the road, none of the guys drove that, so he wrote it off as one of the workers. Some of the team had already arrived with their families, and the party was just getting started when Shea entered the backyard.

It was the perfect September day for a party. The sun was shining and the sky was brightly blue as kids ran through the sprinkler, and went down the water slide that Shea said had to be there. He had a pair of shorts in the car, just in case he got to urge to go down it with Ryan, his nephew. As Shea walked through the party, he stopped to say hi to his teammates and their wives, or girlfriends. He looked around the party, and saw James, Grace's husband, holding Amelia in his arms. Shea went straight to them, taking Amelia from him, kissing her loudly on the cheeks. She squealed in delight, kissing Shea right back.

"Hey Shea," James said, Shea smiled over at him. He had always like James, he was a good man, treated his sister well, and was a great father.

"Hey man, how ya doing?"

"Good, Amelia has been a terror about going to bed though, I feel so bad for Grace, she's gotta be tired."

"I bet she is. The party looks amazing."

"Like always she out does herself, she's over there with a photographer." Shea whipped his head around so quickly, that he was surprised he didn't have whiplash. His beautiful sister was wearing a long flowing pink dress, her black hair up in a bun with her big shades over her eyes. She was laughing, and he smiled, but when he looked over at the woman in front of Grace, he lost his breath.

Elli was wearing a beautiful summer looking dress, her hair was down in ringlets, her eyes also covered with sunglasses, but he knew the color of them, since he had been dreaming about them for the past two days. His eyes drifted down Elli's body, she wasn't skinny like most girls Shea went after, but she wasn't fat, she was curvy, sexy. He started walking without thinking, he was pretty sure James said something but he was mesmerized by the beauty in front of him.

Right when he was about to reach the two women, Elli walked off, camera in hand, towards the kids slide.

"Shit," he muttered as Grace grinned up at him, taking Amelia from him.

"She's not your norm, Shea."

"No, she's better," he said as he watched her follow the kids around, taking pictures. Grace laughed, before kissing his cheek.

"I hope something happens between you guys."

"Oh, it will."

The party was going beautifully. Grace Justice was one hell of a party planner. The large brick house was covered in lights, with lanterns hanging above the party. The team colors were everywhere, on every surface. There was lots of stuff for the kids, water slides, games, and even a prince and princess reading stories off to the side in a flower garden. For the parents there was food galore, and drinks to boot. The party was something straight from LA in Elli's opinion.

Elli was getting great shots, the kids, the teammates, everything. It was so amazing to get this inside look on the team, they were such a family. Elli was bending down, taking a picture of the most gorgeous little girl, who happened to be Grace's daughter when she felt someone standing behind her.

"I see you've found the most beautiful baby girl to take pictures of, Ms. Fisher." Elli stood up, and looked behind her, to see Shea Adler looking down at her. She always thought he was tall on his skates, but he was still massive without them. He was such a big man, so strong. Being a defenseman, Elli guessed he had to be huge.

"I did, she's gorgeous."

"She takes after her uncle, right baby girl?" he scooped the baby up, kissing her loudly on the cheeks.

"You're niece?" Elli asked as she turned off her camera, then she looked at the two of them together, and she could see the family resemblance, same blue eyes, dark as night hair. The baby pushed on his glasses, causing him to laugh as he put them back on his face. All the Sports Center guys made fun of his glasses, they were big and black, geeky looking, but Elli loved them, she thought he was geektastic in them. "So Grace is your sister?" she said when she found her voice again, being as close as she was to him was making it hard for her to breathe.

"My twin sister."

"Wow, I didn't know, she didn't mention it."

"I doubt she talks about me a lot," he said with a laugh as the baby tried to get down. "Alright, alright, calm down Amelia, go on baby," he patted her on the butt as she waddled away. "She's a busy one, do you have any kids?"

"Oh no, just a lot of nieces and nephews," he smiled as he looked over at her, his blue eyes set just on her. They stood there staring at each other before his eyes raked over her body making her nervous.

"It's a beautiful party," Elli said breathlessly.

"Yeah, like always, Grace outdid herself."

"She did, this is really nice of you though, having this for the team."

"Yeah, I've done it the past three years, since I became captain, Wavier did it before me." Elli nodded, he smiled, and she blushed. God, she was an idiot.

"Wavier was a good captain."

"He was, I miss his crazy ass," Shea said with a big smile "So you follow hockey?"

"Oh yes, I love it. I have glass seats right beside the penalty box, I go to every home game."

"Do you now?"

"Yup, I'm a big fan."

"That's awesome, is that how you got into sport photography?"

"Yeah, I always bring my camera with me to all the games and take pictures, but when I got the opportunity to shoot for y'all, I jumped on it."

"You did a great job; I saw my pictures this morning actually."

"Oh thank you."

He already saw them? She just sent them in yesterday!

"Have you lived in Tennessee your whole life?"

"Um, yeah, why?"

"Your accent is really thick."

She blushed a little as she smiled, "I'm a southern belle, what can I say?" he laughed, and of course Elli continued to blush. "But you are a Yankee through and through?"

"Oh yes, guilty as charged. My mother always teases me, saying one day I'll be saying y'all instead of you guys." Elli let out a giggle, and Shea just grinned at her, so she bit her lip, looking away.

"So, um-"

"What kind of camera do you use?" He asked looking down at the camera that was hanging around her neck.

"A Canon EOS-1Ds Mark III"

"Cool, I just bought a Cannon Rebel. Maybe you could show me how to use it? I bought it to take pictures of things when I'm on the road and of Amelia and Ryan, my sister's son."

"Oh, okay, sure."

"Awesome, so how about tomorrow afternoon? We could meet for coffee, and go to the park; the park is beautiful right now."

What? Wait? Huh?!?

"Oh, tomorrow?"

"Yeah, are you busy?"

"No, not at all, Sunday's are my off day."

"Okay, so spend it with me"

Elli just looked up at him; he was so blunt, so direct. Holy shit was Shea Adler asking her out on a date?

"I don't know," she said, looking around for something to pull her from this conversation. She was getting butterflies and it was making her nauseous.

"Come on, it's coffee and taking pictures. You like coffee right?"

"Yes, of course."

"Okay and you love to take pictures, right?"

"Yes," she said with a smile.

"So do them with me."

Elli couldn't speak, so she just nodded, which made Shea grin bigger. "Awesome, I'll meet you at the park at one, what kind of coffee do you like?"

"Starbuck's, caramel mocha."

He smiled big, and she couldn't help herself, she smiled right back at him.

"That's my drink too, so I'll see you tomorrow in front of the Parthenon?"

"Sure," she answered

"Alright, Ms. Fisher, I'll see you tomorrow."

He leaned over, kissing her cheek softly, causing all the air to rush out of Elli. He smiled at her before walking away, leaving her standing there looking like an idiot.

What the hell just happened!?

When Elli got home that night, after letting Adler out the back, she called Harper.

"Hey, how'd it go?"

"Good, the party was beautiful. How was the wedding?"

"Great, did you see Shea?"

"Yeah, did you check on the studio?"

"I did, its good, did you talk to him?" Harper asked. Elli was about to bust, so she took a deep breath then basically screamed out the news.

"He asked me out for coffee and to teach him to use his camera and I said yes!"

"What?"

"I know! I can't believe it either!"

"No! It ain't that I don't believe it; it's that you said yes! I'm so proud!"

"I know, I don't think it's a date, but it's going to be just me and him!"

"That's a date, babe! Coffee too? Oh yeah, total date!"

"He kissed my cheek!"

"OH MY GOD!"

"I know!"

"This is huge!"

"I don't know. I'm not really his type."

"What do you mean?"

"He dates skinny blondes."

"Maybe he's moved on to curvy brunettes! Now you listen to me Eleanor Fisher, do not go freaking yourself out or talking yourself down. You are beautiful! He asked you out! You can do this!"

"I can do this," Elli repeated, but didn't believe the words at all.

"You can, now what are you going to wear?"

"I don't know. What if it's not a date and I dress up and he comes in shorts and tee?"

"He probably will, but still I'm thinking the khaki shorts you have, the ones that tie, and that really bright Kelly green shirt you have, you know the one that shows off the girls."

"I wear that to the club!"

"Oh yeah, true, okay what about-"

For the rest of the night, Elli stayed on the phone with Harper, picking out something to wear for the date she still didn't believe she had, trying to get her nerves under wraps.

It didn't work.

Chapter 3

Shea sat on a blanket in front of The Parthenon waiting for Elli. Again it was a beautiful day, and he was thankful for it, since this date would not work if it was raining or cloudy. A drink carrier sat beside him, holding their drinks, while his camera sat beside it. He had bought the camera a couple months ago, and was glad he didn't give it away like he was going to, since he didn't know how to use it, but that was all about to change. Elli was gonna teach him, if she ever arrived. He pulled his phone out of his pocket, checking the time again. She wasn't late, but, like always, he was early. His excitement was causing him to have butterflies; he couldn't wait to get to know her, to find out what made Elli tick.

Last night, after the party, Grace couldn't stop talking about Elli, and it made Shea happy to know that Grace liked her so much, because if his sister didn't like the girl then there was no sense in even trying to carry on a relationship with them. Not as if he'd ever wanted to.

But that was changing.

"Hey Shea."

He didn't even hear her come up, but when he turned to look at her, his tongue almost fell out of his mouth. She was wearing shorts, and his eyes went up and down her legs. God she had beautiful legs. He got up, smiling down at her.

"Hey Elli, didn't hear you come up." She smiled sweetly at him. She had her camera hanging around her neck and she was wearing a little pink shirt with a cardigan over it. Her hair was pulled to the side, curls falling down her shoulders with a pink bow holding her bangs out of the way. She was spectacular.

"Am I late?" she asked, nervously, she was flushed, her cheeks so pink against her pale skin.

"No, not at all," he said with a grin as he handed her, her coffee. "I'm just always early." She smiled, and sat down beside him, taking a drink of her coffee.

"Mmm," with that sound, his eyes went straight to her mouth. Such a pretty mouth she had, she had a cupids bow, with bright pink lips, she wasn't wearing lipstick, just lip gloss. "Thank you, it's wonderful," she said, he tore his gaze from her lips, looking in her eyes. How did someone's eyes get so green?

"You're welcome," he answered, taking a good hearty drink of his coffee without taking his eyes off her. "So how did the pictures come out last night?"

"Great, I got one of Amelia, oh my stars, beautiful! Her eyes are so bright in the picture. I emailed it to Grace so she could see."

"Awesome, she probably emailed me, but I'm so bad about that kind of stuff."

"Bad about what?"

"Checking emails, sending emails, invoices, crap like that, that's why I have an assistant, I.E., my sister."

Elli giggled before giving him a pointed look. "By the way, Mr. Adler, my fee was only five hundred."

Shea gave her a forgiving smile, and of course she smiled back at him. He knew his smile of lethal when it came to women, but for the first time, he actually wanted to make this female smile.

"Maybe I thought that fee was too small. You were at the party the whole time."

"So? I know my fee, I've been doing this a while."

Perfect opening for him.

"How long?" he asked.

"I've been taking pictures for forever, but I've had my business for the past seven years."

"Seven years? So how old were you when you started?"

"Twenty one."

She was only a year younger than him. "So you're twenty eight?"

"Twenty seven, my birthday is in a few months."

"Cool, what did you do before that?"

"Went to school."

"What school?"

"What, trying to see if I'm qualified to teach you?" She said with a grin, he smiled.

"Nah, I know you are qualified, I looked at your stuff online. I'm just making conversation." A small smile crossed her lips as she looked down at her cup, messing with the straw.

"Oh, well, I went to the Art Institute, did you go to school?"

"I did, I went to U of M in Boston."

"Did you grow up in Boston?"

"I did, and you grew up here."

"Yup, southern to the core."

He smiled and nodded, she was so easy to talk too.

"What did you go to school for?" Elli asked in her charming thick accent.

"To play hockey." She smiled as he laughed, "I got a scholarship to play, then I got drafted to the NHL."

"Did you graduate with anything?"

"Nope, I only went for hockey, that's all I wanted to do."

"What happens when you retire?"

"I become a coach; I want to teach kids how to play."

"Kids? Not adults?"

"Nah, adults are drama queens, I love kids." She laughed and he laughed along with her, leaning back on his forearms, the sun was hitting him in the face, he felt warm inside and out. It was a beautiful day with a beautiful girl. "Have you always wanted to be a photographer?"

She hesitated before saying, "Yeah, I guess. I love what I do."

"You're good at what you do."

"Thank you, that means a lot." He nodded, sipping on his coffee.

"Are you an only child?"

"Oh no, I have two older brothers and an older sister."

"So you're the baby?" he said with a teasing smile.

"Yes, and they remind me of that every day it seems," she said with a sad smile. Okay, family, touchy subject.

"You mentioned nieces and nephews, yesterday?" Elli lit up, smiling full on, he had never seen anything so beautiful. Not even Amelia was as beautiful as her smile. It lit up her whole face, her eyes glazed over with happiness and that's when he vowed that he wanted to make her smile like that every day.

"Oh yes. I have three nephews and three nieces."

"Wow, that's a lot of kids."

"Yeah, they are amazing. I love them so much."

"You can tell by the way your face lights up." She blushed, looking down at her hands.

"I'm their favorite. I take them once a month and we go out and have a day to ourselves. We love it."

"Sounds awesome."

"Do you spend a lot of time with Amelia and Ryan?"

"When I can, but they are both really young, so you know, they make me nervous, and I doubt Grace would let me leave with them."

"Are you not responsible?" she said with a laugh, he smiled.

"I am, but they are so little, so precious, I wouldn't be able to live with myself if anything happened to them." Elli smiled big at him again, turning towards him, crossing her legs as she looked up at him. Their legs were almost touching; he could feel the heat from her. He could smell her, something mango, maybe her shampoo.

"I feel the same about mine."

Shea nodded, looking out over the park. "So do your parents live in state?"

Elli nodded as she said "They live in Clarksville, all my family is there. Except my sister, she lives in downtown Nashville."

"Do you stay downtown too? Isn't your studio there?"

"West end, and no, I live forty minutes from here, in Sweetbriar."

"Oh, I haven't heard of that town."

"It's an old farm town; I found my house there and had to have it."

"That's cool. I live over in Harding Place, in a condo."

"Cool, I sometimes wanna live in town because when I am stupid tired after work I hate driving forty minutes home, but I love my house, so does my dog."

"What kind of dog you have?"

"A forty pound pug."

"Jesus Christ!" She almost fell over laughing, which made him laugh too, she was so pretty.

"He's a fatty, but I love him."

"I want a dog, but I don't ever have time for one. I'm traveling a lot."

"Yeah, the life of a hockey player."

"Yeah, are you coming to opening game?"

"Of course, I don't miss games."

"Awesome, I'll look for you." Her cheeks turned red, as she looked anywhere but at him. Since she wasn't looking him in the eye, he looked down at his hands. "So, does your husband come to the games with you?" She whipped her head up, looking at him like he was crazy.

"I'm not married."

"Oh, a boyfriend?"

"No, I'm single."

"Good."

She was still looking at him, making him nervous, maybe that was a little to direct.

"Does your wife come to the games?"

"There is no one in my life, just me."

"Must be lonely," she said, he gave her a thoughtful look.

"It can be," he said with a shrug, because he wasn't all that lonely, he could get any girl he wanted in bed, but no one had ever really mattered.

"So anyways, your camera, ready for a lesson?" She asked, smacking her hands together, with a nervous giggle.

"Absolutely," he said, even though, Shea didn't want to learn a thing about the camera, just about Elli.

Shea was a fast learner, he caught on to everything Elli taught him, and when he did something wrong, he grinned widely at her, causing her to grin even bigger. It was so easy to talk to him, between his jokes, his smiles, and the way his eyes just settled on Elli, it was so easy. As if they had known each other their whole life.

"Hey, look at this one!" he called over to her; he was over by the flower gardens, while she finished her coffee and snacked on the pretzels she had bought. She stood up, and came over to him. She leaned over to him, looking over his arm to the viewfinder. The picture was of her, with the flower garden in front of her. It was actually a good picture of her, and she never thought pictures of her were good.

"Wow, Shea, that's good."

"I got a pretty amazing teacher, I'll hook you up," he said with a wink as he wandered off towards a duck. She watched him with a smile on her face. While it was a pretty interesting to watch a grown man chase a duck, she couldn't help wondering why this was so easy. She had never met a man that was so easy to talk to and get along with. He made her nervous of course, but it was fine after a moment.

Probably cause they are meant to be friends.

Yeah, that's it, so she needed to get this notion out of her head that he liked her. It would never happen. He was Shea Adler, leading defensemen of the NHL, captain of the Assassins, the most gorgeous man she had ever met. When her heart started to ache, she rolled her eyes, what was she expecting? True love?

Please, it's Shea Adler, you are Eleanor Fisher, no man of that stature or that pedigree would want you.

"Hey, you okay?" She looked over to Shea; he was standing beside her, his camera in hand.

"Fine, you done?"

"I am, I got some good shoots, I'm excited to go on the road and take pictures now."

"Awesome, my job is done then," she said with a clap of her hands "So you'll have to email me when you're on the road, show me what you get."

"For sure, if I ever figure out how to use my email." She laughed as he picked up his blanket and their trash. "Maybe you could teach me," he said as she stood straighter, he had that sexy smirk on his face, the one that made her girlie parts scream.

Bad girlie parts!

"Sure," she said breathlessly.

"Cool, where did you park?"

"Over by the Sportsplex."

"Awesome, me too. We can walk together."

She smiled, and they started walking in silence. Not weird silence but comfortable silence. How she had became so comfortable with him so quickly, was beyond her, but she would never let him know. He probably thought they were becoming friends. She was someone to teach him things, since he obviously was an idiot with technology.

She was not girlfriend material.

Duh.

When Elli saw her truck, her heart dropped to her stomach, this was the end. No telling if he would ever have contact with her. He would be nice of course, the occasion hello if they ever ran into each other. But this was the end of probably one of the best afternoons of her life.

"Where's your car?" he asked as she started towards her truck.

"My *truck* is right here," Elli said, pointing to her truck, like always when guys saw her truck, their eyes got big, their mouth dropped open some, and they gave her the 'you gotta be kidding me' look. She expected it, liked it even.

"That's your truck?"

"Yeah, why?"

"I expected you to drive something small, like a Beetle."

"Why cause I'm a girl?!"

"No, well, maybe…that's a big damn truck!" Elli ran her hand lovingly down the side of her baby. Along with her house, this was one of her favorite things.

"It is big, but I like big things if you haven't notice, my dog, my truck-"

"Maybe you're man?" Elli choked on the words that were trying to leave her mouth as her face went deep red in a matter of seconds, he laughed. "Sorry didn't mean to embarrass you."

"I'm not embarrassed," she lied, not looking in his eyes.

"Actually you are. You're bright red!"

"Oh hush," she said, smacking him on the arm. Was she flirting? Jesus, what the hell is wrong with her? She glanced up at him and he was grinning at her, making her feel even more stupid so she looked away to unlock her doors.

"So, can I get your number?" She looked over her shoulder at him as she laid her bag down.

"Oh, of course," she muttered as she rambled the numbers off when he had his phone out. He pushed a button, and then her phone started ringing.

"For when you want to call me," he said with a grin as he did some more stuff with his phone.

"Oh, okay," she said with a nervous giggle as she saved his number, when she looked up from her phone, he was closer to her, his blue eyes piercing into hers. His jaw ticked at the side, and of course her eyes went to his mouth.

Good golly, it was a pretty mouth. Such strong jaw bones, a little scar at the end of his chin. His lips looked so soft, so inviting.

"I had a great afternoon with you Elli," he said, was he whispering? Was his voice husky? Oh God.

"Me too, one of the best ever," she cringed at her nervous babble. God, she was an idiot. Shea gave her a sexy grin that she was starting to think he was born doing, and leaned closer to her. Her breath caught, and he smiled again.

"Can I kiss you?" he whispered in a husky manly, yummy voice. Elli could do nothing but nod, and his lips were over hers within seconds. His lips were so warm, so strong, as his hand came up to her cheek, caressing her softly. She had never been kissed like this. When Justin would kiss her it was quick and rushed, but Shea took his time, tasting her mouth as she did the same to him. When he pulled back, he smiled down at her. "I'll call you later?"

Elli's head bounced up and down like a freaking bobble head.

"Bye, Elli."

"Bye," she said after he was already to his car.

Okay, what the hell just happened?

"He kissed you!" Harper bellowed through the house when Elli had relayed the afternoon to her. "Oh my God! Was it good?" Harper had come over for dinner and a movie. Something they did a lot. Sometimes their other friends came too, and they made a night of it but tonight it was just her and Harper. Sometimes she liked it better that way.

"It was amazing," Elli gushed out. "I don't know why he did it though."

"Because he likes you!"

"Oh come on, Shea Adler? Like me, Elli Fisher, please. I am nowhere near his type; he likes the leggy blondes with big boobs, small waist, and fake faces. I am not that."

"You don't know his type Elli, plus you can give them blondes a run for their money! You're beautiful."

"I'm fat, and I guess okay looking."

"Oh shut up!" Harper said throwing a piece of popcorn at her, Elli giggled as she picked it up, throwing it in her mouth. "I slept with Jakob again."

"Well that came out of nowhere," Elli giggled as Harper just grinned widely at her, "Again? I thought that was a onetime deal."

"Me too, but he kept like calling me, and then he showed up at my condo last night, and I'm like well since you're here come on in and fuck my brains out. You know?"

"No actually, I don't."

Harper giggled. "That's what you should do with Shea, just have him knock your boots off then be done. How long has it been since you've gotten any?"

"Wow, Harper. Um no, I will not be knocking my boots off with Shea Adler, that would be a horror. A big sexy man like him with my dumpy body? Please!" Elli purposely didn't answer the other question. That was an embarrassment in itself. Something Elli didn't even want to venture too.

"Your body is beautiful Elli; you've got sexy curves, something I wish I had. I'm just bones and skin."

Elli gave her a pointed look. "Please don't give me that I wish I was curvy speech, no skinny girl wants to be fat."

"You're not fat!"

"I'm not skinny."

"Whatever Elli, and don't think I forgot about my question. How long has it been?"

"Why does it matter?" Elli asked picking a piece of popcorn apart. When she was nervous she always had to keep her fingers moving.

"I want to know."

Nothing was said for a moment, and when Elli realized Harper wasn't going to let it go, she let out a breath before saying, "Six years."

"What! Since Justin?"

"Yeah, why?"

"Oh my God, you need to get laid, no wonder you're such a bitch sometimes."

"For the love of God, shut up! I am fine."

"You most certainly are not!"

Elli was about to yell some more, when her phone rang. She picked it up and looked at the display.

"It's him," she whispered, looking up at Harper in horror. What the hell was he doing calling her?

"What? Shea? Answer it!"

"No! What would I say?"

"Umm...hello?"

"Shut up!" Elli stood off the bar stool and walked to the living pushing, talk. "Hello?"

"Hey."

"Hey."

"It's Shea."

"I know."

"Oh okay, you sound weird."

"Oh, sorry."

"Don't be, what's up?"

"Um, nothing, what's up with you?"

"This is Elli right?"

"Yeah."

"What's wrong? You sound really weird."

Elli slapped herself in the forehead, trying to get it together, but how could she! Shea Adler was calling her! "Oh, well, I'm just surprised you called."

"Am I not supposed to?"

"Oh, no, it's not that, I just didn't think you would."

Silence.

"Alright, did I do something wrong? Cause I thought this afternoon went great."

"It did, but I thought that was all it was, an afternoon."

"Oh, is that all you want it to be?"

"Oh no you don't, don't put that loaded question on me!" He laughed, and she smiled. Harper came into the living room, throwing herself on the couch, grinning up at Elli, she, of course, gave Harper the death glare.

"Okay, then I will tell you this; I want it to be more. I want to see you again Elli."

"You do?"

"Oh, yeah I do, what are you doing tomorrow?"

"Tomorrow?"

"Yeah, as in the day that comes after today?"

"Smartass." He chuckled, which made her smile "I gotta work during the day, and I have a wedding tomorrow night."

"Okay, Tuesday?"

"Bar mitzvah and work all day."

"A bar mitzvah? You do that?'

"Yup," she said with a grin, Harper just smiled big.

"Okay, I got an event Wednesday, what about Thursday?"

"Wedding."

"Well, shit woman!" she laughed, "I bet Friday and Saturday is a no go."

"Friday, weddings out my butt, but Saturday, I'm spending the day with my nieces and nephews, my assistants are doing the weddings that day, then I have a wedding that night."

"Okay."

"I know I'm stupid busy and-"

"We'll make the time okay? The season opener is Wednesday, and then I'll be wicked busy."

"I know, I understand."

Silence, she guessed he was thinking, because she sure was. She was thinking maybe she could throw some stuff on Harper, but she quickly dismissed that, how could she expect Harper to do her job just so she could go on a date with Shea.

"All I know is that I can't wait till next Wednesday to see you."

Her heart warmed, he was so sweet.

"It is a long time away."

"Yeah it is. I go to practice every day from nine to eleven, your studio isn't far from the arena, maybe we can do lunch?"

"Sure, I don't have my schedule in front of me, but I can text you in the morning, let you know."

"Sounds good, so I'll see you tomorrow."

"I hope so."

"Good, do you have time to talk?"

"Um, well, actually I have a friend over."

"Okay, well, I'll let you go, I'll see you tomorrow."

"Okay."

"Bye Elli."

"Bye Shea."

When she hung up, she looked over at Harper who had the biggest grin on her face. Elli's hand came up to cover her mouth. Was this really happening? Did Shea Adler want to see her? For real? Not as friends? Elli was on the verge of tears, she had never been so happy and scared all at the same time. Her mind was reeling; Shea Adler wanted to date her!

Harper stood up coming over, and wrapped her arms around Elli.

"Told you," she whispered in Elli's ear as she hugged her tightly.

Chapter 4

Okay, how in the world did Shea miss Elli after one date? It made no sense to him, but it was happening. She was on his mind hardcore. Her smile, her eyes, her legs, everything, he just didn't understand. No girl had ever made him miss them, ever. And, after one date with Ms. Fisher, he was hooked. He was worried last night when he called her; the way she sounded was as if he wasn't supposed to be calling. It made him feel like an idiot even thought he was pretty sure she liked him with the way she had flirted with him.

And the way they kissed.

Good Lord, it was heaven.

Shea was hard the whole night. Her perfect little lips on his large ones, the way her soft cheek felt in his rough hands.

Jeez, it was hot.

Shea was in the team workout room, running on the treadmill, thinking about Elli when his phone beeped, he had a text message.

Hey Shea, it's Elli. I can take lunch for 12-2, anytime between then.

He smiled as he texted her back.

I'll see you at 12 then.

He kept running and smiled when he saw she sent him back a smiley face. She had two hours? Well then they would spend the whole two hours together, he thought with a grin. Just as he was finishing his workout, Jakob walked in.

"Dude, there you are!" Jakob yelled.

"What's up?" Shea asked as he turned the treadmill off, and stepping off as he wiped down his face.

"So, that girl I was telling you about, I slept with her again Saturday night."

"Really? How did it go?"

"Great, until she kicked me out again! I just don't understand!"

"How did you even get in her bed, Jakob?"

Jakob was silent for a moment, "I went over there," he said with a shrug of his shoulders.

"Jesus, Jak, you look desperate."

"I miss her, when we're together its crazy amazing, then she goes crazy on me and kicks me out!"

"Well get the hint bro, she just wants sex and that's all."

Jakob hit his head on the back of the wall, closing his eyes as he took a deep breath. This wasn't the first time this had happened; Jakob could fall in love with a hockey puck. Shea's best friend was a hopeless romantic and didn't care who knew, unlike Shea who kept that stuff in the closet. Plus, Shea had never been with a woman that drove him crazy the way every woman drove Jakob...well that was until he met Elli.

Shea walked by him, cupping Jakob's shoulder.

"Let it go bro."

When Shea arrived at Time Stands Still, he took in the beauty of the building. It was an old building, lots of white brick, and when he pulled the door open to the studio, and saw the teal and brown accents, it bought a classic essence to the place. Large photos lined the walls, babies, couples, kids, families, and weddings. He was looking at a beautiful blue eyes little girl when Elli came rounding the corner and again, she took his breath away. She was wearing a teal and green dress, the teal part was a tube top looking thingy and the green had designs all over it for the skirt, it went to mid thigh. Her breast looked so plump, she must have been hiding them the last time he had seen her. Her hair was in curls down her shoulders, with a feathery bow holding up a part of her hair, but Shea had to admit, the best part of the outfit was her shoes. They were some pointy teal heels, and her ankles and calves were screaming to be touched.

Elli wasn't looking up when she came around the corner, she was looking down at her phone when she said, "You caught me when I walking out, how can I help you?" she looked up with a fake smile on her face, since he knew what her real smile looked like, till she saw him, then she grinned for real.

"You can go to lunch with me," he said as he came towards her, she was still grinning as he kissed her cheek, "How are you, Elli?"

"I'm fine," she said breathlessly, he loved when she got that breezing tone to her voice.

"You look beautiful." Her face flushed as she looked away.

"Thank you," she said, still not looking at him, "You look great too." He smiled; he was wearing some ripped up jeans and a tee with his favorite black hat.

"Yeah, but I didn't dress up, I'm sorry, I just came from practice."

"Shea, you look good, don't worry about it, I probably over did it," she said, moving away from him, towards the front desk. She was messing with some papers when he came up behind her. When she froze, he moved her hair off her shoulder, placing a small light kiss on her bare shoulder since he didn't want to scare her.

"I don't think you over did it babe, but then again, it is for my viewing pleasure," he kissed her shoulder again, and she turned, leaning against the desk.

"I'm nervous, so I'm babbling."

"Don't be, you look great, I look okay, so let's go, we're wasting eating time."

Like Elli could eat. Please. She was wearing a dress that showed off too much thigh in her opinion, her breast were about to fall out and the damn heels she was wearing were hurting her damn feet!

Damn Harper, this was all her fault.

Elli should have never worn this dress; she bought it back when she was a little thinner, now she looked like a damn fat man in a little coat. God, she was nervous.

As they rode in Shea's Range Rover, the first thing Elli notice was that it was super clean, and then that he had a picture of him with his niece and nephew. Her heart melted a little at the sight. It was nice to find a man that loved children as much as she did. They arrived at Maggiano's, a really great Italian place on west end. It was actually one of her favorite places to eat, and when they entered the back way, they were personally greeted by one of the concierge; she figured that Shea came here a lot.

"This is my favorite place; I live about ten minutes from here."

"My studio always orders from here."

"It's good food," he said as they lead them to a table in the back. She scooted into the booth, making sure her dress stayed down, as he scooted in beside her. Beautiful music was playing as the concierge went over the wine list.

"Do you want your regular bottle, Mr. Adler?"

"Please," then he turned to her, "You like wine?"

"I do."

"Moscoto okay?"

"Sure, is it good here?"

"Wicked good, I love wine, Grace says I'm a sissy boy for drinking it, but coming here all the time, it converted me." Elli giggled as he smiled bashfully at her.

"I like wine, but a nice cold beer is how I end my night."

Shea's jaw fell open a little as he looked at her lovely, "Marry me, now."

That had them both laughing, as she turned deep red, because she was pretty sure if Shea Adler ever asked her to marry him, she would die of a heart attack. "No, I love beer too, but my classier side, is a wino."

A waiter showed up with a bottle of their best Moscoto and poured both of them hefty glasses. Since Elli knew that it was a desert wine and you were only supposed to get half a glass, she was surprised to see that she had a full glass. Elli brought it to her lips, and took a sip. Both the waiter and Shea watched as her eyes opened in surprise and a little moan escaped her lips.

"My god, that's good."

"Told ya," he said with a wink, and the waiter walked off with a grin on his face. Elli took another sip, and smiled when she saw that Shea was still watching her.

"So, what are you going to get?" she asked, hoping he would look away. He didn't.

"Chicken Parm, that's what I always get."

"I get the tilapia."

"Good choice."

"Usually with the zucchini fritters."

"Sounds awesome."

Elli smiled as the waiter came back, they ordered their food and the waiter ran off to fill the order. They sat for a few minutes, drinking and taking in the scenery. She looked over at Shea and noticed that his hat was low, covering his glasses so she couldn't see his eyes.

"I can't see you eyes."

He looked up at her, with a sheepish look.

"I'm sorry babe, I'm trying to make sure we aren't bothered, or I would take my hat off."

Elli wanted to squeal, he called her babe! She had to keep her composure though, so she took a deep breath before saying, "Oh, fans."

"Yeah, they know I like this place, I don't mind them when I'm by myself, but I don't want any interruptions." She smiled sweetly, before reaching over and pulling his hat off, he looked at her surprised, as he ran his hands through his hair. She loved how it stuck up in all different ways.

"I'll take the interruptions if I get to look in your eyes," she practically whispered, he smiled, scooting a little closer to her, so that their legs were touching. She gazed into his sky like eyes as she took a drink of her wine. "How was practice?"

"Good, I feel good about this season."

"Another cup?"

"Hoping so."

"I believe in y'all." He smiled.

"Then we'll win." She laughed, as the zucchinis were brought out. As the munched they talked about the guys on the team, who was looking good, and about the new goaltender. Apparently he was someone that Shea had played with in the AHL. So he was excited to be on the same team with him again.

"He's bad ass, so I'm really excited."

"Awesome, he played for Washington, didn't he?"

"Yeah."

"Will he take Ryans' place?"

"No, he'll be back up."

"Okay good, I love Ryan." He smiled.

"Is he your favorite player?"

"Nope."

"Oh, really, who's jersey do you wear?"

Elli was beat red and luckily the food was bought out so she didn't have to answer. Shea watched her as the waiter laid the food down and wished them happy eating before walking away. Elli had a feeling he wanted his answer.

"I'm waiting Ms. Fisher."

"How do you know I wear a jersey?" she asked, trying to deflect the question as she ate.

"Cause you are a fan, you have a number. Who is it?"

"I ain't telling. I don't want to make you jealous." He let out a booming laugh, causing Elli to grin as she ate some of her fish. "I'm serious, male egos are so fragile." He kept laughing as she continued to eat.

"Whatever, I bet you like Alex Welch, all the girls like him."

"Nope."

"Tell me."

"No way, maybe first game I will."

Since he would see her, and see the 6 on her arm along with the C above her breast. He winked at her, and dug into his parm. God, he was gorgeous.

"So, you're still busy all week?"

"I am, except Wednesday, but you have that event."

"I canceled it." She looked over at him surprised, he was smiling.

"Why?"

"It was just a radio thingy; Jakob said he would go instead, worked out for me."

"That's cool."

"Yeah, since now I'm gonna get you to go out with me again." Elli looked up at him, surprised and happy all in one. They had only been together an hour and he was ready for another date! She couldn't believe it, but she wasn't going to let him in on the fact she was freaking out inside, so she decided to tease him a little.

"That male ego, I tell ya, assuming I want to go out with you again."

He gave her a sexy, cocky grin, leaning towards her as he put his chin on her arm looking up at her, batting his eyes as he said, "You don't want to go out with me? I was thinking dinner and a movie."

"Mmm. Dinner? Where?"

"Pf Changs."

"Okay to dinner, what movie?"

"Your pick."

"Ooo, smooth."

"I thought so," he said, before leaning back in his seat, taking a sip of his wine "So, can I pick you up at six?"

"I'll meet you at the restaurant."

"Why? I can pick you up."

"I don't want you driving all the way out to my house, just to come back in town."

"I don't mind, I want to," his hand moved to her thigh and she looked over at him, surprised.

"Are you sure? I mean, are you sure you want too-" Harper told her not to do this, not to second guess herself, so she took a deep breath, and smiled. "I'll give you my address before we leave." He grinned, leaning over and kissing her cheek, causing her heart to skip a beat.

"For a second there I thought you were going to turn me down." Elli grinned as she continued eating. "So, what kind of music you listen too?" She looked over at him, and he was looking down at his food. "I bet country huh?" He looked up at her with a satisfied grin.

"Actually, I like all music."

"Liar."

"I do!" she protested, he just raised his eye brows at her. "But I mostly listen to country" He laughed and she giggled as she took a drink, "What do you listen to?"

"Well, since I've been in Nashville, I've started to like country, but I like rock and rap a lot."

"Cool."

"Yeah, what's your favorite movie?"

"Pride and Prejudice, it's also my favorite book."

"Never seen or read it." She looked up at him like he was an alien.

"Excuse me?"

"What?"

"You've never read or seen Pride and Prejudice?"

"No, why?"

"Um, it's the greatest love story ever! Oh my goodness, you know," she started to move out of the booth. "This isn't going to work, I'll see you around," she only made it an inch before he grabbed her arm, pulling her back, horror all over his face.

"Oh, no you don't!" he said, causing a lot of people to turn and look at them. "I promise I'll watch it, and, hell, I'll even read it on the road." Elli smiled fully and scooted back to her spot.

"Good, make sure you have a book cover, or the guys will make fun of you."

"Your right on that one," he said with a grin, "Did you really think you would get far, leaving like that?"

"No, but it was fun seeing the horror on your face."

"Hey, I can't have my beautiful date run out on me, remember my fragile male ego?" he said with a teasing smile.

He called her beautiful…

"Oh, yeah, totally forgot about it" she said with a shy grin. She looked over at him, so happy to be with him. "You are-"

"Excuse me." Elli looked up at a long legged blonde, but the blonde wasn't looking at her, she was looking at Shea. "You're Shea Adler right?"

"I am, and you are?"

"Cindy! Hi, I'm sorry to interrupt your lunch, but can I have your autograph?"

"Of course," Shea scooted out of the booth, and signed her shirt that happened to be an Adler shirt. That's when the swarm happened, everyone came up, asking him for his autograph and of course he signed everything, while sending her a forgiving smile. Elli would smile back, and continued to eat.

When she was finished eating, she looked at her watch. She needed to go; she had an appointment at 3:30. Thankfully, Shea looked over at Elli and she tapped her wrist, mouthing she had to go.

"I'm sorry everyone, I gotta go."

People of course protested as Shea handed his credit card to the waiter, along with his food, so they could package it up. "I'm sorry Elli."

"Don't worry about it," she said as she gathered her bag of leftovers, and followed him out. He opened the door for her, and she climbed in. When he got into the truck, he started it and drove off without a word.

"So, what's your favorite movie?" Elli asked since she still wanted to know some times about him. Shea looked over at her, and smiled.

"Miracle."

"A classic."

"It is."

"This is our time! Their time is over!"

"Their time is over? Come on babe, if you're gonna quote the greatest movie ever, get it right," he said with a teasing smile.

"Oh hush, I got most of it!"

"You did, I'm impressed." She smiled proudly, but her smile fell when he pulled into the studio parking lot. He got out just as she turned to say bye; she watched as he walked around the truck, opening the door to let her out. Elli climbed out, and Shea moved closer towards her trapping her between him and the truck. "I had a great lunch Elli, I'm sorry about the end though."

"I told you it was fine, I asked you to take the hat off, so I was basically asking for it."

"Still, I'm sorry."

"Don't be, it was a beautiful lunch, I had a great time." She smiled sweetly, and he took another step towards her, leaving no room for moment. His hands came up around her waist, pulling her to him as he looked deep in her eyes. Her breathing hitched because she knew he was going to kiss her again, she tried to steady her breathing, but with Shea Adler this close to her, it wasn't working. Shea smiled before covering her mouth with his. He kissed her softly, before slowly teasing her lips with his tongue, asking for permission to come in.

Elli hadn't kissed like that in so long that she was scared out of her mind, but she open her mouth for him, playing with his tongue with her own. His grip on her hips became tighter as he brought her even closer to him. Elli's hands rested on his chest as he kissed the stuffing out of her. When he pulled back, they both were breathing hard. He rested his head against hers as he looked into her eyes.

"Jesus, you're gonna be the death of me baby."

Baby? He called her baby!

"I could say the same about you, Shea," she whispered with a small smile. He smiled before taking her mouth with his again, this time it was slow, sweet. He gave her three more small kisses before letting her past him. "Bye," she said with a small, shy wave.

"Bye, I'll call you." She turned when she got to the door.

"If I don't answer, I'll text you. I have that wedding tonight."

"Okay, bye."

"Bye," she said with another shy smile as she walked into the studio. Once inside, she leaned against the wall trying to control her breathing. At the sound of laughter, Elli looked over at the front desk to see Harper, an amused look on her face.

"I mean, jeez El, ya'll need a room next time."

A room? With Shea alone?

Elli slid down the wall, groaning. Lord, help her if that ever happens.

Elli kissed like a dream. Shea had just left her with a dumb grin on his face as he drove back to his condo. God, she was amazing. So beautiful, so understanding, so amazing, she loved hockey movies! Hell, she loved hockey! Just being with her made him feel so safe, so happy, it had never felt like that before. No girl made him want to call her as soon as he left her, just to hear her voice. No woman ever made his blood boil with just one kiss, one touch.

What the hell was going on?

Shea pulled into the spot in front of his condo, and turned the car off. He reached for his phone and texted Elli, since he knew she had clients.

Am I on your mind, the way you're on mine?

As soon as he pushed send, his phone rang, it was Grace.

"Hello my loving brother," she cooed in the phone.

"Oh Jesus, what do you need?"

"A favor."

"Okay?"

"Bradley Johnson, the guy who sells me my liquor,"

"Yeah."

"He is being a douche and trying to raise my prices, can you sign me a stick so I can try to schmooze him into not doing it?"

"Sure, when do you need it by?"

"Tomorrow."

"Done."

"Thank you."

"You're welcome."

"Didn't you have your date with Ms. Fisher today?"

"I did."

"And?"

"What?"

"How was it!" she yelled, he smiled.

"Great, she's amazing Grace, I don't know how someone so beautiful could be so amazing and not taken. She's so understanding, a bunch of fans interrupted our lunch and she didn't care, she just smiled and ate as I did my thing."

"You didn't wear a hat? God you're dumb, she's sweet, but you're dumb."

"I did! But she pulled it off, saying she couldn't see my eyes."

"Awww!! How sweet! I think she likes you."

"I don't know, I think so too, but she acts weird sometimes, like she doesn't know why I'm calling or when I call her beautiful, she blushes so hard, and looks away. She's just so shy; I'm not used to it."

"Shea, you have to remember, she's not like these gold digging hoes you've dated in the past. She's a real woman."

Shea thought that over for a moment. She was like no one he had ever been with, maybe that's why he couldn't get his mind off her.

"Do you think that's why I think of her all the time?"

"No, I think it's cause she's amazing, and you've finally found your match. Now I gotta go, Amelia is driving me nuts. Thanks for the stick bro, love you."

"Kiss them for me, love you too."

Shea hung up his phone, and sat there for a moment. Met his match? What the hell did that mean? That Elli was his soul mate or something? He hated when Grace did that, say something then hung up, it drove him crazy. His phone dinged and he looked down seeing a text message from Elli.

Well, if I'm all you think about then……yes. ☐

A slow grin went over Shea's face. His match? Yup, he was starting to think so too.

Chapter 5

After sending what Elli thought was a very bold text message to Shea, they talked all night. She felt bad for making him wait for her responses but he told her he didn't mind, he knew she had to work. Elli never thought she could be bold enough to say the stuff she had said in that text message but she was pretty damn sure if they were face to face, she would turn beat red and run. It had been so long since she had been with anyone. Justin had messed her up pretty bad, and she thought she would be alone for forever, but now with Shea, maybe something could happen.

But, just in case it didn't, she wasn't letting her heart get involved. Shea might come to his senses, and not want anything to do with her, and that would devastate her. So she would keep her heart on lock down, yup, that was the plan.

Elli stood at the front the next day, unloading a box of photos when the doorbell sounded; she looked up saying her regular greeting as Shea came in, a smile on his face.

"Hey there, beautiful." She smiled, and thanked God she was dressed cute today. She was wearing one of her 50s style dress, in her favorite color, green.

"Hey," she grinned as he leaned across the desk to kiss her softly on the lips, taking her breath away. "What brings you by?"

"You."

"Me?"

"Yeah, had to see you, these texts get old you know?"

"Yeah," she grinned as she continued unloading. It was so hard to keep your heart on lock down when a man was saying such sweet, amazing things.

"So, have you eaten?"

"Not yet, have you?"

"Nope, that's why I'm here, came to spring ya." Elli smiled up at him.

"What if I had things going on?"

"I was taking my chances, seeing you would have been enough, but eating with you would make my day."

"I actually got most of the afternoon open, you're lucky," she said with a wink.

"Yes I am, come on, let's go." She bit her lip and looked up at him. He was looking delectable in some white shorts, with a black shirt and that same matching hat. His glasses were in place and his grin was unstoppable.

"Let me grab my purse, I'll be right out," she said as she turned to go to the back office. She grabbed her purse, than hit the alarm system as she walked out. Shea was waiting at the door, the same grin on his face as she walked towards him. It was hard to believe that he was still standing there, that this all wasn't a dream, but it wasn't because she felt the warmth of his hand when he took her hand in his, smiling down at her.

"I got us subs from Jimmy Johns, figured we could have a picnic."

Yup, keeping her heart on lock down was gonna be real hard.

Elli looked really pretty today, usually he thought she was hot, beautiful, but today she was pretty. Like classy, something straight out of a 50s show. Her hair was up in a bun with a great big white flower in it. He was starting to think she had the sickest style ever, because the girl had his eyes bugging out of his head every time he saw here. As they sat in the park, eating their subs and talking about the customers Elli had had that morning, all he could do was think how lucky he was to be sitting with her.

"The baby was adorable, a pain, but a beauty."

"Is it hard getting shots of babies?"

"It can be, but I love it just the same," she said with a grin as she wiped the corner of her mouth, and then took a long swig of the water he had bought. Grace was actually the one to suggest the picnic. She had said that she thought it was the perfect day for one, so here he was, with Elli. He had missed her last night when she was at the wedding, she could only answer him once every hour, but she did call on her way home and they had talked, till she had to get back to work on the pictures. He found that she was an extremely busy lady.

"So, tell me this, how does a typical Elli Fisher day go?" She smiled as she took another drink of water.

"Well, I wake up early, if I'm not too tired I go for a run before letting my pup out, than I eat some breakfast, go to work, then go to work again, I'm really boring I swear," she said with a laugh. "You're a pro hockey player, nothing I do would impress you." He smiled as he looked down at his food.

"Elli, anything you do impresses me, you're amazing." She blinked a few times, before looking down at her food. He needed to remember that she was shy and he couldn't be so forward with her, but it was so hard. Plus it was as if he got diarrhea of the mouth when she was around, he would just blurted what he was feeling. Shea took his hat off running his hand through his hair than placed it back on his head.

"Tell me what the typical day of Shea Adler is," she said, he looked over at her, she was tearing apart a piece of bread, he smiled.

"I run in the morning too, maybe we could do that together one time," he suggest, she laughed out loud.

"Please, you would smoke me!"

"I really don't run that fast, I hate running."

"You're in shape, Shea. I am not."

"Yes, you are."

"No, really, I'm not, anyways, go on with your day."

He paused, giving her a look before saying, "Running in the morning, practice in the mid morning, then, lately, lunch with a beautiful girl." She grinned at him before she threw a piece of bread at him.

"Stop your making me blush!" He smiled, and continued.

"Then I usually go home, sleep a little, before doing some more team stuff, right now I'm taking it easy, since the season is about to start and I'll be busy all the time."

"Yeah," she said with a nod. "I have a question."

"Shoot."

"Why do you wear glasses when you're not on the ice? Do you hate your contacts that much?"

"No, it's just my glasses are easy, really, I'm just lazy." She giggled as she laid back on the blanket. There was a nice breeze and the sun was shining, it was a nice late summer day. "I also hate putting my finger in my eye, I have big hands," he said holding them up, she smiled.

"I know, when you held my hand over here, yours swallowed mine." Shea smiled as he reached over and took her hand in his.

"I think it's a nice fit," he said, looking at their hands, she looked down, then back at him.

"Maybe your right."

"I'm always right." She giggled again, rolling her eyes.

"Male ego…" He smiled, as she giggled some more. He loved her giggle, her smile, shit, her everything. "I got another question."

"Ask away."

"Did you always want so many tattoos?" she asked looking at his arms. He looked down at his arms; he had gotten both arms done over the last 8 years. He added things that meant something to him, and he was about done, he had a little room on his left arm, but, for the most part, everything was full.

"Yeah, I started them about 8 years ago, what you don't like 'em?'

"No, I do, I just never knew you had 'em, your jersey covers your arms. And when I saw pictures of you on line, you are always wearing your blazer jacket."

"Yeah, the league doesn't like them much."

"Oh."

"I don't care though, I love them, they are a story, telling of my life. My whole family has something on my arm."

"Really? Where's Grace?"

"Right here," he pointed to two stick figures that stood with their arms around each other.

"Stick figures?" He smiled.

"She likes it; she has the same one on her hip."

"Oh, cool," she made a little face, and he laughed as he pointed to other things. His mom and dad's part which was their names. A hockey stick with a 6 above it, the date he was drafted, then the dates Ryan and Amelia was born. Then there was a bunch of other crap that didn't matter, but looked cool.

"Do you have any tattoos?"

"I do, but I can't show you cause I'm wearing a dress, remind me the next time I'm wearing jeans"

"What is it?"

"You'll see," she said with a sneaky smile, he smiled back, turning onto his stomach, holding her hand in both his. They stayed like that for a long time, Shea messing with her fingers as they talk about everything. Elli's time in college, along with his, their families, but she didn't say much about her parents or brothers or sister, it was mainly about the kids. They were discussing the upcoming season when her phone rang. She dug into her purse till she found it.

"I'm sorry, I gotta answer this," she said as she pushed talk. "Hey Harp, everything okay?" He watched as she listened and nodded at whatever the person was saying. "Alright, I'll be back over there in a few, go ahead and get started. Thanks babe," she hung up and smiled. "My assistant and best friend, Harper"

"Everything okay?"

"Yeah, one of the our clients needed some shots of their daughter for the Miss. Tennessee Pageant, she hadn't called to make an appointment and called Harper for help, so Harper is down at the studio, getting started. I'll come in and look at the shots, if there's anything else I can think of to do, we'll do it"

"Do you need to go?"

"In a few."

"Okay," he said, and then he smiled to his self as she put her hand back in his.

"So I think your friend is dating my friend," Elli said.

"Huh? Who?"

"Jakob Titov."

"Um, no, Jakob isn't dating anyone." She gave him a look, as if she was saying 'you're being difficult'.

"Okay, he is screwing my best friend, well Harper is screwing him, ah, whatever." Shea smiled.

"Harper is a very complex woman that is driving my best friend mad."

"I know, I don't understand it, she usually only messes with them once but I've been hearing a lot about Jakob and that's not on the ice, but rather in the bed."

"He's a good guy, but he's looking for the one."

"Well, Harper is not the one, tell him to watch it, she is a heart breaker."

"Wonderful. Tell her to dump him."

"She tried, but he keeps coming back, and I don't know, I'm not telling you what she says!" Elli blushed as she covered her face. When she peeked at him, he smiled.

"Let's leave them to do what they need to do."

"Sounds like a plan," she said with a grin, "Can I ask you something else?"

"Sure."

"I feel like this has been questions and answers."

"That's how dates go, we are learning about each other."

"True, but this is a silly question…what are you wearing to our date, tomorrow?" Shea had never had a girl ask him that, he just look at her surprised as she bit her lip. Then he laughed out loud, causing her to giggle uncontrollably. "I told you it was a dumb question!"

"It's not! I just never had a girl ask me that."

"I just don't know if I should dress dressy or casual or dressy casual. I'm freaking out!" She threw her hands over her mouth, her cheeks so red that he was pretty sure he felt the heat from them. He sat up, crossing his legs so he could sit in front of her. He took her hands off her mouth, kissing her palms before kissing her lips sweetly. He brought his hands up, cupping her face gently.

"You don't need to freak out about me, I'm easy going." She just nodded, looking dazed. He loved that look on her. "I'm probably going to be dressy since we are going to PF Changs."

"Okay," she almost whispered.

"Now, come here, give me some more of them kisses." She bit her lip before he covered her mouth with him.

If everyday had Elli's kisses in them, his life would be complete.

When Shea dropped Elli off at the studio, they kissed goodbye in the truck since she had clients inside. She didn't want to leave, but had to, and promised to call him later. When she went in, Harper was sitting at the computer with Liz and her daughter, Aslynn.

"Hello all!" Elli gushed as she hugged Liz, then Aslynn. Harper looked at her with a 'what the hell' look, as Liz gushed on how good Elli looked.

"My goodness, has your momma seen you lately? You're glowing!"

"Oh, thank you, Liz"

"You really are Ms. Elli," Aslynn added, Elli blushed as Harper giggled.

"She's seeing someone, ain't you Ell?" Elli's smiled dropped, why would she say that? Especially in front of Liz Martin! Her momma's every-other-day-best-friend!

"Harper!" Elli said with a glare. As soon as Harper realized what she did, she looked towards the computer.

"Oh really! How awesome! Who is he? Please say he is better than that dumb ass Justin you were dating!"

Oh yeah, he is.

"You know Elli, Justin is dating my cousin Annalisa, she is so ugly! I don't know why he left you."

"I left him." Elli said, but it didn't matter because on went Liz and Aslynn about dumb ass Justin. Gossip is what make these southern states run. "How do the pictures look?"

"Perfect!" Aslynn gushed, she was so pretty. Bright blonde hair, big breasts, big blue eyes, she was gorgeous, and young at only 17.

"Wonderful, if y'all would excuse me, I got some paperwork to tend to."

Harper came to the office after Liz and Aslynn had left. She sat down in front of Elli with a sheepish look on her face. Elli knew Harper thought she was mad, but she wasn't. Harper sat down, pulling her knees up to under her chin, and looked over Elli.

"Are you mad at me?"

"I'm not mad, just worried about what my mom will say when she finds out."

"Just don't answer the phone."

"Yeah. I guess."

"I'm sorry." Elli looked up at her, a small smile on her lips.

"It's okay."

Harper smiled big, letting her legs fall back to the ground. That's how Elli knew she was really sorry, she always brought her legs up to her chest, like she was protecting her heart or something.

"So you wanna go to dinner before the wedding?"

"Actually, I need to go shopping, I have a date tomorrow," Elli said with a big grin.

"Wow, so how many times have you been out with him?"

"Tomorrow will be four," Elli took a deep breath, trying to calm herself. "He's amazing"

"And hot, but I hope you're not falling for him El. Guys like him are good for one thing, and one thing only," Elli looked at Harper with what felt like a sullen look because she knew what Harper was about to say "and that's to fuck, so watch it. He's a cool dude, but don't give him your heart, just have fun."

"You feel like that about Jakob?"

"Jakob is different."

"How?"

"I don't know, that is a totally *different* situation."

"No, it's not, how many times have you all been out?"

"It doesn't matter."

"Yes it does! Because you can't tell me not to feel more for Shea, when you are with Jakob, Shea's hockey twin!"

"I am not with Jakob, I'm fucking him, so you, shut up." And with that Harper stormed out the room. Elli just smiled after her.

Jakob was getting to Harper and Harper didn't like it at all.

Elli locked the studio up since she didn't have any evening appointments and left. The wedding wasn't till seven, so it gave her time to go shopping like she wanted. She decided to go to her favorite designer's shop, Melanie Renee because the dresses there were beautiful. Ever since she had opened a Nashville shop, it was basically the only place that Elli shopped. She loved Melanie's designs, they were perfect for her. They were something straight out of the 50s, with a crazy flair to them.

Elli parked her truck in a spot, and then proceeded to go in. She loved the feel of Melanie Renee's store; it was so inviting, so classic. Totally white, with the only color being the clothes and accessories, big white lamps hung from the ceilings and the glass windows were from floor to ceiling, lining the front of the store. Elli went to the first rack, looking through it when her phone singled a text message. It was Shea.

I miss your small hand.

She grinned so big, that she thought her face was gonna break.

"Do we even carry your size here?" Elli looked up from her phone, her smile falling. Her sister, Victoria, stood before her in what she knew was a size extra small of the exact same dress Elli was wearing. Her sister was extremely beautiful. Long light brown hair, that came to the middle of her back, straight as a board, big green eyes, with high cheek bones, and a cupid bow mouth. But even though Victoria Fisher was gorgeous, she was evil, had been making Elli's life a living hell since day she had been born.

"Obviously y'all do since I am wearing the same dress you are, Vicky." Elli knew Victoria hated being called Vicky but she did it anyways.

"We carry cow here?"

"Wow, thanks, my dear sister," Elli said as she moved through the racks. "Why are you here?"

"I work here."

"Lord help us all, what happened to the big modeling gig?"

"It happened, now I'm down on money."

"And you're not living off momma and daddy?"

"No, I can stand on my own feet, thank you."

"Sure," Elli said with a dazed look. "Well, it's been great talking to you Vicky, but I'm busy and I know you wouldn't want me to report to management that you're harassing me, right?"

Victoria glared as she walked away, towards the counter. Elli tried to ignore the stares of her evil sister as she shopped, but it was hard, especially with her words going through Elli's head.

We carry cow?

She kept looking through the racks, because she'd be damn if she let her sister see that she had gotten to her. She was flipping through one of the last racks when she saw a champagne colored apron dress from the 1930s, it had a cute little tie bow in the back, and it was just so cute! She found her size and carried it to the counter where her sister stood, glaring of course.

"Can't I refuse service?"

"You can, but I can have Amy on the phone in a matter of seconds." Amy was the manager of the store, and luckily for Elli, she had taken pictures of Amy's daughter last week, so Elli would be fresh on Amy's mind.

"Whatever."

As Victoria took care to take the tags and security tag off Elli's dress, she looked at the counter where there were cute head bows and flowers to go with the dresses in the store.

"I'll take that champagne colored feathery bow too, please," Elli said, Victoria grumbled something, and then rang it up. After giving her the total, Elli handed her back her bank card.

"Must be nice to drop this kind of money on a dress and a hair bow."

"Well, when you work for it, it does feel nice. Have a nice day, sister dear." Elli grabbed her bags and card, and walked out feeling a lot better since she knew her sister was jealous to the core. When she got into the truck, she started it before she pulled her phone back out, reading Shea's message again. Katy Perry's 'Not like the Movies', started playing and Elli smiled.

What was happening with Shea was kinda like the movies. It was like a dream.

And I miss your big hands swallowing mine. She typed back before putting her phone on her thigh and driving off.

The wedding went great that night, Harper didn't talk to Elli but Elli knew she would get over their little fight earlier that day. Shea had texted her all night, and she enjoyed their little conversation between her working. After the wedding, Elli was walking towards her truck, when Harper fell in step with her.

"I'm not dating him," she muttered.

"Okay, it's none of my business."

"Yes it is; you're my best friend."

"You're right, so be honest with me, you like him?" Harper looked everywhere but Elli's eyes, she had this nervous look to her, which confirmed what Elli thought. Harper really liked Jakob.

"I like having sex with him."

"Well, there's a start to admitting your feelings."

"You like Shea?"

"I do." Harper seemed to think it over, and then she looked Elli right in the eyes.

"Then you better not let your insecurities get in the damn way. You're amazing El, amazing. Any man, even dudes at Shea Adler's caliber, would be lucky to be with you. Don't forget that, and don't let your family fuck it up." She turned to walk away, then stopped to look over her shoulder at Elli. "And don't let past shit with Justin fuck it up either." Harper was gone after that, leaving Elli alone leaning against her truck.

How the hell did she do that? Totally call everything that Elli was feeling scared of then walk away like it was nothing. She smiled as she got into her truck; she guessed that's why she loved Harper so much. Harper knew her inside and out.

Once she got on near the interstate, she was stopped at a red light, when she looked at the clock, it was well past midnight, so she texted Shea to see if he was awake. She pulled onto the interstate just as her phone rang, it was Shea.

"Hey, did I wake you?"

"No," his voice was all groggy.

"Liar, I'll call you tomorrow."

"No, I want to talk to you, make sure you get home okay." She smiled. "How was the wedding?"

"Beautiful, tiring, I'm ready to go to bed."

"Are you on the interstate?"

"I am, I have about thirty minutes till I get there."

"Okay, so did you hear about the Potter trade?" he asked, and that threw them into an awesome conversation of hockey. She loved talking hockey with Shea, he actually knew what he was talking about, unlike her brothers, they were idiots, and they only liked the fights. Elli was home before she knew it; she pulled into her drive and smiled at Adler who was in the window, wagging his little pug tail.

"I'm home," she said after a moment of silence.

"Okay, so I'll see you tomorrow?"

"Yup, seven right?"

"Right."

"Do you still want to pick me up? I'm cool with driving in town."

"I'll be there at seven; I want to see your house."

"Okay, well I'll see you tomorrow."

"Alright babe, bye, sweet dreams."

"You too, bye."

Elli hung up the phone with a grin on her face as she walked up the sidewalk to her house; she loved on Adler as she came in, and then let him out as she moved through the house. After hanging her dress up, and taking her shoes off, she went to let Adler back in. She stood in the doorway, waiting, and looked behind her to her Assassins wall. There was a Fathead of the team's emblem, and then pictures from the game, mostly of Shea, since he was her favorite player. There was also a signed jersey that her uncle had gotten her that year to go with her season tickets. Shea's signature was in the middle, right beside his number. She loved her little entry way, it was totally Assassins' decked out.

"Oh, shit!"

She looked around in horror, she was dating an Assassin and when Shea saw this he would think she was a freak!

"Oh my God, and he's coming here tomorrow!"

Chapter 6

Shea was looking really good in his opinion he thought, as he drove to Elli's house. The suit he had picked out fit him perfectly and he was having a great hair day. He was going to put his contacts in, but he couldn't find them, so that was a no go. He was extremely excited about seeing Elli, even after the conversation him and Jakob had had that day.

"Dude, you're making yourself too available!" Jakob bitched as Shea texted Elli, "You're always talking to her, and she's going to think you're desperate."

"No, she won't, I just like talking to her," Shea said defensively, "So shut up."

"You've seen her every day since Sunday, you're smothering her!"

"I am not! I just want to get to know her," Shea looked back up at him, glaring "and this coming from the guy that stalking what's her name."

"Harper, but I love her."

"Oh my God, really dude? It's been a week!"

"I know *the one* when I see her." Shea stood up, wrapping a towel around his waist.

"You know what, before you try giving me advice on how to date girls, get your love life square."

Shea shook his head just thinking about Jakob declaring love for Elli's friend. It made no damn sense, but it really didn't matter. He was going out with Elli in a matter of minutes.

Her house wasn't hard to find, it was one of six on the road she had given him. He saw her truck before he saw the house. That damn truck, a girl shouldn't be driving it, a man should. He shook his head as he pulled up behind it, and got out. He was so memorized by her truck he didn't notice her sitting on the porch in a rocking chair. She stood up, looking as beautiful as ever in a light colored dress.

"Hey," she said with a wave, crossing her legs, she was wearing some naughty looking boots that had chains on them.

"Hey, I was going to come to the door," he said as he walked towards her, she looked nervous as she came down the stairs.

"Yeah, my dog jumps on people."

"How high can a 40 pound pug jump?" he asked with a laugh.

"Hey, shut up. Let's go." she said pulling him towards the car.

"You don't want to show me the house?"

"No, I'm ready to go, plus I don't want my dog to mess up you suit." She took his hand in hers and started for the truck. He went along with it, if she didn't want him in her house, fine.

 For now.

He opened the door for her and she climbed in, grinning back at him. He returned the smile, and then went around getting in himself. He pulled out of her driveway and they were off.

"I told you I should have just drove," she said from beside him, he looked over at her.

"What?"

"You're mad."

"I am not."

"Yes, you are, you get that tick in the side of your jaw when people irritate you." He had to smile at that, that's how he knew for sure she was a hockey fan, his tick was documented as a way for is opponents to watch the hell out.

"That doesn't mean I'm mad."

"True, but you are irritated. I'm sorry Shea; I'm just not ready to show you my house."

"Can I ask why?"

"I'd prefer ya didn't."

"Okay," he took a deep breath trying to calm his irritation, "but I still want to pick you up and walk you to the door at the end of the night." He looked over at her, and she was biting her lip. He reached over, taking her hand in his. "You look beautiful tonight, Elli. Gorgeous." She blushed and looked out the window.

"Thank you, I like your tie." He smiled as he looked down at his pink tie.

"I thought you might."

Nothing else was said as they drove; it was a nice, comfortable silence. With other women he always felt like he had to keep talking, but with Elli, all he needed was her small soft hand in his and he was golden, nothing in the world could bother him, except for the fact she wouldn't let him in her house.

They arrived at PF Changs right before their reservations, after helping Elli out of the truck; Shea gave the keys to the valet and took her hand before leading her in. The hostess already had their table, and they followed her to the back. Since he couldn't wear a hat tonight, he asked to be in the back somewhere, and of course the restaurant obliged. They were seated at a corner table, were they scooted into the booth, next to each other.

"What's good to drink here?" Elli asked as she looked over the menu, he looked over at her from his menu.

"I was going to get us a bottle of plum wine, it's really good here."

"Sounds good," she said with a nod, and a smile. "Your hair looks extra spiky today." She reached up and tapped his head with her palm, making him laugh.

"Yeah, when I don't wear my hat, I make sure my hair looks good."

"It does," she said with a grin as the waiter came over to take their orders. Elli knew what she wanted and so did he, so they ordered their food too. The waiter smiled thanks before leaving to put in the order.

"So how was your day?" he asked her as he took a drink of the wine another waiter had brought over.

"Good, not that busy. Next two days will be hell though."

"Oh really? No lunches?"

She had a sad smile as she shook her head, "No, I'm booked solid."

"Well that sucks, who am I supposed to eat lunch with?" She smiled.

"I'm sure you can find someone."

"Maybe I don't want to eat with anyone but you." She grinned before taking a drink, her cheeks a bright red. "What are your plans for the weekend?"

"I'm spending the day with my nieces and nephews Saturday, then that night I got a wedding. Sunday is free except in the morning, I got church and at night my friends will be coming over." Her face lit up as she smiled. "My friends and I do this thing every month, where we get together, drink, eat, and play games, it's fun." He nodded as he took a drink and leaned back in the booth.

"Sounds like fun," he said.

"It is," she agreed, taking another drink of her wine.

When their food arrived they talked about foods they liked and didn't like, but they both agreed that nachos were the best hockey food ever. They talked about more movies they liked, then music, and of course hockey. The food was amazing, like always, but the company was even better.

"I need to ask you something, Shea," Elli said as she took another drink of her wine, he nodded as he took a bite of the dessert they had ordered.

"Okay?"

"This is gonna sound stupid, but I need to know." She looked worried; she was biting the hell out of her lip, so of course Shea got nervous, sitting up straighter. He looked over at her as he laid his fork down.

"What is it?"

"Okay, so I know I'm not your regular type. I've always seen you with the leggy blondes, and never with the same girl. I even read somewhere that the same girl doesn't sit in your box more than once, so I guess what I'm trying to say, or ask even is that," she took a deep breath, and he couldn't help but smile at her, she was so sweet. "Is that, we've been out four times now, I'm not seeing anyone else, and I'm not saying that you can't see anyone else, that's not what I'm trying to say, it's more like," she was flustered he could tell, but he also knew to let her get it out, so he sat patiently until it was time for him to answer "Why me? You know? I mean I'm pretty sure there isn't anyone else, if there is, I would like to know, but why me?" He shook his head.

"There isn't anyone else."

"Okay, so why me? You can have any girl with the flick of a wrist. I mean, I guess it just hard for me to believe that you want to spend time with me."

"Why's that so hard to believe?"

"Because I'm me, and you're you. I just a normal citizen, while you're a celebrity. I'm ordinary, while your gorgeous, and-"

"Okay, shut up," he said since he had heard enough, she looked over at him stunned. He smiled, and then reached for her hand, kissing her knuckles. "I want see you because I like you, I like you because your amazing, sweet, understanding, and if I ever hear you say your ordinary I might smack your ass because you are gorgeous Elli. So freaking beautiful that sometimes, like tonight, I find myself speechless of your beauty." She looked down at her hands, then back up at him with a shy smile.

"I don't know it's just so hard to believe."

He smiled before bringing her knuckles to his lips again. "Then I'll just have to work hard to make you believe me."

Elli still didn't feel any better about why Shea was with her, but, hell, what was she supposed to do? He said his piece, she would either trust him, or let him go. Since letting him go wasn't an option now, she would try to trust him. After eating their desserts, Shea paid the bill, and they took off for the movies. She picked an action/thriller movie she had wanted to see, and so had Shea. It was good, but it was even better to hold someone's hand through the movie.

The walk to the truck was quiet, just the two of them walking with their fingers intertwined. After getting Elli in the truck, Shea came around the other side and joined her. The ride out to her house was nice, they talked about the movie, and what they liked and didn't like. They also made fun of the actor who couldn't act worth crap. Elli loved talking to Shea, he was so animated, so funny. So perfect.

When they arrived to Elli's house, Shea got out and helped her down, holding her hand as they walked to the door. Adler started barking as soon as they reach the first step.

"Shh!" she scolded as she turned to look at Shea. He was on the bottom step while she was on the second, so they were the exact height. "I had a wonderful time Shea."

"I'm glad, I did too." He leaned a little closer, wrapping his arms around her waist. Adler chose that particular moment to start scratching like a mad man at the door.

"No treat!" Elli yelled, Shea started laughing, but the scratching stopped.

"You never did tell me your dog's name."

Elli froze, she couldn't tell him the name; he would think she was crazy! So she did the only logical thing she could think off, she wrapped her arms around his neck, and kissed him hard. What was supposed to be a distraction turned into some heavy kissing, his hands tightened at her waist, making her dress tight around the middle. She would have cared any other time, but with Shea kissing her the way he was, she really didn't care. She moved her hands from behind his neck, to his cheeks, feeling the dusting of hair on his cheeks and jaw. It was so sexy to feel a man's face like that. He kissed like a dream, his lips so hard, but soft at the same time, and the way he used that tongue. Jesus, help her. She kissed the side of his mouth, his breathing was hard, and so was hers. As she kissed the side of his neck, a low growl escaped his lips. She had forgotten how much she loved the sounds males could make, so she kissed him again, rewarded with the same sound. He pulled back, bringing her face up to kiss her lips softly, than he leaned his head on hers.

"Jeez, Elli, you're driving me crazy. So unless you want to move this inside, because I doubt you want a show for the neighbors, we need to stop, because my control is slipping," he whispered, against her lips. God, how she wanted him to come in, she wanted to rip his clothes off and screw his brains out. The lust was apparent on his face, he wanted her, all she wanted was to distract him and look what she did! She had not only turned him on, but also made herself hot as ever!

"I'm sorry," she said taking a step back, "I'm so sorry. I don't know what came over me." He smiled, as he pulled her back to him.

"It's called chemistry baby, and we've got it. Now give me a kiss goodnight, but not a naughty one," he said with a grin. She smiled and kissed him softly on the lips.

"Thanks again for dinner and the movie, I had so much fun."

"Yeah, that stuff was fun, but what just happened here…Jesus." He gave her a cocky smile as he walked down the steps. She waved as he got into the truck; he waved back before starting the truck and backing out.

"Well, that was intense," she muttered to herself as she went inside.

Between practice, promos and not being able to see Elli, he missed her the rest of the week. She was right when she said she would be busy for the next two days, not only did they not get to talk much, but she apparently stayed with Harper since she was so tired after all the events so they didn't get to talk on her way home. He was going to offer his house to her because he wanted to see her so bad, but he was afraid it would scare her, so he didn't.

Saturday morning, while he ate breakfast after running on the treadmill for an hour, he decided that it was a decent time to text Elli, so he did.

Hey, whatcha up to?

Hey you! About to get the kids, then heading to the Rising Park. It's the kid's favorite.

Oh yeah, she had her nieces and nephews today. He had totally forgotten about that.

Cool, have fun. I guess text me when you can.

I will, □

Shea laid his phone down as he cleaned up his mess, he wanted to see her today, but he couldn't invite himself to her day with the kids. It would be awkward for him to be there when she has all the kids. When he turned to put the milk back in the fridge, he saw Ryan and Amelia smiling at him from the picture on his fridge. A slow grin crossed his face as he looked at their beautiful faces.

"But if I had the kids," he muttered as he rushed off to the bedroom to get ready.

Shea knew he was driving like a bat out of hell, but he was on a mission. He should have called Grace first, but that would give her time to say no, so he pulled into her driveway and parked the truck beside her van, before jumping out and walking briskly to the front door, letting himself in.

"Hey! Anyone home?" he yelled through the house, Ryan came running towards him, his arms held wide.

"Unky, Shea!" he yelled as Shea picked him up, kissing his cheek.

"Hey bud, where's momma?"

"In the kitchen."

"Wanna go to the park with me?" he asked, Ryan grinned big, his blue eyes bright.

"Yes! Can we play hockey?"

"Maybe, we'll see okay?"

"Okay, put me down, I'm gonna go get my bag."

"Don't bring your ice skates!"

"I won't!" he yelled back as Shea entered the kitchen. Grace sat at the table, her face on her arms with her eyes closed. Amelia sat in the highchair, playing with a puzzle.

"What do you want?" Grace muttered. She looked so tired.

"You're kids. I'm borrowing them." Grace sat up, looking at him through half lidded eyes.

"Huh?"

"I'm taking the kids to the park."

"Why?"

"Cause you need time to yourself. I'll bring them back later."

"Huh?"

"You heard me, where's Amelia's bag?"

"By the door, when will you be back?"

"Sometime later." He unhooked Amelia's chair, and took the smiling baby in his arms. "Hey baby girl."

"Unky!" she squealed as she smacked his face. "Go, Go!"

"We're going, okay, give me your keys."

"Why?" Grace asked looked up at him, confused.

"I don't have car seats, so I'm gonna take the van, I left my keys in the basket."

"Huh? I'm so confused, you never take the kids."

"You're tired Grace, sleep." He walked away with Amelia in his arms, he grabbed her bag as Ryan came booming down the hall in his Assassins' gear, Shea's face on his shirt, with his number on the back, Ryan was his biggest fan.

"I'm ready Unky."

"Alright, bud, let's go."

"Did James put you up to this?" Grace asked as she kissed Amelia then Ryan.

"No, just please promise me you'll sleep today, love you."

"Love you too Shea, thank you." Shea threw her a grin as he left with the kids.

After loading the kids in the van, he had to push the seat all the way back so he'd fit, before rolling out. It only took ten minutes to get to the park, and thank God for that because Ryan was talking nonstop. From hockey, to baby poo, to The Wiggles, whatever the hell that was. When he pulled into the park, he didn't see Elli's truck, maybe she left? He pulled out his phone and dialed her number.

"Hello," she answered, he heard kids in the background.

"Hey, you still at the park?"

"Yup, we'll be here for a while."

"Oh, okay, well I'll let you go." He hung up before she could answer, and unloaded the kids. Holding Amelia on his hip, as he held Ryan's hand, he headed towards the park where it seemed billions of kids were playing.

"Unky Shea, does Ryan Justice sound like a hockey player name?"

"Sure does bud, why?"

"Brandon Owens says it doesn't."

"Brandon Owens doesn't know what he is talking about," Shea said simply as they walked. He heard Elli before he saw her. He could pick out that thick country voice anywhere.

"Max! Please do not pull Penny's hair! Riley if you don't put your sister down, I'm coming after you!"

Shea smiled as he walked towards her, she was looking too hot for words today. A pair of jeans shorts that were ripped up, with an Assassins' tee and his grin got bigger when he saw it was his number on her back. Her hair was pulled into a high messy pony tail, and she had them big glasses on from the first time he had saw her. He watched her for a moment as she fussed over the kids, kissing their cheeks and tickling them. She was beautiful, breathtaking. He read his name over her back one last time, before stepping behind her.

"So, you're an Adler fan huh?"

"Shea!" Elli gasped when she whipped around to tell the person that made the comment about her shirt, that hell yeah, she was, but she didn't expect to see Shea. "What are you doing here?" He grinned at her, hoisting his niece higher on his hip, as he swung his nephew's hand back and forth.

"Grace was really tired, so I took the kids."

"I thought you were scared of them," she said with a teasing grin.

"Unky Shea, I thought you weren't scared of anything," Ryan said looking up at his uncle lovingly.

"I'm not, bud."

"My Unky isn't scared of anything; he won the Lord Stanley Cup last year. He held it over his head as he skated around, he cried but that's only because he was soooooooo happy, hockey players don't cry at any other time."

Elli grinned at Ryan before looking up at Shea, he was actually blushing. "I know he did, I was there, I cried too, I was really happy."

"Wow, really! Where did you sit? Unky had us in a box, with this girl with really big hair, she smelled funny, but she was nice, I guess. What ever happen to that girl Unky?"

"I don't know bud, listen, cool it for a second so I can introduce you." Ryan nodding, hanging on every word Shea said, you could tell he thought his uncle was the bees knees. "This is Elli, Elli this is Ryan and you've met Amelia."

"I have," Elli said with a grin, touching the baby's cheek, before she shook Ryan's hand. "Nice to meet you."

"Nice to me you too, Ms. Elli. Unky can I go play?"

"Of course, go ahead." Ryan ran off towards the play area leaving Shea, Elli and Amelia in his dust.

"He's a sweet kid."

"Runs his mouth all the damn time, but I love him so much. Do you think it's safe for Amelia in that sand box?"

"Yeah, I'm sitting on that bench right there, so it would be perfect," she said with a grin as she followed them over, Shea sat Amelia in the sand box then walked over to the bench, sitting beside her. "It's so sweet of you to watch the kids for Grace; I know how tired she's been lately."

"Yeah," he said with a grin. "Are you mad I came here? Move in on your time with the kids?"

"No! Not at all." She looked at the kids, then down, picking at the fray of her shorts "I've kinda missed seeing you these past two days," she added in a whisper.

"Awwwwww," he teased, leaning into her as he grinned down at her. He looked over at Amelia and Elli felt dumb. Great way to make yourself look needy, she thought as she sat there mentally kicking herself. You don't put yourself out there like that with guys like Shea. God, she was an idiot- "I've missed you too, Elli. A lot. More than I liked to admit, that's why I came today, not to give Grace a break, but to see you."

She sat there, shocked, looking up at him, as he watched Amelia. He had his glasses on; she was starting to think that was the only way he ran around when he wasn't on the ice. His tattoos weren't covered this time, since he was wearing a t-shirt and cargo shorts. He hadn't shaved since the last time she saw him, so the hair on his chin was darker and longer.

"So, when are you going to introduce me to the kids?" he asked, looking over at her. Oh shit, for the first time ever, she didn't even think of the kids. A look of horror crossed her face as she looked towards the playground where her nieces and nephews played.

"Shit."

"Huh? What?"

"Okay, Shea, don't take this the wrong way, but I can't introduce you to the kids, they will go back and tell their parents, and then my mom would find out, and I cannot even deal with my mom about you right now, so we're gonna have to act like you just sat down beside me," she said, frantic, just as Riley and Max came running towards her.

"Auntie El, there's this kid over there, saying his uncle is Shea Adler! Isn't that crazy! You think he's lyin'?" Max practically yelled, Elli gave Shea a sideways glace then looked back at Max.

"You never know honey; I heard that Shea Adler does have a nephew, a niece too."

"Wow, wouldn't that be awesome if we met him! Dad would be so jealous!" Riley exclaimed.

"Yeah, he would, alright run along" she said, shushing them away, they ran off talking about Shea and she took a deep breath.

"Ryan talks a lot." Elli looked over at Shea; he looked upset under his hat. She hated that she was the one to put that look on his face.

"Shea, I'm sorry."

"It's cool; do you want me to go, so you don't have to explain why you're sitting next to me?"

"No! I want to spend time with you." She took his hand in hers, "You just don't understand my family, you haven't met them or, hell, I haven't even talked about them, and they are crazy, so please just bare with me through this."

"Only if you promise me one thing," he said, not looking at her.

"Yeah?"

"Come spend the day with me tomorrow, we'll watch movies, and just hang out, no interruptions, just us." He had the cutest grin on his face as he kept his eyes on Amelia, when she noticed he only had one dimple, she poked it, and smiled.

"You only have one dimple." He covered it with his hand, and blushed.

"Grace makes fun of me all the time for it."

"I think it's sexy," she said with a grin, than she looked out to where the kids were. Should she go to his condo? All by herself?

"So, what do you say?"

"Um, I-"

"UNKY SHEA!!!!!!!!!!!!" They both jumped in shock as Ryan came towards them, his hand in the air as tears ran down his cheeks.

"Ryan, buddy, what happened?" Shea asked jumping up and going to him quickly.

"I,I,I, fell and hurt my hand!" he wailed, Shea cupped his hand looking at it. From what Elli could see, it was only a small scratch.

"Buddy, come on now, calm down. Hockey players don't cry remember," Shea said with a smile as he rubbed Ryan's back. Elli saw it coming but obviously Shea didn't, because when Ryan's face cringed up and he started wailing for his mommy, Shea freaked out. He picked Ryan up, hugging him close.

"I want my mommy!!!" Ryan cried, Elli went over, taking Ryan from Shea, cuddling him close to her chest.

"Oh goodness, you poor thang," she cooed as she sat down on the bench, putting him across her legs. "Let me see this boo boo, honey." He held out his hand for Elli to see, rocks and dirt were mixed with a little blood.

"Its hu,hu,hurts," he stuttered.

"Oh my goodness!" she exclaimed as she dug in her bag for a wipe, then she cleaned off his hand before bringing his palm to her lips, kissing it softly, "All better?"

"Ye, ye, yes, ma'am. Do you have a Band-Aid?" he asked, tears still in his eyes.

"I do, honey," she said, putting a Spiderman one on his hand. He looked at his hand, than her, with a watery grin.

"Thank you."

"You're welcome darling," she said with a grin as he jumped off her lap, grinning up at his uncle.

"Ms. Elli fixed me."

"She sure did."

"You need to learn how to do that Unky, it's good to know."

"I know that now bud, go play."

"Kay!" He ran off with the biggest smile in the world and Shea looked down at Elli with appreciation all over his face.

"You're amazing Elli."

"Why thank you," she said with a grin as she leaned back on the bench. "He's sweet."

"He's a pain," he muttered as he sat down beside her, she loved how he moved, so fluid like. They sat in silence as they watched the kids play. Elli made sure to keep an eye on Amelia since she was so little; she noticed that Shea was doing the same. Elli tore her eyes off the beautiful baby to do a head count.

"Max, Riley, Emma, Penny, Jason, and Jessica, oh, and Ryan," she muttered as she counted each child.

"Are those you're nieces and nephews names?"

"Yeah, Max, Penny, and Jason are Liam's kids, and then Riley, Emma, and Jessica are Noah's kids. We had a child born each year for 5 year; Emma and Max were born within a week of each other."

"Wow, that's a lot of birthdays."

"Yeah, but it's nice, I love them all so much."

"You know, you're always talking about the kids, but this is the first I've ever heard your brother's names."

Elli thought that over, and then shrugged her shoulders.

"My family issues are not a good topic for today." Shea nodded as Penny, Emma, and Jessica came running towards her.

"Auntie Elli, the boys are being mean," Jessica complained.

"They are still pulling my pigtails," Penny cried.

"They just stink in my opinion," said Emma. Elli shook her head, as Shea chuckled beside her. All three guys looked at Shea, and when Elli saw how big Penny's eyes got, she knew that Penny knew who he was. Penny came closer, still looking at Shea as she came close to Elli's ear to whisper "Auntie Elli, do you know Big Daddy Adler is sitting next to you?"

Elli couldn't suppress the giggle that came out of her, Penny walked backwards till she was standing with Emma and Jessica.

"Just stay away from them, girls," she managed through the giggles, the girls nodded than ran off.

"What did she call me?"

"Big Daddy Adler, my sister-in-law is in love with you, and has a picture of you and her at some hockey thing Max had done, it's on the mantel, and Adina calls you that." He started laughing, and Elli joined in.

"That's intense."

"It really is."

"You're really good with kids, Elli," Shea said after a moment, she looked over at him.

"I love them."

"Do you want your own?" She smiled, than looked out towards the kids.

"Yeah, I do. When I was younger, I was convinced I would be married by now with a big ole family, guess God had a different plan for me," she said with a sad smile, than shrugged her shoulders, dismissing the idea. "Do you want kids?"

"I do, but I need a wife first. Luckily, Grace had kids, so my mom leaves me alone." Elli laughed as Shea shook his head. "When I was being traded back in the day, my mom would be so mad at us, saying we needed to settle down, find us a partner, thank God we came here and Grace met Jason."

"Y'all traveled together?"

"Yeah, wherever I went, Grace went."

"Really!? Everywhere?"

"Yeah, she lived with me wherever I went. When I first left, she would have anxiety attack and when she came to where I was, she was fine, so, we just stayed together."

"Wow, I didn't know y'all were that close."

"Oh yeah, Grace is my best friend."

"That's so sweet."

"I guess, I'm just glad she has Jason and the kids. I just want her to be happy." Elli smiled big at him, then looked at the kids some more.

"Are you close to your parents?" she asked.

"Yeah, I talk to my parents at least every day. My dad and I are really close. He taught me to play hockey, plus we love going deep sea fishing too."

"I love fishing."

"I'll take you home, and we'll go out on the boat with my dad, you'll love him."

Elli got all warm inside. He wanted to take her home. To fish. With his dad.

"My mom is crazy, but God I love her. She cooks all the time, I swear I gain 20 pounds every time I go home," he said with a grin, "She spoils me and I'm ten hours away! She sends packages to me of my favorite treats and then she packs stuff for the team. Even Coach Bacter loves her." Elli had to laugh at that, from what she heard Coach Bacter hated everyone. He was always mean-mugging someone in her opinion. He never smiled! Even when the Assassins won! Shea kept on talking about his family, about all their amazing times. Elli could tell he loved them, a lot.

Wish she could say the same about her family.

"I think my mom would love you, my dad would probably steal you away since you love hockey, and mom doesn't know anything about hockey, she always says it a bunch of baboons fighting around on ice."

Elli busted out in a fit of giggles, she loved hockey, but she could see where someone would think that. "They sound great."

"They are," he said with his one dimple grin. It was funny that she never noticed that before, probably because he always sat on the other side of her. They sat the rest of the afternoon talking about whatever came to mind, while watching the kids. When Amelia started crying, Elli went to get up, but Shea was already there, kissing and loving on her.

He was going to make a great dad one day.

Shea brought her over to where they were sitting, and gave Amelia her bottle. She pushed it away rubbing her eyes.

"I might have to go, I don't think she is going to make it much longer," he said looking over at Elli. She smiled, rubbing Amelia's head.

"I understand. Grace got at least a three hour nap."

"She sure did," he said with a grin as he stood up, Amelia on his hip. Elli grabbed Amelia's bag and handed it to him. He looked down at her, and smiled. "Did I tell you that you're sexy in my number?" Elli turned deep red, crossing her legs as she pulled at the bottom of her shirt.

"Shut up," she giggled as she hit him with her arm, she tried to pull back, but he had an arm wrapped around her so fast, that she didn't have time to protest before he crushed his mouth against hers. When his tongue slid in her mouth, she knew she should have felt dirty since he was holding his niece, but she didn't. Her hand slid up to his cheek, and she kissed him back just as hard. She hadn't seen him in two days, that's two days of no smiles, laughs, or goodness gracious, those damn kisses.

"Auntie Elli, why are you open mouth kissing Big Daddy Adler?"

Well, shit.

Chapter 7

Shea watched as Penny looked up at them, her eyes were big as quarters, and her mouth was hanging open. The other kids stood behind Penny, with Ryan right in the mix.

"Oh my goodness, it really is Shea Adler," one of the boys said, another one was slapping the last boy as Ryan just grinned up at him.

"Yup, and he's my Unky, are you ready to go yet? I'm tired," Ryan said.

"Sure am buddy, wanna say bye to your new friends, and Ms. Elli?"

"Bye guys," he said to the kids, then went and gave Elli a hug, looking up at her "Thank you for fixing my boo boo, bye."

"Bye Ryan," she said with a grin, than she looked over at Shea. "Bye, Shea."

"Bye babe, I'll call ya."

"Alright," she said with a shake of her head, Shea looked down at the kids as he began to walk away, they all had their mouths hanging open at the sight of him.

"Bye guys." Their eyes never left him as he walked with Ryan to the car with Amelia on his hip. It seem as soon as he got Amelia in the car seat she passed out. That wasn't the case with Ryan, he was talkative till they got to the house, even up the driveway, and even when his dad came to the door.

"You're a Godsend, Shea. Thanks," James said as he took a sleeping Amelia from him.

"No problem, where's Grace?"

"Sleeping, I figured I'd meet ya at the door, take the kids, try to keep them out her hair."

"You're a good man, James. Good man." Shea leaned over kissing Amelia's head, than he hugged Ryan tightly. "Love you, bud."

"Love you too Unky, thanks for a fun day."

"No problem bud, we'll do it more often."

"Am I still going Wednesday to your game?"

"Absolutely bud, everyone will be there."

"Awesome!" he said with a punch in the air, and then he ran off. James smiled at Shea as he said goodbye and shut the door after giving Shea his keys. Shea walked to his truck, a smile on his face. He felt good, today was a good day, hell, maybe a great one. When he got into the truck and started it, he went through the drive through for some Taco Bell, before he headed home.

It was close to six when Shea finally sat in front of his TV watching Sports Center. He was ready for the opener on Wednesday, ready to play. The thought that Elli would be watching him made him smile, then he started wondering what she was doing. He pulled his phone out of his pocket and texted her.

At the wedding?

He only waited a moment before she answered back.

Yup, bored. Some weddings are awesome, while others are drags, and this one is a drag.

Sorry about that, how was your ride home with the kids?

Interesting to say the least. I just dropped them off, didn't even stay for the fireworks. My mother has called me 10 times.

Shea smiled to himself. Her family probably wasn't that bad, she was the baby, so they probably picked on her.

Wow, sorry about that. It was good seeing you today, can't wait till tomorrow.

Me neither □

Shea smiled to himself as he laid his phone down, he didn't want to keep her busy so he decided to wait till later when she would call on her way home. What he didn't expect was to fall asleep; he guessed the kids wore him out more than he thought. He woke with a jump when his phone started ringing, it was Elli. He answered as he looked at the time, it was past midnight.

"You were sleeping." He smiled as he rubbed his eyes.

"I was."

"Sorry! Just text me your address in the morning."

"Okay babe, I'm sorry, I'm really tired."

"Its fine, I'll see you tomorrow, sorry to call so late."

"No, don't be sorry, are you home?"

"Just left Nashville."

"Okay, text me when you get home, so I know you got there safe. I'll see you tomorrow."

"Alright, goodnight."

"Night baby." He hung up the phone and texted her his address before walking to the back room where he fell face first into his bed. He was almost asleep when his phone went off again, he glanced at it seeing that Elli had made it home, and she would see him tomorrow. With a smile, he closed his eyes, pulling the pillow that was beside him up under his chin, wishing it was Elli as he went back to sleep.

"Hello, brother dear." Shea smiled when he answered his phone, it was his sister, he was cooking lunch for Elli, he wasn't much of a cook, but he made a mean sandwich and heating soup wasn't that hard.

"Hey, you sleep well?"

"Amazing, I haven't gotten more than twelve hours of sleep in God knows how long. So thank you!"

"No problem, only for you," she gave a little laugh and he knew it was coming; Ryan had the biggest mouth in Nashville.

"So, all I heard this morning was, Ms. Elli this, Ms. Elli that, and oh mommy, then Ms. Elli and Unky Shea were open mouth kissing." Shea shook his head, a grin on his face. "Shea, where the hell did my four year old learn about open mouth kissing?" Shea let out a hoot of laughter, slapping the top of the counter with his hand.

"Not my fault, Elli's niece yelled it at us."

"You were making out in front of the kids?"

"No, we kissed goodbye and it got a little hot."

"I mean jeez, protect the younger eyes please."

"Sorry, is he scarred for life?" She laughed, as he smiled.

"No, but he is wondering why Unky Shea and Ms. Elli don't have kids since they kiss like that." Shea was practically choking on his laughter.

"That kid is a trip."

"That he is, so what do you have planned for today?"

Shea smiled, as he turned the soup down.

"Elli's coming for lunch, maybe a little open mouth kissing."

"Let her swallow her food before you pursue that," Shea let out a chuckle, his sister humor killed him, "Have fun though, call me later?"

"Sure."

Grace wished him luck, and then told him she loved him before hanging up, Shea smiled as he finished up everything for lunch. He had remembered Elli saying she liked fruit so he made sure to cut some up for her. He also got some mango ice cream for her, another of her favorites. He was walking through the living room, making sure it was clean when the door bell sounded.

Shea ran his hands down his shirt, then through his hair as he walked to the door. Shea opened it to Elli, who leaning against the door jam, holding up a bag. She looked sexy as hell in a pair of shorts and a little tee that hung off her shoulder. She had big glasses of her face and on her head was an Assassins hat, with her name on it.

"Well, hello," he said looking her over, loving the fact that her toes were purple, team colors.

"Hey," she said holding out her arm, handing him the bag. "For you."

"Ooh, presents," he cooed as he moved out the way for her to come in as he peeked in the bag, to his delight it was a copy of Pride and Prejudice, the 2005 movie version and the book with a book cover.

"Not much, but since you don't own it."

"Thank you," he said pulling her into his arms, and kissing her softly. Her hands came up his arms to his neck, rubbing softly as he kissed her. He pulled back looking into her bright green eyes as she smiled up at him. Her eyes were like fresh green grass, the kind of green that made you stop and look at them when you got even just a small glimpse. They were captivating. He moved a piece of her hair out of her face, tucking it behind her ear and the brim of the hat. "We'll watch it after lunch."

"I was hoping you'd say that, I'm not sure I can date a guy who hasn't at least seen the movie." He smiled as he hugged her tighter to him.

"Come on, I'll show you around." He took her hand, and then led her through the condo, to his office, his bathroom, and his bedroom. Elli was quick to high tail it out of there, even though he had a beautiful view of Nashville through the windows that lined the walls. He took her through the living room to the kitchen; she looked around with a smile.

"Grace did a good job in here, the house its, you."

"Yeah, she knows what she's doing," he said with a grin, he pulled a chair out from the table. "Ready to eat?" he asked.

"Yes, I'm starved." She sat down, and Shea moved around, placing stuff on the table, going back and forth from the kitchen. When he finally sat in front of her, she was smiling as she looked at the spread. "Looks great."

"It's not much, but it's better than the same old takeout we've been eating." Elli nodded as she started serving herself. Shea did the same as they made small talk. Did she find the place okay? Was the wedding good last night? Just little stuff, he loved listening to her talk and he loved when she got excited or found something funny. Her face would get so bright, bright as the sun.

"Are them vintage guitars?" Shea looked over at the wall that Elli was pointing too. He nodded as he looked back over at her; she was getting up with an awed look on her face. "They are beautiful."

He stood up and went beside her, looking up at the nine guitars that graced his walls, "Do you play?"

"Sorta, not good. My instrument was fiddle and a little banjo."

"Wow, could you get anymore country?"

"Shut up, my dad made all us kids play an instrument. When we would all play together," she smiled, but it didn't reach her eyes. "Those were some of the best times of my childhood."

"What did everyone play?" he asked, she cut him a glance them looked back up at the guitars.

"My dad played guitar, Noah played the upright bass, Liam would play the banjo, and Victoria played the mandolin."

"What did you play?"

"The fiddle."

"Oh, did your mom sing? Don't you need a singer for that kind of stuff?"

Elli laughed as she shook her head "No, my momma never had a musical bone in her body, she watched," She looked down at the ground, then back up at him a few moments later. "I used to sing."

"Oh cool, you'll have to play and sing for me one day," he said with a grin, Shea turned and started cleaning the mess they had made as she looked up at the guitars.

"That Gibson Hummingbird is beautiful." He heard her say as he stood in the kitchen, he heard her come up behind him and she sat up on the counter as he loaded the dishwasher. He shook his head as he smiled at her.

"You never cease to amaze me, Elli. You know guitars?"

"I told you I play a little."

"Yeah, but usually women don't know anything about them."

"True, how did you get into them?" He smiled as he shut the dishwasher and leaned against it.

"When I came to the team, Wavier used to call me Boston, saying I was too Boston to live in Nashville, so I decided I wanted to be able to do something that was Nashvilley, so I started collecting guitars. Well one day Wavier came over, and he was impressed with my collection and he said 'Hey bring two down, lets jam.' I froze; I didn't know how to play, when I admitted that, he tore into me." Shea smiled at the memory of his long time friend. He didn't get to see Wavier much but he still loved the guy "But he taught me to play, and now I love it."

"Wow."

"Yeah, so you ready for a movie?"

"I am," she said with a grin as he followed her into the living room. He grabbed the DVD and tore it open, putting it in his DVD player. When he turned, Elli was sitting on the far side of the couch, her knees under her chin. He savored the sight of her thighs peeking out from her shorts, his groin got tighter at just the thought of touching her there. She drove him mad. He had never waited this long to have sex with a woman that he was dating, he usually had sex with them the first night, but with Elli, it was different. They had been dating for almost a week and a half, and he was fine with the fact that he hadn't seen her naked, he just wanted to see her. He smiled as he came over, sitting on the other end of the couch. The movie started, and he looked over at her, at the same time she looked over at him. They busted out laughing at the awkwardness, before stopping to stare into each other's eyes.

"Come here," Shea whispered holding out his hand, Elli looked at him, then his hand, before looking back at him. She bit her lip before taking his hand, and he pulled her to him. She looked up at him, and he covered her mouth with his, kissing her so deeply he was convinced he felt it in his soul. His hand went up into her hair as the other one cupped her face. Elli's hands were at his shoulders as she ate at his mouth, he loved the way she kissed, the way she felt in his hands. Shea moved his hand from her face to her legs, pulling them out from underneath her and laying her back into the couch, where he continued to kiss her lavishly. When he got himself positioned between her legs, feeling her warmth against his hard groin, she pulled back, eyes half lidded as she look at him.

"I really wanna watch the movie," she whispered. Shea stopped and looked at her.

"Watch the movie?" was all he could get out, he was beyond wanting to watch the movie, more like fuck her brains out.

"Yeah, it's a really good movie," she said with a nod as she tried to sit up and move from underneath him. He moved too, letting her up, but she didn't go far, she cuddled into his side with a cute grin on her face. He moved a little, pulling at the crotch of his pants; she looked down then back up at him.

"Sorry, it's a little tight in there, babe," he muttered, which made her blush deep scarlet as she intensely looked at the screen. He had to grin to himself as he readjusted and moved his arm around her. His hand met her hip, and he had to tell himself not to rub it because then any chance of him paying attention to this movie would be shot. So he paid attention and the movie was actually really good. When the ending credit's started, Elli sat up grinning down at him.

"Did you love it!?" she exclaimed, he smiled.

"It was good."

"What was your favorite part?" Shea thought for a moment, the movie was really good.

"The part when that Darcy guy told her he loved her for the first time. I love Elizabeth's face, she was like 'Say what?!'" Elli giggled as she sat with her legs crossed in front of him. "It was a good movie, babe, and thanks for educating me." Her grin continued to grow, showing all her dimples.

"My pleasure, I watch that movie every night when I go to sleep."

"Really?"

"Yup," She nodded as he got up and took the DVD out. "Whatcha wanna watch now?"

"I have this new action movie I've wanted to watch."

"Sounds good," she said as he put the movie in, he smiled to himself, this was nice. He never hung out with a girl, he would hang out with Grace, but he didn't want to sleep with her. With Elli, he wanted to spend time with her and sleep with her and sleep with her, all at the same time. She was intoxicating, so pretty, and sweet.

"What time do you need to go?" he asked as he looked at the movie box, then the time. He didn't want to make her late to see her friends.

"Sixish, everyone will be there at 8." Plenty of time.

"Oh, okay, who is coming over?" he asked as he walked back to the couch, sitting beside her.

"Harper, my friend Jodi, and her husband Derrick, and my gay best friends, Trice and Walter."

"Sounds like a bunch," he said with a grin, she smiled as she scooted closer to him.

"I love them all, they are really great friends."

"Good," he simply said as he started the movie. He didn't let it bother him that she didn't want him to meet her friends; she hadn't said anything about it so he wasn't going to bring it up, but it did remind him of the party for the season opener on Thursday. "I wanted to ask you."

"Sure," she looked up at him, a small smile on her face. She seemed so comfortable, so happy.

"Welch is having a season opener party for the guys and their dates on Thursday, I was wondering if you would go?" she made a face, and looked down. What the hell did that mean? "It'll only be my friends, no crazy big wigs that we would need to impress," he added with a grin when she looked up. "Go with me?"

"What do I wear?"

"Something hot," he said with a teasing grin as he squeezed her side. He loved how soft she was, no bones sticking him in the hand. She just rolled her eyes and leaned her head on his shoulder.

"So you want me to meet your friends in something hot?"

Shea thought that over, and smiled as he said "No, I want you to wear something hot for me, then I'll introduce you to my friends." She smiled at that, but didn't look up at him.

"What time Thursday?"

"What time can you be available?"

"Eight, I have a baby shower from four to six, at Yancy's down the road." Shea nodded, and thought about it for a moment.

"Well, why don't you just bring everything you need here and get ready, then we can be there only an hour after it starts."

Elli sat for a moment, before looking up at him. "Okay," she said, with a small nervous smile, he smiled back, than leaned to kiss her softly. Shea meant to leave it at a small kiss, but Elli slid her hand up his chest to his throat, and he began kissing her harder. Again he maneuvered her onto her back, with him between her legs, and this time she didn't stop him as they kissed and teased each other through their clothes.

"I see how it is, during my movie we can make out, but not during yours," he whispered against her neck as he nibbled and licked. She let out a breathy little giggle as she ran her hands through his hair.

"My movie needs all the attention." He pulled up, lust filling his eyes as he looked down at her.

"Baby, when you're in the room, you're the only thing that has my attention." She had this little grin along with half lidded eyes going on, and he had to suppress the groan that was building at the base of his throat. He leaned down and kissed her again, hooking her leg around his waist, pressing his hard length onto her. She wanted this; she was just as hot as he was. Yes, this was going to happen. Was it too early? Did he want to involve sex in this?

Elli ran her hands down the back of his arms, cupping his elbows, and wiggled a little underneath him.

Yes, yes he did want to involve sex. Right now.

Shea kissed down her neck, moving his hand to go under her shirt when Elli's hands stopped him. He pulled back and looked down at her. Her eyes were wide, and she looked nervous.

Fuck.

"I'm sorry, I need to go."

"Huh? What?" he asked as she moved herself out from underneath him, she stood up, fixing her shorts, than her shirt as she looked everywhere but him, she was breathing just as hard he was. The fall and rise of her chest had him becoming harder by the second. "Elli, wait," he said when he saw her slid her shoes on, then grab her hat.

"I'm sorry Shea, I'll call you." She looked as if she was going to cry, he had to stop her.

Elli had to get out of there. Like ten minutes ago. What was she thinking? He almost touched her skin under the clothes that she hid under. There was no way in hell Shea Adler was gonna see or touch her under her clothes. No way. No sweet words, no amazing hot kisses, nope nothing. Elli reached for the handle just as Shea wrapped his arms around her from behind. She could feel the length of him on her ass, and God how she wanted him.

Bad.

That was the only way she could describe it, but there was no way. Unless they came out with a new way of having sex with your clothes on, but Elli was pretty darn sure Shea wanted her naked when he took her there.

"Baby, slow down, please," he whispered against her ear, her eyes drifted shut, and her heart still banged against her chest. Somehow he ended up in front of her when she opened her eyes. His eyes were searching hers, pleading for her to slow down. The blue was a little darker, not the sky blue they usually were. His hand came from around her, to cup her face. Her two plump cheeks in his massive hands, she wanted to sigh at the feeling, hard against soft, but she needed to go.

"Hey now, you don't have to go. We can watch the movie," he said sweetly.

"No, I gotta do some cleaning, let my dog out, and get ready for when everyone comes."

"I thought they weren't coming till eight."

"Yeah, but Harper usually shows up early, and I just need to go." Elli tried to get away but he wasn't letting her go. She had to get out of there before she started crying. She was beyond embarrassed, this was Shea Adler, he had females throwing themselves at him left and right and she wouldn't even let him grope her. He probably thought she was a freak!

"Elli, please. Look at me." Of course she wouldn't do that! But being the persistent little ass he was, he moved her face up so she had nowhere to look but into his eyes. "Baby, please. Don't let what happen effect what we have going here, it's not a big deal. We can watch a movie, just be together." The tears were welling up, he was so sweet, so amazing. And if she didn't get out of there she would embarrass herself even more by crying in front of him. She caught him off guard and kissed his cheek softly, before turning out of his embrace and opening the door.

"I'll call you," she practically whispered as she ran out, she heard him call her name but she kept going, by the time she hit the stairs, she was fully crying. Big crocodile tears fell down her burning red cheeks. Her mother used to always tease her about how foolish she looked when she cried, Elli had always been embarrassed after that, but when she got her first roll on Broadway, it was because of her voice and the fact that when she cried, the tears were so big that it made it more dramatic, the director loved her, that was until Elli got fat.

When she reached the truck, she jumped in, locking the doors behind her as she just sat there crying, she had to get it out or she wouldn't be able to make the drive home. She could always go to Harper's and calm down, but she didn't want Harper to see her like this. She was so mad at herself. How long had it been since she had been touched or even touched a man? Forever it seemed, why couldn't she do it? Shea was a beautifully made man, he was a buffet, and she could eat him alive! But the thought of him seeing her stretch marks or her pooch made her sick to her stomach with fear.

Elli pulled back and slammed her hands against the steering wheel as she sobbed. She hated this feeling, because no matter how much running or how little she ate she couldn't get rid of the pooch. Shea would be done with her in no time; he wouldn't want to wait forever to have sex with her. Who could blame him? Elli could always get it cut off, she thought, get a nice little tummy tuck, but everyone would know, and she would never give her family the satisfaction of watching her fail. Not anymore. Plus, she couldn't get rid of the stretch marks; they would be forever on her.

She leaned her head on the steering wheel, and watched as the tears fell onto her legs, puddles of them, sliding down the sides of her thighs, thighs that had little dimples and marks too. But they were so little that only Elli knew about them, or so she hoped because if Shea ever mentioned them she would never wear shorts around him again. She closed her eyes, she hated feeling like this. She wanted to be strong, confident.

 This was probably the only time that she wished she was like Victoria. The confidence Victoria exhibited was so in your face, men fell at her feet. Why couldn't Elli be like that? Why couldn't she throw her clothes off, screw Shea's brains out right there on his couch? Victoria would have done it in a New York minute, but Elli, nope, she ran out crying.

How was she ever going to face Shea again?

When Elli was fully calmed down, she drove home. After parking her truck at the very top of the driveway so everyone would be able to get in, she headed up the walk way, hearing Adler freaking out. Elli's phone beep just as she open the door, Adler took off running and Elli just shrugged as she left the door open for him to come back in. Shea had texted her about ten times since she left. He was, of course, being sweet, but she just couldn't do it. Couldn't talk to him, not yet, she pulled out her phone, reading the last text.

Are you okay? You always answer my text, please just say your okay, I'll leave you alone till your ready to talk to me.

She quickly texted back that, yes, she was okay, and that she would call him later. Even though they both knew she wouldn't. She laid her purse and everything down on the sofa before going back to her bathroom to clean up. She ran the water as she looked for a wash rag, when she looked up into the mirror seeing her eyes bloodshot and tear streaks across her cheek, she felt like she would cry again. She remembered when she used to look at herself and think how pretty she was, how any guy would die to be with her.

That wasn't the case anymore, after Justin and his abuse and her family's abuse, now she just felt alone. Felt as if no one would ever love her, or even think she was pretty. Yeah, Shea had said it, but he was probably just trying to get into her pants. She really should watch his sweet and smooth words; he was a famous hockey player, not some regular Joe. What did he want with her? She didn't have anything a beautiful, amazing, geektastic hockey player would want, and with that thought, Elli decided she would cry.

Elli had cleaned up, and gotten dressed just as her friends starting showing up. She had known, Jodi, Walter, and Trice since her Broadway days, Trice used to be her makeup guy, while Walter was the backstage director. They both still worked for the TPAC in Nashville, and loved what they did. Jodi used to act alongside Elli, but when Elli left, Jodi said she didn't love it as much and quit; now she worked as a Drama Teacher for one of the most prestigious private high schools in the state. She married Derrick almost five years ago; Elli was her maid of honor. She loved her friends something stupid; they knew her inside and out. She also looked forward to these nights every month. No matter what, everyone came over to someone's house for game night. It was a time for all of them to catch up, she enjoyed it. Elli just wished that the events from today could be put aside, but all she kept seeing my Shea's pleading eyes.

Jodi had brought sushi with her for dinner, so everyone gathered around Elli's family size table and ate while catching up. Elli felt that she was doing a good job hiding the fact that she was dying inside until Jodi gave her a pointed look, pointing her chop stick at her, before saying,

"What the hell is wrong with you?"

All eyes went towards Elli as she shrugged, looking down at her sushi roll.

"Nothing," she muttered.

"Liar," Trice said flamboyantly, Walter sat beside him nodding his head.

"Elli, darling, we have known you for, like, ever, we know your lying, we knew something was wrong when you answered the door. Now go on, tell your dearest and oldest friends, what's wrong?" Walter said, Harper sat beside Elli, nodding her head, while Derrick watched from the other side of the table beside Jodi.

"Nothing wrong guys, I'm just tired."

"What happen with Shea today?" Harper asked Elli cut her a look of death, before she looked at the rest of the table; it was as if everyone leaned closer to her.

"Shea?" Jodi asked "Who's that?"

"No one," Elli answered, stuffing a piece of sushi in her mouth.

"Liar!" Trice basically screamed again, causing everyone to giggle as Harper grinned at Elli.

"You might as well tell em, El, it's been almost two weeks!"

"Two weeks?" Jodi asked "What the hell has been going on for two weeks and I don't know about it!"

Everyone was staring at Elli, her heart was slamming against her chest and she felt like sweat was dripping down her back. Could she tell them about Shea? She wasn't even sure if this thing with Shea would even still be going on after today? She hadn't been with anyone since Justin, they all knew that and Elli knew they would blow this out the water.

"Um," Elli stuttered as Harper shook her head, laughing.

"Just say it, Elli, it's no big deal."

No big deal? Really? Plus, why was she friends with Harper again?

"Yeah, just tell us," Trice cooed, while of course Walter just nodded. For being two guys that were in love, they sure did look alike. Both blondes with big brown eyes, the only difference was that Trice was a skinny narrowed faced guy, while Walter was huge, not Shea huge but fat. Jodi and Derrick were completely opposite. Jodi was white, with long blonde hair and huge blue eyes, real skinny and pretty while Derrick was a huge, massive black man, that could probably kill Elli with his hands, but he was a sweet guy. These were her people, her best friends.

"Well, I'm kinda seeing someone," she heard herself say, the room went eerily quiet.

"What do you mean *kinda* seeing someone," Jodi asked, breaking the silence. Elli looked up to the faces of her friends, her support system. Some had shocked faces while others grinned with happiness pouring out of their pores. These people loved her, and she knew it, she would never question it.

"Okay, I'm dating someone," a few people gasped while the others just grinned, "but it's not worth talking about."

"What do you mean not worth talking about?" Trice asked, his hands moving with every word "A man, is always worth talking about, especially if they are taking our baby girl out." Elli's cheeks turned red as she moved her food around.

"It's no big deal," she said shyly.

"What's his name? Shea?" Walter asked, Elli nodded.

"That's a nice...sexy name. Where did y'all meet?" Trice added, Elli looked up, everyone was zoning in on her.

"At a photo shoot." Everyone nodded, smiling.

"What's he like?" Trice asked again, Elli face broke out in a smile as she blushed, she couldn't believe she was talking about Shea, to her friends. Even with the events from that day, she couldn't help the words that poured out of her about Shea.

"He's amazin'. Totally nice, he has a niece and nephew that he adores, he has brought me lunch all week, took me out, and everything, we spent the afternoon together, where he cooked and-" she gushed out, smiling, but then she stopped when she almost blurted out how the afternoon ended.

"And?" Jodi asked.

"And, than I turned stupid and ran out his house crying, and I doubt I'll ever see him again," she said in a rush, then she looked up again, "That's why this was not worth talking about, because even though Shea is amazing, and I would want nothing more to see where this is going, I just don't think I'll ever be able to face him again."

"What on good God's green earth happened!?" Jodi demanded "because any man that makes you smile like that Eleanor is a man worth keeping."

"Yeah, so you tell us, let us be the judge!" Trice added.

"Yeah," Harper said "he's great Elli, what could have happened?"

Elli looked at Walter and Derrick; they sat quietly, eating as they listen very intently. She looked at Jodi, Trice, and Harper, than took a deep breath.

"Well, we started making out-"

"Ooh, was it good?" Trice cooed with a grin, Elli laughed.

"Amazing," Elli said with a grin, than looked down at her food "but then it got hot, like he was on top of me, and I felt *everything.*"

"Ooh, it was that good?" Jodi cooed this time; Elli rolled her eyes as Derrick glared at Jodi.

"Words don't describe how that felt," Elli said before going on "But then his hands went for under my shirt and I-" Elli stopped, not able to say it, that she ran like a scared little bitch.

"Ran like a scared little girl? Elli, come on," Harper exclaimed in disgusted. If anyone knew Elli, it was Harper. "Why?"

Elli just got up, taking her plate to the kitchen; she dropped it in the sink, running the water as she tried to get her breathing under control. She wished she could ask everyone to leave but knew that was rude, plus in a way she didn't want to. She loved them all, even with their prying questions. They had a right to know, they were her best friends, plus talking about it would be good for her, especially with the guys, well, manly Derrick's point of view. She turned the water off, before going back in the dining room where everyone was sitting. She stood behind her chair, looking at her friends.

"I ran because the thought of him seeing my stretch marks, or feeling the fat on my tummy almost made me puke. I can't do it. He's so gorgeous, so amazing, I'm not that. I'm not skinny, or super duper pretty. I'm kinda squishy, and not what he is usually with."

Everyone just stared at her, like she was the dumbest person on earth; she was starting to feel that she was when Jodi finally spoke.

"So, let me get this straight," she started as she cleared her throat. "You haven't dated a man in what, how long has it been since dickhead?" she asked.

"Six years," Harper answered before Elli could.

"Six years, and now that a man that you like and are attracted to wants to get up under your shirt, you decide to freak out, run, and then not talk to him anymore because you are not what you think he wants."

Elli just stood there, when she put it that way, Elli sounded dumb, so she just shrugged as she said "Yeah."

"Has he said that you are not what he wants?" Trice asked.

"No, quite the opposite, really," Elli answered

"Okay, so explain to me why you don't want to see him anymore?" Harper asked.

"Because I'm fat," Elli said as she threw her arms up in the air.

"You're not fat!" Everyone yelled at the same time.

"Yes, Elli, you are not a size two anymore, we get that, but honey, you were sick," Trice explained.

"You have already lost a lot of what you gained, you're at a healthy size, baby girl, stop," Walter added.

"Let me tell you something, Elli," Everyone's heads turned towards Derrick, "I am your after friend; I came after the sickness hit, after Justin left, after the studio opened, but I've heard about before Elli, about how outspoken, and crazy she was. Jodi told me about how Justin treated you when you got sick." Everyone just nodded, Justin was such a douche. "But not every man is like him, this guy that you are talking to likes you, not before Elli."

"But what happens when he sees me naked, or sees pictures of before Elli?" she asked sadly, "I can't do another Justin, I can't."

"And no one is asking you too, but do you think he would do that? Have you talked to him about it?"

"No."

"Okay, so how would you know?"

Everyone just nodded, grinning at Derrick than Elli.

"You can't stay hidden El, you're so beautiful, so amazing, so funny, don't hide," Jodi said.

"Yeah, because when he sees the real Elli, the carefree happy one, he'll fall head over heels in two point three seconds," Trice added.

"Elli, he really likes you, Jakob has even said so. Maybe he is tired of the Barbie dolls, and wants something real," Harper suggested "You need to give him a chance, love like you've never been hurt before. You need to talk to him."

"I don't know."

"Is he worth it, Elli?" Elli looked over at Derrick; he had his glass of wine in front of his mouth, a grin on his lips. "It's early, I know, but people always know when something is worth it, do you think he is?"

Elli thought for a moment, she missed him, she did. In the past couple weeks she had never went this long without talking to him, but she was just so damn scared. She didn't want to get hurt again, she didn't want the rejection. In a way she was fine with her life, she had Adler, her friends, her nieces and nephews. What else did she need?

"I know that look Elli; your life could be a lot better, a lot happier. Don't you still want kids of your own?" Harper asked, everyone nodded, and Elli caved. She sat down; put her face in her hands. She did want kids, she did want a husband, a happily ever after. But could she get over her insecurities to try?

"He's worth it, but I don't know if I am."

Chapter 8

The images of Elli running out of Shea's apartment would be forever burned in his brain. The tears streaming down her face, the way she slammed her hands into the steering wheel as she cried. He knew she didn't know he was watching, but he was, he wanted nothing more than to run down there and comfort her. Didn't she know that he wasn't mad, that he was fine without going further, that he just wanted to be with her? Why didn't she understand that? What had he done wrong? Was he moving too fast? He didn't know, he had never been in this situation, never been with the same woman more than once. So he was lost.

He hadn't talked to her in two days, he had sent text messages and she would answer that she was busy and would call when she had the chance, but hour after hour passed, and he never heard from her. Part of him wondered if this was her way of blowing him off, but part of him knew that wasn't true. She was just embarrassed, or so he hoped.

Like always when he was confused about something, he ended up at Grace's. Grace was moving around the house, running her mouth as he sat with Amelia in his lap, playing kissy face with her, while Ryan shot pucks at the new net Shea had brought over with him.

"Unky, watch I can shoot just as hard as you!" Ryan exclaimed as he swung his stick as hard as his little four year old body would let him. What surprised Shea was that he actually got the puck in the goal.

"Way to go, bud!" Shea exclaimed. "Cheer for Ryan, Amelia! Go, Ryan, Go!" Shea lifted Amelia's arms in the air and she giggled as she bounced in his lap.

"I'm amazing, just like you, Unky. That's what momma says." Shea cut a look at his sister, she was grinning bashfully.

"Your momma knows her stuff, huh?"

"Sure does!" Ryan yelled as he went back to shooting, Amelia started getting fussing, so Grace took her, kissing her cheeks.

"She's hungry," Grace explained as she put her in her highchair with some food on the tray. "Are you hungry, Shea?"

"I could always eat," Shea answered as she placed a sandwich and chips in front of him. After a lot of coaxing she finally got Ryan to sit down and eat too. Grace sat across from Shea taking a bite out of her sandwich before giving him a pointed look.

"So what's up?"

No reason beating around the bush.

"I think I messed up with Elli." A lot of emotions went over Grace's face, anger, surprise, concern, then the final one, worry.

"What? What happened?"

"She came over Sunday, and we had a great time, till we started making out and then-"

"Unky Shea, what's making out?" Ryan asked; both he and Grace looked over at Ryan; he was looking up at them with his big, blue, innocent eyes.

"Um," Shea stuttered.

"I'll tell you when you're fourteen," Grace said, and she looked up at Shea. "Keep going, but spell the words that we don't want young ears to hear."

"Okay," he laughed, "Well, I went to put my hand up her s-h-i-r-t," Grace nodding approvingly, "and she freaked. Ran out crying, I don't know what to do, she won't answer my calls, only my texts and they are like 'I'll call you', but she never does. It's been two days, Grace, tomorrow is opening night, and I'm freaking out! And I never freak out!"

"Okay, so you were f-o-o-l-i-n-g around and then when you tried to c-o-p a feel, she ran out like a bat out of h-e-l-l?"

"Yes, and she was crying."

"Hm, I don't know why she would do that?"

"I don't either! That's why I came to you!"

"Jeez, calm down, let me think," Grace pleaded as she put her chin on her hand and thought. "Has she had any kids?" Shea thought for a moment.

"Um, no I don't think so; she says she wants kids in the future."

"You don't know?"

"No."

"Okay, has she been married?"

"I don't know, it hasn't come up."

"What the h-e-l-l do you all talk about?"

"Whatever comes up."

"Don't you think you should have the exes talk?"

"Yeah, but it just hasn't came up."

"You're hopeless. If she won't answer your calls, then go to her, if you're in her face, where can she to go?"

This was a bad idea; Shea should have thought this out more instead of acting on impulse. It was close to eight and Elli still wasn't home. Shea had called Jakob to ask Harper what Elli's schedule was like and with his luck she should have been home by seven, since all she had was a birthday party at three, but she still wasn't home. He was sitting in his truck because when he was sitting on the porch, Elli's dog was barking it's ass off and he felt bad, so he went back to his truck. He felt like he was already in hot water with Elli, and he didn't want to piss her off anymore.

Shea leaned back in his seat, moving his arm around. Jakob had slammed him into the boards earlier that day and he was feeling it now. He checked his phone seeing that it was almost 8:30, and decided to give her until nine, if she wasn't there; he would leave the roses he had gotten for her on the doorstep and drive home. He had to get up early for practice, and he had all kinds of PR before the game tomorrow.

So he waited.

And waited and waited.

At nine, he couldn't bring himself to leave, even when ten rolled around, he stayed where he was playing Angry Birds on his phone. He missed her, a lot, and if him being a little tired at practice would be the outcome of him waiting, then that's what was going to happen.

Shea was getting angrier with every minute that passed, where the hell was she? It was close to eleven and she still wasn't home, was she out with another guy? Did she replace him that fast? He tried to distract himself with his game but it wasn't working. He found himself looking up, then to the clock, back to the road, then her driveway, just in case he missed the truck driving by him. He finally spotted her truck at eleven. She pulled into the driveway and he jumped out, roses in hand.

Shea didn't think she saw him; she was fully out the car, camera in hand and still didn't say anything as he walked up towards her. She looked beautiful. Her hair was up in a twist looking thing, she had on a pretty little blue dress that had yellow flowers all over it. She wore some sexy little heels, and his mouth watered at the sight. Elli let out a little scream covering her heart with her hand when she turned.

"Shea!"

"Hey, Elli," he answered shyly, he didn't know why he was shy, shy wasn't in his vocabulary but there he was shy, it was disgusting really. "These are for you," he said quietly as he held out the roses. She looked down at them, then back at him, before taking them.

"Thank you," she whispered.

"I haven't heard from you."

"I told you I was really busy, you didn't have to drive all the way out here."

"I wanted to see you," he answered, looking down at her, she wouldn't look up at him, and it was driving him crazy being this close to her and not kissing her. He took a step closer to her, and she looked up at him.

"I'm sorry I haven't called, I've been so busy," she said, looking back down at the ground.

"Well, I'm here now."

"You are, how long have you been waiting?"

"Not long," he lied, she smiled.

"The party I was doing ran over, and then there was traffic on I-24." Shea nodded, still looking at the top of her head since she wouldn't look at him. They stood there for what seemed like forever, her looking down at the roses, while he stared at the top of her head.

"So, are you blowing me off?" he finally asked, she looked up at him quickly, and then shook her head. The breath that he was holding came out in a whoosh. That was reassuring.

"I'm just embarrassed, Shea. I don't know where to go from here."

He shrugged his shoulders, "Elli, I just want to see you, talk to you; be with you. I'm sorry if I did something wrong, I was caught up in the moment, I'm sorry."

"Don't be sorry, Shea, you didn't do anything wrong."

"Then why did you run? Why haven't I heard your voice in two days?" She shrugged her shoulders, turning to look at the house.

"Would you like to go sit down? I gotta let my dog out."

"Sure."

Shea followed Elli up the little cobblestone path to her porch. She climbed up, opening the door to let her dog out. Shea tried not to laugh when he saw the porker of a dog running on four little legs, but it was hard and soon couldn't contain himself.

"I know you're not laughing at my dog," Elli warned, Shea smiled sweetly, bending down to pet to oversized pup.

"Of course not," he lied, running his big hand down the dogs back, the dog had a goofy look on its face as he licked Shea's hand. "How you doing bud?" The dog let out a little bark, and took off for the field by the house. He watched the dog for a moment, and then looked up to where Elli was sitting on the steps. He gave her a small smile as he went and sat next to her. He tried to give her space, but he missed her so much, so he sat right beside her, his knee touching hers.

"It's late Shea, I know you have practice in the morning," she said as she watched her dog, not looking at him.

"I don't care, like I said, I wanted to see you."

"You're gonna be hurtin' in the morning," she mumbled just as the dog came barreling up the stairs to sit between her legs.

"I know, but you're worth it." She looked over at him surprised. Had no one ever told her that? Why was it every time he said something nice to her, she looked at him like he was from a different planet?

"Okay," she said, kissing the dogs head.

"You still haven't told me your dog's name," he pointed out; she looked back up at him.

"Adler."

Shea just stared at her, Adler was his last name. Did she name the dog after him?

"Adler?"

"Yup," she said nonchalantly as she kissed Adler's head. She looked back over at him. "I'm gonna show you something, I think it will explain some of why I ran out the other day." She reached into the sweater she had put on after going inside and pulled out a photo. She looked at him nervously before handing it to him. He took the photo from her, and looked at it.

It was a younger picture of her, maybe eighteen, or nineteen, doing some kind of silly pose; she had the same eyes, the same smile, the same hair, her cheeks were hallowed in a little, and her face wasn't as round as it was now, but the only real big difference was that in the picture she was skin and bones. She didn't have the round ass she had, or the curves, or the breasts. She was literally skin and bones.

"How old were you? Eighteen?"

"Seventeen."

He smiled; "You're a baby in this picture." She smiled nervously.

"I was super skinny."

"Yes, you were."

"I'm not now."

It was like a light bulb went on in his head.

She was nervous about her body.

Her perfect, beautiful, mouth-watering body.

Was she crazy!?

"Baby, this picture is what, ten years old?"

"I know, but you like girls that size, and I'm not that size anymore, bigger in fact." Okay, she was pissing him off. He didn't date damn skin and bones, yes he would admit to the Barbie dolls but he did like meat on his women.

"Honey, I haven't dated anyone this size in a while, when I was younger I did. But now, they have meat on their bones." She shook her head.

"Shea, I have never seen you with a girl my size, or even my look. That's why you wanting to date me is so confusing. I'm nothing that you would want-"

"How do you know what I want?" He said cutting her off, she just looked at him, surprised by his tone probably, but she was pissing him off. She had just met him, how was she going to judge him by the women that he put on his arm. "I dated those women as an easy way out, if I had some super model on my arm, people bowed down to me. Not only was I hot on the ice but I had me a hot piece of meat on my arm."

Shea knew he had said the wrong thing when he saw the look on her face. It was a mix of hurt, anger, and just plain embarrassment.

"And again, why would you want to date me? I'm not a super model, nor am I a size two, with fake tits." She said standing up, "I am an overweight photographer, with a forty pound dog, that loves hockey, and lives forty five minutes from town. What makes me worthy of being on your arm?"

"Elli, I'm sorry, what I said came out wrong. I haven't been with a model in a long time. Ever since we won the cup my priorities has changed. I know you think I'm some kind of playboy but I'm not, at least not anymore." He stood up too, taking a step closer to her, but she stepped back.

"I never said you were; I just said that I'm not your type."

"But you are. Baby, please, listen to me." He took her hands, kissing each palm before looking down into her eyes. "We get along so well don't we?"

"I guess."

"Come on, you know we do."

"We do," she said with a small smile, "But if you're not attracted to me-"

"Baby, I like that you aren't a size two, your curves drive me crazy, can't you see that? Couldn't you feel it on Sunday?" he said with a wink that made her smile "I wanted you so bad, I couldn't see straight. I don't want a Barbie doll, I want you, and if I have to prove to you that you are what I want, I will, but I'm just asking, begging really, to just give me a chance. Don't write me off yet."

"Shea, I just don't see this working, you're gorgeous, while I'm mediocre."

"You are far from mediocre, Elli, far from it. You are gorgeous, beautiful, amazing. Just give me a chance, and anytime you feel that you're not worthy just ask me baby, because I want to make you feel beautiful, always."

Shea had her swooning, but didn't she tell herself not to fall for his sweet words? But then again, he seemed so real, so compassionate, the way he was looking at her, made her feel like she was the only girl, the only one that had him in knots. Could she completely trust him?

"I don't know; I'm just so scared."

"Of what?"

Elli felt the tears burning her eyes; she felt her heart beating in her throat. "The rejection, I guess."

"Oh baby, come on."

"No really, like what if you see me naked and you're disgusted, I don't know what I would do," she said with a shake of her head. He cupped her face, kissing the side of her mouth. He leaned back, a small crooked grin on his face.

"Here's what we'll do, when you're ready, we'll go forth on the adventure of getting naked, but right now, I'm fine with a kiss here and there, as long as I don't have to endure two days of not talking to you."

"Shea, be realistic, you love sex."

"Oh, hell yeah I do, but I will wait until you're ready, because these two damn days have sucked," he said with a laugh, "and I don't want to rush this, I've always jumped right into bed with women, then it's over in no time, I don't want that with you."

Was he being for real? Could Elli put all the stories she heard, all the pictures she saw off him partying with hundreds of different women aside?

Shea ran his hand down her cheek to her throat, rubbing his thumb along the base. She had been miserable these past two days, hating that she didn't have the balls to call him, or even see him, but Shea being Shea, so in your face about everything, made her see him and she couldn't be more thankful.

And Harper did say too 'love like you've never been hurt before', so hell, might as well give it a try.

"Okay."

"Okay?"

"Okay," she said with a nod, he grinned before taking her mouth with his. It felt like an explosion went off around her, being wrapped up in his arms, kissed by his beautiful mouth. She missed his big body, his strong arms, and his lips; yes, she had missed them a lot. When they parted, he smiled against her mouth, dusting sweet kisses all over her lips.

"I've missed you, Elli," he whispered softly, he smiled goofily before pulling back some. "It's probably too early to say that, huh?" Elli gave him a sweet smile, pulling him back to her by his shirt, so their mouths were inches apart.

"No, because I missed you too," she said before kissing him again, they stayed wrapped up in each other's arms for what seem like hours, but it was only minutes. When they finally came up for air, Elli smiled as she pushed him away.

"Go home, Adler, you have a game to win tomorrow," she said with a sexy grin as she kissed his cheek.

"Alright, I'll call you tomorrow."

"Alright, thanks for coming to see me."

"I'm the one that should be thanking you, baby, I'll see you."

"Bye."

He gave her one last kiss before walking towards his truck. She watched his beautiful sculpted ass in his fitted jeans, and suppressed a groan. She had never felt the urge to rip a man's clothes off, but ripping Shea Adler's jeans off would be a magical experience if she ever got the balls and the confidence to do it. Elli sighed as she watched him drive off with a wave, man she hope this worked, because for some reason she felt that the crush was developing into something way more for Shea.

Chapter 9

"Hey." Elli looked up from the pictures that had just came in from the imagining company that she ordered from, Harper was leaning against the counter, her hair this week, blonde with purple streaks.

"Hey, what's up?" Elli said with a grin, she was really excited; it was opening day with the Assassins.

"Um, you have two tickets for the game tonight? Or are you taking someone?"

"No, I'm not taking anyone, why?" Harper looked nervous, which made Elli smile. Harper never got nervous, what she was about to asked must be about Jakob.

"Can I go with you?"

"Sure!" Elli all but screamed. She had been begging Harper to go to a game with her for years. "We'll have so much fun! We can get beer and pretzel and all kinds of stuff!!" Elli was practically jumping up and down.

"Whoa, calm down," Harper nonchalantly said, but Elli knew she was excited. "What time are you going?"

"The games at seven, so I'll get there at six, to watch the guys warm up and everything."

"Can we get there earlier? I need a jersey."

"Of course!!! I get a discount at the pro shop, oh my god! I'm so excited!"

"Yay!" Harper said sarcastically as she walked away, then she looked over her shoulder with a grin, telling Elli that she was just as excited but refused to show anyone that she was. Harper was weird like that. Elli went back to separating pictures when her phone rang, it was Shea.

"Hey, you," she answered with a grin.

"Well, hello, sounds like you are in a good mood."

"Oh, I am, its opening night!" Elli boasted, "I'm so excited, I have all my Assassins gear on."

"Oh, do you now," he said with a chuckle, she smiled, "Like what?"

"Well, I have my tee on right now, over my patched up jeans, with my Assassins' undies and socks, and hat." She looked down at herself, proud of her outfit. What she would never admit though, is that her undies had a big six on the crotch.

"Assassins undies, huh? You'll have to show me," he flirted, which made her blush.

"Maybe."

"Mmm..I like the sound of that." She giggled as he went on "So what time you coming to the game?"

"5:30 I guess, Harper needs to buy some gear."

"Okay, so I get to see who your favorite player is tonight, huh?"

"But of course."

"I think I have an idea."

"Really, who?"

"Me."

"God, that male ego." He laughed, as she smiled.

"No really, you named your dog after me."

"The hell I did!" She protested, even though it was true. "I named him after my favorite...toothpaste"

"Adler toothpaste?"

"Sure."

"You're such a liar."

"Whatever." He laughed and she giggled as she carried stuff to the back.

"So you'll be sitting in your seats tonight?"

"Yeah, where else would I sit?"

"In my family section?"

Elli went quiet, dropping what was in her hands as he kept talking, "My mom and dad came in for the game, and Grace and her husband and the kids will be there. I thought maybe you'd want to sit with them."

"Oh, well, I have Harper."

"She can sit up there too; I think Jakob's family is in too."

"Oh no, she would freak." He laughed.

"So are you telling me no?"

"Would you be mad?"

"No, but I'll keep trying. I think you'll like my parents."

"I probably will, but let's give it a little longer before we go introducing each other to our families," Elli said, "My mom leaves me a message every day saying that she wants to meet the man I was open mouth kissing in front of her grandchildren, but I just ignore her."

"That's fine with me, babe, I understand."

"Okay, good." Elli let out a breath; he made her so damn nervous. "Does your family know about me?"

"Grace does, of course, but no, my parents don't."

"Oh, okay, good, so they aren't expecting me or anything."

"Well, I was going to tell them about you."

"Oh, okay....why?" He laughed and she got nervous all over again.

"Because we're dating."

"Did you tell them about the women before?"

"No, Grace did, so no matter what my parents will know about you."

Well, hells bells. Elli sat on the chair in the hall and took a deep breath, she hadn't had to do the parent thing since Justin, and that was horrific all in itself. She wasn't ready for that, she was still scared Shea would reject her; she didn't need the rejection of his parents.

"Baby, why are you quiet? I told you not to worry about it, you don't have to meet them this time around," he said quietly.

"Oh, thank sweet, baby Jesus," she muttered, which made him laugh.

"You're silly, so do me a solid." She laughed.

"A solid?"

"Yeah, a solid."

"Oh goodness, what?"

"Come out into the lobby and give me a kiss for good luck tonight." Elli grinned big as she popped up and walked quickly to the front lobby, where Shea stood, a single daisy in his hand. He was wearing a khaki suit with a blue shirt under the jacket. He looked devilishly sexy with his hair all in spikes, his sweet blue eyes not covered with his glasses. He took his phone from his ear as he grinned at her; she did the same and went to him, wrapping her arms around his neck, bringing her mouth to his. His hands came around her waist, pulling her tightly to him. When they parted he smiled down at her. "You really are Assassins' decked-out, huh?"

"They are my team."

He smiled, kissing her again. "Is there a chance I can see these undies today?" he muttered against her lips, she giggled as she shook her head pulling him down for another long passionate kiss. She could do this all day and night, his lips were that kissable.

"I mean, Jesus! Get a damn room y'all." Elli pulled back from Shea, looking over to give Harper the death look.

"Did I say anything when I found you and Jakob on your desk last week?" Harper just grinned and walked right up to them.

"No, but at least I introduced you," she said in a matter of fact voice. "So, on with it, Ms. Fisher." Elli rolled her eyes, parting from Shea a little.

"Shea, this is my best friend Harper, Harper, Shea Adler."

"How do you do?" Harper said in an overly fake country accent, Shea smiled.

"Good, nice to meet you, I've heard a lot about you."

"Have you now? From who?"

"Oh, from Elli, and Jakob, you're quite the subject." Harper smiled in delight and turned on her heels to walk away, with nothing but a wave. "She's just like Jakob described."

"I hope he described her nicely, because she is...nice I mean." Shea wrapped her back up in his arms, kissing the side of her neck.

"Elli."

"Shea," she gasped as he bit softly.

"Show me your undies." Elli broke out in a fit of giggles as Shea smiled against her neck.

"No way."

"What if I get a goal just for you, then can I see your undies?"

"Do they have to be on me?" she asked, playing along. There was no way in hell he would see her in her undies.

"Yes, they do."

"Hmm....no."

"Come on, two goals."

"No."

"Three."

"Okay, how about three, and y'all gotta win."

"Deal, now kiss me."

"That I will do," she said with a grin as she leaned up on her tippy toes to kiss him deeply.

It was probably the first time; Eleanor Fisher hoped Shea didn't score.

Shea walked into his box where his family was. They always came early so they could eat and visit before Shea had to go get ready. He had left Elli and came straight here, he had hoped she would come with him, but he didn't want to push her into anything. Shea saw his father, Mark, first, standing by the wall, overlooking the ice. His father was aging well, in his opinion, at the age of forty-nine his father didn't look at day over 30. His hair still black as night, he had the laugh lines and a rugged look to him, but he still looked the same as he did when Shea was nine.

"Hey, pop," he said as he walked in, Mark turned around with a smile on his face.

"Hey, son, excited?"

"Sure am, where's mom and everybody?"

"Pro shop, Ryan wanted a new jersey, and Amelia needs a new one too." Shea smiled as he came over, leaning against the edge with his father.

"You still like these seats, right, pop? I can get you another box if you don't like these."

"I love these, son, let it be." Shea nodded, looking down at the ice he would be playing on in a matter of hours. He looked over by the penalty box, where Elli would be sitting and smiled before looking over at his father who was staring at him.

"You alright, pop?"

"Fine son," he said with a nod and grin, "Your mother was wondering what girl we would be subjected to tonight."

"No one," Shea said with a shake of his head as he went to the bar, getting a bottle of water.

"Oh, really?"

"Yeah."

"That's unlike you."

"Pop, I haven't been with anyone since, what was her name...Alyssa?"

"Really? That was game 4 of the quarterfinals."

"Yeah, my priorities are changing."

"Good, your mother will be happy to hear that." Mark came around the bar, grabbing himself a beer, then he smiled "Who is she?" Shea laughed, he couldn't get one past his father if he tried.

"Her name is Elli."

"Elli, short for anything?"

"Eleanor."

"Nice, how long?"

"Two weeks."

"Oh, I thought she came sooner."

"I wish she had, she amazing pop. A real gem." Mark nodded with a smile on his face. Shea knew his father wanted nothing more for Shea than to be happy outside the rink, not with a different woman every night.

"She didn't want to sit up here? Please don't tell me she doesn't like hockey!" Shea laughed, shaking his head.

"No, pop, she had glass seat season tickets, down there by the penalty box."

"No shit," Mark gasped as he looked down at the ice, not like you could see anything but empty seats, but his father still looked. "She's rich?"

"She owns her own business, she's a photographer."

"Wow, how old is she?"

"Twenty-seven."

"Good, she pretty?"

"Gorgeous."

"Smart?"

"Yeah."

"When do I get to meet her?"

"I don't know, she's sort of skittish, I'm trying to take it slow."

"Wow, this girl is nothing like what you're used to huh?"

"Nope, not at all." Shea smiled as he shook his head, "But damn she drives me nuts, with just one look, pop, one look and I'm gone."

"I'm impressed; I want to meet her, soon."

"I'll do my damndest, like I said she's skittish."

"Who's skittish honey?" Shea turned to see his mother, Jenna, coming in with Amelia on her hip. Grace and James with Ryan came in right behind her.

"Hey, mom." Shea said, kissing her cheek, he hadn't seen his parents in a few months, but she hadn't changed. People would say that she was Grace's sister instead of her mom, that's how young Jenna looked. She was only eighteen when she had them, so she was still young, or as she would say 'I'm forever young.'

"Who's skittish?" she asked again as Shea kissed Amelia, then Grace, before picking Ryan up over his head, Ryan's giggles filled the box, and everyone smiled, as Shea chose to ignore her again.

"Unky, where's Miss. Elli?"

Well, hell.

"Who's Miss. Elli?" Jenna asked again.

"Ryan's met her?" Mark asked.

"She was the photographer for Shea's party, pop, she also did the promo shots for the team, that's how they met," Grace said, taking Amelia from Jenna, and giving her a juice box.

"Met? Who? Huh? Someone tell me something before I blow up!" Jenna yelled, everyone starting laughing, leaving Jenna to be confused. Sometimes she could be a little dramatic.

"Mom, Elli is Shea's new girlfriend," Grace said with a grin for Shea, he rolled his eyes.

"Girlfriend?" Jenna said with her hand over her heart, a dazed look on her face.

"We're taking it slow," Shea said sticking his tongue out at Grace. "Don't go planning my wedding, mom."

"How long have you guys been together?" Jenna asked.

"Just a couple weeks, it's new," Shea insisted. "We're just dating."

"She's really nice, Jenna. I met her at the party, she loves kids," James added. Shea cut his brother in law a look, but James just smiled.

"She loves kids! Is she still in child bearing years?"

"Jesus, mom!" Grace yelled, as Shea shook his head. "If you do meet her, please don't ask her that." Grace shook her head, making a plate for the kids as she did it.

"What? It's a logical question!" Jenna insisted as she turned her attention back to Shea. "How old is she?"

"Twenty-seven," he repeated.

"What does she look like?"

"Um, she's about this tall," he said bring his hand to the base of his throat, "Real dark curly hair, cute little nose, these lips, mom, Jesus, they have that little cupid bow look to them, and rosy cheeks, but the best part is her eyes, they are as green as moss, the kind of eyes that make you stop, look and stare." Shea took a deep breath, wishing Elli was there, "She's gorgeous."

Jenna had a dreamy look on her face as she covered her mouth, for a minute there Shea thought she might cry.

"Yeah, mom, all that and get this, she isn't a Barbie doll," Grace added, Shea looked over at her.

"Of course not, she isn't blonde."

"No, I mean, she isn't a size zero, she's got meat on her, she's kinda thick." Shea gave Grace a dirty look, and Grace held up her hands as she laughed "Whoa there, killer, I'm not saying she's fat, but she sure isn't skinny."

"Really?" Jenna asked, as Mark gave Shea a surprised look too. Shea knew this was news, he understood the surprise but still did he really date nothing but Barbie dolls before? No wonder Elli had a complex about this.

"Yeah, I guess," Shea said with a shrug, "I think she is perfect." Jenna smiled, cupping his face.

"Well, good, I can't wait to meet her. Has she been married?"

"Jesus mom!" Grace groaned as she shook her head "Leave him alone! It's only been two weeks."

"Still, he's head over heels for her; I need to know this kind of stuff."

"Whoa, head over heels?" Shea asked, looking up at his mother "What the h-e-l-l does that mean?"

"Thanks, Shea," Grace said with a grin, as she kissed Ryan's head. Ryan had been so bad about repeating whatever anyone said. So everyone had been doing a lot of spelling lately.

"You know what it means, you're in love," Jenna said so sure of herself, that Shea kinda believed her for a split second.

"The h-e-l-l you say!" That had everyone laughing, as Shea got madder by the second. "I care about her, but no way do I love her. I've never been in love; I think I would know if I was in love. I mean it's been two weeks," Shea complained, Jenna just smiled as she leaned her head on Mark, looking up at him lovingly. Shea got disgusted and went to Ryan kissing his head.

"Unky, win for me?"

"Of course," Shea said kissing him again, before kissing Amelia.

"You didn't eat, Shea," Grace complained.

"I'm fine," Shea said through his teeth as he kissed her then went towards the door. Just as he was about to go through, his mother decided that was the time to say, "There will be a wedding this time, next year, I feel it. You guys be ready-"

Shea walked out before he heard anything else. There was no way he was in love. Elli was amazing, perfect even but he didn't love her. Not saying he would never love her, but right now, no…there was no way…right?

 Elli was beyond excited; she had her number six jersey on, while Harper was decked out in number two gear. They both had their faces painted with their favorite guy's numbers and Elli had to admit, they were too damn cute for words. Harper was leaning back, drinking a beer as she looked around the filling arena. Elli was basically bouncing in her seat; she was so excited about the game, about seeing the guys on the ice for the first time since last season, about seeing Shea.

"This is cool, I guess," Harper said, Elli looked over at her, a big grin on her face.

"It's amazing!" She gushed, causing Harper to shake her head.

"Apparently Jakob's family is here from Russia or wherever the hell he's from." She was looking around at the boxes; Elli looked up at what she knew what Shea's family's box.

"Did you meet em?"

"Hell no, we aren't together like that. He asked of course, and I, of course, said fuck no," she said nonchalantly.

"Harp, come on now, y'all are together."

"No, we ain't, we're just screwing around, and he's the one trying to take this to a level it ain't," she said with a shrug.

"I'm gonna point this out because of how you ousted me to our friends, but aren't you wearing a number two on your face along with the jersey?" Harper looked down at her jersey, than back at Elli.

"It means I'm proud of who I'm screwing, plus he said if I wear his number he'll make it worth my while, and of course I want that."

"Oh, of course," Elli said with a shake of her head. Harper was impossible. This was the first guy that had lasted more than a week with Harper, they had been going strong for almost a month, even though Harper wouldn't talk to him for days at a time, Elli knew there was something there. She also knew that Harper was scoping the place out; she was looking for any sign of Jakob, probably seeing if she could find his family's box, which Elli knew was the one by Shea's.

Screaming irrupted, causing Harper to jump as Elli popped up screaming along with the fans because the guys were coming out to warm up. Shea was the last one out and when Elli saw him, she grinned. He looked amazing all suited up, no glasses covering his blue eyes and in a way she missed them. His helmet sat on his head, but it wasn't buckled underneath, something she knew he wouldn't do until the game started. He skated around twice before he saw her, and the grin that came over his face was so bright, it could have blinded someone. He skated over to where she sat, and just smiled, then pointed to his face.

Elli shrugged, saying "So, I'm a fan."

"Turn around." It was hard to hear him, but she heard him and did as he asked, when she faced him again he was smiling extra hard. He pulled his glove off and held up three fingers, then kissed his palm pressing it to the glass; she pressed her hand against his, and then said, "Good luck," before he skated off with a nod.

"Oh. My. God. Y'all disgust me that was straight out of some sappy love story, blah."

"Oh, shut up," Elli said with a huge grin, she loved it.

"What the hell did that mean anyway?"

"He's gonna score me three goals."

"Okay, that's pretty hot, not as hot as Jakob is right now, but hot." Elli shook her head, falling into her seat.

That man was gonna drive her bat shit crazy. She held up her hand ordering another beer, as she watched the show of the guys warming up. They were playing the Sharks tonight, a cut throat kind of team and it was gonna be a good game. People were filing in, getting to their seats as they cheered for the guys. Elli laughed as she saw the females pressing their breast against the glass with Adler written across their chests. She also saw the kids with their signs for Shea, he always made it a point to go give them his stick or a puck, and it was so cute when they would run off to their parents jumping up and down.

"He hasn't even knowledge me yet!" Harper complained. Elli looked up at her, then back at the ice where Jakob and Shea were shooting back and forth to each other.

"Harp, he's warming up," Elli insisted.

"Shea came over, did his little thing, where's my little thing!?" Harper whined, Elli shook her head, aren't together her ass. Harper might have found her match. Jakob was hot as hell, and from what Shea said, a really great guy too. Just then, Jakob looked up, seeing Harper. He smiled, nodding his chin at her, Harper smiled back, turning around to show his number to him. Jakob just grinned, watching as she twirled around for him, doing a little dance. She pointed to her face, before blowing him a kiss which he in returned by making a kissy face back at her.

It was downright disgusting, and Elli couldn't wait to tell everyone.

The guys began skating off, but Shea did give Elli one last look before skating off leaving her breathless. Harper dropped into the seat beside her, grinning her ass off.

"Aren't together, huh?" Elli asked, Harper shot her a look before downing her whole beer before muttering, "Shut up."

"Shit," Elli complained as she walked back to Harper's car, "Shit, Shit, Shit."

"I'm pretty sure you're supposed to be happy when they win, Elli. I mean I know this was my first game, but still I think that's the way it supposed to go." Elli cut her a glance as she climbed into the car. Yup, they had won. Five to two, Shea had scored four goals, and after each one he threw Elli a grin.

"Damn it."

"What's wrong!?" Harper finally yelled.

"If Shea scored three goals, and they won, I am supposed to show him my underwear." Harper giggled as she started the car.

"Now that is definitely hot, you have pretty undies on right?"

"They are my Shea Adler underwear!"

"Awesome," Harper said with a laugh, as she turned onto West End, heading towards the restaurant where they were meeting the guys for drinks.

"He'll see my tummy, Harp."

"No, he won't, just leave your jersey on, lower your jeans just a little, no big deal."

Elli let out a little scream of frustration and smacked her thighs, "Why did I make that bet!"

"Cause you like him," Harper said with a grin as she pulled into PF Changs. They got out the car, and headed inside; giving the name that Jakob had told Harper to give the hostess. The hostess smiled, and asked them to follow her, which they did. They passed some curtains to a booth set for four.

"Can I get y'all something to drink?" the waitress asked.

"A beer, please," Elli said.

"Me, too," Harper added as she placed her purse beside Elli's on the booth. Harper pulled her phone out and smiled. "They'll be here in a few."

Elli nodded as the waitress came back with their drinks and asked if they wanted an appetizer, they declined, saying they were waiting for their dates, and the waitress left with a smile. Elli took a long pull of her beer, completely nervous to see Shea. She knew he was expecting her to own up to their bet, and she would, but it didn't mean she would like it.

"Hey, are you going to that party tomorrow?" Elli looked up at Harper; she was picking the paper off her beer.

Aw, she was nervous.

"Yeah, are you?"

"I was thinking about it, Jakob ask me a while back, but I told him no, and of course he won't accept no and won't quit harassing me about it. I really don't have anything to wear though."

"We can go shopping tomorrow."

"Yeah, maybe." The curtain pulled back, and Jakob came through, a big smile on his face. Shea came in behind him, looking extremely tired, but when his eyes met Elli's, he smiled, and came towards her, kissing her lips softly. After parting, Elli scooted into the booth beside Harper, who was, of course, making eyes at Jakob.

"Hey, Jakob," Elli said, Jakob looked over at her, red dusting his cheek.

"Hey, Elli, how are you?"

"Good thanks and you?"

"Great now," he said before kissing Harper's cheek, which caused her to giggle.

Elli rolled her eyes, before looking over at Shea, he was smiling at her. He leaned towards her, moving her hair behind her ear before whispering, "You know you owe me right?"

"I know," she mumbled, causing him to smile before nibbling on her neck.

The waitress came back and the guys ordered some beer, and then everyone ordered their food. The dinner was nice; it was fun hanging out with Harper and Jakob. They were too stinking cute together, and no matter what Harper said, they were a couple. Shea held Elli's hand through the whole dinner, rubbing his thumb along the back of her hand, or he would move hair off her shoulder just to place a kiss on her neck. It was intoxicating.

"Are y'all ready for dessert?" The waitress asked as she picked up plates.

"No, can we get the check?" Elli asked, everyone looked over at her. "What, y'all are tired, you need to get home and rest, not stay out with us all night."

"Elli," Harper sneered.

"What?" she asked innocently.

"Elli's right, I'm tired as hell. I'm gonna head out." Shea handed his card to the waitress "The whole bill is on that please." The waitress nodded just as Jakob started to complain about paying. "You paid last time."

"Yeah, for you, this is all of us," Jakob complained.

"Doesn't matter."

"I got the next dinner."

"Fine," Shea agreed. "Can you give Jakob a ride home, Harper?"

"Of course, straight to my house," she cooed to Jakob which had him grinning. Shit, there was no way Elli was staying at Harper's house now. Not with Jakob coming over for sexcapades.

"Can you still take me to my car?" Elli asked, Harper nodded as she kissed Jakob's neck.

"I'll take you, babe," Shea said, Elli smiled.

"Are you sure?"

"Of course," he said as the waitress brought back his bill and card. They all thanked the waitress and headed out to the parking lot. After saying bye to Harper and Jakob, Elli jumped into Shea's truck and as she leaned back in the seat, she yawned loudly.

"Tired?" Shea asked as he started to truck.

"Yeah, if I knew that Jakob was going over to Harper's, I would have just skipped dinner and gone home."

"Huh?" Shea asked, she looked over at him, he looked confused.

"I was supposed to stay the night with Harper, but since she has a studio condo, there is no way I'm gonna stay there with sexcapades going on," she said with a laugh, "but it sucks, cause I'm so tired."

"So stay with me." Elli's head whipped around.

"Say what?"

"Come stay at my house, I'm right down the road, we can be asleep in thirty minutes tops."

"Huh?" Elli was confused, did he really think she was gonna sleep with him? Didn't they just have this discussion two days ago?

"Come stay at my house, sleep in my bed. Nothing's going to happen, one, you aren't ready; two, I'm tired, so it's cool. If you don't want me to sleep in the bed with you, I'll endure the couch, but when I lose the game on Friday, its cause you made me sleep on the couch, anyone who has ever slept on it can tell you that thing is the devil on your back."

He was rambling, probably because she was looking at him like he was an alien.

"You want me to sleep in bed with you?"

"Yeah, I don't want you driving home this late, babe."

"Oh, okay," she said looking down at her hands. It was just to sleep, no big deal. "Can we drive by my studio so I can get my bag?"

"Sure, babe." He looked so tired as he turned down 23rd to get to her studio, when they pulled up; Elli jumped out and ran to her truck, opening the back to get her bag and dress bag. Hopefully he wouldn't mind letting her hang up her dress in a closet, he had to have a closet she could use. He popped the trunk and got out; helping her put her stuff in. After that, they got back in the truck and headed over to his condo. Shea insisted on carrying her bags as they walked up the stairs and into the condo.

"Do you have somewhere I can hang up my dress?" she asked as he laid his keys in the basket by the door.

"Sure, come on." She followed him through the house, it was messier than it was last time, and it made her smile to think that he had cleaned up just for her. They came to the same bedroom that she had high tailed it out of not even four days ago; it seemed bigger now that she stood in it. The windows that lined the western wall were so clear; it looked like nothing was there. Just the night sky with the batman building's silhouette. His bed was huge, the biggest bed she had ever seen. The color scheme was a real clean, black with red accents. "You can hang everything in my closet."

Elli didn't move; that seem kinda private? Didn't he think so?

"Your closet?"

"Yeah, I'll make room," he said going into the spacious walk in closet. Elli watched as he pushed things around, leaving a good space for her to hang her things. She looked down to where he was kicking shoes and had to suppress the giggle that was about to escape. He had more shoes that she did! "There you go." Elli looked up, and he was stretching his arms over his head, he had played a hard game and was probably dog tired.

"You can go to bed, Shea. You don't need to wait on me."

"I don't mind, I'm good," he said leaning up against the wall as she hung her outfit for tomorrow and her dress for tomorrow night. She took her makeup bag out and put it above the dress on the shelf, and then she pulled out her PJs, which was a pair of boxers and a tank. She wished she had packed something else, but what the hell was she going to do?

"Okay, well I'm gonna go change," she said as she went to past him in the door, but he blocked her, smiling down at her.

"You owe me, Ms. Fisher."

"I know," she moaned as she finally got past him, she threw him a grin over her shoulder as she went into the bathroom. Elli shut the door and then turned, getting the full force of the bathroom.

"Good golly, Miss Molly!" she stammered as she looked around. The bathroom was massive! Shea had a walk in glass shower with what looked like 900 jets, a claw foot tub, and two sinks with a huge plasma TV hanging on the wall. "Gosh," she muttered as she looked around. She threw her bath bag on the black marble counter and started washing her face. After she was done, she changed into her PJs, nervous as hell. She looked at the mirror and rolled her eyes. Of course her tits were about to fall out and she looked like a hussy! She took a deep breath, blowing it out. Well, damn.

Elli opened the door, and went out, laying her bag on the dresser as she passed. Shea had already turned the bed down, so she climbed in, and sunk into it.

"Oh, good God," she muttered as she nuzzled into the down comforter, pulling the blankets to her chin. She was never leaving this bed. She heard the closet door open and Shea came out, fully clothed, something she knew for a fact wasn't the way he slept. Elli had read in an article once that he liked to sleep naked, but why was she complaining? This was a good thing; she wouldn't be able to handle seeing him naked!

"You sleep fully clothed?" Elli found herself asking anyways, as he walked towards her, he gave her a sheepish grin.

"No, I usually sleep naked but I'm not gonna scare you with all this," he said waving his hand in front of his body, she giggled, and looked away.

"I've seen your half naked body, Shea. I think everyone has."

"Ah, the Jockey ad, that shit was so fake."

"Huh?"

"Yeah, they Photoshoped my body left and right."

"Really?!" She asked, he didn't have the abs? The v-cut? Was all that fake?

"Yeah, I'm ripped, but I have a bunch of scars and shit," he said as he climbed into the bed on the left side.

"Scars?"

"Yeah, I was a busy child, and I got hurt a lot in my younger years."

"Oh."

"Yeah, so you being self-conscious about your body, shit, you should see mine," he said with a shake of his head as he pulled the blankets over his body.

"You're self-conscious? Shea Adler? You?"

"Yeah," he said with a shrug, "I get nervous when I take my clothes off in front of women, I'm afraid they'll think I'm a freak, my scars aren't pretty."

"I wouldn't think you're a freak," Elli whispered as she played with her nails.

"And I wouldn't think your fat."

"Whatever." Shea reached over, pulling her against him.

"So when do I get to see some undies?" Elli laughed, trying to get away from him, but he wasn't letting go.

"Shea! Let me go!" she giggled as she fought against him; he got on top her, pinning her legs down with a shit eating grin on his face. He folded his arms across his chest, and looked down at her.

"I won't touch I promise," he said with a smirk.

"I'll show you my panties, but only a little, you ain't seeing my bra though, since I would have to show you my tummy."

"Fine, get on with it," he said with a wave of his hand, Elli rolled her eyes, then bit her lip as she brought her hands to the top of her boxers, her tank went over the top of her boxers so she knew her tummy was covered before bringing them down to show him the big purple six that covered her mound. A slow sexy grin went across his face as his eyes skimmed her body, what little she showed at least.

"The logo is on my butt; above it says 'Adler'."

"Mm…that's hot, babe." She giggled, biting her lip harder.

"Is that a hockey stick?" he said looking down at the tattoo that covered her hip, she smiled.

"It is." He smiled as he looked his fill, before rolling off her to the side. Elli pulled her shorts up, and turned to her side, facing him.

"Show me a scar?" she asked, he thought for a second, then lifted his arm, pulling the tee up so she could see a jagged scar with holes where stitches had been. "Oh, my," she said, running her finger over it.

"Yeah, I broke my shoulder when I was ten; this kid slammed me into the boards, hard. It sucked."

"They all look like that?" It was gruesome, but she didn't care.

"Yeah, I got this really bad one across my stomach. I was playing one on one against this bad kid in my neighborhood, we wagered hockey cards to the winner, and well, I won. He had broken his stick on the last shot he had tried and he ended up stabbing me with the stick."

"Shut up!"

"No, really, it was bad. Grace was screaming; my mom was freaking out. When my dad found out about it, he went after the kid's dad. It was really scary."

"Oh, my goodness," Elli said with wide eyes, "How old were you?"

"Sixteen."

"Wow."

"Yeah," Shea said with a nod, he looked down and smiled, so she looked too, seeing her breast practically hanging out. "Nice."

"Ass!" she gushed, smacking his chest as she pulled her tank up some. "I didn't plan on sleeping here, thank you, or I would have worn footed PJs." That had him laughing and she soon joined in. "Okay, go to sleep," she said closing her eyes.

"No goodnight kiss?" Elli opened her eyes and Shea was grinning at her, he slid his hand to her ass and brought her closer to him. "Please."

"I guess," she muttered just as their lips met. It was a sweet kiss that ended faster then Elli would have liked, but she knew they were both tired, and things had to stay G rated. He gave her a small smile before wrapping her up in his arms and closing his eyes. Elli watched him from a moment, his eyelashes touching his high cheek bones, his crocked nose, and the dusting of hair of his hard jaw.

God, he was gorgeous.

Elli smiled and closed her eyes, thinking just how great it was to be lying in bed with Shea Adler.

Shea woke up to Elli walking across the bedroom, fully dressed. Something was wrong with this picture. The way he imagine it was that she would be lying beside him, all sleepy and sexy, but nope, she was fully dressed, ready to go. She glanced over at the bed, and gave him a sheepish smile.

"I'm sorry, did I wake you?" Elli asked coming towards the bed, she sat on the edge, looking down at him with a small smile on her face. She was wearing a pair of slacks with a lacey top, her breast were peeking out a little, making his already hard shaft harder.

"No baby, come here," he said pulling her down next to him, kissing her neck, since he wasn't sure if he had morning breath. "You were supposed to be sleeping next to me when I woke up," he mumbled against her neck.

"I gotta go to work."

"At," he looked over at the clock "7:30?"

"I got some paperwork to do before my 10 o'clock."

"Okay, I'm getting up," he said as he nibbled on her neck, she let out a little moan.

"You don't have to," she gasped as he bit harder, "Harper is coming to get me."

"No way, I'll take you," he said, pulling her on top of him. Her body lined up with his, she was so soft, so hot. He wrapped his arms around her middle, kissing her deeply, praying to

God his breath wasn't that bad, but he guessed it wasn't since she kissed his back, cupping his face in her hands. Her legs fell to the sides of his waist, to where she was straddling him, her softness against his hardness, he was convinced he was about to come. "Jesus Elli, you're so fucking hot," he mumbled against her lips as he squeezed her hips in his hands, pressing her harder against him. She blushed, as she closed her eyes and kissed him again.

Then the damn doorbell rang. Elli sat up, and rolled off him.

"Hey, where you going?"

"It's Harper!" she said with a grin as she walked out the room, Shea had never wanted someone as bad as he wanted Elli. "Let me say bye, and I'll be ready," he heard her say as he got out the bed, moving his shaft up so it wasn't too noticeable that he was as hard as a rock. Elli came back in the room, her heels clicking on the hardwood. She came around the bed, wrapping her arms around his neck, grinning up at him. "I gotta go."

"Alright, what time you getting off?"

"I'll probably be here at 6:15, we can leave by 7."

"Sounds good." He slapped her ass, making her jump in his arms.

"Shea!" She giggled as she leaned up to kiss his cheek. "I'll see you later."

"I'll be waiting," he said as she started to walk away, but he didn't let her get far, pulling her back in his arms, he kissed her hard. His hand slid up in her hair, his other hand cupping her sweet, perfect ass as he kissed her with all the passion that was building up inside of him. He wanted her so bad, and he wanted her to know it. He opened his eyes as they parted, staring into her beautiful green eyes. "Have a great day, baby."

Elli giggled, putting her hand over her heart, "Shit, Shea, after a kiss like that, I'm pretty damn sure I will." She leaned up kissing his laughing mouth before leaving with a wave. He heard the door shut and he smiled as he sat on the side of the bed Elli had slept on. He ran his hand down her pillow and took a deep breath as his mother's words replayed in his head.

He's head over heels.

Shit, was he?

Shea looked at clock; he didn't have to be at practice until ten, so he had time. After jumping in the shower and getting dressed, he headed into the kitchen to see a plate of food on the counter, with a note beside it.

Shea,

You're gonna need to nuke the food, but I made you breakfast. Thanks for last night, the win, the dinner, the night in bed, it was all a dream come true. I hope you have a wonderful day, and I'll see you tonight.

I'll be thinking of you,
Elli

Shea grinned as he took his phone out of his pocket and dialed Elli's number. As it rang, he put the food in the microwave and warmed the food.

"Hey."

"You know, I'm not going to let you leave now."

"Huh?" He laughed.

"You're not allowed to go home, you keep my bed warm, even though you steal the covers, and you make me breakfast, you expect me to let you go home?" Elli giggled, he loved the sound, it made him smile bigger.

"I have to go home, Adler is there. His babysitter was only paid for yesterday and today."

"Bring him here."

"No way, he would hate it, he needs a field."

Shea could live out there, no big deal.

"Fine, but that leads me to a question."

"Oh goodness, should I be nervous?" he laughed.

"No, but anyways, did you name Adler after me?"

She went quiet for a moment, and then let out a sigh.

"I did."

"So I am your favorite Assassins player?"

"You are," she huffed out.

Shea didn't think he could smile any bigger.

"So are you only dating me because of my employer?" he teased.

"Come on really, Shea? You know why I'm dating you."

"Why?"

"Cause you are hot, duh." He laughed as she giggled, he heard her moving around the office, and he had never felt so comfortable. Something about her made this so easy.

"I think you had your eyes on me since day one, your plan was to flirt with me, to get me in bed."

Elli was fully laughing by now, and he was laughing just as hard. "For one, I didn't flirt at all, if I remember correctly, I was a complete idiot, and second, you're the one that got me in your bed."

"Very true, it's a good place for you," he said with a laugh "and you weren't an idiot the first time we met babe, you were sweet."

"Sweetly stupid, I'm surprised you even understood what I said to you." A phone rang, it must have been in her office because she said, "I gotta go Shea, I'll text ya later."

"Alright babe, thanks again for breakfast, bye."

"Anytime, bye."

Shea ate his food as he watched the morning news, then cleaned up before leaving. After getting into his truck, and starting it, he drove off towards his sisters. Grace was probably gonna be livid to see him so early, but he needed to talk to her. When he pulled up to her house, he saw her at the window, in front of her computer feeding Amelia. Good, she was awake. He shut off the truck, and started up the driveway, before opening the front door and going in. Ryan came from the hall, and ran right for him, jumping into his arms.

"Unky!"

"Hey, bud," Shea said kissing his cheek, before walking to the living room where Grace was sitting cross-leg with her hair in a mess on top of her head, and a pencil in her mouth. She was still in her pjs, the joys of running your own business, he guessed.

"Hey, Shea," she said not looking up as he kissed Amelia's chubby cheeks, he put Ryan down, and kissed Grace next, before sitting beside her. "What brings you by?" she asked as she typed something then took a drink of her coffee.

"Do you really want to know, or are you too busy to talk to your only twin brother." Grace rolled her eyes before shutting the laptop and turning towards him.

"I'm having some problems with this wedding I'm planning, my regular photographer is a dimwit and is pissing me off, I'm about to fire him, but the wedding is next month and I doubt I can get someone to take his place."

"Call Elli, she might be able to."

"Maybe, but I don't want to start using her a lot and you guys break up or something."

"Since you brought Elli up," Shea started, Grace shook her head.

"I didn't-"

"Do you think I love her?" Grace just looked at him with a look on her face.

"Say what?"

"Do you think I love her?" he repeated himself.

"No, I heard you; I just don't understand the question. How would I know if you love her?"

"You're my twin."

"I know that."

"Well, what do you think?"

"I don't know! I haven't even seen you guys together but that one time."

"So we'll come over for dinner and you'll tell me?"

"Really Shea? I'm swamped with weddings and parties right now, and you want me to cook a dinner for you and your girlfriend?"

Shea stood up with a grin on his face, "Thanks, you're the greatest, how about Sunday evening, since I'm leaving Monday for a week."

"Are you kidding me!?" she yelled as he kissed the kids.

"No, come on, I need to know."

"You're nuts."

"Yup, about you babe, see ya Sunday, let me know if you need anything."

"I will; your credit card number since I'm hiring a cook!" she yelled as he shut the door.

God he loved his sister.

Chapter 10

"I don't know why I need a dress; can't I just wear some jeans?" Harper complained as they browsed through Marine Renee's store for a dress. Harper hated shopping and definitely hated anything but jeans. Elli on the other hand, loved to shop, and definitely loved to dress up. Elli had already bought a lilac tube top dress with a scalloped chest lapel that went to her knees for the party, she was gonna pair it with a bone color cardigan and bone colored, peep toe Jimmy Choo heels. She was excited, which was odd since she was never excited about trying to be cute in front of a bunch of hockey players who happen to be the friends of the guy that she was dating, but she was. For the first time in years she had a great night's sleep without her DVD's help, she felt great, refreshed, all because of Shea.

"Because it's a party."

"You can wear jeans to a party," Harper mumbled as she looked through the racks, with a little more force than needed.

"Don't you want to be pretty for Jakob?"

"He thinks I'm pretty no matter what," Harper countered as she pulled out a dress, looking back and forth at it, "This is pretty." It really was, that's why Elli owned it, it was a little pink flower print dress, that was tight around the bust and loose around the waist. It was one of Elli's favorites, but Harper needed something tight.

"It is, but you need something like a tube dress, something to show off that hot body of yours," Elli said as she kept looking, as Harper just grinned.

"Yeah, Jakey would like that."

"Jakey?"

"What? It's my nick name for him."

"Aw, so cute!" Elli gushed causing Harper to gag herself, which in return made Elli laugh.

"Oh, gawd, what are you doing back here? Is there an all-you-can-eat buffet close by?" Harper and Elli both turned to see Victoria standing a foot away with a price gun in hand. Elli cursed herself, she could have swore she hadn't seen Victoria's car in the driveway. Damn it.

"Ah, it's the wicked bitch of the west! Run Elli!" Harper yelled, Elli rolled her eyes as she went back to looking for a dress.

"Just ignore her," Elli grumbled, turning her back to her sister, but that didn't stop Victoria, she came around, facing Elli.

"So, I think it's totally pathetic that you convinced our nieces and nephews that your dating Shea Adler, I mean really Elli, like he would ever look at you twice."

"I didn't do no such thing, now if you'll excuse us," Elli said turning the other way, but Victoria kept at her.

"Mom says she will make you talk to her, she wants to meet 'Shea Adler'," she said making air quotations around Shea's name.

"You would die if she showed up with him, huh?" Harper asked, "Shit, El, you might have to do it, just to rid us of Vicky here." Elli giggled as she pulled out a dress. It was a black tube dress that was tight all over except for the sleeves; they had pretty eyelet lace on them.

"This is it, Harp," Elli said handing her the dress, Harper had a small smile on her face as she nodded.

"It is," she agreed, picking out her size, and walking right past Victoria.

"You're not really dating Shea Adler, so just drop the act Elli."

"If I'm not dating him, then why are you still entertaining the thought? Just let it go," Elli said simply, "Harp, I'll be in the truck."

"Sure, babe." Elli walked past her sister, and out the store. She hated being around Victoria, she was like a poison or something, so damn toxic. No matter how much Elli wished she had Victoria's confidence, she would never wish to have her values and morals. Elli got into the truck, pulling out her phone to text Shea.

You're real right?

I think so. He texted back, which made her smile. *Why?*

Just needed to make sure, we're really dating too?

Oh, yeah, we are. Hey, can you do dinner with me and my sister's family Sunday?

Sure, I would love too.

Awesome, I can't wait to see you tonight.

Me neither.

Elli smiled to herself, yes, she was dating Shea Adler, and he couldn't wait to see her.

Later that afternoon as Elli was finishing up with an edit on a family shoot, the business line rang. She picked it up with her regular greeting, and then froze in a cringe as her mother's voice rang over the line.

"Eleanor Ray! I have been trying to get a hold of you for weeks! You gave me no choice but to call you at your so called work!"

"Oh, mother, and you wonder why I ignore your calls. I'm busy working, are you dying?"

"No."

"Okay, so I'll talk to you later."

"You hang up on me, I will tell your father!" Olivia warned, darn it, her dad would be so mad at Elli, that's why she usually just ignored the calls. Elli talked to her father at least once a week, she loved her daddy, but that was probably because he wasn't crazy like the rest of the family.

"Fine, mother, I got four minutes before my next appointment comes in, what do you need?"

"I need to meet your boyfriend!"

"I don't have a boyfriend, mom."

"So you are making out with random men at the park in front of my grandchildren!"

"He wasn't random, mom, just a friend."

"What, are you are trollop!"

"For the love of God," Elli muttered, putting her face in her hand, "Mom, he's a guy I'm dating right now."

"What's his name?"

"Shea."

"Shea, as in hockey player Shea? The one that covers the walls of that small house you own?"

And people wonder why Elli didn't answer her mother's calls.

"Yes, mom."

"Victoria says there's no way."

"Victoria is a bitch, and I'm not going to defend myself, believe me or not, I don't care."

"Such, language, bring him to the house for dinner."

"It'll be a cold day in hell before I subject Shea to you people."

"Eleanor Ray! You will bring him to dinner; he is the first guy I have heard of since Justin."

"There's a reason for that," Elli commented as she fixed a red spot on the baby's face in the picture. "I don't really like family dinners with you people."

"Eleanor, you heard me. Dinner, next month, since this month was canceled."

"Mom, I don't even know if this will last past this week, plus if it does, I don't know if he'll be in town."

"Find out, and give me a date that he will be in town, sometime next month. You have till next Sunday to give me an answer Eleanor, dear. Or I will sic your father on you!"

"Okay, mom." Elli sneered. She was not happy, and her mother would know it.

"I'm pretty sure I can convince him to drop you from the will."

"Whatever, dad loves me more than you, he wouldn't do that, he would just be mad at me, and you're lucky I don't want that."

"Whatever you say darling, love you. Tootles!"

The line went dead and Elli closed her eyes, that woman drove her bat shit crazy just like her sister. Hell, her whole family did, except her daddy, and the kids, they were the only normal ones. Elli thought she could always call and beg her dad not to make her do it, but then he would want to meet Shea, and no telling how that would go since the last time he saw Justin he had pulled a shotgun on him.

Well, hells bells.

"So, killer," Elli looked up to Harper leaning against the doorframe. "How was last night? You seem extra happy this morning."

"It was nice, I guess."

"Please don't ever tell Shea that you called sex with him nice."

"We didn't have sex," Elli informed here as she saved the pictures and shut the program down. When she looked over at Harper, she was just staring at Elli.

"What do you mean y'all didn't have sex? I picked you up from his house."

"We didn't, we just cuddled, slept, what?" she asked when Harper was looking at her crazy.

"That's depressing El, you have a fine piece of man meat lying right beside you and you didn't even touch him?"

"We made out a little, then went to sleep," Elli said with a shrug as she passed by Harper. Harper, of course, followed her down the hall to the front room and stood by as Elli set up for the newborn shoot she had.

"Are you crazy? You're still trying to hide your body aren't you! I thought you talked to him about it."

"We did, but it doesn't mean I'm gonna have sex with him now, I'm scared, Harp, let me be."

"Sex is nothing to be scared of, do it, you'll like it, I promise."

Elli shook her head, of course she wanted to have sex with Shea but the thought just drove her crazy, "I probably wouldn't even know how to do it," she admitted quietly, "It's been years, Harp. Not only would I be scared because he'd be seeing me naked but then I would be crazy nervous I would mess something up."

"El, it's pretty cut and dry, one thing goes in the other and magic happens, plus it's like riding a bike, you never forget," she said with a devilish smile, while Elli rolled her eyes, "But if you're nervous about it, just do it in steps, tell him your ready to take making out to another level but not ready for sex."

"Does the next level of making out involve me showing him my body?"

"Why, yes, it does."

"Then I'm not ready," Elli said as the door open and a young couple came in with a bright pink car seat, that no kidding, had feathers on it.

"Hello! Welcome to Time Standing Still, I'm Elli." And off she went, into photographer mode, putting her issues of sex and Shea in the back of her mind as she worked, but like always Shea managed to make an appearance, especially when the father of the baby, kissed the mommy's neck, it made Elli think of him, since he loved doing that. Elli sighed as she positioned the beautiful baby girl on a bright pink flower pillow, what would it be like if this was her baby, and Shea was standing behind her kissing her neck?

It would be her happily ever after.

Shea sat in his condo, waiting on Elli. She was running late, but she had texted and already warned him, saying the baby shower ran over a little. He sat in his black Armani suit, with a light blue shirt underneath it with no tie, just the first 2 buttons open; he had his favorite black chucks on and of course his glasses, since Elli didn't mind them. She kind of liked them, which made him happy since he hated his contacts. He got up, going to the kitchen for a glass of wine, when the door open and Elli sailed through going straight by him to the bed.

"I'm so sorry!" she called as she rushed into the room, shutting the door. He shook his head with a smile as the door opened back up and she stood there gawking at him.

"Damn, Mr. Adler, you're looking mighty fine." He smiled, smoothing his jacket down.

"Why, thank you." She gave him a wink then shut the door; he smiled and poured himself a glass before going back into the living room to wait. It seemed so normal, so comfortable. Him, waiting on his girl, he liked it, he thought with a shrug and a smile. He watched all of Sport Center before Elli finally emerged, looking so damn hot; it was hard for him to breathe. Her hair was in big curls, framing her face and shoulders. Her pretty little thighs were peeking out the wide skirt, and her beautifully sculpted ankles were brought out by the high heels she wore. God, she was gorgeous.

"Jeez, Elli, I can't take you out in public, I'll be fighting everyone at the damn party." She grinned, coming towards him, he noticed her lips were painted red, and luscious was the only word that came to mind. He wrapped her up in his arms, pressing her closer against him.

"I could say the same about you, you know."

"You could, but you don't have too, because I got eyes only for you."

"Sure," she teased as she leaned up, kissing him softly against the lips.

"Mm, come back here," he said when she pulled back, he covered her mouth with his, kissing her the way he had been wanting to all day. He had missed her, a lot. Waking up with her in his house had kept her on his mind all day. If it was like this now, without the sex, no telling what it would be like when they finally did it. He probably would be like a hemorrhoid, never leaving her ass alone.

"Mm, goodness, do I even have lipstick still on?" she asked as she looked up at him, she giggled as she wiped his mouth. "I guess not, you might want to wipe that off, while I reapply," she said as she walked back into the bedroom. He had a crooked grin on his face as he wiped off his mouth, when she reappeared, new lipstick applied, they gathered their things and left.

Alex Welch and his wife, Mary Ann always held the opening game party at Union Station, which was a ritzy hotel in downtown Nashville. Shea loved the place, thought it was beautiful and the food was amazing. He was really excited about taking Elli there because he was pretty sure she hadn't been there before. After giving his truck over to the valet, Shea led Elli inside, his hand on the small of her back. As they walked through the beautiful hotel to the meeting hall, he could tell that Elli was nervous. She was doing that lip biting thing, along with moving her hands a lot. He finally took her hand in his, squeezing lightly.

"Its going to be fine, baby."

She smiled nervously, "I'm just nervous your friends won't like me."

"They'll love you," he reassured her; she gave him a small smile as they entered the hall. All his friends and teammates were there, with their wives or girlfriends, some were talking, while others danced. Dinner hadn't been served yet, so everyone was snacking on the hor' dourves while they drank. When Shea saw Alex and Mary Ann, he led Elli towards them. Alex smiled when he saw Shea, before turning Mary Ann a little to greet him.

"Hey, Bro," Alex said, shaking hands with Shea, Mary Ann smiled big, leaning up and kissing Shea's cheek. Mary Ann used to be a model or something like that but when she and Alex got married, she gave it up to have children and to be a wife. She was stunningly beautiful and very sweet; Shea liked her best out of all the wives.

"Shea! How are you!" she said in her thick country accent, she had grown up in Nashville.

"I'm good, Mary Ann, I want you guys to meet my..."

Shit, his what? He looked over at Elli and she smiled nervously, taking Alex's hand. "His date, Eleanor Fisher, but I go by Elli," she said, shaking Alex's hand, Alex looked surprised but smiled as he returned the gesture.

"Well, hello, this is my wife Mary Ann."

"Hi," Elli said, Mary Ann smiled, hugging Elli instead of shaking her hand.

"Hi! How are you! You're just too beautiful for words! I love your eyes!" Mary Ann was also very loud, but she meant well.

"Thank you so much. Your maiden name is Ryan right?"

"It is!"

"I've seen your work, a friend of mine used to shoot for you back in the day"

"Alli Richardson?"

"Yup, I went to school with her."

"Wow! Small world huh?!"

"Sure is," Elli said giving Shea a grin, and off they went, into a very elaborate conversation about this person and that person, Shea and Alex stood for a few minutes before they both didn't know what the hell the women were talking about so they excused themselves, going straight for the bar. Alex ordered them both a beer, and the men stood drinking them, as they made small talk.

"She's nice, Shea," Alex said with a nod towards Elli and Mary Ann.

"I think so."

"She was the photographer from the team pictures we did, isn't she?"

"Yeah, that's where I met her."

"Okay, I was thinking she was new because I haven't seen you with anyone in a while."

"Changing it up, I guess."

"You can say that again, she is not your norm, Shea, not at all. Mary Ann loves her." Shea smiled, watching Elli talk with her hands, before letting out a gut busting laugh. She was intoxicating; she looked over at him giving him a smile, which he returned.

"She's something."

"Is it serious?" Shea looked over at Alex, he had known Alex for a very long time, they both joined the Assassins the same year, and they both played in the amateur league together, too.

"I think so, but you know me," Alex nodded, and then Shea said "but then again, she's the only thing I want right now."

Alex nodded his head, then grinned up at Shea. "That's great man, I hope it works out."

"Me and you both."

Elli was beyond nervous when she walked into the Union Station. She had been here before with her family for family events, but that didn't help her nerves. First she was running late, which made Shea late, but he didn't seem to mind, then she was meeting his friends, his people. What if they didn't like her? Thought she was a fat cow or something?

But that all changed when she met Mary Ann Welch, Mary Ann was stunning, big blue eyes, almost white blonde hair, with a face to remember, high cheek bones, beautiful lips, she was amazing inside and out. They talked about everything from modeling, to photography, to kids, when she felt Shea watching her. She loved that he only stared at her, even if it did make her self-conscious.

"Oh, Jakob is here," Mary Ann said with a big grin, "I love him dearly, he stayed with me and Alex for a while when he went through his divorce a couple years ago. He's our kid's god daddy, we just adore him," Mary Ann gushed.

Divorce? Harper didn't tell her that.

"He's bringin' someone tonight; someone he says is 'is the one'. Bless his heart, but he could fall in love with a rock, but he seems pretty sure of this one."

It took everything for Elli not to laugh because she knew for a fact that Harper would never get married, or even consider it, but then again Elli never thought Harper would see the same guy more than once.

So what the hell did she know?

"Ooo, she is super pretty!" Elli turned seeing Harper and Jakob make their way towards Mary Ann. Mary Ann wrapped herself around Jakob, kissing his cheek loudly as Harper stood by with the what-the-hell-is-this-chick-doing look. Elli shook her head, but Harper was getting madder by the minute.

"Harper Allen, Mary Ann Welch, she's married to Alex, they're the ones I was telling you about, I'm the kid's godfather."

Harper faced went from mad to understanding in two second flat. "Oh, yes, I have heard a lot about y'all," she said, and then Mary Ann hugged her tightly.

"I'm sorry Elli!" Mary Ann said turning around, and grabbing Elli's hand, "This is Elli Fisher, she's Shea's date."

"We know each other Mary Ann, Harper is my best friend and my assistant photographer," Elli said with a grin as Harper smiled at Mary Ann, basically wrapped around Jakob. He was beaming, and Elli had to admit, Harper was just as happy, maybe things were different for her and Jakob, maybe Jakob was her person. Elli smiled at the thought; she didn't want anything more then for Harper to find her happily ever after.

The four talked for a little longer before Jakob walked off leaving the girls with Mary Ann. Elli could see that Mary Ann was testing Harper out, but Harper didn't seem to mind, she answered any question Mary Ann had, with not so much as a blush. Harper always amazed Elli; she was so fearless, so beautiful. After a while, dinner was called to be served, and luckily the three couples were at a table together, so they were able to keep the conversation going.

The food was divine, Elli knew it would be, but gosh, Mary Ann had great taste. The pork loin was spectacular, but the potatoes were the most amazing potatoes she had ever put in her mouth. Elli almost moaned every time she ate one, they were so delicious. She took another bite, and saw Shea staring at her from the corner of her eye. She blushed as she covered her mouth, looking over at him.

"Stop staring at me!" she whispered, he just smiled leaning closer to her to place a kiss on the side of her mouth.

"I can't help it, you're so hot when you eat." Elli giggled and everyone looked over at them, smiling.

"Y'all are too stinkin' cute! Aren't they Alex?" Mary Ann gushed as she drank her wine.

"Yes, honey, yes," Alex teased in a fake country accent that had everyone laughing.

Elli loved Mary Ann and Alex; they were funny, and real. They got into a fight right in front of everyone about the seasoning on the meat, but two seconds after it, they kissed like two teenagers that couldn't get enough of each other.

It was the second time that Elli had seen Harper with Jakob, and it still blew her mind how Harper acted towards him. She wasn't cold like she was with other guys, and she wasn't hateful either, she was nice, not lovey-dovey like Jakob was, always touching her face, or holding her hand, but she was nice to him, smiling and kissing him whenever she had the chance. It was weird, but a good weird.

As for her and Shea, they were perfect. That was the only way Elli could put it, he would move her hair off her shoulder, or kiss her neck, or hold her hand, kissing her knuckles. He didn't care that they were sitting with four other people; all he cared about was her. It was weird, but an amazing, over the top, awesome weird.

As desert was served (a three layer chocolate cake with a white chocolate sauce…yum!), Mary Ann and Alex excused themselves, to go thank people Elli guessed, but all she cared about was the cake, it was fantastic! She knew Shea was watching her, but she was too busy stuffing her face to care.

"My goodness, this is wonderful" she muttered as she ate.

"It really is," Shea agreed, she smiled at him, and looked over at Harper, who was also stuffing her face.

"It's amazin'," she gushed as Jakob laughed, that when Elli noticed that his plate was still full of a cake and it hadn't been touched.

"Why aren't you eating?" Elli asked pointing her spoon at his plate.

"I don't like chocolate." Elli dropped her spoon.

"Say what?" Shea chose that moment to drink his beer and started choking on it at Elli's complete and utter shock. "What do you mean you don't like chocolate? I'll have to run 5 miles tomorrow, but I don't care, this is God's gift to me." Jakob smiled and he shook his head while Harper and Shea laughed.

"It's not my thing, and Mary Ann knows this, that's probably why she skipped out," he said with a laugh, Shea nodded his head, chuckling as he said, "Probably."

Elli just shook her head, *didn't like chocolate? That was a sin*, she thought as she took another huge bite. A microphone was bumped and Mary Ann's voice filled the room.

"Hey, everyone! We just wanted to thank everyone for coming out, and bringing your dates out. I have met so many new people this year, and that just awesome to me!" she gushed; Alex took the mic then and smiled at the crowd.

"Like my beautiful wife who has had a little too much said," everyone laughed while Mary Ann pouted, "Thanks for coming out, we hope you guys have enjoyed the food, and the dancing to come. Go Assassins!"

The hall filled with everyone repeating 'Go Assassins' even Shea and Jakob did it, leaving Harper and Elli out, not that they minded, they were too busy eating Jakob's piece of cake. The music started as Mary Ann and Alex made it off the stage. Some people got up to dance, while others went to the bar as the waiters came around picking up plates.

Shea leaned closer to Elli as she licked the spoon she had, making sure she didn't leave any of the most amazing cake she had ever eaten. She was gonna have to ask for the recipe, it was fantastic. "Hey," he whispered in her ear, knocking her out of her chocolate haze.

"Hey," she said, leaning her head over a little so he had full range of her neck.

"Do you like to dance?"

"I love to dance," she answered with a giggle as he sucked on her earlobe. "Do you?"

"Yeah, I like to get down with a pretty girl every once in a while," Elli smiled as he looked into her eyes, with a crooked smile, his glasses a little crooked too since he had his face all in her neck, "Wanna dance with me?"

"Hey El, wanna get a drink with me?" Both Elli and Shea looked over at Harper who was standing up; with one look Elli knew she was mad.

"Uh, yeah" Elli said, she looked at Shea with a shrug and then lean over kissing his cheek. "Sorry," she said as she stood up, and followed Harper to the bar. Harper was fuming; Elli was trying to figure out what happened since they were joking about chocolate not even 5 minutes ago. Crap, things were going so good! Harper ordered a Jack and Coke, while Elli settled for a beer. They both leaned on the bar, looking out at the crowd that was dancing while Jakob, Shea, and Alex stood with two wingers and the backup goalie at their table. Elli looked over at Harper; she had drunk half her drink.

"So, what's wrong?"

"I wanna leave."

"Why? Aren't you having a nice time? I am," Elli said turning towards Harper, she looked like she might cry but since Elli hadn't seen Harper cry since they were nine, she highly doubted that would happen.

"He just doesn't get it."

"Who? What? Jakob?"

"Yeah, he told Mary Ann I'm his girlfriend." Elli just looked at Harper confused, was she missing something?

"Okay?"

"Its sex, Elli. That's all. Just regular sex when I want it. Nothing more, I'm not his girlfriend."

"Okay," Elli said with a nod before taking Harper's hand in hers, "Harper, y'all are so good together, are you sure it can't be more?"

Harper just shook her head, "No, I don't want a boyfriend. I like it the way it is, he stays at my house and we do it all the time."

"And you've told him this?"

"Yeah, but he can't get it through his head, he says he can change my mind on that, but I'm serious, he can't, I don't want that."

"I know," Elli said with a nod, she knew it was too good to be true. Harper would never change. It wasn't who she was, she was crazy, fun loving, different man screwing, Harper Allen. Not a one woman type gal, Elli felt so bad for Jakob, he just didn't get it.

Elli looked over to her right and saw two girls staring at Harper and her. Elli looked back over at Harper, who was shaking her head, as she took sips of her drink, and then she looked back at the girls. They were beautiful girls, one had brown eyes while the other had green, and both were blondes, with extremely huge boobs and no waist at all. They started making their way towards Elli, and she looked back over at Harper, who saw them coming.

"Oh, come on," she complained as the girls plastered big, fake grins on their faces.

"Hi! I'm Ellen Rochester, I'm married to Bryan Rochester, number 62." The one with brown eyes said, holding her hand out to shake Elli's and Harpers, they took her hand, shaking it as green eyes went into her spill.

"And I'm Roxy Adams, I'm engaged to number 31, Matthew Parra," she said also shaking their hands. "Who are you girls with?" Roxy continued.

"Oh, I'm Eleanor Fisher, I go by Elli though, I'm here with Shea Adler."

Both girls just looked at her, before raising their eye brows, "Shea Adler? The captain?"

"Yeah," Elli said slowly with a nod.

"We thought she was with him," Ellen said as she pointed her skinny little finger at Harper.

"You've got to be kidding me," Harper said, looking up at Ellen, Ellen had about a foot on Harper, but Elli didn't think she cared. "No, actually I'm here with Jakob Titov."

That made the girls giggle, "No, wait, you're kidding right? We had this all wrong, didn't we Rox, we thought it was the other way around."

"Yeah, Shea usually doesn't date girls of your-" Roxy looked Elli up and down, "Stature?"

Oh hell, this was about to go bad. Elli knew it when she heard Harper's loud intake of breath.

"Are you fucking kidding me right now?" Harper asked, stepping towards Roxy.

"Harp, please, its fine. Come on," Elli said, pulling on Harper's arm.

"What are you trying to say? What that Shea doesn't date beautifully sized women; or that Jakob couldn't get someone as hot as me?" Roxy took a step back, but Harper followed

"Because if you're thinking what I think your thinking, I might have to break that fake nose of yours, you dumb bitch."

"Okay, now, come on, Harper."

Jakob came out of nowhere, wrapping Harper up in his arms, walking her away, Shea was right behind him, sending a look at the girls, then Elli.

"You alright, babe?" Elli nodded as Shea looked over at Roxy and Ellen. "What's going on guys?"

"We don't know? She flipped," Roxy sputtered, as Ellen pulled her arm, and then they were gone.

"What the hell is going on?" Elli shrugged her shoulder, completely embarrassed for one, and a little hurt. This was what she had tried to tell Shea would happen. People wouldn't understand why he was with her, she wasn't his damn type.

"They didn't believe that I was your date, Harper got pissed, and did the only thing she knows how to do, go off at the mouth." Elli went to turn around, but Shea stopped her, pinning her against the bar.

"Why don't they believe you're my date?"

"Because, what was Roxy's words?" Elli thought, than she nodded "You don't like girls of my stature."

Shea scuffed as he shook his head, "She's just jealous cause I wouldn't give her any of my time, babe, you gotta keep your mind straight with these kinds of people, know that I'm with you because I like you, a lot. Don't listen to any of them, they're jealous."

Elli looked down at her beer, which she held at her waist, he took a step closer; bringing her face up by her chin, "Elli baby, I like you, a lot, don't you get that?"

"I do."

She wouldn't look at him, so he put his face in her view, making her look at him, which made her laugh. "Only you," he said sternly, as he held her face, "I promise." She nodded once before he kissed her softly. When he pulled back, Elli open her eyes, seeing his beautiful smile, she loved the imperfect things about his face that made it perfect. Like the way he had a scar by his lip or the one above his eyebrow, she loved the little bump on his nose that told her it had been broke a few times. He had only one dimple but it was so big that it made up for the fact that there wasn't another one on the other side. His eyelashes were so long, they almost touched the glass of his glasses, and his eyes, gosh they were so damn blue. He was perfect to her, and he liked her, only her. He promised.

"I like you too," she whispered, which made him grin.

"Good, now, come on, let's dance."

She nodded as he led her to the floor, Sean Hayes 'Powerful stuff' started, and Elli grinned as Shea mouthed the words, taking her hand and raising it above their heads as he moved his body against hers to the music. He was an amazing dancer, and Elli hoped she could keep up. She bit her lip as she moved against him. Elli eyes drifted shut a little as his hands went down her body bringing her closer to him, and Elli thought at that moment, that nothing could get better than this.

The night couldn't have gotten have been any better, Shea thought as he and Elli drove back to his condo. They had danced until the party had ended, and he had never loved dancing with someone more until he had danced with Elli. She had moves, and when she bit that plump bottom lip, he really wasn't sure if he was going to make it. She was sexy, beautiful, and amazing; he couldn't get enough of her. He parked beside her truck, and got out, going around to help her out. He held her hand as they climb the stairs to his condo. After unlocking the door, and throwing his keys in the basket, he turned to see Elli standing by the door.

"You can come in, babe."

"Yeah, but, I'm stupid tired Shea, is it okay if I stay again? I promise it'll be the last night!" she said with a hand up, a little red dusting her cheeks.

"I hope it's not the last night," he said with a grin, "of course you can stay, babe."

"Okay, I'll have to leave like crazy early though; I gotta go home in the morning and get clothes."

"So, no breakfast?" She laughed, smacking his chest as she walked by.

"Probably not," she said, but she didn't get far before he wrapped his arms around her waist, pulling her against him, he kissed her shoulder, then her neck, before turning her in his arms, to kiss her hard on her lips. When they parted, she smiled up at him, "Can I borrow a shirt?"

His breathing actually hitched at the thought of her in his shirt, he could only nod as he walked with her still in his arms, she laughed out loud almost tripping a few times, but he had her, she wasn't going anywhere. When he threw the bedroom door open, Elli's laughter stopped as she looked up at him. He backed her up, until her legs hit the bed.

"Still not ready?" he asked, cause he was ready, so ready. She shook her head, biting her lip. His head fell back, as he looked up at the ceiling, trying to control his breathing. "Okay," he said, he looked down at her and kissed the side of her mouth before walking to the dresser to get her a shirt.

"I can still leave, Shea, I'm sorry."

"Baby, its fine," he said as he found one of his old JR League shirts, he handed it to her, not really looking at her as he went toward the closet, he stopped at the door. "Do you need to take a shower?"

"Yes, please, if that's okay."

"Absolutely, I'll take one after you." She looked like she might cry, which wasn't what he wanted. "I'm gonna go get a drink, catch some highlights while you're in there, let me know when you out."

She nodded then hurried into the bathroom. Shit. He mentally kicked himself as he went into the kitchen to get water out of the fridge. Elli drove him crazy, he wanted her so bad, but he had to get himself in check, before he scared her away, made it where she would never talk to him again. That would be hell, since, now that she was in his world, he couldn't imagine her not in it. The thought actually made it hard to breath, he couldn't fathom it.

Shea went into the living room, turning the TV on as he sat down on his leather couches. He heard the water running in the bedroom as he turned ESPN on. He watched the highlights and it actually calmed him. He had been in overdrive since the beginning of the night, and watching his favorite thing, sports, made him feel better. He was so nervous about how to act around Elli that it was driving him mad. He didn't understand it really; no woman had ever done this to him. A woman who didn't want to have sex with him, fine, on to the next, but he didn't want the next, he wanted Elli. What if, after he has had her he didn't want her anymore? The thought scared him so badly, he had to turn off the TV and cover his face with his hands. What if this was about the chase, because she said no.

But it couldn't be because when she was away, he missed her, and when she was with him, he felt so good. He didn't need the sex, he just needed her, her smiles, her country twang, her giggles, her, Elli. When they finally did it, it would do nothing but make whatever was going on with them stronger, yeah, that's it. There was nothing to worry about, nothing...he hoped.

Elli came into the living room just as Shea stood up, putting the remote on the table. "I'm done," she said, he then saw that she had a pillow and blanket from the bench at the end of his bed.

"What's that?" he asked, nodding his head toward her hands.

"Oh, I was gonna sleep on your couch."

"Elli, I told you, this couch is hell on the back, call anyone, they'll tell you."

"Oh, I'm fine."

"Fine, don't sleep on the couch because I want you to sleep with me."

"Shea.."

"No, stop, when you walked through my door, where did you think you were sleeping?" She kicked the floor, looking down at the bundle in her hands. "With me, right?"

"Right."

"Okay, so I asked if you're ready to fool around, you say no, and that causes you to sleep on the couch?"

"I just don't want to disappoint you anymore, Shea, I feel like that's all I do. I'm not like the girls you would date, I won't put out, I mean, I suck!"

"You do not, how many times do we need to do this Elli?" he hated that he was getting mad, but she was pissing him off, and she started yelling first. "You are the girl I want, I mean, yeah, I would love for you to put out, but I'll live until you're ready!"

"I just don't know if this is going to work, I think I'm fucked in the head, and I'm sorry, but I just don't know."

"This is going to work Elli, stop thinking so much, we're fine. Now when I get out that damn shower, you better be in my bed, or I'll come in here and sleep on this God awful couch with you," he said stepping towards her, "Because if you are in the same place I am, I will be beside you." He kissed her hard before going down the hall to the bedroom. He grabbed his night clothes and went into the bathroom. After getting cleaned up, and using the bathroom, he threw his clothes on and went out of the bathroom to see Elli laying in the bed, watching TV. He smiled to himself as he hung up his suit before coming back into the room, climbing into the bed with her. He laid on his side, looking at her as she turned off the TV.

"Why was Harper mad earlier?" he asked, she looked down at him, and smiled, as she put the remote on the night stand.

"Jakob called her his girlfriend, she didn't like that much."

"I thought they were?"

"No, Harper is really weird; she's all about sex, and only sex."

"Jakob isn't like that."

"He knows she is though, he thinks he can change her, but Harper Allen will never change." He took her hand in his, playing with her pink nails as they laid in the silence. He felt so good, so complete. Elli did this to him, he wanted more. So much more with her.

"When I introduced you to Mary Ann, I wanted to call you my girlfriend, Elli," he looked up at her to see her eyes were wide, "I've never had a girlfriend, so I'm not sure if I'll do the boyfriend/girlfriend thing right, but the thought of you being with someone else, or me with someone else, actually hurts my gut, so I guess what I'm trying to say is," he took a deep breath, this was huge, and he thought he sounded stupid but with the way her eyes were glazing over, maybe he was doing this right. "I was wondering if you wanted to be my girlfriend." She smiled at him lovingly, cupping his face in her hands.

"Are you sure? I'm kinda crazy." He laughed, kissing her palm.

"I'm sure."

"Then yes, Shea, I would love to be your girlfriend."

Chapter 11

The next couple days flew by, even with all the weddings, baby showers, and birthday parties, all Elli could think about was the fact that she was Shea Adler's girlfriend.

Sitting in her glass seats, watching her hunky boyfriend (Yes boyfriend!) play the night before was awesome, it was ten times better than it had ever been. He would give her little smiles, or hit the glass with pucks or just come over and smile at her, which caused people to talk around her, but she didn't care!

She was Shea Adler's girlfriend!

Elli was in her truck, driving to Shea's so they could go to his sister's for dinner as she listen to her new mix cd. She was wearing a pair of jeans with a cute purple plaid short sleeved shirt. It was getting chiller, but not cold enough for fall clothes yet. She loved fall in Tennessee, it was so rich with color, so beautiful, it was one of her favorite times of the year, and she couldn't wait, but it also meant that hockey season would be in full swing, and that meant that Shea would be traveling a lot.

He was leaving tomorrow for a week; he had games in Dallas and Tampa Bay, then he would be home for two weeks, only flying out for two games before going back out for a week, but November, that was a whole other story. Shea would only be home for 2 home games, needless to say she was not looking forward to November, but then she thought that she had to bring Shea home for dinner, after that he would probably drop her like a bad habit, and she would never see him again.

Hells bells.

Elli sighed as she pulled into the parking spot beside his truck, and climb out. She walked up the stairs to his condo, and knocked. Shea open the door with a grin; he was wearing a pair of jeans with a Rolling Stone's tee, and a black hat. Yummy, as always.

"There's my girl," he said pulling her against him to kiss her senseless.

"Hey you," she said against his mouth as he held her tightly against him.

"Come on in for a minute, I need you to do me a favor."

"Sure," she answered as she followed him in, "Hey, do I look okay? I brought a dress just in case."

"Yeah, you look great, its casual, babe."

"Good," she said as she followed him into the kitchen. He went to the island and turned around with a piece of paper and a key.

"Grace is really busy this time of year with Halloween and crap, she usually waters my plants and makes sure the condo is good when I'm gone, I was wondering if you could do it for me."

Elli nodded, taking the key and piece of paper with the code to the condo and door from him, "Sure."

"Great, thanks babe, next month will be crazy and with me not being here much, I'm gonna need your help."

"No problem."

"Great, ready?"

"Yup," Elli said with a grin as he took her hand. They left, getting into his truck and driving over to Grace's house. They talked about the week ahead, and what Elli had planned, which was a bunch of weddings.

"Well, if you get tired babe, you can stay at the condo. I don't mind."

"Oh, I don't know."

"Its fine, if you had planned on staying with Harper, why not just stay at my house, at least my bed will stay warm."

"I do love your bed," she said with a grin, he smiled back at her as he pulled in Grace's driveway. They got out the car and walked up to the house hand in hand. Shea open the door, calling out that they were here. Grace came from the kitchen, Amelia on her hip and a grin on her face.

"Hey guys!" She gushed before she kissed Shea's cheek, and gave Elli a sideways hug. "How are you Elli?" she asked as Shea took Amelia, kissing her loudly on the cheek.

"I'm great, and you?"

"Wonderful, come on, come meet my husband," she said walking towards the kitchen; Elli and Shea followed just as Ryan came barreling down the hall, screaming for his Unky.

"Unky!!" he yelled, jumping up and down.

"Hey, bud," Shea said picking him up, holding him in his other arm while still holding Amelia.

"Unky, I played hockey with daddy this afternoon, I won."

"That's my nephew," Shea said as he ruffled Ryan's hair, which of course the 4 year old protested to. With that Ryan was back down the hall, slamming his door when he reached his destination.

"Ryan Michael Justice! I told you about that slamming!" Grace yelled, causing Shea to cringe.

"Sorry mom!" Elli smiled as Grace shook her head.

"Jesus, Grace, you sound just like mom," Shea said walking past her into the kitchen. Grace looked over at Elli, exasperated.

"Do you have brothers?"

"Yes, and a sister"

"Jesus, do you ever want to kill them?"

"All the time," Elli answered simply, making Grace laugh.

"I like you Elli, you're good people." Elli smiled as she followed Grace into the kitchen. Shea stood at the island with Amelia on his hip, beside him was James. Elli had seen him at Shea's party, but never met him. He was a good looking guy, big brown eyes, with brownish blondish hair, he had high cheek bones, and a pointed nose, but he was cute. Not someone Elli would think that someone as beautiful as Grace would settle down with, but really who was she to judge. Shea Adler was her boyfriend, it was like beauty and the beast. Elli was the beast.

"Hey, Elli, this is my brother-in-law, James, James this is my girlfriend, Elli Fisher." The room went quiet as Grace and James looked back at Shea, then to Elli.

"Hold on, what did you say?" James asked, as Grace went, "Did you just say girlfriend?"

Elli blush deep red, looking down at the floor till she heard Shea's booming laugh, "Yes, I said girlfriend, because she is."

"When did this happen?" Grace asked, still looking confused.

"Thursday," Shea answered, kissing Amelia's cheek and putting her down, "Why are you looking at me like that?"

"Shea, I think the last girlfriend you had was Alyson Jacobs, in 12th grade, I'm sorry if I'm a little shocked," Grace said, leaning against James. Shea smiled then looked back at Elli, she just shrugged her shoulders, not knowing what to say, or do. "Wow," Grace said shaking her head, then she smiled, "Well, come on, let's eat."

After that, it was easy. Grace was amazing, but Elli had already known that, James was funny, but serious all in one. He would get so mad when Shea and Grace teamed up against him, and they did it a lot. It would be about the kids, or Ryan's hockey, or Amelia doing dance, anything James said, Shea and Grace went against it. It was really funny; especially when James' face would turn beat red, that had Elli laughing so hard, she couldn't breathe.

"Oh, you just wait Elli, Grace is nice to you now, so was Shea to me when we were just dating, but as soon as you guys get married, it all goes to hell and you're an outside to the Shea and Grace show." Everyone laughed at that, but Elli just smiled, moving around some of the amazing three cheese mac and cheese Grace had made. Like Shea would ever marry her. It had taken him what, 11 years just to get a girlfriend, shit; he would probably never get married.

"We aren't that bad," Grace said with a shake of her head, "but he is my twin, and I do love him a lot. So we tend to go into our twin mode."

"I think it's cute," Elli said with a smile, taking another bite of steak.

"Yeah, well you just wait till you meet the rest of the Adler clan, their mom, jeez she's a hoot, and their dad is amazing, the best father-in-law ever." Grace leaned over to kiss James' cheek as Shea nodded.

"My dad is pretty awesome," Shea agreed. Grace nodded her head, taking a sip of wine.

"How about your family James, do they live here?"

James shook his head, "My parents died when I was nineteen, I have Grace and my kiddos, that's it."

"Oh, I'm so sorry."

"It's fine, thank you though. When I found Grace, everything fell into place, so I'm good now." Elli smiled as Grace leaned over again and kissed him loudly on the cheek.

"How about your family Elli, do they live here?"

"Not in Nashville, but in Clarksville."

"Both your parents?"

"Yup, they are still married after 32 years."

"That's nice, you said you had three siblings?"

"Yup, my brothers, Liam and Noah, then my sister Victoria, I'm the youngest."

"Are they all married?"

"Victoria isn't, but Liam and Noah are, both have three kids."

"Does Victoria have children?"

"Jesus, no, she hates kids."

"Wow," Grace said with a laugh, while Shea chuckled.

"Yeah, I on the other hand, love kids. I take my nieces and nephews once a month to go hang out, I love them so much."

"That's so nice!" Grace gushed, looking over at Shea, "Shea did that for me a couple of weeks ago, and then my son came home talking about open mouth kisses." Elli had taken a drink before Grace started to speak and promptly spewed her drink everywhere with Grace's comment. Everyone burst out laughing, as Elli wiped her mouth.

"Oh, my goodness!" Elli laughed, Shea was about to fall out his chair while Grace held her gut, and James turned bright red with all of them laughing their butts off.

The rest of the dinner was awesome; they talked about hockey, about the kids, and about Shea leaving tomorrow, which Elli really didn't like talking about. Elli helped Grace with the dishes as Shea and James went to play with Ryan outside, hockey, of course. Elli was washing a dish and watching Shea slap shot a puck at his brother-in-law when Grace walked up beside her.

"He likes you, you know." Elli looked over at Grace; every time she looked at Grace she saw how much she and Shea looked alike. They had the exact same eyes, and nose, except Grace's didn't have a bump, same hair, and same cheek bones, everything was the same. Grace was a beautiful woman, while Shea was a gorgeous man.

"You think so?"

"Oh, I know so, I've hear about you every time I call him." Elli smiled, looking back down at the dishes, "I like you too Elli, a lot."

"Aw, thanks Grace, I just adore you and your family."

Grace smiled warmly, "I'm glad, but let me tell you, don't hurt my brother." Elli looked up quickly, shaking her head.

"I never would think of it."

"Good, I didn't think you would, but he seems smitten with you, and that scares me, considering he never has been, smitten, I mean."

"Grace, I'll be honest with you, I haven't been with anyone in six years, so for me to be with Shea is a huge step, I promise I will not hurt him."

"Good."

Just then the guys came in, and Grace put on a huge smile. "Have fun big guy?" she asked, kissing Ryan's cheek.

"I did, momma! Unky gave daddy a bruise."

Grace shot Shea a look while he shrugged, "He got in the way."

"I did not! You aimed for me!" James complained, showing off a nasty bruise on his bicep.

"Shea!"

"What Grace, he's fine. Right, Ryan?"

"Yup, no crying in hockey, daddy," Ryan said simply, causing everyone to laugh.

Having Elli at his sister's house was amazing, having all the people he cared for under one roof was awesome, and fulfilling all at the same time. Leaving tomorrow would suck, but at least he would have this moment to warm him at night when he was alone on the road. Grace and James walked them out, and when Grace wrapped her arms around Shea, she kissed his cheek before whispering in his ear.

"I think so."

"Huh?" He asked pulling back, looking down at his best friend, his twin.

"What we talked about earlier? I think so."

When it clicked in Shea's head that Grace was basically telling him that he was in love with Elli, they were already on the road, going back to his house. It hit him like a ton of bricks, and he actually veered off the road a little, but regained control when Elli let out a screech.

"Sorry, babe." Elli just smiled shaking her head as they pulled into his driveway, beside her truck. They sat in the truck for a moment, not moving. "Can I ask you a favor babe?" Elli looked over at Shea, with a small smile on her face.

"Sure."

"Will you stay?"

"My bag is in the truck." He smiled, leaning over and kissing her before jumping out, to help her out. She grabbed her bag and followed him upstairs. After showering, Elli laid in bed watching Shea pack.

"I'm such a procrastinator," he said with a grin, she smiled.

"You just don't want to go," Elli teased, he smiled.

"Your right," he said with a wink as he closed up the last of his suitcases, he would only be gone for five days, but still it felt like a life time.

"Where's your bag?"

"They already have it at the rink." She nodded as he climbed into bed beside her.

"Why does Ryan call you Unky?" Elli asked as she laid across Shea's chest, looking down at him. He moved his hand through her hair, cupping her face.

"This girl I was with last year told Ryan he had a Hunky Unky, and he's been saying Unky ever since, luckily he dropped the hunky, that would be awkward." Elli giggled as he smiled, closing her eyes as she leaned her face in his hand. "You know we haven't done that whole exes talk."

Her eyes flew open, "Do we need too?"

"I would feel better if I knew some of your past." She bit her lip, looking down at his shirt.

"Okay."

"Have you ever been married?"

"Nope, have you?"

"You're my first girlfriend of my adult life, no." Elli laughed.

"True."

"Have you been with a lot of men?"

Elli shook her head, "No, even when I was super skinny, I was really weird about who I dated. I've only had sex with four men." Shea looked away, completely embarrassed, "I know you've been with more Shea; it's okay."

"Yeah, so anyway, have you ever loved any of them?"

"I thought I loved the last one, but I learned later that I didn't."

"How?"

"When we broke up, I didn't cry, I didn't even feel anything but relief."

"Wow."

"Yeah, have you loved anyone?"

"Nope, never. In high school I had the puppy love, but I've never loved a woman, I just used them I guess."

"Maybe."

"I'm not using you though," he said quickly since she made a face, but she smiled, smacking his chest.

"I know," she said with a shake of her head, "But I need to tell you something, Shea."

"What?"

"I haven't been with anyone since that last guy."

"Okay."

She bit her lip again, and messed with the bottom of his shirt. "That was six years ago."

"Say what?" Elli turned bright red; even her eyebrows were red. "You haven't had sex in six years?"

She shook her head, still not making eye contact. "I was really big Shea, and guys didn't want me, so when I lost a lot of the weight, I figured guys still didn't want me, until you."

"Come on, I know guys hit on you babe, all the guys at the party said you were hot."

"Well, yeah, but I didn't believe that they really liked me, you on the other hand, are very persistent." He smiled, moving his fingers through her hair.

"Well good thing for me, huh?"

"Yeah," she said with a nod, "You think I'm a freak, huh?"

"Not at all," he pulled her closer to him, "So since we're done with that, come here and kiss me." She complied of course, bringing her lips to his for a long lusty kiss. He laid her back, his body of top of hers, her legs on either side of him, kissing down her neck, than back up. He kissed back up her jaw, letting their lips meet again for another long kiss. Her hands came up his side, cupping his neck, then his face. He parted taking a deep breath, looking down at her beautiful round face, the puffy pink lips that were kissing the crap out of him.

"Jesus, El, you drive me nuts." She gave him a little half smile, pulling him back down for another kiss. He could feel the heat from between her thighs, so he knew she was hot, just like he was, but just like the last time, when he went to put his hand under her shirt, she freaked, moving out from underneath him.

"Don't you have to leave early tomorrow? Shouldn't we go to sleep? Yeah, I think so," she said so quickly his head spun. She went under the covers, and gave him a small smile. "Can you hold me again?" she asked in a small voice. Shea exhaled loudly, and ran his hands through his hair, but he nodded, wrapping his arms around her, holding her tight against him.

"Sorry if I poke you," he whispered in her ear with a chuckle, she giggled.

"I like it," she whispered after a few moments, he smiled, and pressed himself harder against her. Her soft curves felt great under his hands, and her butt cushioned his hard on perfectly. He was in heaven, so he closed his eyes, and the next thing he knew, he was out.

Elli leaned against the truck, watching Shea load his truck up with his bags. Yeah, it sucked, and next month she would have to say bye for the whole month, of course, she had to break her years of no dating to date a guy that would be gone a lot. Wonderful.

"I don't like that look on your face, baby," he said, she didn't even realize he was watching her, she smiled, and he returned it. "I like that better." He pinned her against the truck, nuzzling her neck, causing her to giggle. Shea wrapped his arms around her, pulling her closer to him. She closed her eyes as she held on to him, gosh, she didn't want him to go.

"I don't want you to leave," She whispered, he smiled against her neck, placing a soft kiss against it.

"I wish I could take you with me, you can't quit for a couple months?" She laughed, kissing his neck before he pulled back to look down at her.

"I would never quit, I love my job, the same way you would never quit."

"True, so we'll have to settle with Skype and phone calls?"

"And texts," Elli added with a grin, he grinned back, kissing her softly.

"It's just a week."

"But next month, it will be a month."

"True, but we'll be fine. I promise." Elli smiled at the grin on his face, then kissed him long and hard. He kissed her twice more before backing away, kissing her palms before walking away. She watched as he walked to his truck, got in, and started it. He waved, and she waved back as he drove off. When she felt the tear fall down her cheek, she became disgusted with herself and jumped in the truck. It wasn't like he was crying, or anything. He was good, he was used to this. He was used to the goodbyes, but she wasn't, and she didn't know how she was going to deal with it.

Chapter 12

Elli missed Shea.

She missed him a lot.

Of course, he called every chance he got, but she was only four days in, and she was lonely. Elli tried to stay busy with the weddings she had, and the baby showers, but nothing seemed to take her mind off the fact that Shea was not in the same state as her. He couldn't just walk in with that goofy smile on his face, bringing her food, nope, he was in another state, kicking ass. They had won Tuesday's night's game, Elli had sat at the house, cheering them on, and she swore that Shea would look in the camera just for her, and when she told him that after the game, he laughed saying he had hoped she noticed. Things were so great between them, even with him gone; he was just as amazing as he was when he was home. Elli smiled at the thought of his grin as he laughed; it was always so big, so full of life. She missed seeing it. God, she was pathetic.

She was sitting at her desk, returning phone calls for appointments, and to schedule consultations when her phone rang, she looked at the display seeing it was her daddy, Michael.

"Daddy!" she gushed, moving some windows around on her computer, "How are you!"

"Elli bug, I'm good darling, haven't heard from you this week."

"I know, I'm sorry, I've been terribly busy."

"So I hear, the Adam's wedding you just did, that was one of my old college friends' daughter. She was the bride."

"Oh, really? Small world!"

"It is. He had nothing but good to say about you. He went out of his way to call me."

"How nice, that makes my day brighter." Daddy chuckled as Elli finished with a couple of orders that were pending on her website.

"So, I was calling because your mother is on me like white on rice about this family dinner with this man you are dating."

"Oh God, really? I thought maybe she forgot," Elli groaned.

Daddy laughed, "No honey, the grandbabies came home saying you were open mouth kissing with Shea Adler, even if it wasn't him, I'm pretty sure your mother would be on a mission. We haven't met anyone since Justin."

"There hasn't been anyone," Elli added, as she pulled up her email, glancing at a few things, "No big deal, Shea comes home Friday, I'll ask him."

"So it is Shea Adler?"

"Yeah."

"How did y'all meet?"

"When I did the team-shoot for Uncle Bryan."

"That's nice, is it serious?"

"Yeah, it's been almost three weeks, he's amazing, daddy, just amazing."

"I'm happy for you, Elli bug, after Justin I didn't think you would recover."

"Me neither, daddy, but Shea, he's just..." Elli thought for a moment, a contiguous grin going across her face, "He makes me feel....."

"Wonderful, so, I will expect to meet him sometime this month?"

"Yes, daddy," Elli said with a groan, he laughed, telling her how much he loved her before hanging up. Elli smiled down at the phone after she hung up. Harper walked in, falling face first into the couch that sat in her office. Elli looked over at her, noticing Harper's hair was brown this week, before raising an eyebrow.

"What the hell is wrong with you?' she asked, hanging up the phone and clicking a few things on her computer.

"I miss sex!" Elli rolled her eyes, moving some paperwork around, fixing the pictures of her nieces and nephews on her desk.

"What do you mean? You can have sex with anyone."

Harper sat up quickly, looking over at Elli, her eyes look crazed. Elli moved her chair back just a little, trying to put distance between them, "If you laugh, tell anyone, or even smile, I'll throw something at you."

"Okay?"

"I miss sex with Jakob, I miss….him." Elli tried so hard not to smile, but her eyes lit up as she covered her mouth, trying to keep the 'aw' in.

"Oh," she muttered through her hands.

"I've never had this problem, but that damn Russian brought his big ole penis into bed with me and now no other man even measures up! I miss my Jakey!" And with that Harper started to cry, Elli pushed her chair back more, scared shitless. Was this for real? "I don't know what my problem is, I never get like this with guys, but I just miss him, you know? Don't you miss Shea?"

"Oh, yeah," Elli scoffed, "but I'm in a relationship with him."

"Well, yeah, but I mean, I don't know! I just miss Jakob."

Elli had to smile, she was so sweet and clueless, she was hopelessly in love with Jakob and she didn't even know it.

"You're smiling," Harper said, putting her face in the pillow. Elli just grinned, leaning back in her chair. She watched Harper hit the pillow a few times, before hearing her computer ding, signaling an email. She leaned back up to the computer, hitting her mail, to see the message was from Shea. She smiled big, opening the email titled, 'thinking of you'.

Hey you,

So I've been listening to that music you like…country…and well I don't know if you've heard this song, but it made me think of you, so here is the video.

I miss you, babe.

Shea.

Elli smiled, and clicked on the video, Lady Antebellum, 'Just a Kiss' video started playing. The song was about a kiss being enough, that they didn't need anything else, they didn't want to move too fast, keep things slow. She smiled as she watched the trio sing, she loved this song, but never thought of it in regard to their relationship. Gosh, he was amazing. She typed him back a little message, telling him thank you, then went to her phone carrier's site, and downloaded the song for her ringtone when he called. She smiled as she thought that it was their song now.

She had a song, with Shea.

Elli debated with herself for over 30 minutes, before just doing what she knew was best. That was going to Shea's for the night, since Harper was at her moms, and it was almost midnight, and she just knew she couldn't make it home. She pulled into his driveway, and grabbed her bag from the back before locking the doors and heading up the stairs to his door. She dug his key out of her purse, and put it in the lock, unlocking the door. She made sure to lock the door, and turned on some lights as she made her way through the living room.

Elli headed back to his bedroom, where she laid her bag on the bench at the end of the bed. She looked around the large room as she undid the buckles on her heels. The room seemed so much bigger when Shea wasn't here. Gosh, she missed him. She finished undressing before putting on her favorite shirt, his old AHL tee. After washing up in the bathroom, she went back out to the living room to get her movie so she could fall asleep since apparently, the only time she didn't need the movie was when she slept with Shea.

Pathetic, she knew.

Elli looked through his movie collection, which was massive, before grabbing the Pride and Prejudice movie she had gotten him. She shut the doors to the cabinet, and turned to go back to the Shea's bedroom when she saw some photo albums sitting under a wall table. She had never noticed the table before, so she stepped closer to see a picture of Shea and Grace when they were younger, then another when they had graduated high school, one of them at what appeared to be Grace's wedding with James, and then two of when the kids were born.

Shea loved Grace so much, it was sweet. There was a picture of him and Grace with two older people that Elli assumed were his parents. They all had the same smile, big and beautiful. His father was just as handsome as his son; his mother was beautiful, with the exact same dimple on the right side of her face. Elli smiled, looking closer at the picture before she noticed another picture out the corner of her eye; it was the one of her at the park that he had taken on their first date. She picked it up, looking at herself sipping on her Starbucks. The picture was classy, so pretty, and it just blew her mind that he had it framed and it was in his house.

Wow.

Elli put the picture down, and got a bottle of water, before heading back into the room, to go to sleep. After putting the DVD on and shutting the door, she crawled onto her side of the bed, and cuddled in. The bed was huge without a 6'3 man beside her. Shea would be home the next day, but it wasn't coming quick enough in her opinion. The Assassins had lost that night, he was a little bummed when she talked to him, and she tried to cheer him up, but he said nothing would cheer him up till he was able to kiss her again.

Just the thought of that made Elli warm from head to toe; she smiled as she cuddled into the bed that smelled just like Shea as she started the movie. Elli was asleep before she knew it.

Elli figured that the next day was a thing of luck, or maybe fate. She had a wedding that night, so she wasn't gonna be able to see Shea till afterwards, but the bride got cold feet and called the thing off. From what the maid of honor had said, the bride had a little more fun the night before then she should have. She had slept with the groom's best man. Oops, Elli hated when that happened, but today she couldn't be happier, since she stood in Shea's kitchen, frying chicken for a welcome home dinner.

Shea wasn't due back till around six, and it was 5:30. Elli kept an eye on the chicken as she started the mac and cheese. Shea had once said that he wasn't very familiar with country cooking, and since Elli was an expert at it, she figured she'd educate him. She smoothed out the apron she had brought over, it was her Mamaw Ally's and it was one of her prized possessions. Mamaw Ally was the one who had taught her to cook; she was also the one who had taught Elli to sing. A sad smile went across Elli's face as she thought about the old woman that had given her so many good memories; she missed Mamaw Ally so much. She had died when Elli was 12, so she never got to see Elli succeed in her career as a singer. Her daddy always told Elli that she reminded him of her, which made Elli feel good inside. Mamaw Ally was an amazing woman.

Since Elli was cooking country for Shea, she decided to dress the part. Since she had to run home to get her cast iron pan, she changed, putting on a white eye let dress that had big flowy sleeves along with her black with white swirls cowboy boots. She had her hair up since Shea liked it like that; he had once said he liked her neck in plain view which was fine by her.

Elli was so excited to see him, she couldn't see straight. The week had gone by so slowly, when she had done the books this morning and saw how much money she had made, she thought that would have meant that she was so super busy, and she was, but all she could think about was Shea, and what he had been doing. He had been so busy, he hadn't been able to talk to her much in the last couple of days. He had had so much promotional stuff to do and with all the baby showers and weddings she had, she had missed his calls a lot more then she would have liked.

But tonight was about them, Elli had gone out and bought new plates for him, to butter him up before asking him to go to dinner at her parents. Fate was working in her favor and she was gonna spend the night with her man.

Her man, she smiled at just the thought.

Elli was just starting to set the table, when she heard the doorknob rattling.

He was home!

Shea was hurting, badly. His shoulder was aching; he had a cut along his collarbone, where that idiot, Mattias Ohlund had slashed him with his stick. Asshole, but then again, Shea did hit him in the boards a little harder than necessary, but, oh, well. Shea threw his bag on the ground as he looked for his keys, he was so happy to be home. Elli had a wedding tonight, but she promised she would come by afterwards, which was awesome, he had missed her so much.

He found his keys and put them in the door, looking forward to the hot shower that awaited him on the other side. When he pushed the door open, he was hit by the strong smell of fried chicken.

What the hell?

Shea threw his bag on the couch, walking towards the kitchen where he heard sizzling, and movement. When he rounded the corner, his country cutie stood in front of the stove in a cute little apron, with her hair in a messy bun. Man, she was gorgeous. She turned with a big grin on her face, before she squealed and ran to him, wrapping herself around him.

"Welcome home!" she gushed, kissing his lips loudly. He smiled against her lips, holding her close to him. She smelled like mangos again, something he found he missed a lot while he had been gone for the week. She was so soft, so warm in his arms.

"Mm, I've missed you," he nuzzled her neck before biting lightly. "Did you miss me?"

For some reason he needed to know.

"Of course!" she gushed with giggle as she brought his lips back to hers. He kissed her hard, pulling her as close to him as he could.

"I didn't expect you to be here, what happened to the wedding?" he asked, still not letting her go.

"Bride slept with the best man, so no wedding, it's all fate, I think I was meant to be here when you got home, making you chicken." He smiled, kissing her nose.

"It smells fantastic." She smiled, looking over her shoulder at the pan.

"Thank you, let me flip this," she broke from his arms and flipped the chicken. Shea decided he wasn't done holding her so he came up behind her, and held her from behind, putting his chin on her shoulder.

"How was your week?"

"Long, lots of crap going on, good week though, money wise at least," she said, checking on what appeared to be mac and cheese.

She was a Godsend.

"That's good."

"Yeah, you need to take a shower?"

"I do, I'll be quick."

"I'll be waiting," she said with a grin, he smacked her butt, making her squeal as he walked away.

"You better be," he teased as he went into the bedroom. He noticed her pink and green bag sitting at the end of the bed and smiled, hoping that meant she was staying the night. He went to his closet, grabbing a pair of sleeping pants and a tee, before going into the bathroom and jumping in the shower. It felt amazing with nine jets of hot water hitting him from every direction. He closed his eyes, letting the hot water hit his aching naked body, it was almost as great as having Elli in his arms, or playing hockey, it had to come in at the top three.

After washing up, he dried off as he stood in front of his mirror, looking at his chest. The cut was deep and dark with the black stitches holding it shut, bruising surrounded the cut. Fucking Ohlund. He shook his head as he got dressed before taking out his contacts and putting his glasses on.

When Shea came out into the kitchen, Elli was transferring food into the living room. He followed her into the living room, and stopped. There was enough food to feed an army! And where did that plate setting come from? He had white, plain plates; these were pretty blue ones with silver swirls. His table looked like something out of Better Homes and Garden, pretty napkins, a big vase of white flowers, place mats.

"Where'd the plates come from?"

"I bought em, I didn't like the white ones, with the blue and silver in the kitchen, I thought these went better. Do you not like 'em?"

"No, their nice, I was just wondering." he picked up the plate and made a face at it, it was very girlie.

"If you don't like em, I'll take em back."

"It's just they are kinda girlie," he said honestly, she smiled, before taking the plate from him, and picking up the other one, and returning to the kitchen. "What are you doing?" he asked, following her back into the kitchen.

"You don't like em, so I'm gonna take em back. I'll bring you a gift card and you can go pick out some different ones."

"No, it's okay. I like my white ones."

"Oh, okay then," she said putting the plates next to the box that he hadn't notice earlier. She turned with two white plates and a bottle of wine, smiling. "Shall we?"

"Yeah," he agreed as he followed her into the living room, he pulled out her chair, and she smiled her thanks as she sat down. He sat across from her, and they dug in. He took a bite of the chicken and moaned loudly.

"God, this is good." She smiled before looking back down at her plate.

"I'm glad you like it, since my gift was a bust." He looked up at her, her face was scrunched up between her eyebrows, she seemed mad.

"You're not mad are you?"

She shrugged her shoulders, "No, I just wanted to get you something nice, and I apparently suck."

"No, you don't, I just like my white plates, always have."

"I shouldn't have, I just wanted you to have something that when you saw it you thought of me, and since you love to eat, it seemed like the perfect gift."

"Baby, it is, thank you," he took her hand in his, kissing her knuckles. "I got you something, too."

Her face lit up, "You didn't have to."

"I saw it and thought of you, I'll give it to you after dinner."

She nodded and then smiled as they started eating dinner. The food was amazing, just as the conversation was. Elli had some crazy things happen to her all week, and with every crazy story, he fell for her more. He missed her a lot when he was gone, but being in front of her, listening about a woman that went into labor at her baby shower, and the soon to be father freaking out, made him feel complete.

Dinner was amazing, even though the plates were a bust. Shea loved the food Elli cooked, and he held her hand through most of dinner which she thought was so damn sweet. After getting everything cleaned up, they went into the living room, where Shea started going through his bag. When he pulled out a little blue box, her breath caught. Elli knew that box color; it was Tiffany & Co. Justin had gotten her God awful engagement ring from there.

Shea smiled over at her, before sitting down beside her, and handing it to her. "I saw it in Dallas when Jakob and I went shopping; I had to get it for you."

Elli's hands were shaking uncontrollably as she pulled the white ribbon, letting it fall to her lap, before pulling the top open. Inside, on a little white pillow, was a diamond incrusted hockey stick on a platinum chain. Her hand went over her mouth as she gasped.

"Oh, Shea," Elli lifted it out the box, and held it up watching it sparkle in the light. It was beautiful. She unclasped it and put it around her neck, trying to clasp it back.

"Do you like it?" he asked, she just grinned at him.

"Oh, gosh, do I? This is the best gift anyone has ever given me!" She gushed, turning so he could clasp it for her. He took it from her and clasped it together before leaving a trail of kisses along her shoulder.

"I'm glad you like it."

"I love it," she turned and kissed his lips, "but you didn't have to."

"I wanted too, so hush," he teased with a smile, as he pulled her against him. They leaned back on the couch, cuddling in silence, just basking in the fact that they were together. He kissed her hair, nuzzling his nose in it as she fingered the hockey stick that hung from her neck.

"That Tampa Bay game was intense."

"Intense isn't the half of it, I can't believe we lost."

"Can't win 'em all."

"Be nice though." She giggled and he squeezed her tighter against him, "That asshole, Ohlund, messed my collarbone up though." Elli sat up, turning so she could look at him. She had worry all over her face; she hated the thought that someone had hurt him! She wanted to rip that man apart. If she ever saw that asshole, she would.

"Let me see," she said looking him over, "did he get you anywhere else?"

"Nah," Shea lifted his shirt over his head causing Elli's eyes to about fall out of her head. She didn't even look at his collarbone as he talked about the injury, she was too busy staring at his naked arms; they were perfect. Not too big and bulky, not at all spindly, but sexy. The way his thick, strong shoulders led into his arms was mouthwatering. Then the hollow of his neck, she had kissed there hundreds of times, but never really looked at it, and, boy, was it a sight to see. As her eyes traveled down his neck to his chest, she was getting hot all over. His pecs were well defined, and toned, and his abs, Jesus, they were jaw dropping. Each ab finely defined, toned, sexy, oh, God, she couldn't breathe.

"Elli, you okay? You're bright red?" She looked up at him, meeting his playful grin.

"Yeah, I'm fine," she mumbled as her eyes returned to his chest. He started talking again, but she wasn't paying any attention. She leaned over slowly, placing her lips over his heart. The intake of breath that she was rewarded with set her into motion. She basically crawled on top of him, kissing his neck, his pecs, watching out for the jagged cut along his collarbone as she kissed and licked.

"Baby, that feels amazing," he gasped as she sucked lightly on the column of his neck, biting softly the way he always did with her. "God, I've missed you," he whispered as she brought her mouth to his, kissing him deeply. She pulled back, looking around. She wanted to do more, but she was feeling self-conscious, as always. What if he saw something with her legs like this? She rolled off him, and just as he started protesting, she reached for the lights, and with a flick of her wrist the room went completely dark, except for the faint light of the moon.

When Elli's eyes adjusted, Shea was grinning at her as she crawled back on top of him, straddling his waist. His hands came up her thighs, and she let out a little gasp as he took over, kissing her throat, while he rubbed her thighs. She was self-conscious for about two point three seconds but then his tongue dipped into her cleavage and any coherent thoughts went out the window.

He was so hard, with his PJ pants being so thin and loose, it was all she felt against her white lace panties. His hands were still at her thighs, teasing the lace that came across her ass; while her mouth was busy with his. She couldn't believe she even had the balls to, but she moved her hands farther down his chest, moving her fingers through the little patch of hair that made a line down to his holy land, before freeing him from his pants. He let out a throaty groan, his hands tightening on her ass, as she ran her hand down his length.

"Oh, god," he gasped as his head fell back on the back of the couch. She felt the drip of moisture coming from the tip of his shaft, and her mouth watered. It had been so long, did she even know how to do it anymore? He wasn't expecting it, she knew that and before she could talk herself out of it, she took him into her mouth. Shea jumped in surprised with a low dangerous growl. All it did was fuel Elli to do it some more.

She fell to her knees, between his legs, taking him to the back of her throat; he moaned her name, running his hand up and down her back as the other hand was gripping the side of the couch, hard. She moved up and down his length, taking him deep then going all the way out, licking the tip before going back down. His groans, turned into pants, before his hands came up into her hair.

"Elli-baby, I'm about to come, baby, please," he pleaded, she went faster, taking him deeper, his grip in her hair hurt, but it was a good hurt. "Honey, please, I'm about to come, please, oh God!" When she felt when he was about to come, she took him deep in the back of her throat, feeling the hot thick liquid go down her throat. His grip was so hard on her hair; she thought he was going to rip it out as he rode his organism to the end. When he was finally done, she sat back on the hunches of her legs, looking up at him. His eyes were close, his breathing just as hard as hers. He looked beautifully spent, pants down, shaft lying out, and his hands cupped behind his head as he tried to catch his breath, while the moon shone down on his beautifully sculpted body.

"Jesus, Elli, don't ever do that again," he pleaded, as his eyes closed.

Wow, she sucked that bad at it? She got up, wiping her mouth and going to the kitchen to rinse her mouth out, since she was leaving. How dare him! The first time she throws all her insecurities out the window and that's what he says! She filled up a glass of water and filled her mouth, moving around the cold liquid before spitting it out. When she felt Shea's arms come around her, she froze.

What the hell was he doing?

"God, baby, you gotta warn a guy, I almost ripped your hair out it was so good."

"Oh," she said as she flushed deep red, he turned her in his arms, kissing her swollen mouth.

"I knew when I first set eyes on that mouth, it was going to be trouble," he mumbled against her mouth. "God, Elli." His eyes closed again and then she was in the air, he had picked her up, sitting her on the island of the kitchen. Lifting her skirt up, running his hands up and down her thighs, teasing her mound with his thumbs. God, how she wanted him between her thighs, fingers, tongue, anything at this point. She was dripping wet from making him come, but she just couldn't bring herself to let him do anything. She intertwined their fingers, as he looked up at her. "Let me take your panties off, please, baby."

"No, Shea. I'm good."

"No, baby please, let me taste you, let me lick you, please. It can stop after I make you come, please," he pleaded, his eyes were so dark blue. He wanted her so bad, she could feel it, she wanted him too, but she just couldn't chance him seeing her stretch marks or dimples.

"I'm fine, Shea. Making you come made me come."

"Liar, come on, please."

"No," she whispered, not able to look at him.

"You still don't trust me?" She looked up, his eyes weren't dark with lust anymore, there was only hurt.

"Of course I do Shea, it's just...I can't do it yet." He took a deep breath, turning from her, putting his hands on his head as he walked around the kitchen. "I'm gonna go," she muttered as she jumped off the counter, heading for the door. She didn't make it far before Shea grabbed her.

"No, don't go. I just got home, I've missed you," he said in her hair, kissing the back of her neck, "Please don't leave."

How could she say no?

"Alright."

"Good," he said with a grin as he pulled her closer to him, "God, I've missed you."

"I've missed you too."

Shea laid on his back, with Elli across his chest. Her hair fell across his neck, and he had never felt so damn good in his life. That mouth of hers was going to be the death of him and his mind was still buzzing after the love she gave him. He moved his hands through her hair, down her back, to the short little shorts she wore to bed. His hand grazed her ass before going back up and repeating the process all over.

Shea didn't know what possessed her to get frisky with him, and he would not be questioning it either, he would just enjoy the ride that was Elli. She blew his mind with surprises, she was a sexy little thing, and God knew he wanted more. Shea wasn't even in pain anymore; the cut along his collarbone was forgotten after the show she had put on for him in the living room. He might need to rethink hating that couch, since obviously magic could happen there.

"I need to ask you something." Shea looked down at her as she turned her head to look up at him; he smiled, moving her hair out of eyes. Even in the dark, with only the moon as their source of light, her eyes were as bright as ever.

"Sure."

Elli smiled nervously, before taking a deep breath. "Can you come to dinner with my family the Friday before you leave? I'm gonna warn you, it's gonna be hell."

Shea laughed, and nodded his head. He would basically walk through fire for her right now. "Of course, I can."

"It's Friday night, like I said, you don't have a game and you don't leave town till Monday for the month."

"Sounds good, babe."

"Its gonna be hell," she repeated.

"It'll be fine, how bad could it be?"

"You'll see when you don't want nothing to do with me no more."

He outright laughed at that one, bringing her hand to his mouth, kissing her wrist. "Your family can't scare me away baby, I'm not going anywhere." She smiled sweetly, running her hand down his jaw. "So, this means you'll meet my mom and dad the next time they're in town?"

"If it is after you meet my family, and you actually still wanna be with me, sure." He smiled, turning to bite her hand softly. He loved biting her, she always had the sexiest intake of breath, and it set him on fire.

"Shut up with all that. It's nonsense. I think my parents are coming in for one of the November home games, so I'll set up a dinner if they do."

"Maybe I could cook."

"That would be awesome. My parents are big seafood people; I doubt they've eaten very much southern cooking."

"Sounds good," she said with a smile as she drew circles around his pecs, he noticed that when she looked at his chest, she didn't see his scars, she just saw him, which made him feel so good inside. It just bothered him that she couldn't understand that it was going to be like that for him when he would finally be allowed to see her naked. God, how he wanted that, so bad. "Can I ask you something, and you answer me honestly?" Elli asked, he looked down at her, and smiled.

"Of course, you know I don't lie to you."

She nodded, looking back down at his chest. "Was it good? I haven't done it in years, and I was nervous."

Her nervous babble always made him smile, but when they were talking about something serious, he didn't dare smile. He had never been with someone that needed so much reassurance; he just didn't understand how she didn't realize how amazing she was.

"Ellibaby, it was spectacular. I'll probably be hard for days just thinking about it, really baby, amazing." She smiled sweetly, and leaned up to kiss him. He returned the kissed before she laid down beside him, snuggling into his chest.

"I'm so tired," she whispered into the space below his armpit.

"Me, too."

That was the last thing said before they both were out.

Chapter 13

It was pitch black when Shea open his eyes; all he heard was Elli's soft breathing and the only light in the room was the alarm clock, which read two in the morning. He slid out of bed, trying not to wake her as he went into the bathroom to do his business. He should never have drunk that bottle of water before bed; he was having such naughty, sexy dreams about his Elli which were interrupted by his need to relive himself.

After washing his hands, he went back into the bedroom, climbing into bed quietly as he stretched himself next to Elli. She scooted closer to him, nuzzling her nose into his neck with a sigh, God, she was sweet. Her hands came up on his chest, moving softly as she nuzzled. He closed his eyes, loving the feeling of her soft hands on his chest, her sweet little nose at the base of his throat. He moved his hands up the back of her thighs then back down, before hooking her leg over his hip. Her chest pressed against his, the tank top she wore slid down a little, showing more of her milky white skin, he looked down at the cleavage then back up to her sleeping face.

Shea knew he was pushing it, but he dipped his head down, he had to really, nuzzling his face within the two mounds that drove him mad. He heard her let out a little moan, as she moved her body closer to his, pressing his face deeper into her cleavage.

He was hard within a second of her rubbing her warm center against his thigh. He moved his face to the side, licking up one side of her breast to the other one; she let out a gasp when he cupped her breast, sucking her through the thin fabric to her nipple. He would respect the fact that she didn't want him seeing her naked, fine, it was dark in there, he couldn't see anything, plus she was fully dressed to his dismay.

"Shea?" she asked sleepily as he licked the hard pebble through her shirt, God, he couldn't wait to suck on her with nothing between them.

"Shh, baby, just me," he said, giving her a kiss before going back to her breast, her hand came up, running her fingers through his hair as she pressed herself closer to him. The heat from her core was driving him insane as he gave her breast all the attention in the world. He bit her nipple causing her to gasp then moaned out his name when he sucked and licked it through the thin fabric of her tank. His hand went down her side, cupping her ass as he brought his mouth down on hers; she let out a little meep when he pressed his thigh into her core, moving her against it. He wanted her to come so damn bad he couldn't think straight. He wanted to be the first one in years; he wanted to make her scream.

"Shea," she gasped as he bit her bottom lip, sucking on it before kissing her jaw.

"Yeah, baby," he said against her neck.

Please don't say stop, please don't say stop, he chanted in his mind as he sucked and bit all over her neck and collar bone.

"More, God, please more, please," she pleaded as she rubbed herself against his leg. He almost came at the words, but what the hell was more? Shit, he didn't want to scare her, because what meant more to him was ripping off her shorts and pounding into her, but her more was probably different. He didn't want to ask; she was shy and would probably tell him to stop, so he moved his hand over her thigh, gripping before sliding into her shorts and moving the lace of her panties out of the way. She looked at him with wide eyes just as he slid a finger inside her dripping wet core.

They both let out a moan at the feeling. She was so wet; he couldn't remember the last girl that was this wet. His mind was reeling at the thought that he had done this, that he had made her so wet with want. When Shea felt that there was no hair, his sweet Elli was bare, no hair in the way, nothing, just skin and wetness, he thought she was groaning but, nope, it was him. He slid his finger up to her nub, rubbing softly as her head fell back as deep throaty moans left her lips. He moved his finger back down to her entrance and moved in and out of her, before moving back up to her clit, flicking it with his finger.

"I want you to come, Elli. Come for me, baby," he encouraged in her ear as he nibbled softly on her earlobe, she let out a moan, moving against his hand as he moved in and out of her. He moved his finger back up to the nub and with just one more flick, she hit an organism that shook her whole body with a strangled cry.

They were breathing hard, the rise and fall of her chest touching his as she tried to catch her breath. God, she was hot. Watching her come had made him come like a damn sixteen year old boy in his pants. He should have been embarrassed, but nope, not at all. With Elli cuddling up against him, a sexy little satisfied grin on her face, yeah, he couldn't have cared less.

"Well, then," she whispered, looking up at him, "that was amazing."

"Damn right it was," Shea all but groaned out, she smiled shyly, and nuzzled her nose in his neck, taking a deep breath.

"Thank you," she whispered again, he smiled.

"Anytime baby, anytime."

With the sun shining on Shea's face, he had forgotten to close the curtains; he opened his eyes, taking in a deep breath as he stretched his arms above his head. Elli stirred beside him, but only to cuddle closer to him. He looked down at her; she was sleeping with her face cupped by her hand, looking too sweet for words. He smiled, moving her hair out of her face as he kissed her forehead. It felt so good having her beside him like this.

He hadn't woken up with her beside him yet, every time she had stayed she had to rush off to the studio, so this was heaven in his mind. Especially with what they did early that morning, which reminded him he needed to take a shower. He kissed her neck before climbing out of bed and going into the bathroom. He took his clothes off and jumped in, letting the jets hit him from every direction. As he washed, all he could think about was Elli's little hot body last night, her screams, moans, Jesus, she was hot.

He couldn't remember the last time he came in his pants after only fingering a female, it had to be ninth grade, with Ashley Ryan, a gorgeous red head, with puffy lips, yeah, had to be her. He shook his head with a grin on his face as he came out the shower. While he brushed his teeth and shaved, he couldn't wipe the shit eating grin he had on his face off.

He'd fingered Elli.

Oh, yeah.

Shea shook his head at himself, he sounded like a freaking teenager, so pathetic, he thought with a laugh as he came out of the bathroom.

"What are you laughin' about?" Shea looked over at the bed; Elli was laying against the pillows, the blankets up to her chin, with a grin on her face.

He shook his head, "Last night."

"What so funny about last night?" her grin left, and was replaced with a nervous, shy look. He shook his head again, climbing on to the bed, covering her body with his.

"Not funny, but more like I can't believe I was able to get my fingers inside of you," the blush covering her cheeks made his breath hitch, she was so pretty, "I feel like a teenager, you make me feel like this Elli, baby, it's crazy."

For the first time, Shea felt like he was blushing as she smiled, cupping his face in her hands and kissing his lips.

"It's about time," she said against his lips, "You've been making me feel like one since day one!" He laughed, before kissing her again.

He was falling more and more in love each day and part of him thought maybe she was, but weren't women supposed to be super emotional and tell you everything? Because trying to get something out of Elli was like pulling teeth. He wanted to know if she felt half of what he was feeling, he wanted to hear her say it, but he didn't want to scare her when he said it and he didn't want to tell her and then she didn't say anything.

That would be horrific.

"What time is it?" she asked, moving his hair out of his eyes, he needed a haircut.

"Almost nine."

"Ugh, it feels so early," she complained, he smiled, kissing her neck. "I got a wedding at eleven, then another one at six. Blah."

"Busy girl." She smiled, smacking his butt, moving out from underneath him.

"Wanna go get some breakfast when I get out the shower, if we got time?"

"Sure, baby," he said with a smile as he watched her walk towards her bag, grabbing it before heading into the bathroom.

"Damn," he muttered as he covered his face with his hands, she drove him mad.

They didn't have time for breakfast, Elli said she was having a bad hair day, but when she came out the bathroom, she was looking gorgeous. Part of Shea didn't want to let her go out in her tight black pants and low cut top. For one, the pants made her ass look so damn delectable, he wanted to eat it, and two, he didn't like the idea of anyone looking at her toes but him.

Shea was starting to think he was developing a problem. What man was obsessed with a girl's feet? But he just loved how cute and white they were, all bundled up in high heels with only her big toe showing. Even the purple nail polish on her toes drove him crazy. It was nail polish!

He needed help.

"I think I need help," he said as he handed her a muffin and orange juice in a can, she looked at him weird, then smiled.

"Why?"

"I like your feet." She rolled her eyes, giggling as she came around the bar, kissing his cheek.

"My feet are ugly; I'm on them too much."

"No baby, really. The purple polish drives me mad." Elli just kept smiling, kissing his lips this time.

"I like your neck," she said with a wink that sent heat straight to his crotch, as she walked toward the door, picking up her camera bag. "What are you doing later?"

"I'm gonna be waiting for you to come back, you said Adler was with your brother for the weekend?"

"Yeah, Penny wanted him to spend the night and since you were coming home, I agreed."

"Good, I told you, you can bring him here if you need to."

"He's fine, but thanks. So, I'll come back here after the wedding?"

He smiled, loving how unsure she was, when she didn't need to be, "You better," he teased, pulling her to him, and kissing her deeply.

They parted and he noticed the heat in Elli's eyes. Something he had never seen before, his sweet little girlfriend had a hot streak, yes she did, and he wanted more.

"Mm, damn, you're sexy baby," he muttered against her lips, she gave him a lusty grin, kissing the side of his mouth.

"I have motivation to be." With that she was out the door with a wave.

He was her motivation, as she was his. He had to grin at that.

Harper and Elli leaned up against a wall, waiting for the bride and groom to make their entrance. The Fellow/Ortiz wedding was gorgeous. Kylie had said she wanted a fall festival and, boy, did she get one. It was beautiful, elegant, amazing. The colors, orange and red with brown as an accent filled the hall, and it was beautiful. Elli could only hope one day her wedding would be as pretty.

"God, I feel so good." Elli looked over at Harper, she had a big grin on her face, needless to say, Harper and Jakob had had fun last night. "I don't know if I'm gonna last when Jakes gone for a month, I'm gonna have to go see him, or something, jeez." Elli smiled, looking around at all the grinning faces.

"I'm nervous about it too, I'm gonna miss Shea something stupid," Elli said, a satisfied grin went across her face just remembering the sounds that were coming from the bedroom last night. God, her hockey player was too hot to trot.

"Yeah," Harper agreed, than looked over at Elli. "So what did y'all do last night? Play chess?"

"Funny," Elli said with a glare, than she smiled, "I cooked dinner, and then he gave me this necklace," she said holding out the little hockey stick, Harper grinned as she awed with appreciation. Elli leaned over towards Harper and she did the same to Elli, her eyes dancing with excitement, "I gave him head."

"Shut the front door!"

Elli nodded eagerly, "then he fingered me."

"Say what!"

A couple people turned to see what the commotion was about, but neither girl cared as Elli jumped into details about the amazing night with Shea. Harper listened intently, until the bride and groom walked in, then they went to work, promising to carry the conversation on later. The rest of the night went without a hitch, the bride and groom's night was captured with each click of Elli's camera. Each shot was perfect, the ones where John took such care feeding Kylie her cake, and then the ones where Kylie just slammed the cake in John's face were priceless. The night was wonderful in Elli's opinion, and she just wished all weddings went as well as this one had.

Elli and Harper walked out together, gathering around Elli's truck. Harper was basically bouncing, she had wanted to hear all about what had happen between Elli and Shea, their whole night, and she was ready to bust with questions. Of course, she asked if Shea was stacked and Elli could only blush, causing Harper to laugh her ass off, but after that, she fired Elli with questions and Elli couldn't be happier than to share. It had been so long since she got to have girl talk about sex, so she was basking in happiness!

"So, you think you're ready for the main course?"

Elli thought it over, she was ready, but she was still scared, "I think if it was dark again, I could do it, but not in the light, but then I don't know if I want to, you know?"

"Why?" Harper asked with a scrunched up face.

"What if we do it, and you know me, I'll put my heart into it, and then he meets my family and all hell breaks loose." Harper rolled her eyes, "I mean really, I haven't told him about Justin or being on Broadway, nothing, so I don't know, I kinda wanna wait."

"Well, he's waited this long, when's the dinner? In two weeks right?"

"Yeah."

"Okay, I still think you need to tell him though. About everything because you know your family will bust you out left and right, they are going to try to make you look bad."

"I know, but I don't want to talk about Justin or the Broadway shit, you know? It's my past."

"I know, Elli, but your mom doesn't understand that, she thinks God and everyone needs to know about your failing career, you're failing engagement and your failing life basically." Harper shook her head as Elli nodded, "But you know I don't think its failing."

"Oh, hush," Elli said with a grin, "I know it's not true, but when you hear it enough it still messes with you."

"I know, babe, but look at you now! You're so happy! When are you going to bring him to friend night?"

Elli shrugged her shoulders, and then smiled, "When are you bringing Jakob?"

Harper grinned big, "Actually, they are going to be home next month for it, so I am bringing him then, thank you very much!"

Elli grinned, as Harper bounced up and down, "Well, if he hasn't dumped me, I'll ask him to come."

"He ain't gonna dump you! Come on! He's totally smitten with you." Elli smiled at the thought, she was totally smitten too and Harper was right, she needed to talk to Shea.

She'd do it when she arrived home.

Home?

When did Shea's home become her home?

Well, hells bells.

When Elli got to Shea's condo, talking to him went straight out the window. When she had opened the door and saw the red rose petals all over the floor that made a trail to the kitchen her breath caught. She looked around the room and saw the soft lighting of white candles. Tall candles, short candles on little plates, tea cup candles, and big fat ones that had four wicks to them. They were everywhere; she smiled to herself as she locked the door, and laid her bag down.

"Shea?" she called out as she followed the trail to the kitchen, when she turned the corner and saw the island covered in rose petals with two plate settings, lit only by candle light, she covered her mouth in shock. It was so romantic, so sweet; he had gone through all this for her.

Shea came from the bedroom, with a shy smile on his face. He was wearing a pair of jeans and white button up shirt, with bare feet. His hair was perfectly messy, and he wasn't wearing his glasses.

"I thought you would be later," he said as he came to her, wrapping his arms around her, kissing her softly.

"I guess the bride and groom were in a hurry," Elli said with a grin, she nodded towards the island, "What's all this?"

"I can't have dinner waiting for my beautiful girlfriend?"

Elli narrowed her eyes, with a playful grin, "Are you trying to seduce me, Mr. Adler?"

He let her go to put his hands on his chest with an innocent smile on his face, "Me? Never," he said before wrapping her up in his arms again, kissing her deeply. She basked in his kisses, holding onto him like her life depended on it. He hugged her back, nuzzling her neck. Shea pulled back some to smile down at her before asking, "Are you hungry?"

"I am," she answered, he nodded before letting her go and going to the oven. He pulled out a box of pizza and Elli just giggled.

"What? I can make sandwiches and soup, after that, its take out and pizza."

She just smiled; he was so amazing, "It's fine, pizza is awesome."

"True that." Elli about fell over laughing, he looked at her weird, and then smiled, "What now?"

"True that? Who says that nowadays?" That made him laugh as he sat the box down before bringing a bottle of wine out of the fridge to the island.

"You shut up," he said as he poured her a glass, then himself. "It was a very common phrase back in the day."

"That should be left back in the day, thank you." He smacked her ass as he came around her, to go to his seat. She just grinned up at him as they sat to eat. She noticed that the plate settings were the plates that she had gotten him, and looked over at him confused. "I thought you said you were gonna take 'em back?"

He shook his head after taking a bite of his pizza, "Nah, you got them for me, I like them."

Elli's heart warmed as they continued to eat. Elli told him all about the beautiful fall wedding and the cake fiasco, and Shea told her about him working out most of the day with Alex and Jakob, and then playing a little pick up at the arena. She enjoyed their dinner, loved the conversation, and afterwards they did the dishes together. She had missed him so much during the day, and just being with him now made her feel so complete inside.

"Why don't you go take a bath, I bet your feet are hurting, babe," Shea said as he started sweeping up petals.

"Are you sure? I can help."

He shook his head, "I did this for you, go take a bath."

"Thanks," she gushed, kissing his cheek before heading for the bedroom. When she opened the bedroom door, candle light was the only light in there too; there were white petals all over the bed, and another trail leading to the bathroom. There were more candles, with soft music playing and a tray of bath beads and salts beside the tub. Elli noticed that all the scents were mango, her favorite and she had to smile. He was so thoughtful. She undressed quickly as the water ran, filling the beautiful claw foot tub. After submerging herself in the hot bathwater that smelled like mangos, she thought to herself,

Life couldn't get any better.

That was till she came out the bathroom and her hot boyfriend was laying in his boxers across the bed. Shea grinned up at her, turning the TV off and pushing something on the remote that started the iHome on the dresser. She smiled, crawling onto the bed, beside him as *Powerful Stuff* played, filling the room with the sexy music that they had first danced to.

"Oh, you are laying it on thick, Mr. Adler." Shea laughed, cuddling up beside her.

"Is it working?"

"Maybe," she giggled as he nuzzled her neck, kissing and licking as he made it to her shoulder, where he bit softly. "Mm," She gasped as he came back to her mouth, his body covering hers.

Shit, this was some powerful stuff, she thought as his hands roamed her body. They continued to make out till *Just as Kiss* started, Elli pulled back, looking into his eyes, running her hand down his jaw. This was their song, and she just wanted to look at him. As the female's voice filled the room, Elli wanted nothing more than to sing the words to Shea, and when the guy started singing and Shea's lips moved along with the words, Elli swore she couldn't breathe.

"This is our song," Elli whispered, he smiled, kissing her forehead before nodding.

"I agree."

"I'm not ready to have sex, yet." His smiled stayed on his face as he nodded.

"That's fine baby."

"Are you sure?"

"Yes, I-" He stopped, then closed his eyes before dropping his head to her chest taking a deep breath, when he brought his head back up to look down at her, he looked nervous. "I'm sure."

For some reason, Elli didn't think that was what he was gonna say.

As Shea watched Elli leave Monday morning for work, he still couldn't believe he'd almost told her he loved her. He had missed her all day Saturday, and then after their dinner and just being with her, he really couldn't blame himself for wanting to tell her, but he couldn't. Shea was not scared of much, but the thought of Elli rejecting his love or telling him that she didn't love him, hell, he was pretty sure it would crush him. So he might as well push them feelings way down, wait it out, wait for her to say it.

Like always when things were bothering him, after showering and cleaning up some from the movie day they had had yesterday, he headed over to Grace's. It was as if she knew he was coming, because she was laying out a big breakfast when he walked in. Grace smiled when she saw him as she laid Amelia's plate down.

"Hey, how's your collarbone? I saw that hit," she said, kissing his cheek before going around him to lay Ryan's plate down.

"It's good, sorry I didn't call this weekend."

"Ah, no big deal, I know how it is when someone new comes along and gets all your time. I did it to you with James."

"You did," Shea agreed sitting down next to Ryan. Ryan was shoveling food in his mouth, not even paying attention to Shea. "What's up with him?"

"He's mad at me because I won't let him play hockey with the big kids in the street."

"I am better than they are!" Ryan yelled, and Grace cut him a look that shut him up quickly, it even scared Shea a little.

"I don't care, now eat your food, and return to your room." Grace stomped off towards the kitchen, leaving Shea with the kids.

"Why do you have to go back to your room?"

"I said I wanted to come live with you."

"Man Ryan! Don't bring me in this!" Ryan gave Shea a goofy smile before finishing his food right as Grace came back to the table, he excused himself and ran off to his room.

"Sorry I'm cooler than you," Shea teased when he heard Ryan's door shut.

"Shut the hell up," Grace basically growled as she fed Amelia some more eggs, Shea chuckled. "So what brings you by?"

"Just wanted to see you before I head to the arena for practice, you guys coming to the game tomorrow?"

"We are, Ryan doesn't miss home games."

"So he'll be off grounding tomorrow?"

"We'll see."

"Cool."

"So are you sure your shoulder is okay?"

"Yeah, no big deal, just a deep cut."

"Good, I was worried when I saw it."

"I'm fine sis." Grace gave him a big smile and started eating herself. "James at work?"

"Yup, he left early."

"Thought so."

"How's Elli?"

"Fine, she spent the weekend with me, I think she might come back tonight, I'm not sure."

"That's good, so everything's solid?"

"Yeah," he said with a shy grin, "I almost told her I loved her the other night."

Grace dropped her fork, and shook her head, "It blows my mind Shea, I mean you guys together is amazing, don't get me wrong, but first you drop the girlfriend bomb on me, and then I see you guys together and it's so surreal, the sparks fly when your near each other."

"I love her."

"Good, I want you to Shea, I love her too, but it's only been a month, she's skittish, let it be for a little bit."

Shea thought for a moment, "You don't think she loves me?"

Grace shrugged her shoulder, moving around her eggs, "I don't know, she likes you a lot that's for damn sure, but I don't share a connection with her the way I do with you, so I don't know bro."

"Sometimes I think she does, but I don't know if its wishful thinking."

"Just wait, don't tell her yet."

"Okay," he said before he started eating, they ate in silence before he looked up at her and said "I'm meeting her family the week before the first road trip."

"Really?"

"Yeah."

"Good, will she meet mom and dad when they come in for the first home came in November?"

"She said she will as long as we're still together."

Grace made a face, looking up at him, "Why wouldn't you guys be together?"

"She convinced that when I meet her family, I'll dump her."

"Oh no, are they scary?" Shea laughed, while she grinned.

"She thinks so."

Grace nodded before picking up their plates and Amelia's to take them over to the sink, "Are you nervous about meeting them?"

"No, not at all."

"Have you ever met parents?"

"No."

"Oh, well good luck with that."

What the hell did that mean?

Chapter 14

"And why did I have to come in to cover you this morning?" Harper said with a teasing grin when Elli came in two hours late, two weeks later. Elli had sent a text to Harper the night before asking her to cover for her since she had a morning of shoots and her OBGYN was only able to see her first thing in the morning or she would have to wait five weeks before she was able to be seen, so she did the logical thing which was call Harper. "Did you have to go get some Xanax since tonight is the night?"

Elli stood there for a moment, hell instead of getting birth control she should have went and gotten Xanax since her damn nerves were shot to hell. "Why didn't I think of that?" she said throwing her arms up in the air. Harper giggled as Elli came around the desk, looking at the appointment book. She was book till three then she would be closing shop since she needed to go home, get ready for when Shea would come get her at six for dinner at her family's house at seven. Something she was not looking forward too.

"So where were you?"

"Doctors," Elli answered simply as she turned from the desk and headed for her office, of course Harper followed. Elli threw her purse on the couch, and sat behind her desk turning on her computer.

"Why did you go to the doctors? You okay?" Elli looked up at Harper; she was sitting in one of the teal chairs in front of the desk, her legs pulled up so she could rest her head on her knees. Her hair was still her natural color, brown, had been since her and Jakob had started dating for real. It was weird.

"I'm fine, Harp," Elli said to reassure her as she typed in her password, "I needed a check up, and I got...birth control."

Harper was out of the chair, jumping up and down before Elli even had 'control' of out her mouth. "So y'all are gonna do it!"

"I don't know! Gosh! I just want to be prepared for when we do."

"I knew you wouldn't be able to last much longer! He's too damn hot!"

Elli flashed a playful glare at Harper and just shook her head, Harper was right, getting into bed with Shea and not doing the deed was getting harder and harder every time, and since Elli stayed the night with Shea 5 nights out of the week when he was in town, there was a whole bunch of sexual tension between them. Elli was so ready to tear off her clothes that her insecurities were the last thing on her mind. But then knowing that she had that dinner tonight with her family would stop her, and she would remember that more than likely tonight would be her last night with Shea since she still hadn't talked to him about Justin or her past.

"Yeah, well I might have wasted my time with the appointment," Elli said with a huff as she got out of the chair, and went to her shelf for her camera, her ten thirty would be arriving any minute.

"Everything will be fine tonight Elli, I tell you what, I feel that Shea is real, that he will see right through them, you have nothing to worry about. I mean it's not like you've lied to him."

Elli cringed, had she been lying to him? Was not telling him something, lying? Shit. Elli gave Harper a weak smile as the bell chimed in the front office, her appointment was right on time. As Elli walked to the front, all she kept thinking was that she hoped Harper was right.

Elli bit her lip as she stood in front of her mirror in the bathroom, looking herself over. The high waist black skirt she chose to go with her white blouse that had black polka dots on it with her red belt and heels looked great, but were they good enough so that her mother would leave her alone about the extra six pounds she had put on since dating Shea.

"Shit on a shingle," she said with a huff as she checked the time again, Shea would be there in fifteen minutes, so she hurried to the bathroom checking on her hair. Elli had pulled it up in a cute little up do with a red blossom on the side. She looked like something straight out of a 50s pin up girl calendar, she had loved the outfit when she set eyes on it, and even though it set her back a pretty penny, she had to have it. She smiled at herself, knowing Shea would love it, but then the smile fell because she knew her mom would see the extra weight instantly.

Damn Shea, and his metabolism. The man could eat a whole cheesecake and not gain a pound, Elli looks at it and even though she runs the next day, she still gains a pound! It was so damn frustrating, even more so when Shea would push her to eat with him and when she would make a comment about her weight, he would tell her she is perfect and stuff the ice cream down her throat. He just didn't understand! Bless his heart but still!

Adler trotted behind Elli as she moved around the house, transferring all her crap from her big pink purse to her small black one. Adler whined and Elli bent down to kiss his furry head. She had felt so bad since she hadn't been home lately, so when she was home, she loved on him a lot more to make up for it.

"Wanna go out boy? Before I leave?" Adler took off at the word 'out'. Elli laughed as she followed him to the door, letting him out and walking out onto the porch just as Shea pulled up. He grinned at her as he got out, and she smiled back, checking him out. Of course he came dressed to impressed, he was wearing a nice tailored black suit, with a black shirt and light blue tie and of course those damn chucks.

"I swear Shea, your chucks kill me every time." Shea chuckled as he looked down at his shoes then back up, he wasn't wearing his glasses, so his eyes were extra bright and blue, it might have been the tie that made them shine or maybe it was her?

"Hey, what would you have me wear? Cowboy boots?" Elli giggled at that, Shea in cowboy boots!

"Lord no, even though I would pay to see that," she said as he came up the stairs, wrapping his arms around her, kissing her lightly on the lips.

"You look fantastic baby." She smiled shyly, kissing him again.

"So do you."

Adler decided that it was his turn for Shea's attention and started barking as he scratched at Shea's leg. Shea laughed, bending down to love on Adler.

"Hey bud, how you doing?" Of course Adler basked in the love, drooling all over the place as he basically laid out on the porch for Shea to pet his tummy.

"Shea, you're getting hair all over your suit."

"It'll brush off," he said with a grin for her, and then he looked back down at Adler "Right boy, it's just some hair."

Elli just grinned as Shea loved all over her puppy. He was such an amazing man. Shea smiled up at her again, before saying "We should come back and get him, since you're staying the weekend with me."

Elli had agreed to stay with Shea for the weekend since he was leaving Sunday night for the Assassin's road trip. Eleven away games, two home games, he would be home a total of four days, and Elli's heart hurt just thinking about it. She had done fine when he was gone for two nights and she even did fine when he was gone for that week but him being gone for basically a month, she was having a hard time hiding the fact that she was borderline depressed.

Shea was looking up at her waiting for her to answer, "Well I mean if you don't mind that would be great cause then I don't have to shell out hundred dollars to a boarding house in Nashville."

"I have already told you to bring him when you want, I would love to have a dog around," he looked back down at Adler; damn dog had nothing but love in his eyes for Shea, "Wanna come stay when me, bud?" Adler popped up, basically jumping into Shea's arms.

"Adler!" Elli yelled, pulling him down, "No sir, that's a nice suit, come on, say bye to your lover boy and get on in the house." Shea laughed as Elli pulled Adler into the house than shut the door, locking it.

"You're so cute," Shea cooed as he pulled her to him, dipping her before smiling down at her, "You look so classic; I figured you needed to be kissed like this," Shea said then he planted a sweet kiss on her lips. Elli thought she felt like a 50s pin up girl before, she really felt like one now, in the arms of her strapping hot boyfriend.

Could life get any better?

Yeah, but it was probably gonna get worse, Elli thought as she got into Shea's truck. Shea got in and started the truck before grabbing her hand, holding it in his lap as they drove off in the direction that Elli said. Her knee bounced as they drove through the country side to Clarksville, her home town. She felt like she was going to pass out and wish that she had gotten Xanax like Harper had said instead of the damn birth control because she might be dead before she is even able to use it.

"So we're going to have to make the most of this weekend since I won't be able to see you for two weeks." Elli looked over at Shea, and nodded.

"Please don't remind me," she said with a sad smile, "Maybe if I act like it ain't happenin' you won't leave."

"Oh I'm leaving baby, so please, don't replace me while I'm gone," he said with a teasing grin, she smile squeezing his hand tightly.

"Shouldn't I be the one saying that?" Shea shook his head, then brought her hand to his lips.

"I got eyes only for you, baby."

She loved his term of endearment for her, baby, it just rolled off his tongue so perfectly. She loved it, and loved that he only called her that.

"Same goes here."

Shea just smiled as they drove listening to the radio, when they hit the Clarksville city limits, Elli's heart picked up and her palms got sweaty. Shea rub the back of her hand with his thumb; bringing her hand to his lips again.

"Baby, don't be nervous, everything will be fine."

"I hope," she said directing him towards her parent's estate. "You're not nervous?"

"Nope."

He sure didn't look nervous, damn hockey player!

"So what did you do today?" he asked, probably trying to keep her mind at ease.

"I had a doctor's appointment this morning and then four engagement shoots and two newborn shoots."

Shea looked over at her puzzled, "Why did you need to go to the doctor? Are you not feeling well?"

"Oh I'm fine, it was just a check up, and I, Um, I got some put on birth control." He looked over at her again, a surprise look on his face, "Well you know, I know we haven't talked about it in the past two weeks but I just wanted to make sure I was safe in the pregnancy department since I'm pretty sure you don't want to have a baby with me and-"

"Elli."

"Yeah?" she asked looking over at him, he smiled.

"I'm glad you went," she smiled and looked down at their hands, "So how long does it take for it to be active?"

"A month."

"Okay, so when I come back..."

"More than likely I will be jumping your bones." That had them both laughing, which smoothed some of the tension.

"Sounds great to me, just let me know when you're ready."

"I will."

"Because I am."

"Oh I know you are," she said with a teasing grin as he laughed. Just the other night he was almost brought to begging after they fooled around, he kept telling her he just wanted to be inside her, while it made her hot beyond believe she just couldn't take her underwear off. She had never met a man like him, usually guys would get theirs and were done, but not Shea, he wanted it all, even after getting his.

When Shea turned down Fisher Rd, Elli was full out having a panic attack. Shea looked over at her and started laughing.

"Baby calm down," he said with a shake of his head just as Elli saw the black steel gate that line the property of the house she grew up in. "Where's all the other houses?"

"There isn't any," Elli said as they followed down the road, when the front gate came into view with the security house, Elli wanted to ask Shea to turn around, but she didn't, she pointed saying "Turn in there."

"Where?"

"Right here," she said, he turned into the driveway that would lead up to the main house after getting past security. Rick Harris, the security officer that had been with the Fisher family since Elli was born came to Shea's window, his hand on his gun, and Shea rolled it down with a grin on his face.

"ID please sir, what brings you by?" Rick asked, Shea looked over at Elli surprised, and she smile nervously at him as she moved across him to look at Rick.

"Hey Mr. Harris!" Rick smiled big, taking his hand off his trusty gun.

"Well Eleanor! Aren't you a sight for sore eyes, darling you're glowing!"

"Thank you! You're looking great, is Margret feeding you, your lookin' a little thin."

"Ah you know, she says I'm overweight." Which he was, but Elli just grinned.

"Never! Come on over to my house I'll cook for you."

"Bless your heart Eleanor, always such a sweetie." Elli smiled got brighter as she felt Shea smiling at her, "Here for dinner?"

"Yes sir," she said with a nod, "Mr. Harris, this is Shea Adler, my boyfriend."

It felt so good saying it to someone else that it almost calmed Elli's nerves...almost. Shea shook Rick's hand, a grin on his face.

"Nice to meet you."

"You too son, you look familiar, do I know you?"

"He plays on the Assassins' Mr. Harris," Elli commented, Shea smiled at her, and she smiled back.

"That's how I know you! My grandson is a big ole fan, says he's the next Alex Welch."

"We'll need one when Alex retires; you make sure to tell him that." They shared a laugh as Rick hit the gate button, so it would open.

"I sure will Mr. Adler, and please, take good care of our Eleanor, she really is a magnolia." Elli's face warmed as both men smiled at her.

"Will do, Mr. Harris," Shea said, still not letting his eyes leave Elli's.

"Good luck in there," Rick said with a wave as he walked towards the security house. Shea hit the gas, driving through the gate. They drove for a good ten minutes before the large plantation house came into view. Shea took in a sharp breath, before looking over at Elli.

"You never mention that your family was rich."

It wasn't the first thing she hadn't told him, or the last.

Shea had seen plantation houses before but Elli's parent's house was probably the biggest he had ever seen. The driveway went around a huge white fountain that had to be at least twenty feet tall, Shea parked behind a red BMW, and got out going around to let Elli out, before looking up at the house. Big maple trees surrounded the house, but all you could look at was the six huge white pillars that held the second floor balcony up. It seemed as if the windows were floor to ceiling windows, and the door was just as huge. The white hardwood floor made the blue of the window shutters and door stand out brighter, it was really beautiful. If he had his guess, he would say there were at least thirty rooms, the place was huge!

It was something straight out of Gone with the Wind.

Elli cleared her throat and he looked down at her. She looked so beautiful tonight, but she was so nervous it was making him nervous, even though he told her he wasn't. "It's kinda big."

"Kinda?" he asked looking back up at the house, hell mansion. Through the big window above the door he could see the huge sparkling chandelier. "Jeez, El, it would have been nice to prepare for this. I mean you never once said your parents were loaded."

"It never came up."

"Yeah, I guess," he said taking her hand, "Well come on." Shea started walking, basically pulling her along.

"Now remember, my mother is crazy, my sister is a bitch, my brothers are morons, but my daddy is amazin'." He loved when she got nervous like this, her little twang got thicker, and he just wanted to eat her up.

"And the sister in laws are nice, but stupid for dealing and breeding with your brothers," he said with a grin as they climb the stairs.

"I love when you listen." He laughed as they walked up to the door. Elli took a deep breath before opening the wide door, he didn't know how she got it open it was damn huge but she did, and he walked in behind her. Shea look up as a very pump white lady came through a door, a tray full of glasses.

"Ms. Eleanor! Look at you!"

"Mrs. Harris!" Elli gushed, running over to the older lady, kissing her plump cheek, "I saw Mr. Harris, he said you ain't feedin' him."

"Now ain't he a lie, I feed that man, don't you listen Eleanor, he just wants you to fuss over him."

Holy crap, did he come to Clarksville or back in the day to Tara from Gone with the Wind?

"You know I will too!" Elli gushed, kissing her again.

"I tell you what Ms. Eleanor, you havin' that boyfriend I've heard about is doing wonders, you look fantastic."

Shea had to smile at that, he like knowing that he was the reason Elli look fantastic.

"Why thank you, since you brought him up, Shea, this is Ms. Harris, she was my nanny." Shea smile, waving awkwardly since it wasn't like he could shake her hand, they were full with the tray.

"My, my, Ms. Eleanor, he's a looker." Elli grinned back at Shea, winking at him.

"Damn right about that one." Elli turned from Ms. Harris coming towards Shea as Ms. Harris laughed and started from another door. Elli took his hand in hers, and then looked up at him nervously. The girl that was just talking to Ms. Harris was gone, and back was the nervous Elli.

"Okay, you have met the two people out of three that will be the nicest to me, I'm warning you Shea, it's not gonna get better than that."

"Ellibaby, come on."

"Don't say I didn't warn ya". She turned, leading him through two more rooms that held family pictures of the grandkids. When Shea spotted some of Elli, he stopped.

"Hold on," he said as he looked up at what look like a collage of her. There were her school pictures along with other candid shoots. The best one was one of her on a stage, her arms above her head as she sung something; she looked so happy it was breath taking. "What was this?"

"Um, a school thing I did when I was seventeen."

"So you were in musicals?"

"I was."

"Why did you stop?"

"I gained all that weight."

"Oh," was all he got out before Elli was pulling him along. Elli stopped in front of a huge white door; since the room was red; it stuck out like a sore thumb. She took a deep breath, before pushing the door open. The room was full of chatter, everyone talking at once not paying attention that they had just walked in. Shea took in everyone, he could tell they were Elli's family; all of them except for the two blondes had the same features Elli did, except they were all bone skinny. With all of them dressed so classy, it was intimidating and Shea was so glad he wore his suit.

The oldest woman in the room, even though she didn't look old enough to have four kids, or even six grandchildren, turned and looked at them. She rose slowly as everyone else's' eyes turn to look at him and Elli. Everyone had different reactions, the two blondes took in a deep breath, while Ell's brother's mouths dropped, and Elli's sister had an evil look on her face, while her mother just stared at them. Elli's father stood up, the happiest out the bunch, came towards them with a grin on his face.

"Elli bug, darlin', aren't you looking too beautiful for words." he took Elli's hands in his, kissing each of them before kissing the side of her mouth. Elli was beaming as she turned to look up at Shea.

"Daddy, this is Shea Adler, Shea, my daddy, Michael Fisher."

"Nice to meet you sir," he said taking Michael's hand in his, he had a good grip.

"I've heard nothing but good things Shea, it's good to finally meet you. I've seen you play, and I've been impressed with you since day one."

"Thank you," Shea said with a nod as Michael turned since the older woman came up beside him.

"Shea, this is my mother, Olivia Fisher, mother, this is Shea Adler."

Elli being so proper was messing with Shea's head, but watching her mom look him over was worst. She took his hand, shaking softly as she looked him from head to toe.

"So you're Shea Adler," she stated, not asked.

"I am."

"And you're dating *my* daughter, Eleanor?"

"Mother," Elli said with a bit of warning in her voice, Shea looked at Elli, a grin on his face.

"Yes, I am, for almost a month and a half now. Right Elli?"

Elli smiled up at him, "Right."

"Humph, have you met my daughter, Victoria?"

Olivia moved out of the way as the leggy brunette came over to them, she was walking with a little more sway then needed. She was all legs, small breast, and nothing but skin and bones. She had the same features as Elli but her features were sharp while Elli's were soft.

"How do you do?" Victoria basically cooed as she took his hand in hers. "Wow, you have big hands." Shea could feel Elli getting madder by the second.

"Nice to meet you," he said dropping her hand, even when she tried to hold on. Shea looked past her as Elli's brothers came up with their wives on their arms.

"Shea, my brother Liam, his wife, Adina, Liam, Adina, my boyfriend Shea Adler," Liam took his hand in his, shaking just as strong as his dad did, even Adina had a good strong hand shake.

"Nice to meet you."

"My other brother Noah, his wife, Lauren, Noah, Lauren, my boyfriend, Shea Adler," Noah shook his hand hard, while Lauren just stared at him with her mouth hanging open, she must be the one that was in love with him. He smiled sweetly at her, causing her to blush deep red before she high tailed it out of there.

"My wife is a big fan," Noah said with a grin, Shea smile.

"Yeah, Elli told me when I met the kids," Shea said, taking Elli's hand in his.

"Ellibelly it's so weird hearing you be called Elli," Liam said to Elli before looking at Shea, "We never call her just Elli, it's always been Ellibelly or Eleanor."

Shea nodded, looking over at a very embarrassed Elli, "Daddy calls her Elli bug," someone said, "Yeah but that's daddy," someone else said, Shea wasn't paying attention, he hated that Elli was getting embarrassed even though Grace had said it would happen. His sister warned him about this kind of stuff, but for some reason it still bothered him that Elli wasn't comfortable. He wanted to leave because he knew she wanted too.

"Well come on now, dinner is almost ready from what Miz Harris says," Olivia said still staring at Shea, she was looking at him like he didn't belong, or maybe she was looking at Elli like that, hell he didn't know, the woman was creeping him out.

Everyone walked ahead, leaving Olivia and Michael with Shea and Elli.

"Shea son, would you like a drink?"

"Yes, please," Shea said, Michael motion for Shea to follow him before he did, he looked down at Elli, kissing her cheek before pulling her along with him.

"You want a beer Elli bug?" Michael asked, Elli was about to answer but her mom beat her to it.

"Now honey, the girl has gained weight, it's probably all the drinking she does," Olivia said, Shea whipped his head back at Elli's mother. She was looking Elli over with nothing but disgust all over her face. He looked over at Elli, and saw the heat creeping up on her face.

"None of that now, Livie, leave Elli bug alone," Michael said, handing Elli and Shea a beer.

"Whatever, when she gets as fat as she did, don't say I didn't warn y'all," Olivia walked over to where they stood by the mini fridge, looking Elli over.

No wonder Elli doesn't like her mom.

"Livie, please," Michael said taking a good long swig of his beer; Shea did the same, as Elli downed hers.

"I mean Eleanor, why don't you belch at the end honey! No wonder you're gaining weight again, how much have you gained? Six, eight pounds?"

"For the love of God," Elli muttered, throwing her bottle in the trash, "Isn't it time to eat?"

"We might need to skip it to save you from yourself."

Elli looked up at the ceiling; it looked like she was counting. Shea didn't know what to say or do, he felt so helpless.

"Now that's enough Olivia, not another word," Michael said grabbing a hold of her arm and directing her out the room, "Come on now kids, let's eat." Shea watched as they walked before turning to Elli, who was grabbing another beer. When he turned her, he saw the tears in her eyes.

"Baby, don't let her get to you."

"Just let it be, Shea," she said walking past him.

Great, this was going to be fucking great.

It was going just as Elli thought it would go, straight to hell. How the hell her mother knew how much weight she had gained would always be a mystery to her, but the woman always got it right. And of course her brother's would bring up her god awful nickname, and Victoria's attempts at flirting with Shea were expected, but what she didn't expect was Shea to just completely ignore her.

God, he was perfect.

They all gathered in the first dining room since it was bigger, and classier as her mother always said, it also sat fifteen people if needed. The room was straight out of Better Homes and Garden. Classy white, with light blue accents, some of Elli's prints of the kids hung on the wall, not like her mother would ever own up to it though.

Shea pulled out Elli's chair when they reach the table, and Elli flashed him a smile as she sat, the smile fell when she saw her mother sit next to her and Victoria in front of her.

Great.

Everyone else sat down, her daddy at the other end of the table, beside Adina and Lauren since Liam and Noah wanted to sit beside Shea. As Mrs. Harris and the rest of the kitchen came out to serve dinner, the guys started talking hockey. Liam and Noah were dumbass about hockey so they basically listen as Shea talked about the last Assassins' game and how they won. When all the food was laid out and after her daddy said grace, everyone dug in.

Shea was looking around the room as he ate; he did that a lot Elli noticed. Always took in the scenery, another reason she just adored him, because she did the same.

"I have to say, your children are beautiful," Lauren and Adina grinned big as Liam and Noah kept eating.

"Thank you, Riley and Max just adore you, Jason's still a little young, but he does love himself some hockey," Adina gushed, as Lauren blushed.

"You guys will have to bring them out to Kids night, my nephew comes, they got along pretty well when we met at the park, don't you think babe?" he asked turning to Elli, she smiled big,

"They sure did."

"They would love that, thank you Shea," Adina grinned, Shea nodded towards the pictures.

"They look like your work baby, did you take them?"

Bless his heart; she would adore this man for forever.

"She did," Olivia said, before Elli could say anything, and that's all she said.

"We have a lot of Elli's work through the house, not only pictures of the family, but she did some really nice black and whites of tree for my office. They are the best things in my office," Michael said, Elli grinned widely at her father, and he gave her a wink as Shea nodded. "So aren't you about to go out on a road trip?"

Shea nodded as he took a drink of his beer then said, "Yes sir, I leave Monday."

"Yeah, Bryan said something about y'all leaving, he was gonna fly out to some of the games, ask if I wanted to go. Maybe we can go together Elli bug."

Elli nodded, "Sure daddy."

"Bryan?" Shea asked, and then Elli dropped her fork.

Shit, shit, shit, shit.

"Yeah, Bryan Fisher, the owner," Michael said, Shea looked at Elli, then back at her daddy.

"You know the owner?" Shea asked, she could tell he was confused as everyone laughed.

Shit, shit, shit, shit.

"Oh course I do son, he's my brother, Eleanor didn't tell you."

Shea took a deep breath, and then looked over at Elli. She couldn't tell if he was pissed or shocked, it was probably both.

"It must have slipped her mind."

"Yeah, that why she has them amazing seats, and she's at every game. Elli belly is Uncle Bryan's favorite," Liam said, "he hates the rest of us."

"For good reason," Elli said, "Y'all name drop like a mother, I don't, plus I actually like hockey."

Everyone rolled their eyes, as they continued to eat. Uncle Bryan was a touchy subject; he only talked to Elli and her father since they were the only normal ones in the family. Shea hadn't started eating again, he was just staring at his plate, and Elli wished she could beg him not to be mad, but it was bound to get worst, so she just picked her fork back up and started eating again.

"So Shea," Elli looked over at her mother, as Shea did, "Do your parents live in Nashville?"

"No, they live back in Boston where I'm from."

"That's nice, what do they do for a living?"

"Mom," Elli groaned, Olivia gave her a look.

"What darling? It's a simple question."

"Its fine Elli," Shea said, looking back at Olivia, "My dad is a college professor at one of the private colleges in Boston, while my mother is a teacher at the local high school."

"Oh, that's nice," Olivia said, basically pushing her nose even farther in the air at Shea. If Elli could kill someone it would be her mother, mean old bat. Olivia laid her fork down, and then looked back at Shea "Are you going to continue dating Elli while you're gone?" Everyone got quiet, looking down at Olivia, as she gave Shea a pointed look, "You know she is just so busy with that picture taking business of hers, and she won't be able to go with you."

Elli's face fell into her hand, as Shea cleared his throat, "I know, but that doesn't mean we can't talk on the phone every night or text, or Skype, we did just fine while I've been traveling the last month, we'll do fine this time too."

Elli's heart warmed as she looked over at Shea, he wouldn't look at her, but he had to feel her staring at him. She slid her hand onto his lap and he took it tightly in his.

"Well that's just silly, you'll get so lonely."

"Olivia," Michael warned, Elli looked down at her plate as Olivia let out a frustrated breathe. They went back to eating, small talk about a bunch of nothing was tossed around until Elli reached for more greens, they had always been a favorite of hers, and she couldn't cook em the way Mrs. Harris did, so she was going to get her fill while she was here, that was until her mother stopped her with a smack on the back of her hand. Shea quick intake of breathe was louder than Elli's as the room went completely silent.

"Now Eleanor, I'm not gonna let you get to the way you were, you're done." Elli had never been so embarrassed in her life; she looked up at Victoria, who was grinning ear to ear.

"Yeah Elli belly, you get fat again, there's no way Shea will stay," she said with a laugh, causing everyone else to laugh. The tears were stinging in her eyes, as she looked over at her mother.

"Victoria Renee!" Michael said sternly.

"I was sick, that's why I got fat," Elli said as strong as she could.

"Oh I know you were sick, but still we don't want to chance it, for all I know you ate yourself into a coma up in New York cause of all the nerves of Broadway."

Shit, shit, shit, shit.

"Broadway?" Shea asked, everyone turned to look at him, except Elli.

"Oh yes, Eleanor has a voice of an angel," Michael said with a grin, Elli couldn't help but smile, her daddy was her biggest fan "She didn't even go to college first, Bryan had called one of his director friends up in New York and Eleanor audition at seventeen, next thing you know she's on the stage, starring at Fanny Price for Funny Girl. She was, and still is amazing."

Shea looked over at Elli again, and like before she couldn't look at him until he squeezed her hand causing her to look up at him.

"Another thing that must have slipped her mind."

Elli bit her lip as her mother laughed.

"Oh no, she probably didn't tell you because she got kicked off Broadway when she got fat. It was terrible I tell you Shea, she was close to what Victoria? 200 pounds?"

"Yeah it was crazy," Victoria added with a disgusted look on her face.

"It was, poor Justin, he just couldn't take it, that's why he broke the engagement."

Oh, hell.

Shea had to of heard Elli's mother wrong, "Engagement?" he asked.

Shea felt Elli tense up beside him.

"Yes," Olivia said, taking a drink of wine, "She was engaged to Justin Yates of Yates Financing, such a fine man."

"Until Elli got crazy fat and he left her for a college student," Victoria added.

"He didn't leave me, I left him," Elli said, but no one was listening since they kept going on about Justin.

"They were engaged for what momma, four years?" Liam asked

"One year," Elli said

"No I think it was three," Olivia said, completely ignoring Elli.

"Yeah, they were together forever though, eight years?" Noah asked

"Five years," Elli said, laying her fork down and taking a pull on her beer.

"Yeah eight years, honey," Olivia added.

Shea looked around the table. Michael had his head down, shaking it, as Adina and Lauren looked at Elli with nothing but sympathy in their eyes. "It was so sad to see him go, that's why Shea honey, I'm not really getting attached to you, I don't see you staying with Eleanor, you know between her weight issues and her so called career; she isn't really good enough for you."

"Wow mother, thanks!" Elli said causing everything to look at her, she threw her napkin on her plate, standing up, causing her chair to fall back. "And this is why I don't come home, I'm leaving." She looked over at Shea, tears welling up in her eyes before walking out the room. Michael stood up calling after her before he sent Olivia an evil look and rushed out the room. Shea stood up slowly, throwing his napkin on his plate.

"Oh no, Shea honey, don't leave," Olivia said, standing up, "She'll be alright, she'll come back when Michael tells her too."

Shea was trying so hard to breathe, and not blow up Elli's mom, he counted to three before looking at her, "I apologize if this comes out rude Olivia, but what the hell is wrong with you people? That woman is the most amazing person I have ever met, there is no weight issue, she's beautiful, and her career, I mean do you even know she is one of the most prestigious photographers in Nashville? Why are you guys doing that to her?" He shook his head, "You guys have issues." Shea stepped out from the table looking down at Lauren and Adina, "It was nice meeting you, ladies. Everyone else, I could have went on without watching you tear Elli to pieces, let me say this, you're lucky you're her family." With that he walked away, when he got to the front room, Michael was walking back towards him.

"She's calling a cab apparently," was all her father said as he passed by, Shea was pretty sure Elli's family was about to get a lashing, they needed one that was for damn sure.

"It was nice meeting you sir," Shea said turning to look at Elli's fathers back.

"You too Shea, now please go get my baby." Shea nodded as he turned and walked out the big doors to see Elli pacing by his car, he walked down the steps and when he got close enough to where she heard him coming, she looked up, her big green eyes full of tears, some started to fall over, rolling down her cheeks. His chest clenched at the site and he had to look away.

"I'm calling a cab, so you can leave."

"Elli, get in the truck," he said, going around the truck, and opening the door. She looked at him, then back down at the floor.

"You're mad," she stated

"Yup, pissed as fuck, so don't test me, get in the truck."

Shea thought she was gonna fight him on it, but she didn't, she got into the truck and he slammed the door before going around and getting in his self. They drove off the property and nothing was said until they hit the interstate.

"I mean do I even know you Elli?" Shea asked, the tears were falling fast and Elli didn't even look over at him, "You never told me your family is rich or that your uncle is Bryan fucking Fisher, my boss. You didn't think you should have told me that?"

"It never came up."

"Apparently nothing came up! Elli your uncle is my boss; don't you think I needed to know that?" When she didn't say anything he kept going "What if he trades me when he finds out, what if we broke up and he got pissed and fired me then blacklisted me! What then! Don't you think these are things I need to know!"

"I'm sorry Shea, I should have told you about my uncle, but Uncle Bryan isn't like that."

"I don't care; it is still something I need to know Elli!" She wiped her face, looking at her skirt that had little spots from her tears, "Broadway Elli? Really?!"

"It was a long time ago."

"I mean, I didn't even know you sang for a living, and you were sick? It's as if you kept a part of your life from me, hid it from me. I've told you everything, I mean damn, it's as if I don't know you and in one night I meet the family from hell and find out a bunch of shit about you."

All Elli could do was nod as she cried, "I can't believe this, it just blows my mind, but the kicker Elli," he did say anything till she looked over, she saw nothing but hurt and angry in his eyes as he said "You were engaged, you were fucking engaged, which means you lied to me, because I asked if there was someone important but you lie and said no."

"He wasn't important Shea, he was a convenience."

"Did you have sex with him?"

"Yes, but-"

"He was important then, you said yes when he put a ring on your finger."

"But I broke it off cause I didn't love him."

"But you said yes, so he meant something at the time!" he yelled, scaring the piss out of her, she looked back down at her hands, and nothing was said the rest of the way to her house. When he pulled into her driveway and didn't get out, Elli started crying harder.

"I should have known something was up when you wouldn't even let me in your house, wow, Elli, wow. If you didn't want me to know who you are, then why did you let it go this far? Why did you even bring me around your parents when you knew they would throw all your shit out? I mean shit Elli, damn."

Elli didn't look at him; she just reached for the handle and got out, shutting the door behind her. She didn't even look back when she heard him whip his truck out of her driveway; she just walked up the step as sobs ripped out of her. When she unlocked the door and went in, Adler started barking but then went silent as she went through the house, bawling as she ripped her clothes off. When she got to her bathroom, she filled the bathtub up before crawling in it, dipping down so the water was to her chin as she cried.

He was totally right, she set herself up for this, she ruined their relationship, and he had no choice but to break up with her.

She was a liar.

She thought she had prepared herself for what was bound to happen.

Nope, what a stupid idiot she was.

Shea was pissed, pissed because Elli lied, pissed because her family is a bunch of idiots minus her father, and pissed because he wasn't sure, but he was pretty sure he just broke up with her. He drove down the road, digging his phone out of his pocket to call Grace, she answered on the third ring.

"Oh no, it went bad."

"Bad isn't even going to cover the fucking mess I just left."

"Oh no Shea, where's Elli?"

"I fucking left her at her house and I think I fucking broke up with her."

Grace took in a quick intake of breath then said, "Shea, calm down, pull over."

Of course he did what she asked, shutting the car off and letting his face fall to the steering wheel. His eyes shut as he replayed the way Elli looked as she cried her heart out in his front seat. He actually felt like crying and he never wanted to cry!

"Now tell me what happen."

So he did, he told her everything, about Elli's so called family, her sister, brothers, her so called mother, Shea made sure to say nothing but good things about Michael, since he was a really nice guy. He also told her about the stuff he had learn, and Grace being Grace just sat there listening even after he was done, she didn't say anything, and Shea knew she was processing what he had said.

"Okay, so you're mad because she hid stuff from you right?"

"Yes, she was on Broadway Grace, she apparently can sing, then she was sick and that's how she gained all kinds of weight apparently, and then she was engaged, Grace. She told me there was no one worth talking about in her fucking past! Not to mention her Uncle is my damn boss."

"Okay, I get the being pissed about the Uncle thing, that's huge but she never really talked about her family, and now you see why, and I agree with you being mad about the engagement, but did you give her a chance to explain?"

"No, she didn't even try, she just cried."

"Shea, come on, she was just torn apart by her family in front of you, how do you think she feels?"

Shea sat for a moment, Grace was right; he slammed his hand into his steering wheel. "I should go back."

"You should go back, because I'm telling you, she isn't going to chase after you, she knows she did wrong. Plus she doesn't even think she's good enough for you, I'm telling you, God Shea, this is a mess, and you're going regret not going back if you don't."

For the hundredth, millionth time, Grace was right.

When Shea pulled into Elli's driveway, he noticed her house was dark. He glanced down at the clock; it was only nine, and he knew Elli wasn't asleep. He got out of the truck, taking off his jacket and undoing his tie before shutting them inside his truck and walking up the drive. He was undoing the top buttons of his shirt when he noticed the buckets of fall color flowers that aligned her walk way, Elli must have just put them out because they weren't here last time he was here. He bent down, picking a purple one and continued up the walk way. Adler was sitting in the window watching and started barking when Shea reached the porch, but no lights came on.

Shea was worried for about two seconds before the door open and Adler came running out, leaving Elli standing in a bright purple robe that had the team logo on her breast, and a 6 above it. Her hair was wet, going down her shoulders, and her face was splotchy, she had obviously been crying. She looked everywhere but at him as she stood in the doorway.

Shea didn't know what to say, so he just stuck his hand out, offering her the flower. She looked at it, and then up at him as a huge tear rolled down her cheek. She reached her hand out taking the flower, than pushed the door open, before calling Adler.

"Come on Adler," The dog came running up the stairs at speeds Shea was sure a forty pound pug shouldn't be going and Elli turned to look at him. "Are you coming in?"

Shea nodded as he walked past her, waiting in the foyer for her to close the door and hit the lights. When she did, his eyes adjusted and went wide when he saw his self looking back at him. His jersey that he had signed was hanging right beside an action shot of him shooting a puck. He looked around the room, taking in all the pictures of him and the rest of his team mates. There were pictures of them playing, celebrating and then the best one, the one of him with the cup above his head, tears going down his cheeks as he kissed the cup.

"God Elli, this picture is amazing; I need a copy of it."

"Sure."

"Make that two, my mom would want one too," he said with a grin as he turned to look at her, she looked down, nervously messing with the tie at her waist.

"Alright," she swallowed and looked up at him, "This is why I didn't want you to come in my house, I thought you would think I am a crazy stalker fan." He chuckled, looking around the room.

"Baby I've seen worst, this is awesome, I love it." She smiled weakly and started for the hall.

"Do you want the tour?"

He nodded as he followed her through the hall, the left wall was of the kids and the right was a time line of Harper and Elli. "I didn't know you and Harper had known each other since childhood."

"Yeah, since we were five."

"Wow," was all he said as they reached the end of the hall that went into a large beautiful yellow living room. She had black couches with glass tables with big black vases full of yellow flowers on them. Her walls were line with black and white photos of Adler, than random things like a butterfly, a tree, and a brick wall that had a heart drawn on it. When Shea turned to the south wall and saw a TV that was as big as his, he just grinned, it had to be for the away games. Under the TV was picture of the kids along with others of her friends, he guessed, but none of her family, well except her dad.

He turned to see her waiting by a open door that's frame was painted black, it looked so great with the yellow, "This is the kitchen and dining room," she said as he peeked his head into the purple kitchen, he could see that the dining room was a soft purple, more a lavender with a big white vases of lavender on a large black table.

"You're color scheme is bright."

"Yeah," she said as she walked past him to the other side of the living room, he followed her down a hall as she open doors, showing him her office, done in pink, the bathroom, done in a very soft green, and the playroom for the kids, done in red, then came her bedroom.

 Elli's bed sat about five feet off the ground, the headboard consisted of 4 huge squares, two baby pink squares and two hot pink ones. The bedding was a mixture of all kinds of pink swirls, and she had to have about nine hundred pillows. Frilly little lamps hung from the ceiling and glass night stand sat beside the bed, one stand had a big bouquet of sweet peas, while the other had a pink alarm clock, along with her pink iHome, which was playing

Adele if he was correct, and a photo frame. When he got closer, he saw it was a picture of him looking as if he was about to kill someone.

"Out of all the pictures you can put beside you bed, the one you chose is the one of me mean mugging someone?"

Elli laughed, picking the frame up, "This was at one of the playoff games last season, I can't remember who was in front of me, but you looked up at him with this look and I got this shot right before you plaster him into the glass in front of me. When I printed it out and put it beside my bed Harper asked why, I told her it was for you to scare all my bad dreams away" She let out a empty laugh, "Stupid huh? Wanna run?"

He smiled, taking the picture out of her hand, putting it back on the night stand before wrapping his arms around her waist, "I'm not going anywhere," He pressed his forehead against hers, "I'm sorry Elli for freaking out on you"

"You had every right," she whispered, he watched as a tear fell over her cheek, the sight of it made it hard for him to swallow, "I'm so sorry Shea. I mean all of it, I should have told you a long time ago, but I was so embarrassed of my failures."

"But baby with me you shouldn't be, your past has made you who you are, and I adore you, everything about you."

"I feel the same about you."

"Okay, so don't hide things from me, tell me everything."

She bit on her lip, before looking deep into his eyes. "Okay, but not tonight." She cupped his face in her hands, running her thumbs up and down his cheeks as she searched for God knew what, but he stayed where he was, holding her close as Adele crooned in the background about loving someone.

"Dance with me?" she whispered as she moved her hands to the back of his neck, all he could do was nod, he was spell bound with the way she was looking at him, it was as if she was telling him how much he meant to her with her eyes. He had never felt so cherish in his whole life, than he did in the moment standing with Elli, her gaze fixed on his.

God, she was beautiful.

Her hair was drying so it was in a mess of beautiful curls, she smelled like a ripe mango, her scent filling his nose as she laid her head on his chest as they moved to the music. His hands rested on the small of her back, holding her close to him as they swayed back and forth. They stayed like that through three songs, before Elli broke away from him, going to the door, shutting it, before shutting the light off. His eyes adjusted just as she came back into his arms.

Naked.

Chapter 15

Shea knew everything, and now Elli stood in his arms naked as the day she was born. It was dark so she knew he couldn't see anything, but he could feel and it only took a moment for his hands to start roaming. Shea's hands were shaking as they moved down her side, over her hips, onto her bare butt. She looked up at him, the only light was the stars and moon, so she could only see a little bit, but she saw the grin. She smiled back, as she slowly moved her hands up his chest to the top buttons of his shirt. With every button open her heart beat went faster.

She was doing this, she was about to have sex with Shea.

Elli moved the shirt off his shoulders, pressing her bare breast against his chest, wanting to feel skin on skin. Shea took in a quick breath then let it out through his teeth as he held her close, watching her move her hands along his side. She pulled back a little and undid his pants, letting them fall to the ground with a thud from his belt. He took a step back only for a second to toe out of his shoes before coming back for her. It was heaven feeling his skin on her skin, his hard length against her stomach.

Shea brought his mouth down to hers, kissing her so long and deep that when they parted she couldn't breathe or form a coherent thought. He smiled as he slid his hands down to her butt then over the back of her thighs, before lifting her up. She let out a little scream, wrapping her arms and legs around him as he chuckled, bringing her to the bed, and laying her down. He kissed down her neck, biting and nibbling as he went; when he took her nipple in his mouth she closed her eyes, running her hand through his hair as the other one gripped one of the many pillows on the bed. He moved to the other breast, giving it the same love he had given the first one before dipping his head down lower, kissing her belly, dipping his tongue in her belly button, before biting her hips, then licking them when she would let out a soft moan.

He was driving her bat shit crazy and he loved it. With every little scream, moan, or meep that would leave her mouth, he would chuckle, or gasp as he continued what he was doing. Elli could feel him shaking, as his hands moved along her body, like his control was slipping with every moment that passed. When he trailed kisses down her hip bone, kissing the wetness between her thighs, he looked up at her, and she took in a breath. His eyes said it all, he wanted nothing more than her. Shea wasted no time, he took her whole in his mouth, biting, licking, fingering, everything, until he brought her to the point of no return. His tongue flicked so softly over her nub of nerves, as he moved a finger in and out of her, then he would suck her swollen nub into his mouth, making her scream in pleasure as he slid another finger in her. He kept changing it up, driving her crazy. Elli screamed his name when she came, hard, closing her legs around his head, trying to move him out since he wasn't stopping, when she finally succeeded, he looked up at her, licking his lips as he pulled his fingers out of her.

"Mm," was all he said as he started kissing her thighs, moving back up her body. Her wetness covered her body from his lips and fingers as he kissed and touched her, he covered her mouth with his causing her to taste herself on his lips, and for some reason it turned her on even more. He moved his self between her legs, rubbing his hard length against her core, making her gasp and squirm underneath him. "I didn't come prepared baby," he whispered against her lips as he looked down into her eyes, "I didn't know this was going to happen."

"Neither did I," she whispered, she looked over at the night stand that held all her stuff, "There are condoms in the night stand."

He was off of her in a matter of seconds, opening the drawer and pulling out the box she had picked up after going to the doctor. He opened the pack, pulling out a condom, tearing the package with his teeth, before sheathing himself. Elli watched as he took a deep breath, before looking over his shoulder at her. She blinked twice, scared out of her mind as he grinned, moving slowly back over her. He nudged her legs open again, placing his self between her, positioning his shaft in the right direction. Shea looked up from where they were about to be connected to look down into her eyes. Elli felt the tears burning her eyes, even though she was beyond ready to have sex with him, she was scared. What if she didn't do it right? What if he didn't fit!? What if he can't get off because it isn't good with her?

Shit, Shit, Shit!

"I'm scared," she whispered as a tear leak out, going down the side of her face into her hair, he closed his eyes, leaning his head onto her forehead, before opening them again to look down at her.

"Don't be baby, I..I..," he closed his eyes again, taking a deep breath before opening them again, "I will go slowly; I'll try not to hurt you."

"I'm not scared of the pain; I'm scared you won't like it."

He smiled sweetly, before covering her mouth with his and pushing into her. It was like fireworks went off behind her eyes as he pushed himself to the hilt, groaning with every inch. It was a tight fit, but a welcome, glorious one.

"Oh God, how could I not love this?" he groaned as he moved out, then back in. Elli watched his face as he tried to keep his eyes open, looking down at where they were connected, but he couldn't, his eyes kept drifting close, so did hers. She started to move along with him, meeting every thrust, until he started going so fast and hard that all she could do was lay there basically screaming out his name as she hit her climax again. He only slammed into her twice more, before he was shouting with his own climax, falling onto her, breathing just as hard as she was. Sweat dripped from his body onto hers as their breathing started to slow down.

Shea put his hand down, lifting himself up a little to look down at her. He smiled, and then gave Elli a long lavish kiss before moving off her. She watched his prefect ass moved from the bed as he walked to the bathroom, she heard the snap from the condom, and the water running as he washed his hands. She sat up, throwing her arm over her breast as she reached for her robe.

"What are you doing?"

She looked up at his gloriously naked body and tongue basically fell out of her mouth as she tried to form words, finally she said "I was gonna put my robe on."

"No you're not, get back in that bed, we aren't done."

"We ain't?"

"Not at all," he said with a grin as he covered her body with his, "There are still parts of you I want to taste." He kissed her neck, then her ear as he licked and nibbled back and forth.

"Like?"

"I think I missed your elbows, the back of your knees, and I will have those toes in my mouth before the night is over."

Elli giggled, his obsession with her toes was crazy, but it still made her hot, "So I guess it's safe to say it was as good for you as it was for me?"

"Good?" he shook his head, a cocky grin on his beautiful face, "It was epic, Elli, *epic*."

That was the last coherent sentence that was made for the rest of the night.

Shea's eyes drifted open as the sun warmed his face, he looked down at the beautiful woman that filled his arms, and sighed. Having sex with Elli last night felt like coming home, she was hot, perfect, sweet, did he mention hot? It had been so long since he had been with a woman, hell it had been a long wait just to have sex with Elli, but God was it worth the wait. All the past worries he had about not wanting her after their first time was nowhere to be seen as he looked down at the profile of her face, since she had her back against his chest.

He moved out of the bed and went to the bathroom since he had to go. After using it, he went back to the bed, crawling in it as he glanced at the clock. It was only eight; his body was so used to getting up early that he did it even when he didn't need too. Shea ran his hand up Elli's thigh, then back down. Maybe he could get some morning sex out of her, and then they could sleep the morning away since they both had the whole weekend off. He placed a kiss on her hip, then one in the middle of her back, before trailing them up till he reached her shoulder.

"Mm," she moaned softly as she looked over her shoulder, she smiled, and then rolled onto her back looking up at him. "Good morning."

"Morning beautiful.'

She smiled before yawning, gripping his bicep in her hand, "What time is it?"

"A little after eight."

"Ugh, why are you waking me?"

He gave her a devilishly smile, and she smiled back as lust filled her eyes. Elli pushed his arm out from underneath him causing him to lay flat against her naked chest, before kissing him deeply. She pulled back to soon, then she was gone, looking over the side of the bed.

"What are you doing?" he asked, but then he heard it, her phone was ringing. Since her assistants were the ones working the weddings and other parties she had this weekend, he understood the urgency of answering the phone.

"Shit, it's my daddy," she said, lying back in bed as she answered it, "Hey Daddy."

Shea watched as she talked to her dad, she was so cute, calling him daddy, and smiling so shyly when he kissed her shoulder.

"Um, I don't know daddy, I can call and ask, I don't know what he has planned for today, okay, I'll call you back." She hung up the phone and Shea laughed.

"Can't tell daddy I'm here?"

"God no! He wouldn't have it, he likes you, I don't want to mess that up," she said with a giggle, "He wants to have brunch with us."

"Okay, just him?"

"Yeah, at 11."

"Okay, where at?"

"In Clarksville, I don't think you'll have time to go home and get dress, I'll just tell him no."

"No, isn't there a mall somewhere close? I'll go get some clothes, then we can go."

Elli smiled big, covering his mouth with hers, kissing him lavishly. When they parted, she looked at him with such love that he was sure was going to say she loved him, but nope, she hop out of bed, running to the bathroom with a giggle, saying something about not looking at her, but he did anyways. Shea took his fill of that luscious ass of hers, the hips that drove him mad, the bumps of her spine, and her long dark hair that went down her back.

Beautiful.

He smiled to himself as he got out of bed, going to the pile of his clothes moving them around to get his boxers before pulling them up and walking out the room. Adler met him at the door, looking up at him with his big brown eyes. He really was a cute dog, fat, but cute.

"Need to go out boy?" Adler took off. Shea laughed as he followed him to the door, letting him out before going to the kitchen for coffee. He found what he needed and started up Elli's coffee maker. After getting out two coffee mugs, he opened her fridge to see what she had as she came down the hall in a towel.

"Did you let Adler out by chance?" she asked, coming up behind him, wrapping her arms around his waist. He closed his eyes, basking in the feel of her.

"I did, do you want to wait to eat?"

"Yeah, might as well or we won't be able to eat at club," she kissed the middle of his back before walking off, disappearing down the hall that led to the front door. Shivers went up his spine, God the things she did to him. She came back into the kitchen taking the cup of coffee from him. He watched as she took a medicine bottle off the counter, and took two pills from it before popping them in her mouth, chasing it with her coffee. She looked over at him with a smile, "What?"

"What was that?"

"Oh, nothing, just some pills I gotta take."

"For what?"

"Um, you know to keep things right I guess, it helps with my hormone levels."

"Oh."

"Yeah, no big deal, so the bathroom's open if you want to take a shower."

"I think I will," he said, kissing her cheek before walking down the hall with his coffee in hand.

He loved her house, he could see his self living here, but they would have to keep the condo since they both worked in Nashville, or maybe they could find another house like this one, since he really did like this layout.

What was he thinking? He has sex with Elli once and he is already thinking about moving in with her?

He needed help.

Shea shook his head as he showered quickly. When he looked in the mirror he glared at the stubble on his chin but it wasn't like he came prepared, so he threw on his clothes from last night. He was tying his shoes when Elli came back in; she was wearing a brown skirt with some ivory tights and an ivory blouse that hung big off her shoulders. Her hair was still up in the towel as she breezed by his smelling like the mango shampoo he had just used. He was gonna have to get some of it, so he would always have her scent on him.

Shea was sitting on the porch watching Adler run through the yard when Elli stepped out in some brown heels. She smiled at him before calling Adler in.

"So isn't it called the walk of shame when you are caught in the clothes from the night before?" He laughed as he stood up; Elli locked the door then turned to look at him, laughter dancing in her eyes.

"Maybe for other people, but I would never walk in shame after last night," he said, wrapping an arm around her waist as they walked down the stairs, "By the way, you look good."

"Why thank you," she said with a grin as she climbed into the truck after he open the door for her. He went around the car, got in before driving off. They went to the mall in Clarksville, and even though everyone in the Gap gave him a look, he wore the clothes he bought out of there. He had picked a yellow button up shirt with some nice khaki pants since from what Elli said about the club, it was pretty classy. He was a little nervous about his chucks, so he went ahead and got some canvas shoes to while he was there.

They left the mall and drove about 15 minutes before driving down the drive for the Clarksville Country Club. Shea was starting to think every place had a long drive way in this town. After driving past golfers and tennis courts they finally pulled up in front of the pretty large white building. It had large windows that line the place, with double glass doors, and flowers galore. Shea got out as the valet help Elli out, he came around the truck handing the valet a tip before taking Elli's hand in his.

As they walked, people would stare at Elli than looked up at him before whispering to each other. He wasn't sure if hockey was popular in Clarksville, so he didn't know if they knew who he was, but they definitely knew who Elli was.

"Ms. Fisher," a tall balding man said as he walked in front of them, Elli smiled nicely.

"Hello, Mr. Johnson, how are you?"

"I'm fine darlin', vistin' your daddy?"

"Yes sir, we are late, so if you'll excuse us," she said pulling Shea along towards a lady that stood behind a podium. "Ugh, I hate this place," she muttered before giving the lady her dad's name, the lady smiled at Shea than led them out onto the Terrence. The room was large, filled with about ten tables; the walls were blue with brown trim that lined the floors, windows, and doors. It was very classic, a lady sat in the corner playing a harp as people enjoyed the brunches. As Elli and Shea past each table, people would look up, staring at Elli, but not him. He was used to everyone staring at him that it was new having everyone stare at Elli. Not that it was bad, but different that's for sure. Elli's dad, Michael, was sitting at a table on the other side of the room, by a large window out looking the front nine. He stood as they got closer, a big welcoming grin on his face.

"Eleanor," he said, kissing her palms, than the side of her lips, it must be the way he always greeted her, it was nice. He smiled up at Shea, shaking his hand hard, "Shea, how are you? So glad you could come."

"I'm good, thank you for having me," Shea said as he pulled out the chair for Elli beside her dad, Elli smiled up at him as she sat, Michael sat down as Shea pulled out the puffy chair and sank down it. It had to be the most comfortable chair he had ever sat in. He looked at Elli and Michael to see if they thought the chairs were awesome, but they were just settling in, not paying attention to him or basking in the awesomeness of the chair like he was. Nothing was said as a waitress came up, getting their drink orders.

"I'm surprised you're not working Eleanor," Michael said after taking a drink of his water, Elli looked up from her nails that she was picking at. He was starting to notice that as a nervous habit of hers.

"I took the weekend off since Shea is leaving tomorrow night. Alice and Ryan are doing the weddings I had today, and Jack, Alice's brother is doing the birthdays."

Michael nodded his head, "Where's Harper?"

"She took off this weekend too, her boyfriend is actually Jakob Titov, so she is spending the weekend with him too," Elli said with a grin, Michael smiled.

"Boyfriend huh? Interesting."

"To say the least." They shared a laugh, before Michael looked over at Shea.

"I really am glad to see you Shea, when I called Eleanor this morning and she said she'd call you, I have to say I was surprised. I could have sworn after last night you would run for the hills," Shea smiled as Michael laughed, and Elli looked nervous. "Sometimes I wonder about my family, me and Eleanor here are the only normal ones I think, would you think so darling?"

"Yes daddy," Elli answered with grin as the waitress came back for the orders. He ordered different from them; he went for the classic bacon and eggs with pancakes, while Elli and her dad got sausage, eggs, and grits. Even though he lived in the south, he couldn't do the damn grits, they were disgusting in his opinion. Elli smiled at him, knowing what he was thinking since they had had this discussion before.

"You know Shea, Olivia is quick to point out Elli's failures, but not her accomplishments."

"I noticed that," Shea said reaching for his glass of orange juice. "Why is that?"

"Oh, it's simple, she's jealous." Shea found himself choking on his orange juice that was probably the last thing he expected Michael to say.

"Excuse me?"

"It's simple really, she wanted to be on Broadway, and she wanted to marry into the Yates family. When Elli done both, Olivia was livid, but then Elli got real sick, and she wasn't kicked off Broadway like Olivia tells everyone, she was asked to lose the weight but couldn't so she never went back, and even when she did lose the weight, she was already in her new career and I guess she never wanted to go back."

"It isn't that I didn't want to go back, daddy, it's just I don't know if I'm as good as I was, I mean I used to sing every day, now I only do it in the shower or when I'm driving."

"But you're happy?" he asked, Elli looked over at Shea. She beamed at him, before looking back at her dad.

"I am."

"Then it is done with, but for some reason your mother can't let it go," He reached for Elli's hand, squeezing it lightly as he looked at Shea, "and then the thing with that piece of shit Justin, thank God, she got rid of him, he told everyone he left her, but I know he would never leave her, he had it too good with her," Michael lean back, letting the waitress give him his food, Elli was looking down at her plate, a little red covering her cheeks. After the waitress placed their food down, Michael continued "You know, with the trust fund and the inherence from her grandparents and the inherence she will get from her uncle, then the part from me, she is a valuable thing to have, not only money wise, that's not what I mean darling."

"I know daddy," Elli said with a smile just for him.

Michael looked back at Shea, and said, "But because she is the most amazing girl in world, right baby girl?"

"Daddy..," Elli groaned with blush covering her cheeks.

Whoa, Shea was missing something. He looked over at Elli as Michael looked over at her too.

"Now darlin' I haven't embarrassed you have I? I'm sorry."

She shook her head, smiling weakly at him, "No daddy, I just haven't told Shea all that."

They both looked at him as he placed his fork down, "So what? Are you loaded or something?"

Elli shook her head yes, "I didn't think it matter."

"It doesn't, but you know I'm loaded," he didn't want to argue with her in front of her dad, but damn it! She has kept so much from him. "Babe, you haven't told me anything."

"I have, I didn't tell you about my past or my money, everything else is what's important. Is this going to be an issue?"

He narrowed his eyes at her, she had a little sass to her voice, and it was pissing him off, "Should it? Because since you didn't tell me, you must have thought I would make an issue of it."

"No I just didn't tell you cause you see the way these people around here treat me, I don't want you to treat me different."

"Oh come on Elli, like I would."

She shrugged her shoulders, "You're right, I didn't tell you cause I don't tell anyone in Nashville, the only people that know is here in town, my family don't even know how much I have, or will have, they just all know I have money."

"Only I do," Michael said with a small smile, "What can I say Shea, she's a complex gal."

"You can say that again," Shea agreed as he started eating again. They were going to have a long discussion tonight, well on second thought tomorrow probably…on the way to the airport.

When he felt Elli's hand reach for his, he looked up at her. She gave him a weak smile, and he squeezed her hand. He couldn't be mad at her, he loved her too much.

"Shea, did I hear right yesterday, your family lives in Boston right?"

Shea nodded his head as he looked up at Michael, "My mom and dad do, my twin sister lives in Nashville."

"I've heard of her, she's a big party planner."

"Yes."

"She married James Justice, his family owns a lot of real estate up in Nashville and some surrounding counties right?"

Okay, should he be creep out?

"Yes, how do you know that?"

"I know Jason's family, me and his father play golf. He had made the comment that you were his daughter in laws' brother."

"Oh, I thought maybe you did a background check on me or something," he said with a nervous laugh.

Elli laughed, and then smiled at her father, "Hell, don't put it past him Shea, he probably did."

Shea looked from Elli to Michael, Michael was laughing, "Oh I did, but can you blame me? My daughter is dating you."

Shea smiled nervously, "I guess not."

"Daddy your creeping him out, quit," Elli said, smacking Michael playfully on the arm, Michael let out a booming laugh, and started eating again. Shea looked over at Elli and she was smiling sweetly at him, he smiled back, taking her hand in his since she had moved it to the table. They continued eating, talking about Elli's business, the weddings she had been doing since apparently a lot of them were clients or friends of her dad. They talked hockey, which was cool since Michael kept up with him and Elli. A fruit parfait was brought out while Michael was in a story about Elli singing for the first time when she was three. Shea happen to look up, and saw his boss walking towards them, a big grin on his face.

"Oh, hell." Elli and Michael looked him questionably as Bryan Fisher's booming voice greeted them.

"Eleanor Fisher, you best on get up and give your Papa a big ole kiss and hug," Elli whipped her head around, and then stood up quickly, wrapping her arms around Bryan with a squeal. Bryan was bigger than Michael, he had more muscle to him, but seeing them together, you couldn't deny they were brothers. Which pissed Shea off; he should have noticed the family resemblance sooner so he could have went to Bryan, talked to him about dating Elli. Michael stood up as Shea did, shaking hands with Bryan, then giving him a back slapping hug.

"Well I'll be, you're the last person that I thought would be sitting at this table, Shea Adler," Bryan said shaking Shea's hand tightly, while giving him a look that scared the living shit out of him. "I thought when Michael told me one of my players was dating my Eleanor it had to Jakob or Sergei, not Shea Adler." Bryan went around the table, sitting between Michael and him. Shea looked over at Elli, and she looked nervous, but had a smile on her face.

"What Papa? I ain't good enough for Shea Adler?" She teased boldly, Shea smiled before looking over at Bryan.

"Oh no sugar plum, you're way too good for him, but here's my question," He paused for dramatic effect, because Bryan Fisher loved nothing but the dramatics. Bryan then narrowed his eyes at Shea, he felt his heart pick up in speed, this man was his boss, he signed the million dollar checks that Shea got, "Is this serious or is she just like all them other girls I've seen coming in and out of your box."

"Papa, leave him alone," Elli complained, grabbing on to Shea's hand, and giving him a forgiving smile, "Papa is a little hard to deal with when it comes to me," she bit her lip and smile nervously, "I guess I should have told you that huh?"

"It would have been nice," Shea said with a laugh, "And no, Bryan, she isn't like those women. I think we both know she's different."

Bryan laughed loudly, turning heads of the other patrons, "Oh I know that, I'm just making sure you do."

"I do."

"Well good, I really hate to get my ass kicked when I try to kick my 6,3, 230lbs star captain's ass, I'm pretty sure that wouldn't look good." Everyone laughed at that, and with that breaking the tension, the rest of the morning went great, that was till Elli had to go to the bathroom. She left the guys at the table after shooting her dad and uncle a look. Nothing was said as all three men leaned back in their chair, looking each other over.

"So here's the deal Adler," Bryan finally said, leaning onto the table, Michael sat back in his chair, shaking his head. "You're too good of a hockey player for me to ruin your career so I'll just break your pretty little face if you hurt my niece, I should just go ahead and do it because you weren't even man enough to come and tell me you were datin' her."

"He didn't know about you Bryan, Eleanor didn't tell him."

Bryan shook his head, "That girl." Shea sat up straighter, looking Bryan in the eyes.

"If I would have known about you Bryan, I would have come to you, yeah my track record with women isn't the best, but I have always been honest and straight forward with you on anything you ask me."

"You have, that's why when I came in and saw your damn mug I was pissed as hell, I just don't understand how Elli even met you, I am pretty good at keeping her away-" It was like a light bulb went off in his head, then he smiled, "The team shoot."

"I saw her, and I can honestly say that I couldn't breathe," Shea said, laying his heart out for the two men to see, "I am in love with her, no, I haven't told her but I will tell you two. You guys have nothing to worry about. I don't want to hurt her."

Both men thought it over as Shea looked at the bathroom, where the hell was Elli?

"You might not want to hurt her Shea, and I believe you on that son, but that girl is emotional and insecure as hell, she's got some issues and I want nothing more than for my baby to be happy, but I'm just worried," Michael said, shaking his head. "Her mother and siblings have messed her up bad, and that son of a bitch Justin didn't help either."

"I'm not going to hurt her," Shea said as he looked Michael in the eye, "I can't, because if she left me, I don't know what I would do."

Michael and Bryan laughed, as they both leaned back in the chairs, going on two of the legs, it was so country in the classy place that Shea was worried they might get kicked out.

"Damn, he's got it bad," Michael muttered, Bryan smiled over at Michael, smacking his arm.

"Can you blame him? It's our Eleanor, she's captivating."

Captivating, what a great way to describe her.

"Harper! I have to go, Shea is out with my daddy and Papa, I gotta go!" Elli yelled as she washed her hands, Harper had called while she was using the bathroom.

"Tell me what happen!"

"My family did what they always do, and then Shea yelled at me all the way home for keeping things from him-"

"I thought you told him about everything!"

"No I didn't tell him shit!"

"Then all that you brought on yourself."

"I know!"

"Okay, so keep on."

God, she drove Elli crazy. "Then he dropped me off and drove off basically breaking up with me-"

"Oh no!"

"I'm with him now Harper, I mean you know it works out."

"I know but still, your heart must have hurt when he left."

The tears came hot and fast to her eyes, but thankfully didn't fall, "It did, but it was my fault. He came back about half an hour later, I showed him the house, he didn't think I was a crazy stalker fan and then...we had crazy monkey sex all night!"

"SAY WHAT!?"

"Now I must go! He's out there with my Papa, Harp, Papa."

"Ahh, you better call with details later!"

"I will, bye." Elli hung her phone up and headed out towards the table. Things were going well, nothing too bad. Except for her Papa showing up, that was unexpected and totally her daddy's fault, but Shea was handling it well. Elli headed to the table just as everyone started standing; they all turned when she reached the table. Shea reached for her jacket, holding it out for her.

"We're leaving?"

"Yes Ellibug, we have meetings this afternoon, Shea said something about a dinner with his sister."

"Yeah," Elli nodded before wrapping her arms around her daddy's waist. "Thanks for brunch."

"Oh baby, anything for you," he whispered, kissing her cheek. She released him, hugging her Papa hard.

"Wanna go to one of the away games with me darlin'? Maybe the one in Florida, spend some time on the beach?"

"Sure, let me know the date, and I'll work something out if I have an event."

"Which you will, like always," Bryan said with a grin as he kissed her cheek, "I don't think I scared him too bad," he whispered in her ear as he hugged her tightly.

"Hopefully not," she said as he shook hands with Shea, they all walked out together and waited for their cars from valet in silence. Elli shivered since it was started to get crazy cold, gotta love Tennessee weather since last week it was 80 and this week it 60. Shea wrapped his arms around her from behind, hugging her close to him. She smiled at the feel of his hard body against her soft one, when she saw her daddy and Papa watching them, she became nervous but hell they might want to get used to it, Shea wasn't going anywhere, she hoped.

After leaving the club they drove back to Elli's house, were they gathered up her bag and Adler, before jumping in separate cars and driving back to Nashville. Shea had complained about her driving, but when he left how was she supposed to get home? She wanted to see him off at the airport and she needed a car to get home, he agreed but was not happy about it.

When they got to his condo, she put her things in his room, as he stayed in the kitchen setting up Adler's bowls. It was so cute how much he adored Adler, he was just as excited about having Adler at the house as Adler probably was about a sleep over somewhere else.

"Baby, we need to go get him a dog bed, we forgot his at the house." Elli rolled her eyes as she came out of the room.

"Shea, he can sleep on the floor for a night."

"No, I want him to feel at home, we'll run to Pet Smart real quick, he can go with us." Adler looked up at Shea lovingly, and Elli again rolled her eyes.

"Whatever, what time do we need to be at your sister's?" she asked as she grabbed the leash and hooked Adler up, he started running in circles from excitement making her laugh as Shea chuckled.

"Six, so we have time to run out and then come back and relax, maybe-" He pulled her to him, and she grinned up at him, "Maybe I can seduce you?" he wiggled his eyes brows at her causing her bust out in a fit of giggles.

"Shea Adler!" she pushed him away and started for the door, when she reached the door she looked behind her and he was grinning at her. "We'll see."

"Oh will we now?"

"Maybe."

After a trip to Pet Smart, Shea, Elli, and Adler walked out with over two hundred dollars in stuff that Shea insisted on paying for. Elli shook her head as she watched Shea load everything into the car. New bed, leash, collar, bowls, a dog car seat, a 40lb bag of the best food in the store, toys, toys, and more toys, oh and some bones and treats.

"Shea you over spent on a dog that doesn't even live with you."

"Hey, Adler is my bud, so if I want to spend money on him I will, plus when you need to stay at the condo while I'm gone, Adler can come."

"You're ridiculous."

"And you like me."

"I do," she said with a huff as went to put Adler in his new car seat. She had been wanting one for him but never got around to getting one. She was jealous that Shea was the one to buy it for Adler and not her. The dog already adored him! Anytime he was around, Elli didn't even matter, damn traitor dog!

After loading everything up and going through the Taco Bell drive thru, they headed back to the condo, where Shea unloaded everything and played with Adler leaving Elli to watch on the couch. After about thirty minutes of watching them play catch, Elli cleared her throat.

"What happen to playing with me?" she asked, Shea laughed while petting Adler's head.

"Awe, is your mommy jealous?" he asked Adler, Adler let out a bark, and Shea nuzzled his nose against Adler's head, before crawling over to Elli, putting his head in her lap as he laid on the couch. She moved her fingers through his hair, as he looked up at her, smiling. "I love your dog."

"I know, he loves you too." They sat for a moment watching Adler run back and forth bringing all his toys into the kitchen where his bed was. "Was my Papa and Daddy real bad when I went to the bathroom?"

Shea shook his head, "Not really, Bryan threatened to break my pretty face, but other than that nothing too bad."

"He's just over protective of me, he never had kids."

"I know, that's why I'm not letting it bother me."

"It means a lot to me that you went today and last night." He looked up at her, cupping her cheek.

"Elli, don't you get that you mean a lot to me?" She shrugged her shoulders, and he dropped his hand into his lap, he looked at her for a moment, and then asked "Do I mean a lot to you?"

"Of course you do."

"You never say I do, and like I'm bursting with feelings for you, I feel like a damn girl," Elli smiled, "I just need to know if you feel what I feel."

"I do Shea, if I didn't I wouldn't be freaking out about you leaving, or hello, I had sex with you."

He smiled as he gave her a very naughty look, "Yes you did, and for the first time ever I don't want to leave for the road trip."

"Really?" she asked with a small sad smile.

"Yeah, I wish I could take you with me."

"I wish that too," she took a deep breath trying to keep the tears at bay, "I'm gonna miss you so much."

He cupped her face again, looking deep in her eyes, "Not as much as I'm gonna miss you," he then brought her down for a sweet kiss that curled her toes.

Elli was gonna miss Shea something stupid, and in a way she didn't know how she was going to handle it.

For the first time ever, Shea was doing dishes by hand. He hated doing them that way, and wondered why Grace didn't just use the damn dishwasher, but it was her house, who was he to tell her how to wash her dishes but then again,

"You need to use your dishwasher," he complained as he handed her a plate for her to dry.

"You hush," Grace said with a grin as she looked out the windows where the kids were running around the yard with Elli. James was in his office on a conference call while Shea and Grace did dishes. "She's so good with kids."

"She is."

"Everything okay with you guys?"

"Yeah, we had sex last night."

After making a face, she tried to smile but it didn't work and Shea just laughed, "Sorry but hearing about you having sex is still gross to me."

"Stop being a baby," he teased as he handed her another plate, "she went on birth control."

"Wonderful," she said sarcastically with another disgusted face.

"I've never done it without a condom."

With that statement Grace dropped the plate she was holding, "I mean really Shea! Ew!"

"What?"

"I don't want to know about you penis!"

"Shut up, I can't talk to anyone else about this, so you're the lucky contestant on 'Shea is going to have sex without protection and its freaking him out' show."

"Oh my god, you named the show?"

"Shut up, what if I blow in a minute after getting in her."

"Oh God please, go talk to James."

"No! He'll laugh at me!"

"So you want to make me gag! Come on Shea, I don't care what you do in bed."

"I'm worried though, dad always told me 'Don't be a fool, cover your tool' so I have."

Grace just look at Shea with nothing but disgust all over her face, "Are you kidding me right now? Come on, please."

"No really Grace, I'm really worried about this."

"So talk to Elli about it! Not me!"

"Fine, you're no damn help."

"You should have known that when you started this damn conversation!" She spat back as she picked up a plate and started drying. Shea just shook his head, damn woman was no help.

They continued on the dishes in silence, with the occasional scream from the kids or Elli outside, Shea looked over at Grace, "She's rich."

"Who?"

"Elli."

"Really?"

"Yeah, like wicked rich."

"Wow, I always thought she dressed too nice to be photographer, she has a sick style and it isn't a cheap one."

"Yeah, but that was another thing she has never told me. This morning I saw her take some pills, she said they were for hormones."

"Hmm, maybe she's just secretive."

"I don't like it."

"Well now that all her shits on the table just ask if there is anything else."

"I will," Shea handed her the last dish, when she was done drying it; he took Grace's hand in his. "Do me a favor?"

"Sure," she said turning to face him.

"Keep an eye on Elli for me, call her and stuff."

"Of course."

Just then the door open and Elli came in with Amelia on her hip and Ryan's hand in hers. "I think we're done," Elli gushed, breathing hard, Amelia kicked to be put done so Elli obliged. Amelia took off past Shea and Grace, down the hall to where James was coming up.

"She's her daddy's girl," Grace said with a shrug as Ryan took off running, "So I was thinking we'll go to the Adventure Science Center tomorrow with the kids before you leave."

Shea shook his head, grabbing Elli's hand, bringing her to him. She nuzzled into his side, wrapping her arms around his waist. "No can do, we're spending the day together."

"Oh."

Elli looked at Grace then up at Shea before looking back at Grace, "Or we can come with you."

"Baby, I want to spend the day in bed before I gotta go on a road trip."

"It's fine Elli," Grace said a little sharper than normal. "Things change when a new person comes in your life, spending the day in bed is way more fun than spending the afternoon with your family."

"Wow Grace, guilt tripping me?" Shea asked, Grace just looked at him with anger filling her eyes.

"You're going to be gone for two weeks, then mom and dad will be here and you won't have any time for us."

"I'm gonna go in the living room," Elli said as she dropped her arms, trying to get away.

"No, its fine baby," Shea said, wrapping her back up, "Grace, really?"

"What?"

"Stop, if I do remember correctly, I didn't see you for three months when you and James first got together."

"That was different, I was pregnant."

"So you being pregnant made it okay to not talk or see me for three months? But me spending the day with my girlfriend in bed instead of going with you is not okay? When I call and come see you at least every other day?"

"Whatever Shea, I'm not arguing with you."

"Cause I'm right."

"Whatever," Grace stomped out the room and Elli looked up at him.

"Maybe we should just go; I don't want to piss her off."

Shea put his finger on his lips, just as Grace came back in the kitchen just as he knew she would, she looked at Elli than Shea. "I'm sorry, I'm just not handling you leaving this time very well cause for some reason I feel like something is going to happen, so just be careful, but like I said I'm sorry," Shea let go of Elli to wrap Grace up in his arms. He knew that was the reason why they were fighting, when Grace got really nervous or worried about him, she took it out on him by fighting. She had been up his butt ever since he had gotten slashed on the collar. He loved her so much, so he took what she threw at him, she had been doing this to him since they were younger. No telling what Elli thought, probably thought they were crazy, "Just please be careful."

"I will, I'll call every night."

"You better."

Chapter 16

"How did you know Grace would come back?" Elli asked as they drove back his condo a couple hours later. After a tearful goodbye from Ryan and Grace, Shea had to get out of there. He hated when Ryan cried but seeing Grace cry; he couldn't handle it.

"When she gets real worried about me, she gets like that. She had been a little testy with me the past couple weeks."

"Wow, I'm glad you knew what was going on because for a second I thought she hated me."

Shea laughed, "No baby, she's just nervous."

"I am too; I don't want you to leave."

"I know," he said taking her hand in his; they drove the rest of the way home like that.

Nothing else was said until after they were washed up from the day, Adler was fed, and they were lying in bed together. The light was still on; the bed was turn down as they laid on top of the blankets. Shea was wearing just his boxer while Elli was wearing his AHL shirt and panties. She was lying on her back, while he laid on his side, tucked up against her side, running his hand up and down her thigh.

"Hey," he said since her eyes were closed, she opened them then smiled, "How did you get sick?"

She bit her lip, than shrugged her arms as she looked up at the ceiling, "I don't know."

"How old were you?"

"Nineteen."

"What happen?"

She shrugged her arms again, "It all happen so fast, like one minute I'm on top of the world. I was Roxie Hart for Chicago, it was my second show and I was so excited cause I had just signed my contract for a third show. I was dating a Yates, something my mother had wanted me to do since I was born, I had this beautiful apartment in New York, and I was spending more money than I should," She let out an empty chuckle as she moved her hands under her thighs, he guessed since she was picking at her nails. "I woke up and my jeans didn't fit, and I was like what the hell? So I stopped eating the way I was and went on an intense diet and started running, but I kept gaining. When I finally got to the doctor, I was already topping over two hundred pounds, had already lost my job, was packing up to come home and Justin was livid but he still stayed with me, which made no damn sense then, now it does, but still. Anyways, I got diagnosed with hypothyroidism, and I have been on medicine ever since."

"When you got on the medicine did you start losing the weight?"

"Yeah, but it was slow, it took 3 years for me to get where I am, and I still have problems. I still get real tired, and weak sometimes if I don't take my meds, I gain weight so stinkin' fast if I don't watch it, and depression sticks its head into my life every once in a while."

"Wow, but you're okay now right?"

"Yeah, if I take my meds and stay away from my mom," she said with a smile, he smiled back, kissing her temple.

"Will you get better? Or well you have to take the pills forever?"

"No, I have to take them for the rest of my life."

"Does it scare you?"

Because it scared the living shit out of him.

"No not too bad, I'm used to it now I guess. I guess when I get pregnant I'll probably be worried, since if I don't take my pills and take care of myself it could hurt the baby."

Shea nodded as he looked her over, she was so beautiful, he hated that something like this could happen to her, but in a way he was happy it did. He knew it was selfish but her going through what she did brought her to him, and now that he had her, he could never imagine her not being there.

"Do you miss it?"

She shook her head, he was surprised she knew what he was talking about; he guessed they were just that connected, "No, when I was singing I thought I would never be happy doing anything else, but I love what I do. I love taking pictures of people for them to keep that moment forever. I make good money, I can pay my employees, and pay all my bills and still have money for my shopping addictions, I have a beautiful house that I love, a dog that loves me when you are not around, and for the first time in a very long time, I'm happy." He smiled as she turned on her side, putting her hand on his cheek and the other on his neck. "Its cause of you, you know."

He gave her a sheepish grin, because if she knew how much she changed his life, she would probably run, he wanted to scream at her that he loved her but instead said, "Really?"

"Yes Shea, I have never loved my life, but you came along and flipped it upside down and I couldn't be happier. You make me happy."

His hand slid down her back from her hip, and he pressed her closer to him, meeting her mouth with his, kissing her hard. She melted against him, kissing him just as hard as she wrapped her arms around him, basically molding her body with his. He moved his hand up her body, pulling her shirt up as he went, and she let him causing him to smirk against her lips. She smiled back as he moved himself over her, pulling her shirt off and throwing it on the floor. Her arms folded over her stomach and she looked up at him with worry in her eyes.

"Shut the lights off," she said, he shook his head as he kissed one side of her mouth, then placed a kiss on her lips, bringing his lips to the other side of her mouth kissing it.

"No, I want to see you," he whispered as he sat back on his hunches, her thighs were touching his as her legs wrapped around his waist.

"Shea, I don't want you to see me naked in the light."

"Oh but baby," he said as he tried moving her dead locked arms away, he smiled down at her, "I want to see you." He finally got her arms moved and looked over her naked chest, her perfectly voluptuous breast, with her rosy hard nipples, her smoother than silk skin.

"Don't look at my stomach." she complained, trying to cover it again, but he wouldn't let her. He looked down her ribs to her soft looking belly. Her little belly button was surrounded by little white jagged lines; they ran along her hips too. "Shea quit, you're making me self conscious." He looked back up at her beautiful face.

"Show me what you think is a problem."

"I know you can see em, stop looking and kiss me."

"No, show me."

She let out a frustrated breath, and pointed to the marks around her belly button, "They are disgusting." He smiled, leaning his head down, placing feathery light kisses against each one of the marks. She let out a breathy sigh as he followed up her hips, to the side of her breast before taking her nipple in his mouth. He gave the same attention to her other breast before reclaiming her mouth with his. He pulled back too look down at her beautifully pink flushed face.

"I think your beautiful," he kissed her again, before pulling back to look deep in her eyes, "I love every imperfection on you, because they make you perfect, Elli." He kissed her nose as her eyes went wide, and tears rushed to her eyes, "You're perfect to me."

A tear leaked out the side of her right eye, and he smiled as he leaned his head down, kissing her with all the feelings that were welling up inside him. Kissing her before he bore his heart to her, telling her everything he was feeling, that he loved her with every ounce of his being, that he would never want anyone but her.

He slowly left her mouth, going down to her neck, where he suck and bit his way down to her collar bone, going back to down to her nipples, where he took her between his teeth as he gently kneaded and stroked her other breast. Her breathing picked up, coming out quick and shallow as he feasted on her swollen breast. When he got his fill he moved down her body, kissing her stomach, before pulling her panties off and continuing the kisses onto her hip bone. He placed soft wet kisses along her damp, moist needy place that he wanted nothing more than to be inside. He slowly opened her, and became harder at the site of the slick wetness of her excitement. He dove in, licking and sucking as he drove her to the edge. Her breathing was more erect, along with the hottest moans he had ever heard. She drove her hands through his hair pulling him closer to her, as her leg went over his shoulder, her other wide and open just for him. When she reached the edge, she came, wildly, explosively under his mouth as he just grinned cockily, he loved making her squirm and come just for him.

He bought her leg down, looking down at her body that was glistening with sweat. Her eyes were half lidded as she looked up at him with a small satisfied grin. "Damn, you're hot," he said as he reached into his night stand, ripping off his boxers as he grab a condom out the drawer and sheathed his hot, bulging shaft. He was rock hard, and ready to be inside her. She looked down at the evidence of his arousal with a sexy little grin, before turning over, getting on her hands and knees, looking over her shoulder at him.

He almost came at the sight.

He moved behind her, giving her a grin as he moved his hand over her sweet round ass, then to the inside of her thighs before sliding two fingers inside her, getting her even hotter than she already was. She let out a deep, shuddering moan as he moved his fingers in and out of her. He watched as her fingers tighten around his pillow and couldn't take it no more. Without much warning, he replaced his hard fingers with his even harder shaft, taking her inch by inch, slowly till he was inside her fully with a ragged gasp. She took in a breath as he moved out, then slammed back into her, losing all control as he moved into her lower body in a frenzied fervor.

Elli met every thrust with a soft sound of pleasure as sweat dripped down Shea's back. She looked over her shoulder at him, and he leaned forward taking her mouth with his, kissing her sloppily as she came uncontrollably, shuddering against him as her body clinched around his hard swollen shaft. With that he pulled back, grabbing a hold of her hips, and slammed into her once, twice, then a third time before he let out a cry of satisfaction as he released inside her.

He fell onto her as she fell onto the bed, her face in the pillows as his face buried into her hair. He fought for his breath, as did she as they laid, still connected with him on top of her. When their breathing finally returned to normal, Elli moved her face to the side so she could talk. "Shea."

"Yeah baby," he muttered in her hair.

"I can't breathe."

He chuckled as he removed his self out of her, rolling off her lying on his back. "Jesus, that was amazing."

"Epic, so damn epic," she said as she nuzzled into his side, kissing his chest, licking his nipple before looking up at him.

"I need to clean up, but I can't move." Elli smiled, kissing his chest again.

"Shea," she whispered, he looked down at her as she looked up at him, with a small smile on her face, "You make me feel so special."

"Baby, the word special has a lot more meaning when it comes to you."

Elli laid across Shea's chest in completely ecstasy. What in God's name was she waiting for? This man was a sex machine, sex on legs, a sex god! She had never come so hard in her life, he did things to her, and she wanted more. A lot more.

Shea ran his hands through her hair, then down her back, over her bottom, then went back up and started it all over again. It was hypnotic and soothing all in one. God, she adored this man.

She was gonna miss him so much.

"Tell me something I don't know." She smiled, before looking up at him; he had that satisfied grin on his face, along with his eyes only be partially open as he looked down at her. "I want to know everything."

"Umm? Well," she popped her head up on her hand, her other finger tapping her mouth as she thought. "My middle name is Rey."

"Eleanor Rey?"

"Yes, it's after my Papa."

"Gosh you're country as hell," he said with a laugh, she smacked his chest as she giggled.

"You love it."

"Oh I do, my 'country cutie with rockin' roll booty'," he said quoting one of her favorite country songs at the time.

"What's yours?"

"Ryan."

"Aw, was Ryan named after you?"

"But of course, kids awesome, I'm awesome, it was a done deal." Elli giggled as she rolled her eyes; he smiled, running his hand through her hair, putting behind her ear. "Tell me something else."

"Have I ever told you when my birthday is?"

He thought it over for a moment, "No, that's weird. When is it?" he said with a laugh, she smiled.

"In a month and a half, December 17."

"Really?!"

"Yeah."

"Well damn, good thing you told me, I'll have to get you something special, take you out somewhere nice. Make sure you have that night off, hell that day," Elli blushed as she shook her head.

"Don't even bother with it, my birthday has not been a big deal since I was six, my dad is the only one that makes a big deal about my birthday, and my friends have a dinner for me."

Shea shook his head aggravated, "Well it's important to me, so just planned to be spoiled that day."

"You don't even know if you'll be home."

"Oh I'll be home."

"You're gonna miss a hockey game for me?" She knew he was off, it was at the end of one of his breaks, and he had a home game two days after her birthday.

He smiled bashfully at her and then shook his head, which made her laugh. "But I promise we'll do something if I do have a game." She rolled her eyes, and laughed.

"You don't have a game; it's at the end of your break."

"Awesome, I was worried for a second there," She continued to laugh as she gathered her in his arms, so they were facing each other. "Mine was in May."

"I know, May 16th."

"Oh yeah, I forgot, crazy stalker fan," She gave him the meanest look she could but failed when she started giggling. He smiled, placing a sweet kiss against her mouth. "What am I going to do without you for two weeks?"

A sad smile replaced her wide happy one, and she shrugged her shoulders, "Probably the same thing I'm gonna be doing."

"Which is?" he asked with a playful gleam to his eyes.

"Go crazy."

Like always Shea wasn't packed to leave, Elli and Adler sat on his bed watching him run back and forth throwing things in his bag and then disappearing into the closet. Elli shook her head as she took a deep breath, letting out a sad sigh as she picked up his wrinkled clothes and folded them, putting them back in his suitcase neatly. She needed something to keep her hand busy or she would pick her nails all to hell. They had laid in bed all morning, feeding each other breakfast and just being with each other, both of them watching the clock as the morning progressed. Shea being Shea waited thirty minutes before having to leave to take a shower and pack. He wasn't even dressed as he ran through the condo like a chicken with his head cut off.

"Do you need help?" she asked sitting on the edge of the bed with her legs open, holding his shirt between her legs.

"Um, no baby, thanks," he said quickly as he went back into his closet. When he came out he was wearing one of his suits, and that's when it really hit Elli that he was leaving. She took another deep breath in, and got up leaving the room. Adler was on her heels as he followed her into the kitchen, where she got a bottle of water out of the fridge and started drinking it as leaned up against the counter. She glanced over at her phone that was lying beside the sink, it was blinking. She picked it up and there was a text from Harper.

So...this sucks. I don't want him to leave.

Elli shook her head, and typed back quickly.

I don't either, I feel like if I cry he'll think I'm stupid.

Harper answered back quickly.

Elli, I've been crying all morning, I'm pretty sure Jakob thinks I'm crazy.

Aw. Elli just smiled, she was so happy for Harper, loved that she had finally found her someone that meant something. Elli's phone beep again and she looked down to see another text from Harper.

I told him, I love him.

What!

I know, but I do. He said he loved me too.

Oh my god, Harper, that's awesome babe.

I'm so scared.

Don't be. He's amazing.

He is, but what if I cheat on him?

Okay, with anyone else that would shock them, but not Elli. She knew Harper would be nervous about that, but Elli would be there for her, like Harper had always been there for her.

Won't happen.

You sure?

Damn sure.

Thanks Elli, I'll see you soon?

Yeah, waiting on Shea to finish packing.

Elli laid her phone down just as Shea came into the kitchen, carrying his bags and laptop case. He laid everything on the couch, and bent down picking Adler up, hugging him close to his body. She was going to complain about Shea's suit but he wouldn't listen anyways.

"You take care of your mom, okay bud? See you soon," He kissed Adler's head before putting him back on his feet, looking over at Elli.

"Ready baby?"

Elli nodded, and they left, packing Shea's stuff in the back of his truck. Elli was nervous about driving it back from the airfield, but Shea assured her she would be okay. They rode in silence, Elli's hand in Shea's as he drove with their hands on his thigh. She was trying so hard not to cry but when they pulled up to the airfield and Elli saw the plane, her heart just broke. She knew she was being a baby, but it just sucked, she didn't want him to leave. Shea took in a deep breath, kissing the back of her hand before jumping out and opening the back of the truck, pulling out his bags. Elli got out of the truck, and went around the truck to help carry something. He gave her his laptop case, before shutting the back of the truck, and handing her his keys. She pocketed his keys as they walked up the walkway through the building to the strip that would take him to the plane.

Women and children stood around their hockey player, kissing and crying as they hugged them tightly. Elli saw Harper and Jakob making out and her heart broke at the sight of Harper's face, blood shot eyes with tears running down her face. Jakob had her face in his hand, trying to kiss away the tears that kept falling. Mary Ann stood with Alex, with their four little girls surrounding him, smiling with tears in their eyes. A man came up and took Shea's bags from him. After telling him thank you, Shea turned to look at Elli.

"So like I said, stay at the condo when you need too."

She nodded, "I will."

"I'll text before I call, just in case you're busy."

"Okay, I'll make sure to do the same," She looked down at the floor as the tears rushed to her eyes, she hated goodbyes. "You better keep you're GP up, I want you to get the Norris this year."

He laughed, pushing his glasses up on his face, "Will do, you'll be watching right?"

"But of course, I don't miss a game."

"Good," they both stood there, not touching or looking at each other, both not knowing what to say. "God, this sucks," he said in a sigh, making Elli smile.

"It really does."

She watched as his converses came a little closer to her canvas shoes, feeling his arms wrap around her waist. He nudged her face up with his fingers under her chin, making her look up at him. "I'll be gone for two weeks don't keep that face hidden for me," Elli gave him a small smile but she couldn't keep in the tears that leaked out and ran down her cheek in. She soaked in the sight of his face, the scars, the one dimple, his beautiful blue eyes, the glasses that drove her crazy, and the way his hair fell into his eyes. She wanted to make sure she wouldn't forget, even though she knew she wouldn't. Not only had she taken pictures of him all weekend, but his face would be forever burned into her memory. It was like he was doing the same, taking in everything about her. She wished she had done something with her hair, instead of throwing it up in a bun. Wished she had put on some better clothes, but she felt so comfortable in his shirt and her favorite jeans.

"I'm gonna miss you something stupid, Shea." she blurted out as the tears started falling faster, "I'm sorry, I'm such a baby," she complained wiping her eyes, and laughing. He took her hands down from her face, cupping her in his hands, running his thumbs along her cheeks as he looked deep into her eyes.

"I'm going to miss you more Elli, so much more."

Elli's lip wobbled as another round of tears fell down her cheeks, he brought her lips to his, kissing her long and hard. She wrapped her arms around his neck, pulling him closer, wanting to climb up his body and live in his arms as she kissed him. She wouldn't be able to kiss his beautiful mouth for two weeks, so she was gonna get her fill.

And boy did she.

When they finally parted, Elli noticed that people were walking back to their cars, wiping their eyes, and trying to calm their children. Elli looked back up at Shea, and he was looking at the plane before looking back down at her.

"I need to go, they are boarding."

Elli nodded, as she brought her lip between her teeth. "Be safe, and come home in one piece."

He nodded slowly before kissing her deeply once more, he took a step back, kissing her knuckles, and then looking up at her. "Don't go getting a new boyfriend," he teased with a wink as he started walking away, their hands still connected.

"Never."

He stopped, and then pulled her back to him, kissing her again. She savored it, not rushing him even though everyone was basically on the plane. He pulled back again, and this time he went, dropping her hand as he walked away from her. Elli watched every step he took, tears falling with every step, her heart pounding in her chest as she watched him board the plane, and the door shut. Since she was pretty sure watching the plane leave would break her, she turn and walked back to Shea's car. She heard the plane start, and then she heard it take off.

And he was gone.

Shea had to fight the tears that were threatening to fall. Walking away from Elli was his undoing; he didn't want to leave her, not even the thought of kicking some ass made him want to leave Elli. He wanted to be back in bed with her, her wrapped in his arms, giggling or moaning, whichever came first.

"Yo, Adler, who was that girl?" Shea looked up and over at Sergei, who was sitting next to Alex. Jakob was sitting next to him and what an ass he was; he hadn't even greeted his best friend yet.

"My girlfriend."

"Girlfriend? Shit Shea, who am I supposed to pick up chicks with now?" Shea shook his head, shrugging his shoulders.

"Not me, I'm a taken man."

"Wow, I thought I would never see this day. Shea Adler has a girlfriend, shit." Sergei shook his head as he put his headphones on. Shea look back down at his hands, wishing Elli's hands were in them.

"Sucks huh?" Jakob finally said, Shea nodded his head.

"I didn't think it was gonna be this hard."

"Me neither, Harper cried all morning."

"Elli didn't start till we got here," Shea shook his head, dropping his face in his hand. "I should have told her I loved her." Jakob took in quick breath. Shea looked over at him, giving him a cocky smile, "Yeah, I love her."

"So why haven't you told her?"

Jakob was probably the only guy Shea would ever say what he was about to say, because he knew Jakob wouldn't laugh, he would support Shea. "Because I'm scared she doesn't love me."

Jakob nodded, opening his computer, where a picture of him and Harper smiling looked back at him. Then he shrugged his shoulders as he said, "Well maybe she's waiting for you to say it, maybe she is scared too."

"Maybe, but I'm too chicken shit to put myself out there."

"Well than, you'll never know my friend."

That was the last thing that was said the whole trip to Phoenix, it seemed the whole plane was a little sullen, no one was talking like usual, everyone was focused on their computers, or eReaders. So Shea pulled out his computer, opening it, looking at his favorite picture of Elli in the park on their first date. He got his computer out to play a game, but all he could do was stare at Elli's picture.

It was going to be a long two weeks.

Chapter 17

Having Shea back in Elli's arms was heaven. He was so warm, so thick, God she loved holding onto him. She nuzzled her nose in his back, he was a harrier than the last time they had been together, but she didn't care, he was in her arms, and she had missed him so much. She took a deep breath in, and then woke up coughing her ass off.

"Adler!" Elli screamed as she pushed Adler out of Shea's bed, "I've told you a billion times! Shea's bed is not for you! He bought you a bed, now go on!"

Adler gave her a sad doggy look before running down the hall. Elli fell back into the bed, with her face in her hands.

She was losing it.

Dreaming of Shea, thinking he was Adler? Pathetic. Elli threw the blankets back and got out of the bed in a huff. After making the bed, she went into the bathroom, showering and doing her morning routine. She walked across the room to the closet, getting dress for the day in a pair of red tweed pants and a black blouse that had red flowers all over it. After strapping her red Jimmy Choo peep toe pumps, she went down the hall towards the kitchen.

She had been doing this for the past week.

In Shea's condo.

Yup, she hadn't left. She had went home after leaving Shea on Sunday, but after sitting in her house all alone for about ten minutes, she found herself packing a bag of clothes and grabbing Adler before high tailing it back to Nashville, to Shea's condo. She felt so much better there with all Shea's stuff surrounding her since she missed him so much. They talked every chance they got, which if Elli had it her way it would be all day, but she did have to work during the day, and he had to work at night, so they were stuck talking into the wee hours of the morning.

With the holidays coming up, Elli calendar wasn't full with outside events like it had been the last couple months. Her weekends were booked solid but she had been home by seven every night since Shea had been gone. Which figures, now that she had a man that wants to spend time with her, and she actually has time to be with him, he's gone.

Elli shook her head as she poured her coffee in one of Shea's travel mugs; she hadn't realized that it was gonna be this hard being away from him. They had only been together for two months but she was acting as if they had been together for ten years or something. Moping around, crying when things would remind her of him, wearing his shirts to bed, not cleaning up the messes he left just so she could feel like he was there just a few minutes before her. Whoever thought up the phrase 'Absence makes the heart grow founder' was an idiot.

Absence makes a bitch go crazy.

Elli grabbed the leash for Adler, hooking him to it before going out into the freezing cold weather. There was no in between in Tennessee, it was either stupid cold or stupid hot, except for when it's pretty for like two days. It drove Elli crazy, but she would never leave Tennessee. She loved it too much.

Adler was okay staying at Shea's which had surprised Elli, she thought the dog needed a field but obviously he could do his business wherever and be happy. When he was finished, they headed back upstairs where Elli packed up her things to leave and Adler went to his bed, getting comfy.

"Now you stay out of Shea's room, stay in your bed, I'll be home later. Mommy loves you, bye." She locked the door and headed to work, she loved only being ten minutes from the studio. It was great to sleep an extra hour and not rushing through rush hour traffic in the mornings and evenings. It was nice, the only thing she needed was Shea and things would be perfect.

The studio was empty when she arrived, Harper would drag her ass in around noon, complaining about how not having sex was ruining her life, and then start crying because she just couldn't cheat on Jakob. She was getting on Elli's nerves but being the best friend she was, she dealt with it. Holding Harper when she cried; or assuring her that the guys would be back before they knew it, it seemed to calm Harper down some, even though it did nothing for Elli. She was convinced that the next seven days were gonna drag just like the first five.

After turning on the lights and the iHome so soft music played, Elli headed back to her office for her appointment book. She couldn't remember who she had today, but she did remember someone being there for a three hour shoot. After turning on her computer, she waited for it to boot up as she drunk her coffee. She glanced at the clock, it was almost nine, Shea was in Los Angeles, it was only seven there, so she would wait to call, or he would call when he got up.

When the computer loaded up, and a picture of Shea and Elli smiled at her, she smiled back before clicking on her icon for her appointment book. When the page came up for the day; she read Harper's name just as Harper came in the studio, calling her name. Elli was confused as she went out from behind her desk, and started for the hall.

"Harper, why are you in my appointment book, taking up my whole-" She stopped talking when she saw Harper had her two sister's with her. Reese and Piper had always been close with Elli, all four girls had grown up together, and would always say that Elli was the fourth sister. So the biggest grin went across her face as she went up to the girls, hugging them tightly.

"Oh my god! When did y'all get in!? I thought you weren't coming in till the end of the month," she gushed, as they grinned back at her.

"We finished exams early, and rolled out," Reese said, she looked a lot more like Harper than Piper did. She had the same dark brown hair down to the middle of her back, big brown eyes, with pouty lips, while Piper had blondish brown hair, cute little brown eyes, and plain soft lips, but Piper was just as beautiful as Harper and Reese, just in a soft kind of way, while Harper and Reese were in your face gorgeous.

"Yup, they are home early so I brought them along, since you know Reese is bad ass at makeup and Piper does some mean ass hair, huh sis?" Harper said wrapping her arms around her little sisters. They both beamed up at her, nodding back at Elli.

"Why? What's going on? Why did you shut out my whole morning?" Elli asked as all three girls just grinned at her.

"Because Eleanor dear, we are doing a photo shoot, and we're the models."

"Excuse me?" Elli asked as Harper threw the bag she was holding down to the ground, and unzip it, pulling a sexy little purple number.

"We are doing a shoot for the boys, they will love it!" Harper gushed, bouncing up and down. Elli started giggling, there was no way in hell Elli was putting on a damn bra and panties set and taking pictures of herself for Shea.

"No fucking way."

"Yes!" all three girls yelled at her.

"Elli, you've lost so much weight, this will be awesome." Reese gushed.

"You're so stinkin' beautiful, we got some hot heels to go with each outfit. We even made sure to get some with lace that will cover your belly if you don't want to show it!" Piper added with a huge smile.

"Yeah, and Shea would love it, you know he would."

"No."

"Yes," Harper said with a little more force "You're doing this, because if you don't I'm breaking up with you!"

"Excuse me?!" Elli said, "What are we six?"

"I mean it Eleanor Rey, I worked all week on this, I paid for my sisters to come in early, you are taking damn pictures with me for our boyfriends, and you're gonna fucking love it!"

Elli smiled, looking over at Reese and Piper, before looking at Harper, "Did you just say that Jakob is your boyfriend?"

Harper froze, she had yet to admit that they were together, yeah she told him she loved him, but still had not admit that there was a relationship. "If I say yes will you take pictures with me?"

"Yes, and you have to change your Facebook relationship status too."

Harper narrowed her eyes, Elli swore she would call the whole thing off, but nope, she pulled out her phone, poked around at it for a moment, then she turned it to Elli, showing her that she had changed her relationship status. "I am Jakob Titov's girlfriend."

"You suck, I swore you were gonna crack," Elli complained smacking her arm as everyone giggle.

"Let's get started!" Reese said with a clap of her hands, and that was just the beginning of a crazy day.

Shea skated around the practice rink in Los Angeles twenty nine times before stopping for a drink. He found that if he works his self to the point of exhaustion, he was able to sleep better since ever since he left Elli five days ago, he couldn't fall asleep because he was thinking about her nonstop. Shea didn't know he could miss someone so much, even with being away from his parents, sister, and the kids, he never missed them the way he missed Elli.

It was crazy, really, Shea hated not being around her, not being able to feel her body against his, hold her soft small hands, kiss her beautiful, naughty mouth, kiss that sweet neck of her, shit just be with her! At night he would toss and turn wondering who she was with or if some guy had talk or flirted with her that day. He knew he was crazy for thinking the things, but it still messed with his head. He was so worried that while he was gone she would find someone else that he would drive himself mad, texting and calling just to see what she was doing and who she was with. He hated that he was doing it, but he couldn't help it.

Shea had called Grace about it the day before, and she just told him that it happens, that when you love someone that sometimes your mind can mess with you, even when you know in your heart that person will be waiting for you. He knew Elli wasn't the type to cheat or be deceiving but for some reason he just kept thinking that some hot successful business man, that didn't travel would approach her, and she would forget about him.

Shea shook his head at the thought. He was going mad, and it wasn't fair to Elli to think that way. He trusted her, he did, he just didn't trust, Bill...yeah he named the imaginary successful business man that didn't travel, that was gonna steal his sunshine away.

Yup, the Assassins' captain was going bat shit crazy.

He stood beside the boards, disgusted with himself, drinking his Gatorade, when Jakob and Alex came out the ice. Of course Shea was the first one out, he always was, he was also warmed up, and now he had to wait for the rest of the team to warm up too.

"Adler, what's up with you dude?" Alex asked as he skated around for a moment, "First on the ice, first to bed. It's weird. You okay?"

"I'm fine," he answered as he put his drink down, grabbing his stick before heading out to the middle of the ice.

"No you're not, what's up?" Alex said again, looking over at Jakob, Jakob just shook his head.

"Leave him alone, Welch. He's obviously in a mood," Jakob said, skating off. Shea sent Alex a look before following Jakob around the rink for a second warm up.

After practice Shea sat back at the hotel while everyone else went out for lunch. He made it a point everyday to send Elli an email with a video attached of a song that reminded him of her. He was looking through his playlist when Jakob came into the room, throwing himself on the bed beside Shea's. Jakob and him always shared a room on the road, had been doing it for years.

"I thought you went out with the guys," Shea said, scrolling down his list.

"Nah, thought you needed to talk." Shea looked up, confused.

"Huh?"

"You know, talk, where your mouth moves and words come out."

"Shut up asshole, I know what talking is, I just don't know why I need to talk."

Jakob shook his head, a small smile on his face, "Dude, your moody as hell lately. I don't know what your problem is but let it go. Did you and Elli get into a fight or something?"

"No, I just...I don't know."

"What's going on with her dude? You don't call to go out no more, you are always with her, is it really that serious?"

"Yeah, it is."

"Really?"

Shea looked up at his long time best friend. He knew it was weird for Shea to be in a relationship but he was, he had changed.

"Things are different now Jake, I'm not the guy I was six months ago."

Jakob laughed, "Well no shit Shea, I knew that, but are you seriously for real about her? I mean we all know I'm for real about any girl I get involved with but are you?"

Shea didn't even have to think, he just nodded, "I am, I love her."

"Good, you're getting older, you need to settle down."

Shea cringed, "I never said anything about marriage, Jake."

Jakob laughed, pulling his computer out from under the bed, "You didn't have to; you love her, so it will only be a matter of time. Since this is the one and only girl you have spent more than a day with."

Shea just shook his head, "You sound like my mom."

"Cause she's a smart woman."

Shea just smiled as he looked through his playlist, Jakob was so easy going, so easy to talk to. That's probably why he was Shea's best friend; he had always been good to Shea as Shea was always good to him.

Everything was quiet till Jakob started screaming, he jumped up, tearing apart the room.

"What the hell are you doing?"

"I need my phone!" he yelled, Shea pointed to the TV, where his phone laid right beside Shea's. "Ahh, thanks!" he yelled picking it up, he then pushed some buttons, till a huge smile came across his face.

"Hey there," he said into the phone as he sat down, "I saw your status, oh no you don't, don't deny it baby girl, I saw it! Haha, I hate to say this baby, but I told you so. Haha, okay, love you, alright, bye."

Jakob smiled over at Shea, "Harper changed her relationship status to dating me."

"Wow, that's awesome dude."

"I thought so."

They sat back in their bed, looking at their computers. Shea decided he would make Elli a playlist and send it to her for her iHome, he was just beginning it when his phone rang. It was Grace.

"Hey sis."

"Hey! How are you doing today?"

"Good, tired, about to take a nap after I send Elli this email."

"Cool, I'm so glad you have learned how to use that stuff. Ryan just loves his emails from you."

"Yeah, it's was about time, huh?"

"Well past it," Grace said laughing

"Have you seen Elli or talked to her?"

"No, I've been meaning to but been so busy, I'll call her Monday, maybe she'll want to do lunch with me and the kids, then go shopping for a little while."

"Sounds good, make sure you do. I miss her."

"I know you do," she acknowledged, "Ready for the game tonight?"

"Yup, you guys gonna watch?"

"But of course, thinking you might win tonight?"

"I hope too."

Since they have lost every game since they had been on the road. He just didn't understand it, it was like his head wasn't in the game or something. He hadn't had one point the whole time they had been out, nothing. It was embarrassing actually.

"You need too; you haven't been playing too good."

Leave it to Grace to tell him the truth, he knew he had been sucking lately, and even Elli wouldn't comment on it, she just ignored the whole fact and talked about something else.

"I know, I don't know what's going on."

"You're love sick, missing your woman, you big sap!"

"You shut up," he muttered, even though she was right.

"You need to leave your feelings off the ice Shea, don't let your emotional issues mess with your game. You gotta learn to separate them. I know it's hard, you've never had to do this before, but it's time to put your big boy pants on and step up to the plate...I mean blue line, and play some damn hockey. My brother doesn't suck, so get your shit straight and play the damn game!"

The talk with Grace was what he needed because his head had been everywhere but where it needed to be and that was in the game. He just hoped he would remember that when he went out on the ice that night.

"Oh my god, Harper, your boyfriend is ridiculously hot," Piper giggled as she leaned back on the couch with a glass of wine, and a bowl of popcorn between her legs, "Like stupid, crazy hot. You lucky bitch."

"Oh girl, let me tell you, you should see him naked," Harper giggled, taking a hefty drink of her wine. It was the first time in days that Harper was happy. It was probably the first time in days for Elli too, they just loved Piper and Reese. They were two little balls of sunshine.

"I wish," Reese agreed while she shared the bowl of popcorn with Piper, Elli and Harper sat on the floor at the coffee table looking over the pictures as they watched the pregame on Shea's humongous TV. They were clicking through Harper's pictures, picking out her favorites, which included boobs, a little bit of lace, and crotch-less panties.

Yeah...

"Ooh, I like the black."

"Yeah...hot," Elli said, trying not to look, she had seen naked Harper all day, and she had seen more than she wanted of her best friend, but she had to admit, the pictures were hot. Piper had done an amazing job with Harper's hair, doing it in big curls, pulled up on one side with a huge black flower, while Reese did her makeup very bold. Needless to say, Harper was one hot mama when they were done with her, and Lord knew the girl wasn't shy. She was posing in ways that Elli didn't even know existed.

After picking out her favorite poses, Elli started editing. Between her and Harper, she was the best at it, and usually done all the edited for the studio. She could make people's skin look like a newborn baby's; she could make them skinner, hell she could do just about anything.

Elli was in the middle of erasing one of Harper's birth marks when Piper screamed out, "Holy shit! Is that him, Elli!?" Elli jumped at the ear piercing scream, and looked up at the screen to see her boyfriend laughing near the boards with one of the Kings' players. He looked positively scrumptious in his away uniform and it made Elli's mouth water at the sight.

"Why, yes it is," she cooed, watching as he hit the guy in the shin with his stick before skating off.

"Oh my god," Reese gushed, while Piper looked back and forth between the TV and Elli.

"Elli, he is gorgeous," Piper gushed, "I mean way hotter than Justin."

"I know, I can't believe it either," Elli laughed as Shea skated around, they were talking about his no goals in the past three games, which was nothing really, he was having a cold streak, he would pick it up in no time.

"Oh I can, it's about time," Reese said, Elli looked over at her.

"What do you mean?"

"I mean that it's about damn time that you realized that you deserve a hunky man, because darlin' you're beautiful." Elli blushed, as Shea went off the screen.

"Whatever Reese, hush," Elli giggled as she looked back at the laptop, bringing up her pictures. Harper started giggling beside her, which made Reese and Piper come look too.

"Oh my goodness! You look so hot, El." Elli shook her head. She thought she was pretty but not smoking like Harper had been. Reese had made her eyes smoky, making the green of her eyes stand out a lot more than usual, and had also put bright red lip stick on her lips. Her hair was up in a very intricate up do, with a white blossom on the side of her head. In the picture she was wearing a purple get up, lace covered her belly as the bra made her natural Cs turned to double Ds. The panties were cute little lace boy shorts, and to top the outfit off, a beautiful pair of purple Manolo Blahnik pumps, that had a diamond studded heel. In the picture she was laying on her back, with her legs crossed showing off the heel of the pumps, with her arms crossed under her head, looking at the camera with a come hither kind of look.

Elli had to admit, she was cute.

"You do El, gosh look at them legs! They go on for days!" Piper gushed, as Harper just grinned looking through the various poses she had put Elli in. Standing, sitting, open legged, which was all messed up since Elli started laughing because she felt so stupid.

"Perfection Elli, I'm so proud, let's pick some out!" Harper exclaimed, Elli went along with it, knowing damn well Shea would never see these pictures. He would laugh his ass off; skinny girls did this, not chunky ones that had cellulite on their legs. "I know your staring at your legs Elli, they look amazing, so shut up." Elli cut her best friend a look and kept on looking through the pictures, only picking seven poses out of the thirty-two they had taken. Jakob was gonna get an email full of pictures since Harper had picked out almost thirty pictures, and all of them were amazing, and he would love them.

"The game is starting," Piper said, Elli looked up just as the puck dropped.

"Are you going to send the pictures to Shea now, Elli?" Elli shook her head, keeping her eyes on the screen.

"I will later," she lied as she shut the computer.

"Well give me the computer; I want Jakob to have his when he gets back to the hotel tonight."

"Sure," Elli said handing the computer over to her, and getting comfortable in Shea's couch. She called Adler over, and he cuddled up under her feet before promptly falling asleep while the girls watched the game. Shea was doing so good tonight, knocking people into the boards and shooting the hell out of the puck. There were thirty-two shots on goal and he had to be twenty of them! He was doing so good! She was so proud!

"All done," Harper said, laying Elli's computer down during the third period. Elli paid her no mind, watching as finally Shea's puck made it passed the goalie, getting him his first goal in 3 games!

"Yes!" Elli gushed, throwing her arms in the air, causing Adler to fly off the couch and run to his bed in the kitchen. She should of felt bad, but she didn't, she was too happy for Shea. She loved seeing his big ole' hockey-grin as he hugged his teammates, before making his way back to the bench.

"God, he is pretty," Piper basically moaned.

"Pretty freaking hot," Reese added as the camera crew did a close up as Shea's beautiful face. He was sweating something crazy, and he had that in the zone look, something Elli loved.

"I have to admit, he is," Harper agreed, Elli's grin took up her whole face, before she looked over at the three girls who were watching the screen.

"And he is all mine."

"I'm so proud of you! You did so great tonight!" Elli gushed while Shea stood in the terminal waiting for the team bus to pull up. He grinned as she went on about how amazing he played that night, which he had. He was in the game now, thanks to Grace.

"Thanks baby, I'm so glad that shot went in though, I was sucking for a minute there."

"You sucking? Never," she reassured, "You're the best of the best!"

"Gosh, whenever I'm down, I'll know who to call huh?"

Elli giggles rang over the line and he wished he was with her, holding her close to him. "I miss you babe."

"Aw Shea, I miss you more. What are you doing?"

"Waiting to board this damn bus to go up to Anaheim for the game tomorrow, I'm already sick of the hotels."

"Aw, poor baby. What can I do to make it better?" she cooed in the phone, making it a little tighter in his jeans. God, just her voice drove him nuts.

"Oh baby, don't ask to do things to make it better in less you're going to follow through."

She giggled, and he smiled, "Who said I wouldn't follow through?"

"Fine, get on the first plane out and meet me in Anaheim."

"Now we both know I can't do that."

"Well that's what would make it better, you being in my arms, in my bed for that matter."

"Shea Adler! You naughty man, you." He laughed, and closed his eyes, imaging her standing right in front of him, her big green eyes looking up at him with her arms wrapped around his waist, pressing her body to his. "Plus what would we do with Jakob?"

"Kick his ass out," he scoffed as she giggled.

"We only have seven more days."

"It seems like a life time away."

"Yeah, it does," she agreed just as the bus pulled up.

"Shit babe, I gotta go. The bus is here, do you want me to call you when I get to the hotel?"

"No, call me in the morning before you go to practice, I have an early morning so I'll be up, I'm going to bed."

"Alright baby, I miss you, oh did you get my email? The playlist?"

"I did, thank you, I do miss you more Shea."

"I don't think so, but hey listen to number eight, that's how I'm feeling right now."

"*Home*, by Blake Shelton? I've already listen to the list four times Shea, I know it all." He smiled, feeling good that she enjoyed his list and emails, "I want you home just as much as you want to be here. Get some rest hot stuff, goodnight."

"Goodnight baby," Shea said as he hit end, and walked towards the bus. Everyone was loading up, grins everywhere since they had won. He felt good, a win, a goal, and a goodnight call from his girl.

Life was good.

When the bus pulled up to the Hilton, Shea should have known that Jakob would start bitching. "I wanted to stay at Disneyland!" he complained as they walked off the bus, taking their room cards from the receptionist that stood at the door waiting for them.

"Jakob, we're here for a night, why does it matter where we sleep?"

"Cause I like Disney, I wanted to see Mickey!"

"You're hopeless dude," Shea said with a laugh as they walked towards the elevators. "I'm so damn tired."

"Me too, good game though."

"It was," he agreed as they loaded the elevator with a couple of the other guys, heading up to the floor that held their rooms. After getting off the elevator and entering their room, Shea promptly made his way into the bathroom since he had won the coin toss to take a shower first back in the locker room. After getting all cleaned up and shaved since Coach had bitched about the up keep of his face, he came out to see Jakob gawking at his computer.

"You alright Jake?"

"No dude. I can't show you, because that would be rude. But let's just say Harper took some pictures for me," he whistled through his teeth, "Some hot pictures."

Shea laughed as he put a shirt on, "That's nice, I guess," he said, and he had to admit, he envied Jakob. He doubt Elli would ever do that for him, but if she did, he would probably have a heart attack. Maybe he would ask her to do it for him, since having something he could look at every night before going to bed would probably help him sleep a lot better. Jakob got up, taking his computer into the bathroom with him and Shea just laughed as he shook his head. It didn't take a lot to guess what Jakob was up too.

After getting under the covers, he brought his laptop out of his bag, and loaded it up. He wanted to send Elli an email before bed, so when she checked it in the morning it would bring a smile to her face. He also wanted to send one to Ryan, since Ryan loved getting email's from him. When the computer loaded up with a cute picture of him kissing Elli's cheek, her eyes bright with excitement, he clicked on his email, and waited for it all to load.

He heard the shower start up just as his email came up saying he had mail. He clicked his inbox and saw it was from Elli, with a title of 'For you'. He clicked the email, and then clicked the attachment for it to download as he read the message.

Miss you a lot, hope you enjoy.

Love, Elli.

Love? Hmm. Should he read into that, or was that just a simple closing? When the computer ding saying his attachment was downloaded, a picture of Elli in a bright purple lingerie came up and Shea's jaw dropped.

Holy Shit.

Chapter 18

Elli had woken up early and went for a run before heading into work. She felt refreshed and ready for the day; she had a full morning, and hoped that Shea would call before things got crazy. Elli had two newborn sessions that morning, and then two weddings late that night. She would have had the assistants cover the newborn shoots, but the two women requested her since she had done their engagement, weddings, and pregnancy pictures, so of course Elli obliged. She was walking into the studio when her phone rang; it was Shea, which surprised her, since it was six where he was.

"Hey!"

"Are you trying to kill me, Eleanor Fisher?" Elli stopped where she was, turning the lights on.

"Um no, why?"

"What did you think was going to happen when I opened an email from my beautiful girlfriend in nothing but lace?"

Air rushed out of Elli as she braced herself against the doorframe.

Harper! She was gonna die!

"I mean hot damn baby, I was hard all night! Couldn't sleep at all!"

"Oh…sorry?"

"Oh hell no, don't be sorry, you are just lucky we are over 2,000 miles away from each other, cause if not, I would have you on your back so damn fast your head would spin."

"Jesus Shea!" she laughed, but she did get a little hot.

"No baby, really, I've been staring at the damn pictures for hours, I even put them on my phone. You're so freaking hot baby, so hot."

Okay so maybe she wouldn't kill Harper…but she would cuss her out, "I'm glad you like 'em, I wasn't sure about sending them to you."

"What?! Why not?"

"Cause I didn't know if you would like 'em."

"Like them? Baby, I love them."

"Well then good."

"Yes, good. Oh god, I've been waiting all night to call you."

"You're crazy."

"Crazy about you babe, thank you, jeez, thank you."

"Hush! You're making me blush!" she giggled as she listen to him breathe heavily into the phone. "What are you doing? Shouldn't you be asleep?"

"No, I needed to call you."

"You're impossible, call me later."

"You hush; tell me about what you have planned today, are you busy?"

"Yeah, really busy actually, it seems no one wants to do anything during the week now. It's always like this in the winter months."

"What do you mean?"

"The winter hours are always hard, I'm busy on the weekend with outside work but on the week days, it's slow. I've been home by seven every night."

"Figures, I leave and you're home at a decent hour now."

"I know."

"So hell you're done by six? That's crazy."

"No, I'm done by seven."

He was quiet for a moment, then said "But I thought you said you were home by seven, I'm sorry, it is early, but what are you doing babe, flying home?"

Shit, shit, shit.

"Um, well, I've been staying at your place," she began, "but I mean, I could start going back home if that's a problem, it's just been easier and I kinda miss you a lot and being at your house helps, I know that's crazy, that I am basically living in your house, and I mean we haven't even had that kind of conversation about it, and I'm sorry I didn't tell you-"

"Jesus Elli, it's too early for you to be rambling," he laughed as she felt even more incompetent. God, why didn't she tell him sooner, or even better, why didn't she go home! Be a big girl for once! "Baby, you staying at the condo is wicked awesome. At least I know my bed is staying warm for me, and I mean if you want to move in that's fine with me, I love coming home to you."

Wow, she didn't see that coming.

She actually dropped down in the chair by the desk, trying to control her breathing. Was this really happening?

"Really?"

"Yeah, I love the thought of you and Adler living in my house when I'm gone and definitely when I'm there."

"What about my house?"

"We can live there too; when we want to get away we'll go to your house. I'll bring some clothes over, and you can bring some to my house. We can do the exact thing we were doing when I was home, stay at both places."

He made it seem so easy.

The door open and in came her first appointment, and she wasn't even ready.

Shit.

"Shea, I gotta go, my first appointment is here. Call me after the game?"

"Sure babe thanks again. Have a good day."

"You too, bye," then she added "I miss you!"

He laughed, before saying, "I miss you more babe."

Elli hung up her phone, putting the hugest smile in the world of her face since she was unprepared for her first appointment, something that never had happen before.

"Hey Amber, Peyton! Let me see her!" she gushed, going over to the little bundle of pink Amber was holding.

"Here she is Elli, Charlotte Ann."

"Oh god, Amber, she's beautiful." and Elli meant it, the baby had the softest, most beautiful skin, no red splotches or anything, just clear skin, she was gonna photograph well.

"Thank you," Amber beamed, Peyton stood beside her, in full proud daddy mode.

"Y'all did good," Elli gushed as she moved away trying to get things set up, "Excuse me guys, my boyfriend is away right now, and I'm running a little behind since he called this morning."

"Oh girl, you're fine!" Amber gushed, with a wave of the hand, "I was gonna feed her anyways."

"Awesome."

As she prepared for the baby, all Elli could think about was Shea asking her to move in. Was he serious? Wasn't it too early? What the hell was he thinking?

Well, hells bells.

The next couple days were extremely busy, Elli didn't even have time to talk to Shea much, never less think about the fact that he has asked her to move in with him. That was probably best since she would analyze it all to hell. After cleaning the hell out of the condo, and running the following Monday morning, her phone rang, she didn't recognize the number, but answered anyways.

"Hello?"

"Hey Elli, its Grace."

"Oh, hey Grace!"

"Hey girl, I was just calling to check in with you, see how are you doing?"

"Good, how are you?"

"Good, thanks for asking. What's your day look like?"

"It's looking pretty bleak. My assistant is running the studio today, so I was gonna clean and run errands."

"Well that works out for me, want to do lunch and shoe shopping? I need a new pair of pumps for dinner with my parents Friday. They flew in last night so I have someone to keep the kids while we are out."

"Wow, sure! I would love too."

The thought of Shea's parents in town made her nervous, but it wasn't like she would run into them, in less they came to his condo! Shit! Maybe she would go home? Crap.

"Awesome, want to meet up at the Mexican restaurant on third?"

"Sure, sounds awesome."

"Cool school, and don't worry I won't bring my parents. I'll let Shea do the introductions!"

"Oh thank God! Thank you!" Elli said relieved, while Grace just laughed.

"No problem, see you soon!"

When one goes to lunch with her boyfriend's sister, what the hell does she wear? It was all Elli could think about as she stood in front of the eight outfits she had at Shea's condo, she really needed to go get more. She decided she would do that after spending the day with Grace, even though that meant she was basically moving in, which was weird. Wasn't it too early? They had only been together two months.

Well hell, who knew?

She threw on a pair of jeans and a cute little red tee, going for the lazy chic look, since she put on a pair of her D&G black pumps to top the outfit off. She was in the middle of curling her hair when he phone rang, it was Shea.

"Hey baby," he said, when she put him on speaker phone.

"Hey you! You make it to Columbus yet?"

"I did, its freaking cold, that's why I'm staying inside while everyone else went shopping. What are you doing?"

"Getting ready, I'm going to lunch and to shop with Grace."

"Awesome, I'm glad you guys are hanging out."

"Me too," Elli gushed as she curled her hair, piece by piece.

"So we haven't talked much this weekend."

"I know; I'm sorry I've been so busy."

"I know, but have you thought about what we talked about the other morning?"

Elli laid the curling iron down, since she didn't want to burn herself in case he said something to shock her. She leaned against the counter, holding the phone in front of her face, staring at the picture of him grinning at her. "No, not really."

"Do you want to talk about it?"

"Now? Maybe we should wait till you get home."

"Yeah, I guess."

"Yeah, let's think about it some more before we make a decision."

"Okay, does that mean you don't want to live with me?"

She rolled her eyes, shaking her head, "No it's not that, it's just a big step, are we sure about this?"

"I am."

Well, okay than.

"Okay, well let's just wait till you get home okay?"

"Fine," He sounded mad, but he just went on saying, "So what do you want to do for your birthday?"

She laughed, laying her phone down and picking the curling iron back up, "I don't know, I haven't done anything for my birthday in a long time."

"Well let's do something this time."

"I mean whatever is fine, Shea. Dinner and movie. whatever. I don't care. It's just another day."

"I don't like that, it's your special day, so it should be special."

She laughed as she pulled her hair up on one side, "I guess."

"Well think a little and we'll discuss it when I get home."

"What time should you be in?"

"Probably around five, I think Grace is making dinner for seven, so I'll have enough time to get ready."

"Alright, I'll have to shop for something nice to wear."

"Not nice babe, hot." She laughed uncontrollably.

"Like I would meet you parents in something hot, please."

"Oh god, please do. Oh by the way, you have that purple number right?"

She didn't, it was with Harper but it was easy to get, or maybe she would get something hotter today, so she said "Yeah, I do."

"Oh thank God, good. Please wear that under whatever you buy, I can't wait to have you naked baby."

"Gosh, you're so horny," she teased as she giggled, trying to apply her makeup.

"Only for you, baby, I'll let you go, call me later. It's my off day."

"I will, I miss you!"

"I miss you more."

Elli smiled as she hung up the phone, and finished doing her makeup. She cleaned up, and then went into the bedroom picking up all her outfits to hang them up. Afterwards, she took Adler outside. After standing in the cold for fifteen minutes waiting on him, they finally made it back in just in time to catch Elli's phone ringing. It was Grace, canceling, because Amelia was running a fever. Elli wished Amelia well, and asked if they needed anything, Grace informed her that there were plenty of hands to help, and thanked her anyways, before hanging up, promising to reschedule another day.

Since Elli was already dressed and ready to go, she left. She drove around town running the errands she needed to run before heading out of town to go to her house. After parking the truck in her driveway and walking up the walkway, Elli found that she had missed her little house, but then she went in, and felt completely alone. So after making sure the house was in one piece and grabbing some more outfits and shoes, she left, packing up the truck. She checked around the house, and then made sure everything was locked before getting in the truck and driving off.

As she drove, she started thinking about living with Shea. She loved her home, she did, and even though he said they would stay there when they could, it wouldn't be the same as her going home every night like she had done for the past five years. She would be going to Shea's condo every night, not that she hadn't been doing that for the past couple weeks, but still, she would be officially living with Shea. Could she do it? Was she ready for that?

Elli found herself parking in front of the studio, and getting out to go see how things were going. When she open the door, and step inside, Harper stood up from behind the desk with a huge smile on her face.

"Welcome to Time-" she stopped, and shook her head, "I mean really Elli, can't stay away for one damn day?"

"Oh hush, I was bored," she grumbled as she walked towards the desk, and sat in one of the chairs behind it. "Anyone coming in?"

"Not for an hour."

"Good, I got a bone to pick with you!"

Harper started laughing, "He loved it! And I know for a fact he did!"

"That's not the point Harper Allen! You sent it without my consent!"

"Oh well, you'll live."

"I can't believe you."

"I am helping you out, so hush."

"Uh! You make me sick!"

"I do not."

"Whatever," Elli said with a huff, "So on another note,"

That made Harper laugh, they both knew Elli couldn't stay mad at her.

"Yes?" Harper asked, as she picked up a packet of pictures and started sorting through them.

"Shea asked me to move in with him," Harper stopped what she was doing and looked over at her, surprise all over her face.

"You're kiddin'."

"No, I am not."

"Wow, what did you say?"

"I said I don't know; that we'd talk about it when he got home."

"That's crazy, what are you thinking?"

"I don't know, I mean I stay there five days out of the week anyways, but that was when we were crazy busy, now we ain't, so I wouldn't need to stay there like I did, but every time I go home, I get lonely."

"Okay, well why do you have to say you moved in? Why can't y'all just go the way you've been going?"

"I think he wants it to be official."

"Oh, well I don't know babe."

Elli let out a frustrated breathe, and dropped her face into her hands.

"I mean Elli, do you even love him?"

"Huh?" she asked lifting her head to look at Harper's profile, since she was looking down at an order form.

"You heard me, do you love him?"

"Why?"

"Because I thought you did, but now I don't know because if Jakob asked me to move in, I would because I want to be with him all the time."

"You would move in with Jakob?"

"In a New York minute, that man drives me nuts. In a good way, of course."

Elli kept staring at Harper in total astonishment, "Who the hell are you? And where is my best friend?"

Harper giggled, still not looking at Elli as she packaged up some pictures. "He said he would change me, I guess he was right. It takes the right person to change you."

"I'm speechless."

"You'll be alright," Harper said standing up, and walking around the desk to put the picture packages in piles. "But really Elli, do you love him?"

Elli thought for a moment, before shrugging her shoulders, "I don't know, how do did you know?"

"I don't know? This is new to me! All I know is that Jakob is the only man I want, so hell that must be love," Harper giggled as the most beautiful smile went over her face. It had to be love, because Elli had never seen Harper smile like that. "He's the first thing I think of when I wake up and the first thing before I go to sleep. I want him, always, and the thought of being with anyone else actually hurts my heart."

Elli felt the exact same way about Shea, so did that mean she loved him? Wasn't it too early for that? Of course she cared for him deeply, but did she love him? She must not if moving in with him scared the living shit out of her, but that didn't feel right, because sometime she felt the words right on her tongue, ready to say them to him, he made her feel so good, so special. So she had too, but then why did moving in with him scare her so bad?

Because she was crazy, that was the only logical answer.

Chapter 19

Elli was in her living room, eating her favorite hockey food: nachos, when it happened.

The day had gone easy; she had talked to Shea that morning when he had arrived in St Louis. She even went and bought a beautiful black sweater dress to go with the studded black Christian Louboutin heels she had bought the day before for the dinner with Shea's parent's that following day. Harper had declined coming over to watch the game since she was cramping and wanted to watch the game back in her bed.

Elli didn't think anyone saw it coming, but with hockey, no one ever does, but she was out the door and in the truck driving to Harper's because she knew Harper was gonna need her. She just wished she had put on some pants first, because it was colder than the North Pole out with only her little plaid shorts on.

When Elli pulled into Harper's apartment complex, she saw Harper in the window on the phone. Shit, she had forgotten her phone at home. She ran up the stairs after locking the truck, and pounded on Harper's door. Harper threw the door open, tears streaking her face, snot running down from her nose.

"I can't get a hold of anyone!" she cried as she threw herself in Elli's arm. Elli held her close, even though she was freezing, and moved her hands up and down Harper's back.

"I'll call Papa, let's go in," Elli said soothingly as she moved Harper inside.

"It looked bad Elli, so stinkin' bad."

"I know," Elli said with a shake of her head, as she locked the door, and sat Harper on the couch before taking her phone from her.

The hit that Jakob took was honestly the worst Elli had ever seen. Elli wasn't even sure who the guy was that took Jakob out, all she knew was that Jakob had done a full flip before hitting the ice, face first.

And Jakob doesn't wear a face guard.

"Did they get him off the ice?"

"Yeah, about ten minutes ago. Shea isn't in the game anymore either."

"He isn't?" Elli asked looking at the screen to see if she could catch Shea's number as she dialed her Papa's number. Bryan answered on the third ring.

"Eleanor I can't talk right now."

"Is he okay?"

"We don't know, they are taking him to the ER now."

"Is Shea with him?"

"I think so."

"Okay, I'll call him."

"Okay." Elli hung up, dialing Shea's number, but he didn't answer. She looked over at Harper to see her still crying her heart out, which who could blame her? Elli would be a wreck too if her boyfriend was the one that had gotten hit. She went over to the computer, looking up the number for the hospital by the arena. After talking to four nurses and waiting for over ten minutes Elli hung up the phone in complete frustration. No one would tell her anything.

"Anything?" Harper asked as she hiccupped before wiping her face with her shirt.

"No babe, but someone will-" The phone rang, and it was Shea. "Shea, is he okay?"

"No, not right now, but he will be. He took a bad hit to the knee, and broke his nose. They are running x-rays right now, we'll know more in a few, but I wanted to call and tell you guys that he's going to be okay."

"Okay." Harper had come over and stood beside Elli, she relayed what Shea had just said, and Harper nodded her head, trying to keep the tears at bay.

"Should I go down there?" Harper asked as she took deep breaths.

"Should she?" Elli asked.

"She could, I'm not sure how long he'll be here, it might be just overnight."

"Okay, when will you know more?"

"Soon, I'll call you at this number."

"Alright." Elli hung up, and gathered Harper in her arms. "It's okay Harper, knee injuries can be fixed, he'll be okay," Elli said as Harper sobbed in her arms.

"I've never been so scared in my life. I just want to see him, hold him."

"I know Harp, I know." Harper pulled back, looking up at Elli.

"Can you manage tomorrow? Maybe we can call Alice, she can come in to assist."

"Sure, go pack, I'll look for a flight."

Harper ended up leaving an hour later which was for the best because Jakob had a complete tear of the MCL in his knee, and wouldn't be able to leave the hospital for a couple days. Elli had called Alice when she was driving back to Shea's from the airport, and she was more than willing to come in a help the next morning. When Elli had arrived at the condo, she walked Adler before going back inside to go to bed. She crawled into bed just as her phone rang, it was Shea.

"Hey."

"Hey you, Harper get off alright?"

"Yeah, she should be there at 10:15."

"Okay, I'm gonna head to the airport in a few, then bring her back here."

"Thanks, she's a mess, so beware." He chuckled, and Elli's heart swelled. She missed him so much, and was so excited to see him tomorrow, but all she kept imagining after dropping off Harper was Shea getting hurt, and her being the one in a ball of tears.

What in God's name possessed her to date a hockey player?

"Its fine, it was a scary hit, we are lucky it's only what it is, it could have been worst."

"Yeah."

Nothing was said for a moment, and then Shea said "Hey you're okay right?"

"Yeah, it was just scary, Harper's a mess."

"I know baby, but getting hurt can happen, we all know that when we lace up our skates before each game."

"I know, but still, I couldn't imagine if it was you. I probably would have flipped out."

"Oh baby, don't think about that. You'll worry yourself sick."

She already had.

"Okay."

"Alright, well go to bed. I'll see you tomorrow."

"I can't wait."

"Me neither, goodnight."

"Night."

Elli hung up just as the tears started to fall. She was crying for Harper, for Jakob, and for the simple fact that this could happen to Shea. The thought tore sobs out of her, because she was so scared. The uncertainty of what could happen to Shea scared her shitless, and the fact that he wasn't with her made it worst. She couldn't hold him to guarantee herself that he was fine at that particular moment, so she cried, and cried.

Until sleep came.

Shea had gotten back to the hotel late the night before after taking Harper to the hospital, so when he woke up late and missed the bus back home, he went to the airport and jumped on the first flight home. He was surprised no one came looking for him, but then again they probably thought he was still with Jakob, which normally he would have been if Harper wasn't around.

Since he had taken the airplane home, he three hours early. After landing, he took a taxi to his condo. Shea wanted to shower before heading over to Time Standing Still to surprise Elli. When he walked into the condo, Adler came barreling from the kitchen to greet him.

"Hey boy!" Shea said bending down to pet and hug the pup. He didn't realize how much he had missed the dog, but he had. He rubbed the top of Adler's head before shutting the door, and taking his bags back to his room. Nothing had changed, he noticed as he walked through the condo, but it was easy to tell that Elli had been living here. Cups were in the sink, along with the trash being full, and her shoes were everywhere. He shook his head as he threw his bags on the bed, he would unpack later, he was too eager to see Elli. After taking a shower and throwing on a pair of jeans with a t-shirt and sweat shirt over it, he was out the door, in his truck on his way to Elli's.

When Shea pulled up to Time Standing Still, no one was in the parking lot except for Elli's truck and one other. He prayed that no customers where there as he got out the truck and headed for the door. He kicked himself mentally for not picking up flowers first, but he was in such a hurry to see her he had forgotten. He threw the door open and a blonde haired girl stood up, saying the regular greeting.

"Hey, is Elli here?" he asked, the girl smiled nicely, but obvious didn't recognize him.

"She is, and you are?"

"Shea Adler, her boyfriend."

"Oh! Hi! I'm Alice, one of her assistants! So nice to meet ya!" she said holding out her hand, he took her small hand in his and smiled.

"Nice to meet you too," he said, "Is she in her office?"

"She is. Would you like me to page her?"

"Um, can I just go back there?"

"Sure!"

"Thanks," he said with a grin as he started down the hall for her office, he was half way there when the door open and Elli started towards him, looking down at a piece of paper she was holding. He stopped taking in the beauty that was her. Her hair was up in a crazy mess of curls, she was wearing a white button up shirt that had a green tie that wasn't tied, with a green plaid skirt, with black tights and green high heels.

She looked like a naughty school girl.

And she was all his.

"Jesus woman, you are too hot for words."

Elli jumped, startled, throwing the papers she was holding in the air. She looked up at Shea, as a slow grin went over her face.

"Shea!" she gushed, running to him, wrapping her arms around his neck before pressing her lips to his. He wrapped her up in his arms, picking her up off the ground a little as he passionately kissed her. When she wrapped her legs around his waist, he groaned as he started walking towards her office. God, he wanted her.

So fucking badly.

He pushed the door close with her back, before pressing his rapidly growing erection into her core. She gasped as she pulled at his sweat shirt, trying to get it off. He pulled back, pulling his shirt and sweat shirt off at the same time, before reclaiming her already swollen lips. As he fed himself from the sweetness of her mouth he undid each button of her shirt, before capturing her breast in each of his hand. She let out a moan as he tweaked her aching nipples through the sheer fabric of her bra.

"God I want you," he gasped against her mouth as he molded her breast in his hands.

"Take me," she practically moaned as he kissed down her throat, "Please," she added when he moved his hands from her breast to her half bare bottom. He pulled back and lifted her skirt, since he was confused. Her legs were black, so he though she was wearing tights. When he saw that the tights came to mid thigh and that she was wearing nothing but lace, he almost came.

"Jesus, you're so fucking hot," he groaned before ripping the fabric off her. Elli let out a small little meep before he took her mouth with his again, undoing his pants. He wanted to give her more foreplay, but he wasn't going to last, he had to be inside her. He reached in his pocket pulling out the condom he had brought with him, before letting his pants fall.

He tried to open the condom while still kissing Elli, but it wasn't working, he couldn't concentrate, so he pulled back, looking at the package, to see what he was doing. Elli leaned against the door, watching him with come get me eyes as he sheathed himself. He didn't even wait; he picked up one of her legs and entered her fully in one deep thrust. She let out a deep satisfied moan, but then covered her mouth as she looked up at him.

"We have to be quiet," she whispered, he wanted to laugh. He was pretty sure Alice knew what was going on in Elli's office, but if Elli wanted them to be quiet, he could do quiet.

"I'm not the one we got to worry about," he teased as he took her mouth with his, circling his tongue around hers as he started to move in and out of her. He pulled back, his grip on her leg tight as he slammed into her to the hilt. She screamed out a little, and Shea stopped, a smile pulling at his lips.

"Shh," he teased, she smacked his arm and he began to move again, when he started to pick up the speed, her nails dug into his biceps as she tried to keep quiet, but anyone outside of the office knew what was going on. She bit down on his shoulder when she came, shuddering uncontrollably, as he drove into her not worrying about the smacking noise from her ass hitting the door. With a final thrust, he came slapping his hand against the door, with a harsh groan of masculine satisfaction. He dropped her leg, leaning his body against hers as they tried to catch their breath.

"Alice so knows what we just did," Elli said into his throat, before kissing it then the spot where she bit him.

"Oh yeah."

Shea pulled back to look at her, she was smiling, so he smiled back, before kissing her beautiful swollen lips.

"I've missed you," he said when he pulled back.

She giggled before pushing him back, detaching herself from him, "Me or the sex?"

He gave her a sheepish grin, "Can I say both and you not get mad?"

She laughed as she pulled her skirt down, "Yes," she said with a nod as she started to button her shirt. "Hurry up and get dressed."

"Why? I was thinking we can do it on the desk next," he said wiggling his eyebrows at her, she smack his arm, bending over to pick up his shirt.

"Hell no, I got customers coming in! And now I gotta figure out what I'm gonna do cause I have no panties," she complained as she bent over to pick up her mangled panties.

He laughed taking in the delectable view of her bare ass when her skirt came up, "Don't bend over or someone will get a show." Elli flew up, pulling the back of her skirt down, glaring at him.

"I mean goodness! You're impossible!" He smiled as he put his shirt on, pulling his jeans up.

"And you love it, come here," he said, pulling her to him, kissing her again, she melted in his arms holding him close to her. Something beeped, breaking their kiss and Alice's voice filled the room.

"Um Elli, you're two o'clock is here."

Elli pulled away from him, blushing deep red as she pulled her skirt down father. "I'll be right out Alice," she said as Shea laughed. She smacked him before looking in the mirror, looking herself over. He came up behind her, wrapping his arms around her waist.

"If you're wondering how you look, let me just say," he placed a kiss to her neck, before grinning up at her in the mirror "You look like someone who was just ravished by a man that has missed you so much it hurts. You look beautiful baby."

She smiled before turning in arms, kissing him long and hard. She pulled back to early in his opinion and smiled before breaking out of his arms.

"I gotta go. I'll meet ya back home at five?"

"Sure babe, want me to leave first?"

"Yeah," she said with a shy grin, "Bye."

"Bye," he said with a wink as he walked out the office, shutting the door behind him. He walked down the hall, passing by the desk that Alice was sitting at, grinning hard at him.

"Bye Mr. Adler."

"Bye Alice," he said as he passed a lady that was holding a small toddler in his arms, he smiled at her before leaving and he swore he heard the two women giggling.

Not that he cared much.

"Well, give Jakob my best, and let me know when y'all will be home so I can plan to come get you from the airport," Elli said as she pulled into the parking lot beside Shea's truck. Just seeing his truck gave her chills thinking about what they had did against the door of her office. Alice had grinned at her all afternoon, it was totally embarrassing but she didn't care.

She felt great.

"I will, thanks babe," Harper said, she sounded much better than she did the day before, Jakob was doing better and would hopefully be leaving in the next two days.

"No problem, bye Harp."

"Bye." Elli hung up her phone just as she reached the door, digging for her keys. She unlocked the door and went in as Adler jumped around greeting her.

"Hey honey," she gushed as she bent down to kiss him, "Have you been out?"

Shea came around the corner, shirtless. "Yup, took him out before I got in the shower," he said, before leaning over to kiss her lips softly "Hey baby."

"Hey," she grinned, gosh she didn't realize how much she had missed him till that moment. The whole coming home and being greeted by both her men was heaven. "Sorry the house was a mess, I was hoping to get home before you so I could pick up some."

"No worries, it's cleaner than I ever have it," he said with a grin as she laid her purse and things on the couch. She walked straight to him, wrapping her arms around him.

"Do you think people would think I was crazy if I just stayed like this all weekend?" she asked, Shea smiled down at her, before kissing her nose.

"Probably, plus it's going to be real hard to skate like this when you're attached to my waist." Elli started to giggle before placing a kiss in the middle of his chest. She looked up at him, before noticing the bite mark she had left earlier.

"Goodness I got you good."

He looked over at his shoulder, then back down at her with a smirk on his face, "Oh yeah you did, I like it."

She giggled, smacking his chest before pulling away and kicking off her shoes. "I need to get in the shower." She started for the bedroom but stopped in the kitchen when she saw the largest bouquet of pink calla lilies she had ever seen. "Aw, Shea!" she gushed, leaning over to smell the flowers; she picked the card out, and smiled at his messy handwriting.

You're amazing Elli, simply amazing.

Love, Shea

Shea came into the kitchen, grinning at her. "You smooth talker you," she gushed, leaning over and kissing him. When they parted she was still smiling as she reread the card. "I love them, thank you."

"You're welcome baby," he said going around the island to the fridge. "I told my mom we would come over early since I got home early."

"Oh yeah, sorry I got distracted. I'll be quick," she said, putting the card back into the bouquet and heading for the bedroom as Shea chuckled. She started to take off her clothes as she made her way to the bathroom, when she reached the bathroom; she started the shower as she took her hair down. When she stepped in, she let out a satisfied sigh as the nine jets hit her from every angle.

God, she loved this shower.

She heard the door open as she was washing her hair, and then the sink running and clanking as Shea got out his bag from the drawer.

"Whatcha doin'?" she asked as she lathered her hair up.

"Shaving, my mom doesn't like my beard."

"Oh."

Elli went under the main jet, washing the shampoo out of her hair. As she came back out to apply the conditioner, Shea said, "So it was nice greeting you when you came in." Elli's hands stopped and she looked out the glass at him. He was lathering up his face, not looking at her.

"It was."

"It could be like that all the time, you know."

Scheming man.

"It could."

She then watched as he leaned against the sink, looking up at the ceiling, he had shaving cream all over his face, his razor in one hand as his other one moved, kinda like he was saying 'Come on' with his hand. She shook her head, going under the water to wash the conditioner out.

When she came out from under the water, he said "So do you want to move in? Or maybe we could look for another place, a bigger one." She closed her eyes, why couldn't it be an easy 'Yes! I would love too!' instead of her freaking out. She shut the water off, grabbing a towel as she open the door. She wrapped herself up as she stepped out. He was facing the mirror again, not watching her as she dried off, which was good because she was still a little naked shy around him.

"I don't know Shea, I mean like I said that's such a big step. We've only been dating for two months."

Shea turned looking over at her, only half of his face shaved, the other half white from the shaving cream, "I know, but you're already here a lot."

"That was when I was busy but I'm not no more, so I could go home a decent hour now."

"But you haven't left the condo since I left."

"Because I missed you, being with your stuff made me feel better."

"Okay, so when I'm home for good you're not going to want to stay here?"

"I don't know Shea, why do we need to label it? Can't we just go as we are?"

"I mean we could, but wouldn't it be easier to have all your clothes here, all your shoes? Some of the pictures you've taken?"

"It would, but I don't think I'm ready for that."

He made a face, "What does that mean?"

"It means that moving in is taking a big step, how would I explain that to my daddy, or Papa, they are gonna wanna know where the ring is."

"What do they say now?"

"They don't know!" she yelled throwing her arms up in the air, losing her temper. He was so damn persistent; he couldn't just let it be. "I mean what do you want me to do Shea, say no? Cause I don't want too, I just want to keep on as we are."

Elli watched as Shea nodded, hurt filling his eyes. He turned looking back at the mirror to continue shaving. She stood watching him shave, waiting for him to say something.

"Can you go get ready? We need to go."

That was not what she wanted him to say.

She let out a frustrated huff and headed out in the bedroom, going into the closet. She grabbed her dress and her shoes out of the box before leaving the closet to lay everything on the bed. She went to the drawer that she had been putting her panties and bras in, and grab one of each, along with a pair of black sheer tights. As she got dressed, she couldn't help thinking about their conversation. Elli didn't want to fight with him while he was home, what was the big deal? He wanted her to move in, she basically already had, so what was the big deal moving in some more things?

Because she wasn't ready, and Shea didn't want some of her things, he wanted it all. He wanted to mix their things, make a home, together.

No matter how much she wanted to make him happy, she just couldn't do it. Even though she didn't want to live in her house because she was lonely, the thought of moving everything out of it, actually hurt. What would she do? Sell the house, so they could get a bigger one? Did she even want to truly live in Nashville? She would miss her porch, her flowers, and hell, the whole house. She loved her house.

Why was being in a relationship so freaking hard? It seemed everything that meant the relationship was growing, made Elli almost break out in hives. Maybe she wasn't ready to be in a relationship. Maybe she needed to rethink this. She needed to go home, instead of staying here.

She should pack.

She pulled the sweater dress over her head, and sat on the bed, looking around the room that was filled with her and Shea's stuff. A pair of her heels laid in the corner, along with one of her flats, the other one was on the floor beside his side of the bed. Her hair bows were laid across his dresser, while her bra's that she had just washed hung on his mirror. Her iPod laid beside his iHome, and random pieces of clothes laid with his on the floor.

It seemed to all fit, like it was meant to be there. Her stuff mixing with his, but even though everything looked good together, it still made her nervous. Did he have a problem with it? No, he wanted it there. Elli couldn't help but remembered how Justin and her things mixed so well, his house looked like something straight out of an expensive classic designing magazine, but he still had no problem kicking her out when he got mad, throwing her things out on the lawn. What if Shea did that?

Shea came out the bathroom, going into the closet. When he came out he was putting on a white shirt, before sliding on the fall colored striped sweater she had gotten him from Macy's when she had went shopping for her dress. He fixed the bottom of the sweater, before looking up at her.

"Thanks for the sweater, I like it a lot."

"It looks good on you," she said when she found her voice, "real good." He gave her a small smile before heading towards the door that led to the hall. "Hey." He turned looking back at her, leaning against the door, "Are you sure you're ready for us to move in together?"

He nodded before saying, "Yes."

"How do you know though? Aren't you scared?"

He shook his head, a small smile going across his face. "No baby, not at all. Because I think-" he stopped, looking down at the floor, kicking the door frame. Then he looked up at her, his sky like eyes boring into hers, she actually had to catch her breath from being under his intense gaze.

"Because I'm falling in love with you, Elli and I want to be with you, always."

Well, she sure didn't see that one coming.

Chapter 20

It seemed like hours passed when really it was only seconds as Shea looked down at Elli. She was pulling in deep, shuddering breaths as she looked up at him. He refused to look away, daring her with his eyes to do anything before answering him. He watched as she went to say something but stopped herself, still taking in the deep breaths.

Finally, when he thought he couldn't take it anymore, she said, "How do you know?"

"What?" he asked, "How do I know what?"

"How do you know that you're falling in love with me? I just don't understand it, I mean, how does one actually know when they are in love? Does it just hit them? Do you just know? I mean how does it happen? I mean-"

"You're rambling Elli," he said, closing his eyes as he like out a frustrated sigh.

She didn't love him.

"I know! Because not only do you want me to move in, but you are falling in love with me! You couldn't wait to drop the love bomb on me till after we were done with the moving in one?" she said standing up, and moving her hands with every word that came out of her mouth.

God, he loved her even though she drove him crazy.

"What do you want me to say Elli, I'm sorry? I'm sorry for feeling the way I do? Sorry for wanting to be with you every fucking moment of the day, for wanting only you? I mean what would you want? For me to be a fucking douche, cheating on you, not telling you I actually feel something for you? I mean for the love of God, Elli, what do you want from this? Is this relationship actually going somewhere?"

She moved her hand over her mouth as she looked down at the ground. He expected her to say something, not start crying. She moved from the bed, walking on insanely high heels to the bathroom, shutting the door behind her. He let his head fall into the doorframe, hitting it a few times before walking over to the bathroom door.

"Elli, why are you crying?" he asked, he heard her blow her nose.

"Because you right Shea, I don't know anymore. I mean first it was you being gone, now it's the fact that I'm scared to move forward in the relationship while your hell bent on moving. I just don't know anymore."

"Don't know what? What do you mean?"

"I mean that maybe we should take a break."

Okay, that came from left field. Shea felt like she was hitting him with a pound of bricks, he braced his self against the door frame trying to control his breathing.

"Okay, so I tell you that I'm falling in love with you, and you break up with me? Right before we leave so you can meet my parents."

The door flew up, and she stood there, the same height as him, tears streaking down her face, as she tried to keep the sobs inside her.

"I don't want to break up, but I feel like I'm holding you back, you deserve someone that will give you what you want, and I'm not sure I'm that person," she said putting her hands on her chest.

"Why do you fucking do this? Why do you over analyze, over fucking think everything! We are great together! If you don't want to move in, fine. If you do; great, if you don't love me, that's fine, but I do love you, and I will wait for you to love me, Elli."

Her lip wobbled, before more tears streamed down her face. "Don't do this, don't over think, just feel baby, don't you feel what I feel when we are this close to each other? Don't you have fun with me? Don't you miss me when I'm gone? Don't you want me?" He cupped her face with his hands, her tears running over his big hands, she had such big tears something he couldn't help but love, because even when she cried, he thought she was the most beautiful person on earth, "Tell me no to any of those questions Elli, I'll let you break up with me, hell I'll even help you pack, I'll let you go, even though-" he took a deep breath, tears welling up in his eyes, because if she did say no, he was done for, "Even though it would kill me."

Shea had never cried in front of a woman, okay well he did cry in front of Grace once, and his mom was always there when he cried, but he had never cried in front of a woman he was dating, but he felt like the tears were about to fall. He tried so hard to keep them at bay because he didn't want to seem weak, but she wasn't saying anything, she was just looking at him, tears rolling down her cheeks onto his hands. He could except the fact that she didn't love him, because he knew she would later, but the fact that she wanted to break up, no he couldn't except that, wouldn't except that.

She took a deep breath, and then said "I don't deserve you Shea."

His heart melted, "Of course you do baby."

"No I really don't, you're too patient; too nice. You deal with my craziness, my insecurities, why Shea? Why do I deserve you?"

He smiled, moving his thumbs back and forth against her cheeks, "Because, I said so," he said with a wink, "Now stop over thinking us. I'll leave the moving thing alone; let you make the decision, okay?"

She nodded before wrapping her arms around his middle, nuzzling her nose in his neck, getting snot and tears all over him, but he didn't care. He held her close, kissing her wet hair, inhaling her scent. They stayed like that for a long time, just holding each other until his phone rang. He pulled back a little pulling the phone out of his pocket, it was Grace.

"Shit," he said, "Its Grace."

"Crap, I gotta finish my hair!" she placed a quick kiss to his lips before turning back around going to the sink.

"Hey."

"Where the hell are you?"

"We're running late."

"I mean Jesus, can't you guys wait until tonight?!"

"For your information we weren't having sex, we did that earlier in her office."

She let out a disgusted cry, "Wonderful, now if I'm ever in her office that's what I'll imagine."

"Hey, it was good stuff."

"Ugh, anyways, when will you be here? Mom is waiting…and she is not happy about it."

"Sorry, we'll stay later, Elli's doing her hair now, we should be out of here in…hey baby how long you going to be?" he asked Elli.

"Give me fifteen, I promise I'm hurrying."

Yeah right, fifteen minutes?

"We'll be over within the hour," he said instead.

"Fine!" Grace hung up, as he shook his head.

Damn women in his life drove him nuts!

Elli wanted to call Harper, not go to Grace's house to meet Shea's parents. She was still on edge from their fight, from almost throwing away the most amazing man in the world. She just didn't understand what her problem was, why couldn't she just let it go. Shea's was not going to hurt her, but it didn't matter how many times she told herself that, it still sat in the back of her mind.

Elli wasn't happy with the way she looked either, she only had time to straighten her hair when she wanted to put big curls in, and she didn't get to spend much time on her makeup, so she knew Shea's family was gonna think she was a ugly, frumpy, gold digging whore not worthy of their amazing son. She was more nervous about meeting his family than she was about him meeting hers.

Gosh, this sucked.

When they pulled into Grace's driveway, Shea cut the truck off but didn't get out. He still had her hand in his, moving his thumb back and forth on the back of her hand as he looked up at Grace's house. He looked over at her, and she looked at him, nervously.

"Are you nervous?" he asked.

She gave him a shaky smile, "Yeah."

He smiled back, taking a deep breath. "I'm not, they're going to love you, I just hope they don't embarrass me too much," he said before kissing the back of her hand and getting out, coming around to the other side to help her out.

Elli really should have rethought the heels, yes, they were super beautiful, but her feet already hurt, and it was just the beginning of the night. As they made their way up the walkway to the door, Shea held Elli's hand, running his thumb along the back of her hand. She was starting to think he was lying about not being nervous.

The door open before they even reached it, and Grace stood with her hands on her hips.

"I mean people around here do like to eat," she said with a huff.

"Be quiet; we're what, fifteen minutes late?" Shea said, kissing her cheek before pulling Elli past her and into the house. He let go of her hand when who she guessed was his dad came into the room, with grin on his face that was as big as Shea's. "Hey Dad!" Shea said wrapping his arms around his dad, giving him a back slapping hug before pulling back. Shea reached for Elli and she came willingly to his side, smiling up at his dad.

"Dad, this is Elli, this is my dad, Mark." Elli held out her hand, and Mark took it eagerly, grinning ear to ear at her. Mark was a good looking man, tall like Shea, not thick but not skinny, he was a good healthy size. Shea and Grace must have gotten their nose and eyes from Mark, since his eyes were the exact same color as Mark's.

"Hey, how are you?" she asked with a nervous grin, Mark started laughing, looking over at Shea.

"You weren't kidding about the country accent, it's thick," he looked back at Elli as she turned deep red, "I'm fine thank you, and you?"

"Good, thank you."

"It's about damn time!" Elli turned to see Shea's mother coming in the room. Elli had remembered Shea saying that people thought she was Grace's sister instead of her mother, and it was the truth. She didn't look a day over thirty. When she set her eyes on Elli, she grinned so fully that Elli thought she was gonna be blinded by the whites of her teeth. "Well hello! I'm Jenna Adler, you must be Elli." Elli nodded as Jenna took her hand in hers, shaking it slowly, looking Elli over.

"Yes, ma'am I am, it's nice to meet you."

Jenna grinned widely up at Shea, and Elli saw where Shea got the one dimple from. Jenna had hers on the exact same cheeks as he did, and it made Elli smile.

"Shea told us you were southern, but I wasn't expecting it to be so thick, I like it though." She added quickly.

Elli smiled, "Yes ma'am, I'm country to core."

Shea smiled, wrapping his arm around Elli, "I love her accent."

Both his parents beamed and Elli looked up at him, biting her lip. He smiled down at her, before bring his finger to her lip, pushing it out of the hold her teeth had it in.

"Obviously, can we eat?" Grace said. Shea looked over at her, glaring.

"Grace, what's your deal?"

"I'm freaking hungry!"

"Obviously. God!" Shea complained as he put his hand on the small of Elli's back and walked into Grace's dining room as everyone laughed.

They all sat down as the people Grace hired came to bring the food out. Elli slowly slid her shoes off, running her aching feet along the hardwood of Grace's floor. The floors were so cold that it soothed Elli's feet, and she found herself sighing in pleasure. Shea cut her a questioning look.

"You okay?" he asked, leaning over towards her.

"My feet are killing me."

He gave her a cute little smirk before his mother started talking, "So Elli, you take pictures for a living right?"

"Yes ma'am. I've been doing it for almost seven years now."

"Wow, I've seen some of your work. You're very good, I must say."

"Thank you," Elli gushed with a grin; Jenna smiled sweetly before reaching for her fork.

 Elli looked over at Grace, and she was giving her a sweet smile. "I meant to tell you Elli, I love your shoes."

Elli smiled back, "Thank you, they are Christian Louboutin and let me tell you, they hurt like the dickens." Grace started laughing as the rest of the table joined in, and that's when Elli felt comfortable.

The rest of the dinner went without a hitch, Elli adored Mark and Jenna. They were amazing, she had never seen two people love their children, or even their son in law the way Mark and Jenna loved Shea, Grace, and James. Jenna teased Grace and Shea lovely, and not hatefully the way Elli's family teased her. Mark would always make it a point to talk to James; he would smack him on the arm, or ask him about work. Elli's mom never talked to Adina or Lauren, only time she ever acknowledged them was when she needed to know something about the kids, but not Mark and Jenna, they loved James like he was one of theirs.

They even treated Elli like that, and she had just met them. Jenna fired questions all night, even Mark did. They wanted to know everything, and it wasn't to have information on Elli, like her parents tried to have on Shea, it was to get to know her. Elli actually felt like Mark and Jenna liked her for her, not because of her profession or because of who her uncle was, they liked her.

And it was such a refreshing feeling.

After dinner, everyone went into the living room for coffee and cake. James was in the middle of a story about one of his co workers, when Elli leaned over to Grace asking, "Hey where's Amelia and Ryan?"

Grace smiled, "They are staying with a friend of mine, they attack my parents, and mom wanted to get to know you, so I had my friend take them."

"Oh, that's nice. I was looking forward to seeing them though; I haven't seen them since before Shea left."

"Yeah, well maybe you can visit while Shea's gone these next two weeks. I don't mind, I would love it actually," she said with a grin, Elli smiled.

"I would too."

When Shea moved his hand into hers, she smiled up at him and he returned it just as his mom said, "So Elli, you and Shea would make beautiful babies, do you want children?"

Elli head whip over to Jenna, as Shea used his other hand to cover his face.

"Mom!" Grace complained, "You just met her a couple hours ago, can you not get her barefoot and pregnant in your mind, yet?"

Everyone laughed as Jenna turned deep red, "I was just asking."

"We know baby, we know." Mark said, wrapping his arms around her, kissing her temple.

Shea had done it so many times to Elli that it brought a smile to her face. Elli had always thought Shea was a good man, and now meeting Mark and seeing that his relationship with Jenna has lasted this long, it made Elli's heart swell. She noticed all through the night how Mark would touch Jenna lovely, or how they would share a private joke, causing Grace and Shea to make face while it made Elli smile. Elli wasn't even sure her father really loved her mother, she was convinced her daddy only stayed with her mother because he didn't get her to sign a pre-nup but with Mark and Jenna, it was obvious that they were crazy in love.

Elli watch as Mark moved his hand into Jenna's as she glared at him, then she smiled, as if holding Mark's hand had made the embarrassment of her question for Elli go away. If Shea and Elli's relationship could be anything like Mark and Jenna's, they were golden.

"Elli, the last game we came to Shea showed me your seats, they must be nice. I've never been that close," Mark said with a grin, "Even when Shea played in the AHL, we were always up in a box, I think the last time I was on the ice was when he was in high school, maybe some college."

A small smile crossed Elli's lips, "They are amazin', and I've sat there since the Assassin's started. I love em."

"You're uncle owns the team, is that right?" Mark said looking over at Shea.

Shea nodded as Elli said, "Yes, he has loved hockey his whole life, him and my daddy also played some. My brother's never did play, but I did a little, I wasn't very good though."

Everyone laughed as Shea smiled down at her. "I didn't know you played before." She smiled back.

"Just a little, no big deal," she said with a shrugged, he shook his head, a smirk pulling at his lips.

"You guys are just too cute!" Jenna exclaimed, clapping her hands. Elli watched as Grace shook her head and Shea looked everywhere but at her.

"Jenna, we are talking hockey, quiet now!" Mark joked as he looked back over at Elli, "It's really great having a female in the family that knows hockey," he said with a laugh.

In the family? They already considered her family?

Shea squeezed her hand, and she smiled up at him, showing him that she was okay.

"You should sit with us tomorrow, sweetie." Jenna said, taking a sip of her coffee.

"Oh thank you so much Jenna, but I don't sit anywhere but in my seats," Elli said with a grin, hoping that wouldn't get her kicked out of the family she had just been added too. Mark just smiled, shaking his head.

"I wouldn't sit with us either, if I had your seats."

Elli thought for a moment, Harper wouldn't be going to the game with her tomorrow, since Jakob wasn't coming home till Sunday, so she looked up at Mark with a winning grin on her face, "You wanna sit with me tomorrow?"

Being decked out in Shea Adler gear, when Shea Adler's father sat beside Elli was a tad bit embarrassing but not enough to make her change. She even had Shea's number on her cheek, and a big grin on her face as Mark and her watch Shea warm up. Mark kept his eyes on Shea and the rest of the guys just as intently as Elli did. They had gotten beers and hot dogs before the guys had come out, and the conversation never stopped. Mark was full of stories of Shea's childhood. Shea had once told Elli he was a busy child, and he wasn't lying. Mark had a story for every year of Shea's life, and Elli loved hearing it.

"Did he ever tell you the first time he held a stick?" Elli looked over at Mark, shaking her head.

"No sir, he hasn't," she answered taking a drink of her beer, Mark smiled over at her.

"We lived in a crappy part of town at the time, and Jenna started screaming that there was a rat in the kitchen, she yelled at Shea to go get something to kill it, he was four at the time," Mark chuckled for a moment, reminiscing Elli guessed. "Well I stood in the doorway, shaking my head at my young wife that stood on our busted kitchen table screaming at the top of her lungs. When Shea come barreling into the kitchen with my old hockey stick from high school I actually laughed, but then he pulled back when that rat came out and swung that stick so damn hard, that he killed the rat instantly." Mark slapped his leg as he let out a gut busting laugh, he wiped his eyes after a few moments, still laughing and Elli couldn't help but laugh along, "Poor Jenna, she was freaking out about the rat blood all over the place, while I just stood there gawking at the perfect slap shot my four year old son had just done. I signed him up the next day, and look, hardest slap shot in the NHL for the last three years. I could kiss that rat if it was alive."

That had them both laughing, when Elli was able to breathe again, she looked over at Mark, "That's some story," she said with a big ole grin, "Had Shea told you that he was my favorite player before we started dating?"

Mark nodded, "He did, that's how I knew you are a keeper," he said with a wink. "Plus you have these amazing seats."

That had them both laughing just as the lights went off for the start of the game. Shea skated out when he was announced grinning over at her and Mark.

When she waved at him, something she did at every game, Mark said, "He really likes you."

Elli looked up at him, a shy smile on her face, "I like him too."

"Good, I have a real good feeling about you. You're a good person, something Shea needs."

"Thank you, sir," she said as she turned catching Shea smirking at her just before he turned to get ready for the puck to be dropped, "He's something I need too."

Shea knew he needed to get up and started packing, but he just couldn't let Elli go to do it. He thought leaving last time was hard, this time was gonna be hell. She nuzzled her nose up against his throat just as the sun started coming up. Shea pulled her naked, warm body closer to him, kissing the top of her head. It didn't seem fair, after having such a great weekend with someone, having to leave, but this was his career, and he knew he had to leave.

Shea pressed his lips against her hair once more, taking in Elli's scent before letting her go, and slowly scooting out the bed. He picked up his boxers from beside the bed, pulling them on before going to get his suitcase. When he came back from the laundry room with all his clothes in his arms, Elli was sitting up in the bed, rubbing her eyes, her beautiful milky breast showing for his viewing pleasure.

"Hey," she said sleepily, he smiled, dropping the clothes at the end of the bed, before kissing her cheek.

"Hey beautiful, sorry for waking you."

"Don't be, its fine," she said before pulling the blanket up over her breast, "Do you want me to fold all that while you take a shower?"

A slow grin went across his lips before he leaned over, pulling the blanket down, and nuzzling his face in her breast. She giggled as he crawled on top of her as he became harder with every passing second.

"I was thinking you should join me," he said against her skin as he licked and nibbled. She took in a sharp breath when he took her nipple in his mouth, swirling his tongue around her growing peek.

"We would never get out of here, plus I'm still worn out from last night. So go on," she said pushing him away with a sleepy grin on her face. He kissed her stomach, before getting up. He did need to go, and she was right, they would never get out of there if he got her in that shower. He shot her a smirk before going towards the bathroom as she sat up, looking for her clothes. He admired her naked body, memorizing every curve, all her beautiful skin, everything and anything to keep him warm at night while he was on the road.

After washing up and shaving, he went back into the bedroom noticing that his suitcase was packed and ready to go. He smiled thinking she was a Godsend as he went into the closet getting his suit for the day. He was putting his suit on when Elli crossed the room, going into the bathroom, he stopped for a moment, thinking that maybe he could squeeze in a quickie, but then again, he knew he couldn't. He always took his time, always wanted to taste every part of her, there was no such thing as quickies with Eleanor Fisher, her body was his play land.

After getting dressed and tying up his chucks, he went into the kitchen seeing that Elli had made a quick breakfast of eggs and bacon while he was in the shower, so he sat down to eat, while he waited for her. Adler sat beside him, watching him, and waiting for anything Shea would give him, which was half his plate. What could he say? He loved the damn dog.

"Did your mom take you out yet?" The words had Adler running to the door, jumping higher than a 40lb pug should. After hooking his leash on and putting on his jacket, Shea walked Adler around the condo twice before heading back up, frozen. Elli stood in the kitchen, drinking some coffee and popping her pills when he came up behind her, wrapping his arms around her for her warmth. She let out a little scream, smacking him away as he laughed. "It's cold out."

"I can tell, jeez," she laughed as she took a drink of her coffee.

Shea watched her for a moment, wondering if it was a good time to bring up Thanksgiving and her family. Since Shea never beats around the bush, he asked "Are you going to your parents for Thanksgiving?"

She looked over at him, shaking her head. "I'm going to the club with Papa, daddy said he'll try to meet us for a little bit."

Shea nodded, he knew Elli hadn't talked to her mother or siblings since the family dinner he was subjected too. He also knew she hadn't seen the kids in a while, and she was hurting from it.

"Maybe you can go over for a little bit, at least to see the kids."

She shook her head, "I don't want to see my mother."

"I know baby, but you miss the kids," he said wrapping his arms around her, kissing behind her ear. "And I know they must miss you, even if it's only for a few minutes, you know?"

She smiled, leaning her head against his, running her hands along his arms, "Maybe."

"That's my girl," he said kissing her again before glancing at the clock, "We need to go."

"Alright."

Shea loaded the truck up, as Elli got in. They headed over to the airfield, and watched as everyone hugged and kissed their families. He was dreading going since he was going to be lonely for the next six weeks with Jakob being out for that long. When he was asked if he wanted a new roommate, he said hell no, Jakob was his roommate, he didn't want no one else, even if it was going to be lonely as hell.

Shea popped the trunk and got out as Elli did the same, getting his bags. One of the crew members came over, getting Shea's bag, leaving him and Elli to say goodbye. It was so cold outside, winter being in full swing, so he wrapped his arms around Elli, holding her close to him, not only for her heat but because he wasn't going to see her for another two weeks. He wasn't even going to be able to spend Thanksgiving with anyone he loved since he had a game that night.

Elli nuzzled her nose into the middle of his chest, moving her face back and forth, that's when he noticed she was crying.

"Oh no, no tears Elli, I can't do it this time around." She looked up at him with a watery smile.

"I'm gonna miss you so much, I just hate that you have to leave for so long again," she cried as she nuzzled her nose back into the stuffing of his jacket.

"I know baby, but it's just another two weeks, then I'll be home."

"Yeah but then you leave for another week."

"Yes, but you are coming up that week, we are going to be fine babe," he said with a grin, putting his fingers under her chin, moving it up so she would look at him with them beautiful green eyes. "I'll miss you."

Elli gave him a small smile, sniffing before saying, "I'll miss you more."

"I'll call every chance I get, are you going to keep my bed warm?"

"I am," she said as red dusted her cheeks, he didn't know if it was because she was cold or if she was embarrassed but he loved the color just the same.

"Good," he said as someone called for him to come on, he looked over at the plane and noticed no one was there, everyone had already boarded, and families were making their way back to their cars. He didn't even notice; something that always happened when he was wrapped up in Elli's arms.

"You gotta go," she said as big tears rolled down her cheeks, "Be safe, come home in one piece, alright?"

"I will, remember don't replace me," he said with a wink before kissing her laughing mouth. He kissed her twice more before pulling away, and backing away from her. He wanted to tell her he loved her, but she already knew, and he didn't want to put her on the spot, making her feel like she had to say it back.

When she blew him a kiss as the tears rolled down her cheeks, the words fell flew out of his mouth, "I love you Elli, bye."

She put her hand over her mouth, but didn't say anything as he turned walking towards the plane. He hated leaving her, he did, but he hated that she didn't love him more.

When Shea's plane landed, he had finally finished Pride and Prejudice, the book Elli had given him so long ago, and he knew what he wanted to do for her birthday. While waiting for the crew to load the bus up with everyone's bags, he dialed Grace's number.

"Hey, you land already?" she asked when she answered.

"We did, I figured out what I want to do for Elli's birthday."

"Okay? Why do I feel I'm about to get pissed?"

Shea laughed because she was probably going to get pissed but he didn't care, it was the profession she chose, and it wasn't his fault she was his twin. It also wasn't his fault that she had to do anything he ask, and vice versa. He went on with the theme he wanted, and she didn't say anything for about a minute after he got done talking.

"When's her birthday?" she asked.

"December 17th."

"So you want me to take us back to the 19th century in a little over month?"

He nodded, even though she couldn't see him as he said, "Yes."

"Are you fucking crazy! How the hell am I gonna pull that off? I would have to send the invites out next week just to see how many people RSVP! Then where am I going to have it at? Places are filling up because of Christmas parties! You're positively crazy!-" and on she went, complaining about how she wasn't gonna be able to pull this off as he rode the bus to the hotel.

When he had enough he said, "You can do it Grace, I know you can. You have access to my account. I don't care how much it cost, just make it happen. Invite all her friends from Facebook, invite the team, I'll contact her family, this is gonna be amazing, and when it's all said in done, I'll make sure you get all the credit."

"Damn right I will and I'm gonna charge you an arm and leg!"

He laughed before saying, "You can have all my limbs as long as this is the best birthday Elli has ever had."

Chapter 21

"He's driving me bat shit crazy Elli, I don't even understand how a grown man can bitch and moan as much as Jakob does!" Harper complained as they sat in Elli's office, waiting for a walk-in or their next appointment to come in.

It had been a long two weeks, but Shea was coming home the next day and Elli was super excited!

The first week Elli work a lot, it was a good week for her and the Assassins since they had won every game they played. On Thanksgiving, Elli ended up going to Liam and Noah's house to see the kids before they went to her parents. It was wonderful seeing the kids, they asked her about Shea and when they would see him again, Elli promised to have a day with them and Shea. They loved that, and covered her with kisses and hugs. She ate dinner with Bryan, talking hockey, and of course about Shea. He wanted to make sure Shea was being good to her, which of course he was.

Every time Shea and Elli would get off the phone, he would tell her he loved her. She didn't realize being told that she was loved by someone would fill her so completely, but every time Shea did, it gave her butterflies, but then she would feel like the biggest ass in the world because she would say 'Thanks, bye!'. What was supposed to say though? She didn't want to lie to him. Yes, she had deep feelings for Shea, maybe they were love, but she just couldn't bring herself to say it, not in less she knew for a fact that she did. Which how she was going to know that was beyond her.

The past week was busy with people getting Christmas pictures done in the studio, while businesses hired Elli for Christmas parties. Birthdays and weddings were in full swing again, and Elli wasn't getting home till late again. The holidays always brought in a lot of business, which was good, but Elli was crazy tired by the time she got home.

Nashville was also so beautiful during Christmas time though, lights covered trees, Santa filled the windows of businesses, lights shaped into different Christmas figures adorned every light post along the sidewalks and everyone was just nicer during the holidays, it seemed. There was such a beautiful feeling that just filled Elli up during the holidays. Even with Harper bitching every minute about Jakob, she couldn't help but smile.

"I mean I love him, I do but Jesus, I'm ready for him to go on the road!" Harper complained some more as Elli ordered some toys for the kids on the computer.

"I mean what did you expect Harp?"

Harper threw her arms up in the air, "I was expecting him to not bitch and moan!"

Elli shook her head, "Harp, he's in pain, give him some slack."

"He's a baby," she said in a huff as she crossed her arms, Elli giggled just as her phone went off. She looked at the display seeing it was Jodi.

"Jodi!" she gushed, Harper smiled as Jodi gushed, "Hey Elli!"

"Tell her I say hi!"

"Harper says hi!" Jodi laughed, saying to tell her the same.

"So I'm calling because my water heater busted, my carpets are soaked and there is no way I can have people over this weekend for our dinner, is there any way we can do it at your house?"

"Oh no! That sucks, um yeah, I don't see why not," Elli said trying to think of the last time she went home. She had gone shopping for clothes because she didn't want to go back to her house. She had been missing Shea a lot these past two weeks; she had figured it was cause of the holidays. All she knew was she was ready for him to be home, even if it was only for 3 days.

"Awesome, thanks so much!"

"No problem babe! See ya Sunday," she said before saying bye and hanging up the phone.

"What happen?" Harper asked as she stretched out on Elli's couch.

"Jodi's water heater busted, she was wondering if we can do it at my house," she answered before putting in her credit card information in the right spaces for her order.

"Well shit, do you think Shea would mind having it at his house? Jakob won't make it in the car out to your house."

Elli nodded, "Crap, I forget he can't ride in the car for long. I don't know, I can ask I guess," she said as she looked at the time, Shea was working out, so she would have to wait to call him.

"Cool," Harper said with a nod, then she sat up quickly, "You know what would make me happy and forget that I have a whiny, little brat of a boyfriend at home?"

Elli giggled as she looked over at Harper, "What's that?"

"Let's go out later!"

"Go out?"

"Yeah, let's go karaoking!"

"Karaoking? Is that even a word?"

"It is in my dictionary! Come on! Let's go get our drink on!"

Elli giggled as she shook her head, "Harper I haven't drank in months."

"More the reason to go, we'll have a ball, we always do! Please!"

"Maybe, depends on how the day goes," she said with a grin while Harper's shoulders slumped. She wasn't saying no, she loved going out with Harper, but she needed to clean up a little at the condo before Shea got home, and she had a busy day tomorrow, so she wouldn't be able to drink much if she did.

Her cell phone rang just as she was about to get up to get the receipt that she had printed off the printer. It was Shea.

"Hey you, I thought you were working out," she said as she got the piece of paper, folding it up and putting it in her check book.

"Got done early, what are you doing?"

"Hanging out with Harper in the office, my next appointment isn't for another twenty minutes."

"Cool, I was thinking about you, thought I would call."

"Aw, I'm always thinking of you," she smiled, catching Harper rolling her eyes. She picked up the squishy ball she had on her desk and beamed Harper in the head with it. Harper let out of a scream before flipping Elli the bird.

"What was that?" he asked as Elli laughed.

"Harper being Harper," she said as Harper stormed out the office, "I'm glad you called though I need to ask you a favor."

"Sure."

"Is it okay if I have my friends over for dinner and games on Sunday? I know you leave Monday morning, but Harpers wants Jakob to come and he can't ride in the car for a long time, so my house is out, and Jodi's water heater busted," she said as she drew little hearts on her calendar.

"Sure, I don't mind. I'll like to meet your friends." She smiled as Harper came back into her office a coffee in hand.

"Who said you were invited?" she asked, teasing him a little.

"Oh am I not invited?" he laughed, she laughed along.

"Oh course you are, I think after two months it's time for you to meet the besties, thanks so much for letting me have it at the house. I'll call everyone up and let them know, they'll be excited to meet you," she said picking up the coffee cup Harper had just laid down when she leaned over to see what Elli was writing.

Elli took a sip and Harpers yelled, "Hey!"

"Oh hush!" Elli said back as Shea laughed.

"You guys act like sisters."

"We do," she agreed as her business phone started ringing, "I gotta go, I'll call ya later?"

"Sure babe, I love you, and miss you a lot," he said, and like always her stomach filled with butterflies.

"I miss you too, bye."

When she hung up the phone, Harper had already answered the business line, so she leaned back in her chair, looking up at the ceiling. She wished she knew if she loved Shea or not, sometimes she thought she did, but then Justin would come into her head, causing her to question her feelings. Plus, she decided, when she did know for sure she loved Shea, she didn't want to tell him on the phone but in person.

As Elli watched Harper write some things down, she decided she did need a night out. Girls night with Harper were always a hoot, and she loved to do karaoke, so when Harper hung up and looked up at her, all Elli said was, "What time we going tonight?"

Shea knew he should have told Elli earlier that he was coming home after the game. It was what he gets for trying to surprise her, a taxi ride from the airport to the house. He had called her about ten times, but she never answered. So he got in the cab and went home, but when he got to the condo Elli wasn't there either, and it was well past midnight. He tried to call her again, but her phone just kept going to voicemail.

When Shea went upstairs and saw that Adler was still there, he guessed maybe she was at a wedding, but she never had turned her phone off before, and he could of swore she had said she was coming home early tonight. He stood with his hands on his hips, confused, a little pissed, and even more worried. He reached for his phone again, and dialed Jakob.

"Hey dude," Jakob said when he answered.

"Hey, is Harper there?"

"Nope, she's out with Elli."

Out with Elli?

"Huh? Where did they go?"

"Well apparently I'm driving Harper dog shit crazy, so she left to get her 'drink on', whatever the hell that means," he said, and Shea just shook his head.

"You mean bat shit crazy, and drink on? Where?"

"I think some karaoke bar, *Wanna Do Something* maybe?"

Again, Shea shook his head. Jakob had been living in Nashville almost as long as he had, didn't he know anything about the damn town?

"You mean Wanna B's? You're pitiful Jak," he laughed as Jakob chuckled.

"No I'm drugged up dude, anyways, yeah I think they're there."

"Cool, I guess I roll over there, I was trying to surprise Elli," he said, going to the bedroom to change out of his suit, "Wanna roll out with me?"

"Um, I don't know, Harper might get angry."

"She'll be okay, I'll be there in ten." Shea hung up and threw his phone on the bed, before stripping off his suit to put on a pair of jeans and a button down long sleeve dress shirt. After doing his hair, and putting in his contacts, he was out the door and on his way to Harper's apartment since that was where Jakob had been staying. Harper lived in a little condo building unlike his large one; it was red brick, and old looking. He remembered Elli saying it was huge inside, but it was a studio condo. Something he could never live in, Shea needed a bedroom.

Shea called Jakob, letting him know he was there, and watched as Jakob limped to the truck. Shea cringed watching Jakob trying to get in the truck, he was obviously in pain, but Shea knew not to ask him if he needed help. Jakob was an ass when he was in pain, Shea learned that early, and knew not to mess with him when he was hurting. After buckling his seat belt, Jakob looked over at Shea. His nose was completely healed; only a little yellow around the base of his nose.

"It hurts like a bitch, man."

"I bet, only a couple more weeks though," Shea reassured as he backed out, heading towards Broadway, where the bar was located. When he saw Elli's truck, his pulse picked up. It had been a long, agonizing two weeks. He had missed her so much, and couldn't wait to hold her in his arms, kiss those luscious lips on hers, lay her down in the bed that he had missed as much as he missed her.

Shea parked the truck beside hers, and notice that the place was busy, like always. He waited at the front of the truck as Jakob hobbled his way towards him. They entered and made their way, slowly through the crowed bar. When they got to an opening in the crowd, Shea saw Harper sitting off to the side, waving her arms in the air, but he didn't see Elli.

"I didn't know Elli could sing, she's damn good too," Jakob said, Shea looked over at him, seeing he was pointing up at the stage. Shea looked over at the stage, and that's when he noticed two things.

The first thing was that Elli's pants were extremely tight.

The second was that she was extremely drunk.

"Oh my god," he muttered as he watched her sing. It was the first time he had ever heard her beautiful voice, but he couldn't enjoy it, because she wasn't singing with a smile, no, she was glaring and pointing and basically cussing out some guy by the bar. The guy she was singing too, kind of looked like Jakob as he leaned against the bar, with a smug grin on his face and his arms crossed across his chest.

"Who's the guy?"

"I don't know, let's go ask Harper," Shea said through clenched teeth, heading towards Harper, because Shea felt that if he went over there, the smug grin that was on that asshole's face would be on the floor. Harper was screaming 'Get it, girl' at Elli when they reached her.

"Hey guys!" she gushed when she noticed them. She moved past Shea, wrapping herself up in Jakob's arms, "I missed you," she said up to Jakob, he smiled lovingly at her, kissing her nose, before pointing over to the guy.

"Who's that?" he asked.

Harper squashed up her face, like something didn't smell good, and basically growled out, "That ass hat is, Justin."

Shea whipped his head back to look at Harper, "Justin, as in Elli's ex?"

"The one and only, he actually had to the gall to tell her she looks good. Which of course she does, but she looked good when she was with him too," Harper slurred. Harper's head fell to the side as she looked Elli over, "I'm actually surprised Elli's still dressed."

Shea looked over at her confused, "What? Why's that?"

"Because that girl can't keep her clothes on when she's drinking tequila and she's had a lot!" Shea raised his eyebrows, looking back at Elli, who was only wearing a little tank with her extremely tight jeans. Harper almost fell off the stool she was sitting in, but Jakob caught her before she hit the floor. She was just as smashed as his girlfriend, the same girlfriend that had just threw her mic down, after hitting the last note of the angry song perfectly, and throwing her middle finger in the air as she made it down the stairs, coming towards them.

For the love of God.

"That was awesome babe! Tell that asshole! Because he stole your happy, he made you cry-" and off they went singing the chorus again. People around them sang along, while some cheered them on.

They obviously had fans.

When they finished Harper cheered for Elli again as she grinned widely at her, then Elli let out a squeal when she saw Shea.

"Shea!" she almost fell twice as she made her way towards him, slamming her body into his, and kissing him lavishly. He tasted beer as she swirled her tongue with his, sloppily and had to pull back. She was too drunk to be kissing.

"Hey baby," he said kissing her nose, then the side of her mouth as she smiled up at him.

"You're home early!"

"I am, surprise," he said as she swayed back and forth, "Jesus baby, how much have you had?"

She giggled, before saying, "A. Lot."

"I can see that."

"It started out just beer but then these nice guys wanted to buy us shots of tequila and of course we said yes to free booze!" Harper let out a loud yee haw, and Elli joined in, slapping hands with her.

And he thought Grace was bad drunk. He couldn't count how many times he has dealt with an extremely drunk Grace through his teen years and early twenties. Grace had gotten them in trouble so many times that Shea was surprised he was where he was and not in jail.

"Did you see that ass hat I wasted years of my life too? I wanna go smack him, but Harper said I couldn't. She didn't have any bail money on her, but I said we could always call you, or my papa, but she wouldn't let me," she slurred.

"Thank God," Shea and Jakob said at the same time, they grinned at each other, and then looked back down at Elli. She was chugging a beer along with Harper. Shea shook his head, looking around the bar, noticing that men were watching as the girls drank and giggled.

Shea wondered how many of the guys had hit on Elli, since she had said guys had bought them drinks. He wondered if she flirted back, if she had given them the same smile she gives him, or if she touched them the way she always touched him. His mind filled with the thoughts of what could or what had happen as he assumed the worst, that she had cheated, that she had come out to replace him. She didn't love him, what made him any better than any of the assholes in the bar.

Elli looked over at Shea, and the brightest, biggest, most beautiful smile crossed her face, before she came to him, wrapping her arms around him, looking up at him. He could see the lust filling in her eyes, "Did you know, that the whole time I've been here I've been wishing that you were here, cause I just missed you soooooo much," she slurred as she leaned on him for support, "We should go find a place to be *alone*," she said drawing out the last word.

Shea smiled shaking his head, how could he think those things? His sweet Elli was crazy for him and only him. He could see it in her beautiful, sparkling with lust, green eyes.

He was jealous.

Something he had never been before.

His breath caught, while she just grinned up at him totally oblivious to the fact that he was having an epiphany. He hadn't even realized it had happen, he knew he loved her, but he didn't realize that he was absolutely, completely, and entirely hers, and that she could break him.

She reached her finger up to his forehead, poking him hard between his eyes, "You're thinking too hard," she stated, "about what?" With every word her head nodded, and all he could do was laugh as she beamed up at him, drunkenly.

"Nothing baby, you ready to head out?" he asked as he gathered her in his arms, kissing her cheeks.

"I was thinking I would have another beer or two."

He shook his head, before bringing his lips to her ear, "I thought you wanted to go somewhere to be alone, I was thinking my bed."

There was no way he was having sex with Elli when she was plastered, but if he had to say that to get her out of the bar, he would say it. She probably wouldn't make it home awake.

A slow grin went across her face, and she looked over at Harper, who was making out with the man that was apparently driving her bat shit crazy.

"I'm leaving!"

Harper looked over at her, and glared, "No, no, no, no, you ain't. You're my ride!" she said moving her head from side to side. Shea raised an eyebrow as Jakob just chuckled.

"Baby, I'll drive you home," Jakob said, "Shea can I take your truck home? You can drive Elli's home."

"Sure. Thanks," he said digging out his keys and handing them to Jakob, "We'll come and get it tomorrow."

"Sure dude, thanks."

Jakob put his arm around Harper, and started to lead her out. Shea did the same to Elli, but they only made it halfway before Elli tripped. Shea caught her before she hit the ground as she started laughing uncontrollably. Shea basically had to carry her out of the bar. How did they think they were going to get home if he hadn't of showed up?

When they got outside and the cold hit Elli, she let out a cry and basically climbed into Shea's jacket as he tried to walk. It had gotten colder in Nashville since he left, two weeks ago it was in the lower 50s, but now he was convinced it was only 20 degrees outside. When he reached the truck, Elli had her keys out, and unlocked the doors. He helped her up into the jacked up truck, shutting the door before going around getting in himself. She had already started the truck, and some country singer was singing about drinking.

What else was new in the country world?

They were either singing about being drunk, crying about their women leaving, or about their tractors. But Shea would admit, country boys wrote wicked mean love songs.

Elli sat cross leg, singing louder than necessary as he carefully backed her monster of a truck out of the parking spot she was in. How she drove this truck on a daily bases, he couldn't fathom, the thing was huge!

"Well if I have one, I'll have thirteen, Naw, there ain't no in-between," she sang before stopping, jumping up and down in the seat beside him, "Oh my god! This is my theme song!"

Shea just shook his head as he laughed at his beautifully, drunken girlfriend, "It sure is baby."

Elli threw herself into him, causing him to swerve before breaking down in a fit of giggles. He couldn't be mad at her, she was harmless, but he would monitor her drinking for now on.

"Shea, I've missed you sooooo much," she slurred against his neck, "So much."

"I've missed you too baby."

She grinned up at him, and he returned it before turning off Broadway, heading to his condo. After a few minutes of silence she asked, "You know what?" as she turned the drinking song down.

"What baby?"

"Sometimes I think I love you."

He looked over at her, and she was looking down at her hands, he could see that her eyes were filling with tears.

Aw shit, she was one of those drunks?

"But every time I think I do, Justin comes along and he gets in my head telling me I'm no damn good, and that I don't know how to love a man. He was so mean to Shea, so mean," she said as she shook her head. He didn't know what to say so he didn't say anything, but he did wish he would have at least gone over to the guy, and push him into the wall. "You wouldn't believe half the shit that asshole did to me, and I thought it was normal. I was so naive."

"You were young," Shea stated, hating the guy more and more with each passing second.

"I know, but I should have known better, especially when we had been dating for years, and he never told me he loved me, the day he chose to tell me he loved me was the day my grandparents died and I got my inherence."

Shea looked over at her, "You're kidding."

"No," she said, taking a deep breath, "When we would have sex after I gained all my weight, he would put a blanket over me or turn off the lights, so he wouldn't be able to see anything."

Okay, that was just crazy. "Elli, why did you stay with him?"

"Because he said he loved me," she started to hiccup and he thought she was done talking, but she went on, "before when we were just dating I didn't care that he didn't love me, but after my grandparents died and he said that, I said it back because I was so sad and I felt so alone. We moved in together in New York, and everything was fine, until I got fat. We had moved back home; and my family had turned on me, he turned on me and shit was bad. I craved the 'I love yous', they were slim to none but I tried to do everything to make him happy, but nothing worked. At least once a month I would come home from school and my shit would be outside the house that he owned, Harper would take me in, and then three days later he would show up begging me to come home."

The tears started to fall, and Shea reached for her hand, she took it, using her other hand to wipe her face. "And I did." Shea noticed she was starting to look green when he looked over at her, but she just went on, so he assumed she was fine.

"Finally, I started to notice something wasn't right. I was in school something he said was a waste of time because when we got married I wouldn't need to work since I would be taking care of the babies, which how we were gonna make those babies was beyond me since he never wanted to have sex with me, but whatever-" She stopped suddenly and Shea looked over. "Pull over," he did as she asked, and she opened the door, puking her brains out. Her body shook violently as she threw up on the side of West End Ave. He ran his hand up and down her back, trying to move her hair out of the way as she expelled some of the beer and tequila she had consumed.

Shea had thought Grace was a talented drunk, nope, she had nothing on Elli. Right after she got done, she sat up, grabbed the bottle of water that sat in her counsel, washed her mouth out and went on with her story.

He was amazed once more by her.

"So anyways, we weren't having sex, and he had made me go to one of them stupid dinners through his daddy's firm, when I stepped into that place in my plus size dress without him because he went earlier then me, no one looked at me, that's when I knew that I was nothing." Shea sat listening to her, not moving the truck, he wanted to hear her, plus incase she needed to puke, he was already pulled over. "The night went on, when he would introduce me to the women of the firm; they couldn't even look me in the eye, that's when I knew he was cheating on me."

Shea's heart hurt for her, and it seemed with every word that came out of her mouth, he got madder and madder. When her face turned green again, he was glad he was already pulled over so she could continue to throw up on the side of the street again. She repeated the rinsing of the mouth routine and then went on like she hadn't been throwing her guts up on the side of the road. "So that night," she let out an empty laugh, "he actually had the gall to climb on top of me. I got so mad, that I pushed him off me. Oh Shea, he became so mad. Called me everything in the book, smacked me up against the wall, telling me I was nothing and that no one would love me. I don't know what got into me, it must have been him hitting me, but I swung back and hit him as hard as I could. He fell to the ground and I threw my ring at him, telling him I did not love him, and I was leaving. And I finally did and he never came after me."

Shea wanted to beat the living hell out of Justin. No man lays a hand on a woman, it was disgusting and Shea couldn't believe that he let that man stand beside the bar with that smug look on his face. Let him see him out in the streets, Shea would beat him to a pulp.

"Why aren't you driving?" Shea looked over at her, relaxing his hands from the steering wheel that he was squeezing so tightly his hands hurt.

"Oh I thought you needed to throw up some more," he said pulling the truck back onto the road when it was clear.

"No I'm good. I'm tired now," she said, before crossing her arms across her legs and laying her down.

She was out before they even made it a mile. Her loud snores filled the truck, and even though he was so pissed he could scream, he cracked a smile as he drove, Elli was the most beautiful, strongest, amazing woman he had ever met and he couldn't love her more than he did at that moment.

When they got home, Shea carried Elli over his shoulder up the steps and into the condo as Adler bounced up and down around Shea's legs.

"Adler bud, sit," Shea said as he tried to move by him, Adler of course listen, and Shea made it to the bedroom with Elli drooling down his back.

He just prayed she didn't throw up.

Shea laid her down on the bed, and proceeded to take her clothes off. He thought about throwing her in the shower since she had makeup on and smelt like a bar, but she couldn't even stand, so he discarded that thought and continued to pull her shirt off. It took a lot more force than he thought it would to get her cowboy boots off, but he finally got them off before pulling her pants off. He shook his head at her drunkenness, as he pulled her up in the bed, tucking her into the bed.

He loved learning new things about Elli, but he could have went on without knowing that Justin Yates was a asshole with a death wish, and that Elli was the worst drunk ever, but even with knowing those things about her, he still loved her, probably always would.

Shea undressed before going into the bathroom to wash up and take out his contacts. When he came back into the bedroom, Elli was laying face first in her pillow, with the blankets kicked off her. He laughed as he shut off the lights, and crawled into bed with her. He looked over at her, and smiled, how was she breathing with her face in the pillow like that?

"Baby, can you breathe?" She nodded and he laughed before saying, "Alright baby, goodnight," he leaned over kissing her naked shoulder before saying, "I love you."

When she didn't say anything, like he knew she wouldn't, he closed his eyes. But he opened them again when she said, "Good, because I need you."

A grin cracked across his face, and he closed his eyes.

She needed him.

That had to be one step closer to loving him.

Chapter 22

Shea learned another thing about Elli the next morning, and that was that she was very angry when she was hung over.

When she sat up as he came out the bathroom, her hair was sticking straight up, her makeup smeared across her face, also all over her pillow and drool was dripping from her chin. He still thought she was beautiful though, even when she started cussing him out.

"Why the hell is that window open! For the love of God, Shea! My fucking head is pounding and that damn sun is beaming on me! Ahhh!" she screamed and curled up in a ball, covering her body with the blankets. He couldn't help but laugh as he walked over to the window, shutting the curtains. He came around the bed, looking down at the ball that was his Elli.

"Better, sunshine?"

"Fuck off!" she yelled, but not even a second later she threw the blankets back, and looked up at him, "I didn't mean that, I'm sorry."

He smiled, leaning down to kiss her cheek, "Its fine, you're an angry day after kind of chick, Grace is the same way."

She tried to smile, but shot up, running to the bathroom. When he heard her puking, he went in there to see her hugging the toilet. He went up behind her, moving her hair back. He looked over at the counter and saw a hair tie, so he grabbed it and pulled her hair up in a messy ponytail on the top of her head. When she started crying, he sat down beside her, rubbing her back.

"Oh my god, what man does this?" she cried as she continued to puke, he smiled running his hand up and down her back. When she stopped throwing up, he stood up to get her some water from the sink. She washed her mouth out, but went right back to throwing up. "Ugh, just leave me here to die Shea."

He laughed as he went to the bathtub, filling it up. "Maybe a bath would help?"

"Maybe," she said, lying down so that her face was on the cold tile. "I need to call Harper, what time is it? I have a nine o'clock appointment."

"I already called her; she's fine apparently, she going to go in with Alice."

"Thank you so much. Yeah, she always is, it makes me sick, cause I never am."

"I see that." She opened her eyes, glaring at him but closed them quickly because he guessed it hurt. "Wanna jump in?"

"I will not be jumping, but climbing might happen," she said as she started crawling over towards the bath, he helped her take her bra off, then she slid out of her panties before falling into the water, splashing water onto the floor. He shook his head as he went to get towels to clean up as she apologized. After cleaning up, he made sure she was okay and left her to soak as he went into the bedroom to wash the bedding.

He had an amused grin on his face as he moved through the condo, picking up her mess. Yeah, she drove him crazy, but he wouldn't have it any other way. After last night, he knew why she wouldn't move in with him. It wasn't because she didn't care for him but because that asshole didn't treat her right.

How he could kick Elli out of her home, when she was raw with hurt and scared with all the medical problems she was having at the time was beyond him, and he hated the guy for it, but he wanted to murder the guy for putting his hands on her. No women deserved to have a man put his hands on her, but especially not his Elli. She was too sweet, too perfect.

It all made perfect sense now, and he knew that it was going to take a lot to get Elli past that, but he didn't care. Shea would be there, he would be patient, he would love her, and one day, he just knew she would love him back.

Elli thought men like Shea Adler didn't exist, but they did. Shea had laid beside her in bed watching movies all day, as she tried to recover from the awful hangover she had.

Damn tequila.

She was never drinking again, she swore.

Last night was a blur, she remember everything up to singing Carrie Underwood, after that it was a blur. Shea said that she was puking all over the sidewalk of West End Ave, which was lovely, considering that was the classier side of Nashville. She remembered seeing Justin, but not wanting to fight him like Harper had said she wanted too.

That was another reason she was never drinking again, she didn't remember anything after a certain point!

Shea was so good to her though, bringing her crackers, and rubbing her back when she would get nauseous. He was genuinely a great guy, and Elli didn't know how she got so lucky to have met him.

The next day, they went to see Grace and the kids at the Adventure Science Center after Shea's practice. They had such a great time, even though Elli was still a little sick from the day before. Afterwards, they went to Publix to go grocery shopping for the next day before Shea needed to go home for a nap. Elli decided she wanted to make a Christmas dinner with all the fixing since she wouldn't see her friends till after the holidays, so she got the biggest ham they had since Shea, Jakob, Derrick, and Walter would be there, and they ate like an army.

After unloading the groceries, Elli started to clean while Shea washed his clothes from his suitcase. It was so domestic, they would move around each other with ease, he would ask if she knew where something was, and most of the time she did. Living there for the past month had been so easy, she knew his condo inside and out, and now that he was home with her, moving around the house with her, she really didn't seem as scared as she was before about moving in with him.

She wasn't sure what had changed in the last two weeks, but something had, so maybe she would consider it, or maybe she would just keep things like they are, because God knew her daddy and Papa would freak when they find out. The thought sent chills through her body, she couldn't even imagine it because when she moved in with Justin, they flipped but her mother took care of them and Elli didn't even have to deal with it, but now, she's pretty sure 'the shit would hit the fan', as it was said.

Elli was in the kitchen, getting the ham ready by soaking it in water, when Shea came up behind her, wrapping her arms around her waist. She smiled as he ran his lips up her neck, nipping at her ear lobe.

"So my dining room looks like something out of Country Living, the Christmas Edition," he said, causing her to giggle.

"I know, you don't mind do you?"

"No, I like it, it's just new. So is the Christmas candles you have everywhere."

"I know, but I want it to be pretty when everyone comes tomorrow. I love Christmas," she gushed as she leaned into him.

"I know, but we're missing something." She turned in his arms, looking up at him.

"What?"

"A Christmas tree," he said, "go look in the living room." She beamed up at him before heading into the living room, to see a good size tree sitting in the corner by the TV with bags and boxes of stuff sitting beside it. It was her stuff from her house, she had wanted to go get them but she had been busy.

"I usually don't set up for Christmas, since I'm never home anyway, but Harper had said the other day that it was a big deal for you, so I had her go get your stuff for me, she just dropped it off."

"Oh Shea," she gushed covering her mouth as she turned to look at him, "You're spectacular."

"Spectacular, huh?"

She nodded before wrapping her arms around him, and kissing him hard. When she parted from him, she clapped her hands together with a little hop, "I can't wait to get started after the game!"

Elli stood in the middle of Shea's living room basking in the winter wonderland they had created the night before. All her stuff fit perfectly in his living room, and if it didn't, he made sure to make it. Shea had filled the windows with white lights, covered the bases of the windows with her fake snow puff, placing the candles in the middle of it, with glitter of course. They placed every single one of her snowmen out, and there were a lot of them since that was her favorite Christmas thing.

When they decorated the tree, Elli's heart just filled with such love at the act. She had never decorated a tree with a man, and Shea was the perfect man for her first time. He asked a question about every ornament she had. Elli had been collecting Primitive ornaments since she was fourteen, growing up she had always had a Christmas tree in her room, so she had a lot of old ornaments, and it was nice to reminisce about each ornament. Elli was convinced he enjoyed it cause afterwards he said they should go to the store to pick out some for him, she couldn't agree quicker, which made him smile.

They had hung some of her Christmas photo's she had done when he was in college too, there was one of candy canes made to look like a heart, 'love' written in the snow, and then one of her making a snow angel. She was admiring the one of her when Shea came into the living dressed for her friends that were coming over. He was wearing a pair of nice khaki dress pants, with a dark red button up dress shirt, the first two buttons weren't button, his hair was done spiky, and he had his glasses on, something that still made her heart skip a beat. Even though the guys had lost last night, he had a smile on his face.

"Is this okay?" he asked, running his hands down his shirt. She nodded as she came over, moving herself into his arms; he of course took her eagerly. "What?"

"The living room looks so beautiful," she stated as she leaned her head down on his shoulder, he nodded. "It makes me happy."

"Good, I love the pictures."

"Me too, I was thinking, the first snow fall, we should do a picture together of us making snow angels, Harper would take it."

"Sounds good to me," he said with a grin, as he looked down at her, "Looking good baby, real good."

She looked down at her vintage green with white polka dots dress. The dress was lined with black along the collar and a big black bow around the fitted top, it then puffed out with black netting underneath. She had paired it with stunning, Jimmy Choo, suede black peep toe heels that had matching crystals all over them. She had bought the shoes the first week Shea was gone, it was her pity gift to herself, and she loved them.

"Why thank you, the lady at the store says my eyes sparkle in this dress."

"They do," he said before kissing her softly on her bright red lips. The dinging of the oven broke up their kiss; Elli gave him a small smile before running off to the kitchen to take out her ham and stuffin'. Everything was already laid out, so she added the ham and stuffin' to the island, leaning back to inspect her work.

She had done good.

Shea walked behind her, heading back to the bedroom, so she yelled at him, "Hey, darlin', can you grab the iHome and plug it up in the living room with my iPod?"

"Sure," he said with a laugh, she glared towards the door cause she knew he was making fun of her accent, and continued to move around the kitchen, making sure everything was ready when he came back through with the iHome in hand. "This one right *Darlin'*?" he said in a horrible country accent.

Boston men cannot be country.

"Oh hush!"

Shea laughed as he continued back into the living room, just as the doorbell rang. She assumed he would get it, and went to make sure the dining room was perfect just as she heard Harper's voice rang through the condo. "Jeez! I thought you said you were just gonna set up the tree? It looks like Santa shit Christmas in here!"

Elli rolled her eyes, coming from the dining room to the kitchen. Harper was wearing a tight little red number, with gorgeous peep toe black boots, she looked beautiful like always, and

Jakob stood proudly beside her, wearing a nice little dress suit, with a red shirt, and of course his brace on his leg. "Now you hush! I love my Winter Wonderland!"

Harper laughed, handing Elli the red velvet cake her mother had made, "You're lucky I got out the house with that, Piper and Reese almost got a hold of it."

"Oh! You should have invited them!" Elli complained as she carried the cake into the kitchen, "Shea hasn't met them yet."

"Yeah, they were being brats, plus they always laugh at us when we play our games."

Elli giggled, even though she had been nervous all day about Shea laughing at her when he saw how they played their game. "True."

"Wow, everything looks yummy," Harper said scoping out the food, she ate just like a dude, which made Elli sick with how she could eat and not gain an ounce. "So this is a really nice place."

"It is," Elli agreed as Shea and Jakob made their way into the kitchen.

"Wow, nice spread Elli," Jakob said, hugging Harper into his side.

"Thanks, Jakob."

"I was just telling Elli, this is a nice place Shea, I really like it," Harper said, Shea nodded thanks as he poured wine for everyone.

"I like it for just us," Harper cut a look over at Elli, grinning ear to ear but Elli just ignored her as Shea continued, "but I would like to get something bigger one day. I love Elli's house, but it's a little out there."

"Yeah," Harper agreed, "Jakob and I are actually looking into houses."

Elli dropped the spoon she had in her hand, "Seriously?"

"Yeah, my condo is so stinkin' small, and he lives in an even smaller apartment, so we are looking into getting house," Harper gushed with a grin.

"Wow, that's amazing!" Elli exclaimed just as the doorbell rang, "Someone's here!"

Shea was wicked nervous. He was more nervous about meeting Elli's friends than he was about meeting her family. She actually loved these people! So it meant something if they didn't like him. Elli of course was fine; she grabbed a hold of his hand, dragging him to the door to greet their guest. He loved when she was excited like this, and after setting up the winter wonderland in his living room, she was the biggest ball of sunshine he had ever seen.

Elli threw the door open to a huge black man, and little bitty blonde haired woman. The girls let out a little squeal, wrapping each other up in a hug. "Come in, it's freezin' out!"

They came inside, grinning ear to ear, "Jodi, Derrick, this is Shea," Elli said as the pair beamed up at him, "Shea this is my best friend Jodi, we used to sing together back in school and some on Broadway," Jodi held out her hand, shaking Shea's eagerly.

"So nice to meet you! I've heard some much," Jodi gushed.

"It's great to finally meet you," Shea said, as Elli just stood by grinning.

"And this is her husband Derrick, he looks mean, but he's a teddy bear," Elli said rubbing the man's large belly, when he broke out in a huge smile, Shea finally could breathe. The dude was huge! They shook hands, just as the doorbell rang again.

"Walter and Trice are here, y'all can head into the kitchen, Harper and Jakob are in there." Elli said going to the door, as Jodi beamed back at her.

"Two boyfriends in one day, it's my Christmas wish come true." Shea chuckled as the couple made their way into the kitchen. Elli opened the door to two blonde haired men, one was wearing a pink jacket, (no joke), while the other wore a nice tailored black one.

"Hey guys, come on in."

The guys came in, grinning over at Elli. "I mean goodness Elli, you look fantastical! Radiant!" one of the guys said, while the heavier one nodded his head. "You do darlin'!"

"Thanks guys! Shea," both men turned to look at Shea, both of them looking him over as Elli went on with her spill, "This is Trice and Walter. Trice runs the makeup department at the TPAC, while Walter is the backstage director, guys this is Shea," she said, before the guys took Shea's hand in theirs.

"Well aren't you perfect for our Elli, just the way she describe you. It's nice to meet you," Trice said, Shea nodded as he smiled broadly.

"Same here, thank you," he said, as Elli took his hand in hers.

"Y'all ready to eat? I've been cooking all night!"

Everyone made their way into the dining as Shea and Elli carried all the food in, placing it in the middle of the table that Elli had made into a wonderland too. She had actually dusted fake snow down the middle, with little Santas, snowmen, reindeer, and stars everywhere. The girl loved Christmas, something else he never knew. After placing all the food for everyone to dig in, Elli and Shea sat down and dinner started. The food was amazing of course, but what Shea found surprising was how easy he fit in with Elli's friends.

He was nervous about Trice and Walter, since he didn't really know any homosexuals but the guys were funny as all hell, and Shea enjoyed their stories of the terrible actress they were currently dealing with. Jodi and Derrick were so different that they worked; Jodi was a firecracker that loved the dramatics, Shea was certain the girl would break out in song at any minute. Derrick talked a lot about his job as a teacher at one of the prestigious private high schools in the city, and since Shea's parents were also educators, they had a lot to talk about.

When Jodi stood, clanking the side of her glass, everyone stopped talking, bringing their attention to the cute little blonde. "I just want to make a toast to Elli, the food is define honey, and I don't think any of us could disagree on the fact that Shea is amazing," Elli turned deep red as she smiled at Shea, while everyone agreed holding their glasses up. "Also I would like to say, that I never thought I would see the day when Harper Allen would have a boyfriend, or be moving in with the boyfriend, so here's to you Jakob, for taming the crazy bitch!"

Everyone stated laughing as Jakob kissed Harper's glaring face, but Jodi didn't sit down, and when the tears welled up in her eyes, Elli stood, but Jodi shook her head, stopping Elli in her tracks. "We're all in such good places right now, and this is the best time to tell everyone, don't you think Derrick?" Jodi looked down at Derrick and he smiled, taking her hand in his, "We're pregnant guys!"

Shea, Jakob, and Derrick were left at the table as everyone hugged, gushed, and shrieked over Jodi, congratulating her as they rubbed her belly. Derrick shook his head, smiling over at the guys, "They act like I didn't do anything."

Jakob and Shea had to laugh at that.

After dinner; and Elli yelling at everyone to leave the dishes alone, that she would do em later, they all gathered in the living room. Elli had Shea move the coffee table into the bedroom, since she said they had needed more room, Shea didn't know what for but he did what she ask anyways.

"Is Jakob gonna be able to play?" Jodi asked, Jakob looked up from his cake to Jodi then Harper.

"Probably not, I don't know, we can try, I'm the best here anyways so I'll carry him if I need too," Harper said with a smug grin, Elli rolled her eyes.

"We all know I'm the best, so shut it!" Elli said laughing.

"Whatever, I smoke y'all every time!" Trice added.

"What are we playing?" Shea asked. Elli smiled.

"You've seen Pulp Fiction right?"

"Yeah."

"You know the dancing part?"

"Yeah," he said getting more worried by the minute.

"We do that," she giggled as she handed a dry erase board to everyone; Shea just looked up at her confused. "Okay, so we pull two names from the hat, then a song, the two people get up, the song starts and they start dancing." Shea raised an eyebrow, she had to be kidding. "Now the point of the game is not to smile, if you do, you get points taken off each time. One person keeps up with how many points you lose while the others score you, then we deduct and then we have your final score."

Shea and Jakob just looked up at her blinking. "Okay, let's show em, Elli." Harper said, getting up, and picking up the hat that held the songs, Shea guess. When she pulled a piece of paper out, she giggled, going over to the iPod and finding the song as Elli moved over to the father side of the room.

"This is hilarious, get ready for a show, boys," Trice said as everyone went to the edge of their seats as the girls got ready, when the music to 'Push it' started, everyone died laughing as Elli and Harper started dancing hard with straight faces, even Shea had a hard time breathing when Elli dropped it like it was hot before going into the sprinkler. The sprinkler got Harper, and she smiled, causing Trice yelled, "See that's a point off, since Harper smiled." Shea nodded, turning his attention back to the girls, when the song ended, Elli had made Harper smiled three times, and also burst out laughing, which meant Harper got ten points taken off making Elli the winner. Elli made sure to rub it in Harper's face, but Harper said it was just a practice round, causing everyone to laugh.

Shea figured he had the game that was till he played Jodi. He was basically rolling around on the ground laughing. That girl was a mess, and she knew it. When Derrick got paired against Jodi, he didn't even crack a smile, and it made Jodi so mad, that everyone was laughing as she tried the most ridicules dance moves in the world, but she finally got him with the running man, Shea was convinced it was because she ran into the wall though.

Jakob and Harper went against each other to the 'Skanky Leg' and even Shea couldn't keep a straight face as Jakob just stood there pointing to his bum leg during the chorus. Poor Harper, she didn't have a chance.

Finally Shea was paired against Elli, to some song he had never heard, 'What you know'. The music started and Elli had obviously heard the song cause she stood there tapping her foot as the song started, when the song went into its hard hitting notes, Elli went nuts, while all Shea could do was stand there and try not to crack a smile. When she started moving towards him, he clamped his mouth shut from laughing as he made his way towards her, then they broke it down, Pulp Fiction style causing everyone to laugh, which caused them both to fall over in laughter.

Shea had never had so much fun in his life.

They loved him!

Jodi, Derrick, Trice and Walter, all loved Shea, which set her mind at ease. Not only was she ecstatic that everyone loved Shea, but Jodi and Derrick were pregnant! They had been trying for such a long time. That alone brought the bright smile to Elli's face. The dinner and game night was a huge success, and Elli couldn't have been happier as she stood loading the dishwasher. Shea came in from walking Adler just as she was finishing up, and wiping down the counters. He came into the kitchen, shooting her a smile before filling Adler's bowls up. He leaned up against the counter, watching her put away the left overs, before saying, "I had a great time tonight."

She smiled back at him, "I did too."

"I like your friends, they are good people."

"They loved you and they really are, I've loved them a very long time," she said as she turned from closing the fridge. She had had such a wonderful night that she forgot he was leaving early the next morning. "Are you packed? You gotta leave stupid early."

"I know, I was gonna get everything out of the dryer in a minute."

"It already folded, so all you need to do is pack," she said as she moved through the kitchen, stopping at the hallway to slip her shoes off before going into the laundry room, to grab the basket of his clothes. Shea followed her down the hall into the bedroom, where she laid the basket on the bed.

"You didn't have to do that," he said wrapping his arms around her, kissing her lips.

"I don't mind, now pack," she said smacking his arm, before pulling away, "I'm gonna take a shower."

Elli grabbed her night shirt and panties, before heading into the bathroom. After starting the shower, making sure the water was nice and hot; she started undressing as the bathroom filled with steam. She loved when it was cold outside; the steam just came so much quicker in the winter months. Elli open the glass door, stepping in, letting the jets hit her as she made her way to the end of the shower where the large spout was. She loved this spot, she still got hit with the jets but she was able to shower since the spout got her fully drenched all over, not messing a part of her body.

Elli was washing her hair when she felt Shea up against her back. She turned surprised; she didn't even hear him enter. Elli only saw his broad smile for a second before he had her mouth busy with his. He moved her up against the heated marble, moving his hands along her dripping wet body. Elli decided to get her fill in too, moving her hands over his narrow hips, to his exquisite butt. He smiled down at her when she squeezed his butt before kissing down her neck to her breast.

Elli let out ragged sigh as he sucked the water from her heavy breast, tugging at her nipples with his teeth before moving his other hand to between her legs, cupping her mound before dipping a finger inside her wet, not from the water, folds. He circled her throbbing nub with his large rough finger, catching her moan with his mouth as he began to kiss her mindlessly.

When she came, she came loud. The whole bathroom filled with her agonized gasp that turned into loud, explosively moans. He grinned against her lips when she started smacking his hand, to make him stop since Shea would continue to play with her clit to his heart's content, even if she was to the point of passing out. Since Shea had released her mouth, Elli took it upon herself to explore his body with her mouth, she pushed him against the wall causing him to grinned widely at her as she moved her mouth along his collarbone, to his neck, where she bit softly.

She was rewarded with a hiss through his teeth so she continued biting and nipping at every part of his amazingly sculpted chest. Since he had been gone, he had been working out more so the muscles of his chest, the tightness of his abdomen were so pronounced that Elli was dripping with need at the sight. Not even the scars could keep her from wanting him. "Okay, I need you in me," she said against his chest as she grabbed a hold of his shaft, he let out a harsh rush of breath, closing his eyes as she moved her hand up and down his hot, swollen flesh.

"I forgot to grab a condom, I'll be right back," he said, but didn't move as she moved her hand up and down him, cupping his heavy balls with her other hand. She smiled watching his face as he enjoyed the things she was doing with her hands. His hands came up, rolling her dripping wet nipples with his fingers as she moved faster up and down his shaft.

When his eyes finally open, his eyes were so dark, it almost made her come at the sight of his arousal. He pulled away from her, dropping to his knee, burring his face between her legs, running his tongue up and down her folds, slowly flicking his tongue across her swollen nub. She thought since she had came not ten minutes ago, she would have last longer, but nope, he only flicked his tongue maybe three times before she was coming loudly for him.

"Condom, gotta get a condom. Now."

He went to leave, but Elli grabbed his arm, stopping him. "I'm on the pill."

"Oh," he looked down at her with worry in his eyes, arousal nowhere to be seen, "Yeah, I forgot about that."

"Do you not want to do it without a condom?"

He shook his head no, then smiled sheepishly, "This is gonna sound stupid," he began.

"What?"

"I've never done it without a condom, ever."

They stood there staring at each other as moments past, "Ok, I'm clean."

"Oh I know, it's not that, I'm just worried...performance wise."

Elli had to smile, "Well I'm pretty sure you'll get an A, Mr. Adler, now come here, I want you inside me, nothing between us."

It only took a second for him to have her against the hard, hot marble, lifting her leg and burying himself deep within her. They both groaned loudly at the feeling of nothing between them, he was so hot, so big, and Elli wasn't sure how long she was gonna last, because she felt another organism building.

"Oh God," Shea muttered against her neck as he drove into her. He drove into her only two more times before he exploded inside her, leaving her withering beneath him. He leaned his head down into her shoulder, breathing extremely hard as Elli tried to catch her breath.

"I don't even think I lasted a minute," he muttered against her shoulder, embarrassed.

"Probably not," she answered, he looked up at her, glaring, "but it was the best damn minute of my life."

A slow grin went across his face, before he kissed her long and hard. By the time they got out of the shower, there was no hot water, and Elli never did get to finish washing her hair.

Not that she cared though.

Chapter 23

Elli was packing when Grace called.

"Hey girl! I need a huge favor."

"Sure," Elli said as she threw the new bathing suit she had just bought in her carryon bag, "What's up?"

"I have a party coming up, and the girl ordered matching dresses for her and her friends, well one of the friends is in um, somewhere I don't know, anyways, she is the exact body type as you, so I was wondering, actually, going to beg if you could come over and have this dress alter to you," she said. Elli raised her eye brows at Grace's request, why didn't the girl have the dress shipped to her friend, so her friend could have it altered?

Who was she to ask?

"Sure, when do you need it done?"

"Tomorrow?"

"Oh I'm sorry Grace, I'm leaving for Florida to go see Shea today."

"Oh hell, when are you leaving?"

"I think my uncle's jet is leaving at three," Elli said as she moved around Shea's condo, picking up random things she needed as she went through. She had dropped off Adler to Harper that morning so she didn't fill Adler's bowls like usual as she past by them.

"Okay, its twelve now, can I meet you at the dress shop by one?"

"Sure."

"Cool," Grace said before giving Elli the dress shops information.

They said their goodbyes and Elli hung up the phone before unloading the dishwasher. Elli had been in such a good mood since Sunday, even with Shea leaving Monday, she was doing fine. Hadn't really been crying or anything, just enjoying the last few days before flying out for the game in Tampa. Elli was full of excitement about her mini vacation with Shea; it was hard to contain.

Harper and Alice would be running the studio and the three weddings they had that weekend while Elli was gone, so Elli had nothing to worry about, which was good since this was the first time Elli would be leaving for a vacation. Lord knew, it was much needed. Elli was ready for the days to come, five days in Florida with her hunky boyfriend?

Hell yes.

The only thing bringing Elli down was her health. It always happen around this time of year with the winter air, she always felt run down. That was probably another reason why she was so excited to be leaving, getting away from the cold would be good for her, since it was so easy for her to get sick. Elli didn't want to get sick now, because she just knew Shea was planning something for her birthday. He had been crazy secretive when she would call him, and when he was home, he was always calling Grace, so Elli knew he had something up his sleeve.

It was so exciting, and Elli couldn't have been happier.

Elli threw her bags into the back of the truck, and turned on her GPS with the directions to the dress shop Grace had given her the address for. After getting it all set up, she was on her way. When she arrived at Ann Frances, she wished Grace would have just said the name of the place; it was the same store Jodi had gotten all her bridal wear from, so Elli knew this place well.

After locking up the truck, Elli went inside, just as the door shut behind her, Ryan wrapped his arms around Elli's legs.

"Ms. Elli!" he gushed, smiling up at her with his big, bright blue eyes.

"Hello darlin! How are you?"

"I would be better if I didn't have to come here? Daddy had a meeting and couldn't keep us, so mommy drugged us here, I hate this place." Grace came into the lobby with Amelia on her hip, a great big smile on her face.

"Ryan Justice, you do not hate anything, now stop talking Ms. Elli's ear off, she has a plane to catch. Come on back Elli," she said, as Ryan stomp over to a chair and sat. Elli gave him a smile that he of course returned before following Grace back to the dressing lobby.

Grace pointed to a dressing room, then said, "The dress is in there, go ahead and throw it on, Rita will come in as soon as your ready."

"Cool, but I had a question, why didn't the girl have the dress sent to the friend? Have her alter it in her town."

"Who knows?" Grace said with a wave of the hand, dismissing the thought. Elli shook her head at the inconsideration of people and headed into the dressing room after laying her purse down.

When Elli's eyes fell on the dress, her mouth open fell too as she took in a quick breath. It was a masterpiece, something straight out of the olden days.

The dress was an off-white fine satin material; the bodice was covered in a sheer layer lace that did a 'V' dip in the front. It had a relatively full skirt, with more sheer lace, and a belt covered the seam between the top and the skirt, the belt had a beautiful intricate embroidered swirly pattern with crystals on it.

Elli hurriedly threw her clothes off, taking care as she put the dress on. When she looked in the mirror she felt like Elizabeth Bennet, dressed for the Netherfield Ball where she would dance with Mr. Darcy for the first time. The dress fit her like a glove; the bodice was tight, showing off her breast, the belt sparkle in the lights of the dressing room, as the skirt whoosh every time Elli moved.

She wanted this dress.

She threw the door open, and Grace slowly stood, a dazzling grin going over her mouth. "It's a perfect fit," she muttered as Elli walked up onto the stage where Rita would alter her, even though she felt there was no need for it.

"It really is! Where did she get it? I have to have it, I have no clue where I would wear it but I would all the time."

Grace laughed as she followed Elli up the stairs, circling her as she looked the dress over, "It really is a perfect fit, I did good."

"You did, but really I need this dress. Have you ever seen Pride and Prejudice? Elizabeth Bennet wore a dress like this, and it's my favorite moment in the movie, I need this dress," Elli said, then stopped herself because she was sounding like a crazy person.

"Is that right?" Grace said with a satisfied grin on her face.

"Yes, I love it."

"Good." Grace turned right as Rita started into the lobby, "Rita, it's a perfect fit!"

"Really? Oh look it is! It's beautiful."

Elli beamed at both women, but then her smiled fell when Grace told her to take it off. She did as she was asked even though the whole time she was taking it off, she was trying to figure out a way to get it out of there without anyone noticing. After hanging it back on the wall, since her plot to run with it wasn't going to work. She admired it for another moment; she then walked out to Grace holding Amelia on her hip and Ryan's hand in hers.

"Thanks so much for coming by Elli, it means a lot," Grace said as they headed to the front of the store.

"No problem," she said with a grin as she admired one of the amazing wedding dresses that were on a model in the middle of the lobby. "Gosh that's pretty," Elli said going to it, running her fingers down the satin skirt, it was a total princess style dress, a little too puffy for Elli but it sure was pretty.

Grace giggled, "Already getting some ideas for you and Shea's wedding?" she asked with a wink.

"As if," Elli giggled, "like Shea would marry me!"

Grace's head tilted to the side, "Why wouldn't he?"

Elli felt on the spot, so of course her cheeks turned deep red, and she started digging the toe of her boot in the hardwood floor of the store, "I don't know, it seems unrealistic to me I guess," she finally said after a moment.

"I don't think it's unrealistic at all," she said with a bemused smile as she walked past Elli, "by the way, I look good in purple, see ya!"

Elli couldn't stop the slow grin that went over her face, even if she tried.

Not that she wanted too.

Elli fell back into the comfy plush chairs of Bryan's private jet. Bryan had bought it two years ago, and the darn thing still had the new smell to it. It was spectacular, the inside was completely done in team colors, and even the toilet was purple. Elli always wondered if she should be worried about her uncle and his obsession with purple, but who was she to tell a 65 year old man what color to paint his plane. Plus, Elli loved riding in it; it made her feel like the princess.

 A stewardess came over with a glass of champagne and Elli took it with a grin of appreciation. Elli was ready to go, ready to get to Florida, and really ready to see Shea. Grace's statement still was fresh on Elli's mind, and a grin pulled at the side of her mouth as Bryan sat down in front of her.

"I'm still mad at your daddy for not coming," he said as he leaned back taking his large beer from the same stewardess.

"He had work stuff."

"He works for me," he said with a pout, causing Elli to giggle.

"Stop complaining," Elli said as she took a sip of her drink.

"Has Melody gotten a hold of you about the promotional stuff the team is gonna need in the next couple months?"

"No, but I'm sure she will," Elli said, the thought of working more for the team made her extremely excited, but she didn't want to think of work stuff right now, she was going to see Shea in a matter of hours.

The jet took off right as a text came from Shea; it was a picture of a beach chair with the caption saying:

I have a seat waiting for you.

Elli couldn't contain her excitement. She was ready to see Shea, ready to spend time with him. A shy smile went over her face as red dusted her cheeks when she realized she would be seeing him topless on the beach. Yeah she had seen him naked in the bedroom, but laying on the beach with him, while he was topless, made her giggle from the giddiness!

"I tell you what Eleanor, I always thought you were beautiful, always but goodness me, the last couple times I've seen you, you honestly have taken my breath away," Bryan said, making Elli blush profusely.

"Papa….," she groaned, he let out a loud booming laugh.

"I only speak the truth darlin'. You're absolutely beautiful, and that damn Adler is to thank for it huh?"

"Yes sir," Elli said with a quick grin as she took a drink of her champagne.

Bryan sat there smiling for a moment, before his grin fell and he asked, "What if he got traded Eleanor?"

Elli's head whip back up, staring at him with disbelieve.

"He isn't is he?" Her heart had actually stopped; she couldn't breathe as she waited for him to answer.

"No honey, he's a franchise player, he ain't going anywhere right now, but one day he might, what's gonna happen then?"

Elli let out a whoosh of breath, taking in another deep one. The man was gonna give her a damn heart attack! "I don't know Papa, we're just datin'."

"Now you and I both know that's a lie, y'all are more than just datin'."

"It ain't none of your business, next subject please." Elli said with a sheepish grin, as Bryan chuckled taking a long pull of his beer.

"We need to discuss something darlin'."

"Which is?" Elli said picking at one of the holes of her jeans.

"The reason I asked about Adler was because I'm giving you the team, Eleanor."

Shea was basically bouncing up and down waiting for Elli and Bryan's car to arrive at the hotel. He was ready for their mini vacation, ready to lie beside Elli on the beach and not move, unless to go back to the room where he would have his way with her. Shea was also excited for her being at the game tomorrow; he always played better when he could see her watching.

Yes, he was ready for his girlfriend to come, now.

Grace had called earlier that day, saying that the dress fitting went perfect, and that Elli loved the dress, which put his mind at ease about the party. The dress was the biggest part, since he wanted her to feel like she had stepped back in time and was going to the ball of her dreams. He was so excited about the party, everything Grace had emailed him looked amazing. From the food, to the entertainment, to the guest list, the night was gonna be astonishing, and he couldn't wait to see Elli's face.

Speaking with her family was interesting to say the least, her dad was fine, but Shea decided there was a good chance he would never like Olivia Fisher. She had promised that nothing would happen and that they would be on their best behavior at the party but he was pretty sure she was full of shit, and was just lying because he told her she wouldn't be able to come if she couldn't promise her best behavior. That was the only thing he was nervous about considering the party.

He probably shouldn't have invited them, but he wanted to give them a chance to make amends with Elli. Elli didn't get to see the kids like she had before, and more than anything he wanted her to be happy. So he thought bringing her whole family together would fix things, but he was preparing his self just in case things went to shit.

Shea was leaning up against the wall of the hotel waiting as the ocean breeze hit his face. It was in the high 70s, and Shea was convinced he needed to move here. He had always loved the ocean, and being somewhere where it was always warm made him happy, but he did love Tennessee and didn't really want to leave.

Especially since he had Elli in his life now.

Would she even come with him if he left Nashville? The fact that he didn't know the answer to that bothered him. What did he expect, though? She wasn't clingy; she had been on her own for the past six years. Of course she missed him a lot when he was gone, but she didn't act like her life was over when he was gone, unlike most of the women his friends dated. Elli was different, but would she follow him? Could he ask her too? She was rooted in Nashville.

What was his love compared to her roots?

Thankfully, he spotted Elli getting out of her uncle's car, so he pushed his questions to the back of his head, put a huge grin on his face and headed towards her. Her eyes were bright with excitement, and his grin grew bigger with every step he took. When he wrapped his arms around her, basically picking her off the ground, she let out a little squeal before he placed his lips on hers.

They parted only because Bryan Fisher cleared his throat; Shea looked over at his boss with a sheepish grin, before saying, "Hey Mr. Fisher."

"Adler," he said with a raised eyebrow, before looking over at Elli, "Darlin' I'll have these taken to your room."

"Oh I'm coming, I gotta change, you still wanna hit the beach right?" she asked Shea, but Shea was still confused on the whole 'her room'.

"Yeah baby, where is your room?"

"Um Papa, where is it?"

"Right next to mine," Bryan said without looking at her as he took the suitcases out the trunk, Shea looked over at her, but she wouldn't look at him, because she knew he was trying to figure out why the hell she wasn't sleeping in his room.

"Alright," she said, before looking up at him, "wanna meet down here in a few?"

"I'm already dressed, I can come up with you and then we can leave," Shea said, but wished he didn't when Bryan's eyes cut to him, basically killing Shea with his eyes. Elli noticed the look and shook her head.

"It's alright honey, I'll be done in a sec."

With that she was gone while Bryan still gave him death glares as he walked away. Shea stood there speechless as he watched Elli getting her room key before heading up to her room. He seem to always forget that she had to put on this good southern girl act in front of Bryan and her daddy, but damn, it was annoying as hell. He hadn't been with her in four days, he was hoping to get some before heading to the beach, but it wasn't looking like he was gonna be getting Elli naked until good old Bryan left, which wasn't till Saturday. Which was fine, at least she was there; he had missed her so much.

Elli came down about twenty minutes later, in a cute little yellow sun dress with her flip flops on and a huge yellow hat. He could see that her bathing suit was black and he couldn't wait to see it on her. She came straight to him, a small smile on her face, as she wrapped her arms around his middle, walking with him out the door.

"I sometimes forget I'm with a southern belle," he teased as they walked through the beautiful white sand, the sun was slowly making its way down, and the beauty of the ocean was breath taking, almost as much as the girl that was wrapped around his middle.

"Oh hush, you don't forget, you just hope to be the Rhett Butler of our time, and deflower this little southern belle in front of God and everybody," she said breaking apart from him, giving him a haughty grin as she backed away slowly.

He let out an arrogant laugh as he crossed his arms, "I don't know if you realize this *darlin'*," She glared at his failed attempt at being country, "but I've already deflowered you, many times." He added the last part just for good measures. Her eyes narrowed before pushing him down in the sand, because of course she caught him off balance and promptly starting running down the beach. "Oh, you're gonna get it now!"

And off they went, chasing each other across the beach, at one point Elli's dress and hat joined Shea's shirt as he chased her into the water, grabbing her by her waist, pulling her to his dripping wet chest. The waves ran up against their legs as they held each other, basking in the feeling of each other and the warmth of the setting sun. Elli looked up at him, a small shy smile on her lips as the sun warmed her face. Shea couldn't help but gently run his fingers along her cheek bone, then down her jaw before cupping her neck, and bringing his lips down to hers.

Shea held Elli's hand as they made their way to the beach chairs he had requested for them. Elli threw her dress, shoes, and hat down before sitting down on the chair, looking over at him with grin.

"I love the beach."

"Me too," he agreed as they sun started to make it way down, it was almost completely set, only peeking out a little above the beautiful bluish green water. When Shea felt Elli's hand move into his, he looked over at her, admiring the look of peace that was all over face. "Can I ask you something?" he asked, figuring when the hell had he ever beat around the bush or not ask what he was wondering.

"Sure, what's up?

She looked over at him and he got tongue tied. It was the whole rejection thing all over again, it was crazy how scared he was of her rejection, before he never cared, but with Elli, she could rip him apart with it. "What would happen if I got traded?" Elli's eyes went wide, and he knew he should have gone with another way of asking her, "Not that I am, as far as I know, but what if?"

"It's just crazy that you asked that, Papa had asked me that same exact questions before dropping a bomb on me on the way here."

"What bomb?"

Elli pulled her hand from his, and started picking at her nails as she looked out at the ocean.

"He asked me that because he's giving me the Assassins when he retires."

"Say what?"

She looked over at him, and then shrugged her shoulders, "I'll own the Assassin's in 5 years tops from what he is saying."

Shea sat there speechless, blinking a few times as he stared over at his girlfriend who, if he is still with the team, would be her boss.

What. The. Hell.

"What did you say?"

"I said yes, of course. I love the Assassins; of course I would want to own them."

"What about the studio?"

"I could still do that on the side, I was thinking of selling it to Harper but then I don't know because she is probably gonna go wherever Jakob goes, even though I would want to keep him when I come on, but he might get traded before that, so I don't know, but anyways, if

Harper didn't want to buy it, I would probably sell it, I mean own the studio or own a hockey team, it's not a hard decision."

She was rambling, which meant she was nervous, probably because she was gonna tell him that if he didn't stay with the Assassins, they wouldn't be together.

"Yeah, it really isn't," he muttered as he looked out at the ocean. Off in the distance he saw dolphins jumping out of the water, and he thought that would bring a smile to his face, but he sat with his heart slowly breaking from the mere thought of not being with Elli for forever. "So I guess that answers my question huh? You can't stay with me when you own the team I left," he asked refusing to look over at her.

"Well don't say that, that's like putting a expiration date on our relationship, no telling what will happen in the next few years, what if you retire, or God forbid Papa dies and I get the team tomorrow, because then you ain't ever leaving."

"Yeah."

"Shea look at me," she said, he took a deep breath before looking over at her, she reached over taking his hand in hers, "I'm not saying that we would be over if you got traded but it's not like I could have went with you before my papa asked me to take the team, I have a career here, I can't just leave it."

"But you would sell the studio to own the Assassins but not to follow me to the next place I play?"

She exhaled loudly, and he could tell she was getting angry, good, he was getting pissed. "We're about to get into a fight about a 'what if' situation, you ain't going anywhere at the moment, you are an Assassin, so why ask questions, let's wait till we get there."

"I don't like the uncertainty Elli, I know that you don't love me but I love you, and each day I fall more and more in love with you, so I'm sorry that I want the reassurance that one day, if it happens, my girl will be by my side, going with me."

Elli shook her head, frustrated, "I think you're asking more than you mean too Shea, we've been together for three months, and you're asking for my forever, I don't think you realize that."

"What's wrong with that?"

"So you are asking me to marry you?"

"No!"

She stood up, glaring down at him, "Just what I thought, so come on, let's go. I'm getting cold."

"Wait, we're not done," he said as he stood, grabbing a hold of her hand to keep her from walking away.

"Oh yes we are, cause I don't want to fight with you on our vacation Shea, we're happy, let it be, we'll cross that bridge when it comes." She dropped his hand to pick her things up, so he ran his empty hands through his hair, letting out a defeated sigh. Elli looked over at him, taking his hand in hers."Do you want to do something else? Because if not, we'll need to say our goodbye down here since Papa will be inside and won't like watching you feel his niece up," she gave him a cheeky grin, and he nodded.

"The guys are getting drinks, wanted us to join."

"Cool, let's go than."

So much for reassurance on their relationship.

Elli stood in front of the mirror in the bathroom, checking out the little black tube top dress she was paring with a beautiful pair of sparking Christian Louboutin heels. She looked over her body, liking the fact that she look skinny in the dress, she actually thought she looked good, but then she looked at her face, seeing the red splotches that covered her cheeks, and shook her head.

She had been crying since she left Shea at the elevators.

Why did he have to do this to her? Why couldn't he be happy with the way they were, why did he have to bring up the things that could or would not happen? He wasn't leaving so why did he have to ask her if she would follow. She shook her head, trying to keep the tears that were welling up at bay. Lord, knew she wanted to follow Shea to the ends of the earth, but the truth was she couldn't. When he left, he was gonna be leaving her too, she had too much in Nashville, and it wasn't like they were married. She tried to get that point across to him but he just didn't get it.

It wasn't like Elli wanted him to ask her to marry him, that wasn't it; it would be nice but not right now. They were still young in their relationship, and he wasn't going anywhere! There was no need to stress about it! With that thought, Elli stomped out of the bathroom, pushing all her thoughts of marriage, Shea leaving, and her buying the team to the back of her head.

Shea was leaning against the wall by the elevators when Elli stepped out, he was wearing a nice button down grey dress shirt and black dress pants, his hair was sexily tousled and he had a trouble looked on his face, which meant he was thinking about their conversation that happen on the beach as much as she was. She didn't want their discussion to spoil their night, so she gave him a seductive grin before pressing her body against his, claiming his mouth with hers. At first she was kissing him, but he soon joined in, wrapping her up in his arms, taking over the kiss as she pressed into him harder. When she felt his hands slide down to her ass, squeezing it lightly, she grinned against his lips before taking his bottom lip between her teeth. This time he gave her a sexy grin, before wrapping his arms around her.

"We aren't going to make it into the lounge if you keep at it."

"Maybe that's what I want."

He gave her a skeptical look just as Bryan's booming voice interrupted what could have been the start to a very great night.

"Eleanor, what in the good Lord's name are you doing?" Elli stepped back, rolling her eyes.

"Obviously I'm making out with my boyfriend against a wall, Papa!"

"Well Jesus honey, can you not do it in plain view of my team?"

Elli and Shea eyes cut to the lobby where most of the guys stood, gawking and laughing their ass off.

"Sorry," Elli said, pulling at the bottom of her dress.

"I'm going up to my room; I'll be waiting for you."

"Cock blocker," Shea whispered against the back of her neck as Bryan walked away causing Elli to burst out in a fit of giggles.

"For once I couldn't agree with you more," Elli said as she looked back at him, he gave her a cocky grin before kissing her cheek, and leading her towards his friends.

Her future team.

The Ocean View Lounge was amazing. The walls were painted a beautiful light blue with neat lights shining on the wall that made it look like waves. The bar was completely clear, you could see all the beers that sat in the ice chest, all the liquor bottles, and all the glasses that were in the cabinet, there was also built in fish tanks above the bar. Each table had a bubble in the middle of it that held all kinds of pretty fish; Elli was able to look down into the tank, watching the little fish swim back and forth. It was what was keeping Elli entertained since the guys were acting like she was diseased.

Someone came in saying that Elli was Bryan Fisher's niece, and now the guys were treating her like she was Bryan Fisher. No one would look her in the eye, and when Shea tried to start up a conversation no one said anything. It was as if they were nervous to talk about anything in front of Elli because of who her uncle was. It was weird, awkward, and Elli wasn't having it.

She came for a good time, and she damn well was gonna have one.

Elli slammed her hands against the table, causing everyone to jump as Shea spilled his drink all over the table. "Okay guys, yes I am Bryan Fisher's niece but the guy y'all know isn't the man I know, the man I know is amazing, sweet and kind, the guys y'all know is an asshole, actually he was an asshole to me just a little while ago, since he won't even let me share a room with my boyfriend, so quit, I'm not him, I don't care what y'all talk about, I'm just here to drink, and have a good time with my boyfriend's friends, so I mean are y'all gonna live up to the stories I hear or what?"

Everyone looked at each other before they started laughing. "Fisher won't let you share a room with her Adler? Guess she'll have to sleep with me," Sergei said, causing Shea to give him a look of death.

"Or me, I'm Fisher's favorite," Phillip Anderson said, he was the newly added young forward.

"The hell you say, I'm his favorite!" Sergei argued, and off they went arguing about who was Fisher's favorite when really, Bryan loved Shea, well that was before Elli, she really wasn't sure anymore. Not that it matter because she was finally in, for the next couple hours her and the guys hung out, talked about wives, girlfriends, and the awesomeness of hockey.

Elli, Shea, Alex Welch, and Sergei were playing pool when Elli noticed a group of girls come into the lounge. It was obvious they were ice bunnies, which is what whores that sleep with hockey players just because they can, are called. They all had about two inches of fabric on, and walked with their chest up in the air, for God and everyone to see. Sergei lasted about two minutes before heading over there, leaving Shea, Alex, and Elli to watch as he flirted with some blonde.

"He's hopeless," Alex said as he took a shot.

"He'll grow out of it," Shea said, as he took a pull of his beer, Alex laughed as he handed the stick to Elli.

"Before I would have said you're wrong, but I watched you grow out of it, and I never thought that would happen."

"Fuck off Welch, I wasn't that bad," Shea said, with a little red dusting his cheeks, Alex let out another chuckle as he looked over at Elli, who was also giggling.

"I think he's lying."

"Oh yeah he is, I know all about his old ways," Elli teased as Shea came right for her, wrapping her up in his arms, kissing her lips hard, she giggled when they parted.

"You be quiet," he said still not letting her go as he ran kisses across her jaw line.

"Hey Elli!" Elli looked over to Phillip who was grinning ear to ear at her, "When you done with that, let me know, I'll show you how us forwards take care of our women."

"And how's that?" Elli asked even though Shea was turning red with anger. Phillip had been flirting with Elli all night, and Shea was not happy about it, it didn't bother Elli at all though, Phillip was like eighteen! He was a baby!

"It's simply really, defensemen take care of the back, while us forwards, take good, lovely care of the front," he said with a cocky grin causing everyone to hoot and holler while Shea just burned with angry.

"Shut your mouth Anderson, you won't even know what to do when you finally do get a woman naked," Shea bit out.

"Oh I've had my fair share of women, Captain, oh my captain, and when I get yours, I'll take my sweet ole time."

Everyone got real quiet, while Phillip stood there just grinning as his eyes went up and down Elli's body. Elli felt so bad for him because Shea was gonna kill him. It took all of three second before Shea was chasing a laughing Phillip out the bar. Elli leaned against the pool table giggling while Alex just shook his head.

"Oo wee, he's got it bad for you." Elli looked over at him, "Everyone probably thinks Shea's joking around but I'm pretty sure that kids going to get a talking too, Shea's pissed."

"You think so?"

"I know so."

That made Elli giddy for some reason.

Elli placed her beer on the table and restarted to game with Alex. They were well into the game when she finally noticed that Shea was back in the bar. She watched as he leaned against the bar, laughing with two women, well two ice bunnies. He had two beers in his hand, but had put them back on the bar when one of the girls asked him to sign her, size toddler, jersey. When he picked the beer back up, the other girl wrapped her arms around his arm, and he smiled down at her, than the other one did it, and it took everything out of Elli not to go over there and make a fool of herself. They were fans, they wanted to talk to their favorite hockey player, Elli wouldn't get jealous, it was okay, Shea loved her, he wasn't stupid, he wouldn't do anything dumb, especially with her in the damn bar.

But then, one of the girls leaned up and placed a kiss on his cheek, and he just smiled, which was fine, everyone wanted to kiss their favorite hockey player. No big deal. The other one said something, and he looked over at her and their lips just met. Elli doubt Shea even saw it coming, cause she sure didn't, but Elli found herself getting pissed because kissing on the lips was not okay.

Elli took in a sharp intake of breath as the girl moved her hand up to Shea's cheek, before she stormed towards the door.

Shea didn't pull back.

The damn girl had Shea's mouth sucked into hers, something that had never happen to him before. When he finally pulled back, he felt like the chick had taking his lips with her. "Excuse me," he bit out as he wiped his mouth, "Jesus lady." He saw Elli out the corner of his eye, heading for the door.

"Elli!" he yelled moving away from the women, knocking the beer off the bar as he went to go after her, but one of the girls grabbed onto him again. "Sergei, stop her!"

As Shea tried to detangle his self from the crazy starfish women, he watched as Sergei stepped out in front of Elli, she said something and he let her right by. When he finally got the starfish off him, he ran towards the door. "Thanks a lot Sergei!"

"She said she would trade me!" Sergei yelled back as Shea took off running out the bar towards the elevators. He went inside one, pressing the suite level button and waited as the elevator went up. He didn't understand why he even stayed and talked to the girls! One of them said something about their bother playing back in Boston and that rope him in, he should have known better. He had been playing with ice bunnies his whole life, he knew their tricks, he had fallen to them many times before. When the doors open, he ran down to the room number Elli had given him and started pounding on the door, but Elli never open, Bryan's door did.

"Adler, what the hell?"

"I need to talk to Elli," he said turning his back to Bryan before returning back to the pounding.

"She's in the shower, and it's too late for visitors, you'll see her tomorrow." Shea looked over at Bryan, he stood with her arms crossed, glaring over at Shea, "It's late Shea, go to bed."

"I need to talk to her."

"You can see her tomorrow, bye Shea."

Shea shook his head, he couldn't leave, but if he didn't, he wouldn't have to worry about trying to fix things with Elli, he would be off the team before the beginning of the next week. Shea looked at Elli's door one last time, and then walked away.

Basically making what he thought was the biggest mistake of his life, because when he came back the next morning, Elli was gone.

Chapter 24

The Assassins' had won the game that night without the help of Shea, he was playing like shit and knew it, but the guys still came through and won. Which was great, but Shea was hurting. Elli wouldn't answer his calls, he was freaking out that she had given up on him, and wasn't going to let him explain.

Didn't she understand? He didn't want that starfish freak! He wanted her!

He left for the airport still calling her every two minutes it seemed, and she still wasn't answering. Unfortunately he had to wait three hours before jumping on a plane and heading back to Nashville. When he arrived, he took a cab to the condo to find that Elli had left there too and she had taken Adler with her. Shea fell into the couch and took a deep breath. He couldn't go running over there at four in the morning, she was probably sleeping and would be mad as hell if he came banging on her door. So he laid down, shutting his eyes.

He was out within two minutes.

When Shea woke the next morning he had one hell of a back ache, and his head was killing him. Damn couch, only good for one thing, and it wasn't sleeping. He picked up his phone, dialing Elli's number for the 900th time.

This time she answered.

"What Shea?" she sounded groggy, which worried him since she had probably been crying since she left. He didn't like her crying over him, he wanted her smiling, he loved her smile.

"I'm so sorry baby, please come back to the condo, or I'll come there."

"No, don't."

"Why baby? I don't want them girls, she got a hold of me, sucked my damn lips of my face, I'm sorry, please don't do this," Shea pleaded as he paced the living room, "I want you baby, only you."

"I can't do this right now Shea, I'm not in the mood to talk to-" She started to cough, and it didn't stop for what seem like a good five minutes.

"Are you okay?"

"No, I'm not. Listen I need a few days to myself, a lot happen the other night, and I just need to be by myself for a while."

"Elli, please, don't do that, we can work this out."

"I can't right now, I promise I will call you soon, but right now I need me time. I'm not home so don't go there, I'm at Jodi's. Just let me be for a couple of days, I promise I'll call you soon."

"Like you promised before huh?"

"I promise this time, text me, I'll answer. I just need some time to myself. Please give it to me," Elli started coughing again, "I gotta go."

The line went dead, and Shea slumped down into his crap ass chair.

Why was being in a relationship so damn hard? It seemed like things were easier when he was screwing anything with legs, no one to answer too, no one to worry about, and no one to fucking freak out about! Shea stood up stomping through the house, kicking anything that reminded him of Elli. How could he do this? How could he fuck up the one thing that made him a better person? Elli was everything to him, and he probably lost her. Yeah, life as a single man was great, but life with Elli was spectacular and what he wanted.

When he reached his room, all her things laid everywhere. She must have been trying to find things to bring with her on the trip. His old AHL laid on the floor by a pair of her boxers, he walked over to it, picking it up and bringing it to his nose.

Mangos.

Shea basically crumbled to the floor, a hard feat for someone Shea's size, but he did it, holding the shirt to his nose taking in the scent of his Elli and for the first time ever of his adult life, he cried over a woman.

The next day after his embarrassing break down that no one would ever know about, Shea sat in the living room, watching Pride and Prejudice. He wonder if Elli was gonna talk to him anytime soon since her birthday was only a week away. It would be something if everyone showed up for the party, and the guest of honor didn't show. He would look like a complete idiot. Part of him wished he hadn't planned the party, but somewhere deep in his heart, he knew she would call.

He took his phone out and sent a quick text.

I love you. I miss you a lot.

An hour passed before she answered,

I miss you too.

He smiled, maybe there was hope for them, or maybe she just missed him but had no intentions on getting back with him. He was about to ask her that when his phone rang, it was Jakob.

"Hello?"

"I have a bone to pick with you Shea Adler!" Harper yelled into the phone.

"Harper?"

"The one and only, listen here buddy, why is it that I am taking care of your best friend, but you can't take care of mine?"

"What? What are you talking about?"

"Elli, I can't do both and work, you're gonna have to take one of them!"

"Wait, Harper, what's wrong with Elli?"

She paused, "What? You haven't talked to her- oh God, please don't tell me you don't know she's sick."

"No! I had no clue, she told me she needed a few days to herself, what the hell is wrong?"

"Ugh, damn it, why does she do this? She lied to her dad, her uncle, and now you, wonderful."

Shea was starting to get frustrated so he tried to keep his voice calm when he said, "Harper, what the hell is wrong with Elli?"

"She's sick, it happens every once in the while," she added when he took in a sharp breath, "she starts to feel run down and then she's just down for a couple of days, she had to change her meds this time, so it must have been bad when it happened. She called me to bring her soup and to pick up her meds. I got mad because that's what you should be doing since you are the boyfriend."

"You're right I should be doing that, if I actually knew she was sick!"

"Well now you know, her meds are at Walgreens and she likes the chicken noodle from Panera Bread, holler if you need anything else."

"Where is she at?"

"Home."

"She told me she went to Jodi's," he said through his teeth, Harper laughed.

"She's scandalous as hell; no she's at the house."

"Wonderful."

"Do you have a key?"

"No."

"Well stop on by cause she won't be able to unlock the door, she's stupid weak."

Shea's heart broke knowing that Elli couldn't even move to answer the door, "alright, thanks Harper."

"No thank you, see ya soon."

Shea didn't know why he was nervous when he pulled up in front of Elli's house, but he was. After packing his bag for the next couple days, going to get Elli's meds and five things of her favorite soup, he ran over to the studio for Elli's key. Harper was busy, and told him to grab it off the desk, and go, so he did. The whole drive over to Elli's he thought about what he would say to make everything better between them. He wasn't sure if she was mad still or if she was really just trying to hide the fact that she was sick, which he was not happy about and would address when he saw her.

After unloading the truck, he unlocked the door, and started bringing things in. Adler came barreling out the back room and bark happily as he jumped around and in between Shea's legs. Shea grinned as he bent down, loving on the dog. Shea had missed Adler just as much as he missed Elli. "Hey buddy," he said quietly incase Elli was sleeping before noticing the house.

It was trashed, and something smelled. It was probably all the dog shit by the back door. He walked into the kitchen to find that something must have died in there because it stunk badly. He also saw that Adler had torn into dog food bag, and food was all over the floor.

"Harp, just leave everything in the kitchen, I'll get it later."

Shea barely heard what she said, it was muffled and she was groaning between words. He left everything in the hall, and started down the other hall towards her room. When he open the door, Elli laid face down in her bed, in only a bra and panties, her body was flushed and she was sweaty.

"Harp, please go, I look terrible," she groaned still not moving, Shea moved towards the bed, sitting on the edge and running his hand down her burning hot back. Elli moved her head, looking up at him, her eyes widen and after a moment, a tear ran down the side of her face. "Shea," she groaned, turning her head back into the pillow.

"Harper called, she was busy asked me to go get the soup and everything."

"Please just go Shea; I don't want you seeing me like this."

"I'm not going anywhere, so you can stop telling me to leave. Have you taken anything for the fever?"

"No, I can't move."

"You don't think we should go to the ER?"

"No, this happens sometimes, I just need to lay here, it'll past. I just need the new meds I was prescribed, there should be an antibiotic in there."

"Alright, I'll be right back."

Shea went into the front hall, grabbing the bag with her meds, and tearing open the package. She was right; an antibiotic was in there, along with her new hormone medication. He went into the kitchen, pulling open the fridge to get a bottle of water, but what he found was a great big pan of green stuff that he was sure wasn't supposed to be green.

Well at least he found the source of the smell.

He shut the fridge and went to the bags he brought in, he had bought a bottle of water at the gas station, so he grabbed that and went down the hall to Elli's room. He sat everything on her night stand, and moved her hair off the side of her face. She open her eyes, and he could see that she was hurting bad.

"Can you sit up?"

She slowly shook her head. Shea moved his self into the bed, picking her up slowly, leaning her against him as he grabbed one the meds and the water. Her body burned through his shirt to his skin, and he shook his head. How could she not call him? How did she do this by herself before? "Open up, sweetheart," she did as he asked and he popped the pill in her mouth, then put some water in afterwards. He repeated the same thing with the other med, and then slowly laid her down.

"Thank you," she whispered as he covered her up, he smiled down at her, moving the hair that was stuck to her forehead off and to the side.

"Anything for you baby, anything," he said as he finished tucking her in, "Maybe after I'm done cleaning up, you'll wanna take a shower, the fever might be broken by then."

She nodded before closing her eyes, he slowly moved from the bed, and shut the door quietly as he walked out. When he entered the living room, he looked around and then he slapped his hands together.

Off to work.

It took almost three hours to get the house spotless, he kept checking on Elli making sure she was fine between cleaning, and she mostly was. She was moving a lot as she slept which wasn't really new, but she kept kicking the blankets off and he was afraid she would get cold, so he would cover her back up, just to come back to find the sheets on the floor. He checked on her one last time before heading to the dump and then the local store for food.

When he got back and unloaded everything he made his way to the bedroom, where Elli still laid with her face in the pillow. He was really worried about her but she seemed to know what was wrong, so he didn't push the hospital. Plus Harper said this happen sometimes, which bothered him because when he asked her about it a while back, she said she was fine as long as she took her meds. Shea moved into the bathroom and saw that her bathroom was just as bad as the house had been, she must have been really sick because there was vomit all over the toilet and some in the bath and on the floor.

Jesus, why didn't she call him?

He looked under the cabinet and pulled out all her cleaning supplies, before getting started. When he was done, the damn bathroom sparkle, his mother would be proud. Shea moved back into the bedroom, before sitting on Elli's bed, running his hand up her bare back. She had taken off her bra while he was cleaning the bathroom he guess, the good thing was that she wasn't hot, her skin felt warm, normal.

"Baby, how you feeling?"

"Crappy."

"Okay, you wanna take a shower or a bath? Wash the sickness off as my mom would say?"

"I can't stand and sitting upwards hurts my stomach, so I'll just lay here."

He didn't like the whole her stomach hurt thing, but then again she probably hadn't eaten in a while, there was so much puke in that bathroom, he was surprised it came from her. She had to take a shower, she smelled, and he couldn't let her stay like that. He got of the bed gently, and headed into the bathroom, starting the shower, getting it just right before stripping off his clothes. When he went back into her bedroom, she was basically hanging off the bed, she must of tried to moved on her own.

He slowly removed her panties, then slowly picked her up as she groaned. She let out a little whimpered as he turned her, wrapping her body around his as he carried her into the bathroom. When he stepped into the shower, her grip on him became tighter as he fully emerged them into the shower.

"Can you put a little weight on your legs, baby?"

Elli unwrapped her legs, letting them fall to the shower floor, but still leaned heavily against him, which was fine, he just needed to grab the shampoo so he could wash her. As he washed her, she kept her eyes closed, she didn't say anything, even when he would say something, she would just nod or shake her head. He washed every part of her before shutting the water off and grabbing the towels he had set out for them. He dried her off before taking her into the bedroom, laying her on the bed. He took the shirt and panties he had laid out for her, and started getting her dress. He laid her down before getting the brush and throwing on some boxers. He leaned her against his body, brushing her hair slowly, making sure he didn't hurt her. When he was done, he moved her to the couch that sat in the corner, so he could change her sheets.

Not surprisingly, the only color sheets the girl owned was pink. So he grabbed what he swore was the exact same sheets, and changed her bed. When he looked over at her, she was watching him, her green eyes as dull as her skin, something he never thought would happen. He went over to her, picking her up, bringing her to her bed.

"Do you feel better, baby?" She nodded, but then a tear ran down over her nose, onto her top puffy lip. "Then why are you crying?"

More tears began to fall before she opened her eyes, "I didn't want you to see me like this."

"Oh honey, don't worry about that, you're beautiful even when you're sick, you're always beautiful to me."

"I'm disgusting," she said as more tears fell from her eyes, he shook his head, moving his fingers to catch every tear.

"That is not the D word I was thinking," he said with a grin.

Elli blinked before asking, "What?"

"I was thinking delicious, maybe delectable. In other words, Elli, I want to eat you up, always."

"But I'm-"

"Perfect."

"Shea, I'm far from it, you should leave while you have the chance, these kinds of things can happen, one minute I'm pissed as hell at you, the next I'm on the floor and can't move. Get out while you can," she pleaded as she looked up at him.

"While I can, huh? Who said I could?"

"You should."

"I'm not going. Don't you know that by now? Don't you understand that I'm here, and there is no way I'm leaving? I love you, Elli. I don't know how you were loved before, but I'm going to love you more than anybody ever will or ever has. I'm here for you, because I love you, not your money. Not because your uncle owns the team, or because you have a successful business, that's not what drew me to you, it was your eyes....and your ass," when she smiled, his heart filled with all the love in the world, he loved making her smiled, "but mostly your eyes. I'm so sorry about what happen with them females in Florida."

"I'm not mad, I just didn't understand why you didn't pull back."

"She was sucking my face Elli! I'm surprise I have lips still!" She smiled again, moving deeper into the bed, closing her eyes. "I'm not gonna hurt you Elli, I promise."

She opened her eyes again, looking deep into his before saying, "I believe you."

When Elli woke up the next morning, she felt five times better which was how it usually happened. The first day she would puke her brains out, the second, she couldn't move because the fever set in, and then the third, she was finally able to move but still needed to stay in bed. The next couple days she would be bed ridden, but at least she would be able to use the bathroom and take a shower by herself.

She hated that Shea saw her like that, she hated that he had cleaned her house, her bathroom, and she hated that he had given her a bath. She would be forever embarrassed and hated that too! He really was the most amazing man in the world, and she couldn't believe that not six months ago, he was sleeping with anything with legs. That his idea of having a good time was drinking and sleeping with a random female, but now, lying in bed feeding her soup was what he was doing, and he seemed to enjoy it.

"I can feed myself," she said with a glare as he held the spoon to her mouth, a smirk came across his face.

"Don't be angry; just let me take care of you."

"You're always taking care of me," she countered before she opened her mouth, swallowing the hot, yummy liquid. It was her favorite soup, and it warmed her whole body as it went down her throat.

"Because that's what you do for your girlfriend. You know if I got sick, or if I drunk myself into a stupor, I know you would take care of me, and I wouldn't be embarrassed at all."

"How'd you know I was embarrassed?"

He smiled, feeding her another spoonful of the most amazing soup on earth, God, she was starving. "I know you, Elli. Now that I know the extent of your sickness, I'm pretty sure I know everything."

"You do not."

"I do too."

"You don't know about Justin," she don't know why she said it because Lord knew she didn't want to talk about him but when Shea started laughed, it pissed her off as she raised her eyebrows.

"Actually I do."

"Huh?"

He laughed, before handing her a glass of hot tea, "You told me all about asshat the night you got trashed."

A heavy feeling filled her stomach as she incredulously stared at him, she knew that she had diarrhea of the mouth when she was drunk, but come on! She told him about Justin! "You're kidding."

"Nope, I know all about you now, Ms. Eleanor Rey Fisher."

"You jackass," she sneered as he chuckled, feeding her some more. They sat in silence as he finished feeding her, she didn't know what to say because he did know her insides and outs now, and for some reason, she felt good. Happy even.

"You wanna try to get up? Walk around a little?"

"No, maybe tomorrow."

"Okay," he said standing, taking her dishes in his hands, "I'm going to go clean up the mess I made, do you need anything?"

"Not right now, thank you, Shea."

He smiled, than leaned down kissing her lips softly before leaving. God, she needed to thank his momma. She raised herself an amazing man. Elli reached for the remote, and turned on the TV, waiting for Shea to come back. It was crazy how much she got used to having him around her, and honestly she was glad that Harper had called him. Harper hated taking care of Elli because it scared her really bad, but even though Elli was sure Shea was scared, he still took amazing care of her. Way better than Justin ever did. Justin would just leave her to die basically, he would clean up after her, but he would never shower her, or feed her like Shea had.

So why didn't she loved him?

"Hey." Elli looked over, pushing that question way to the back of her mind, to see Shea standing only halfway in the room, "Okay, so I've been working on something...for you. I was going to do it for your birthday but I think you could use it now."

"What is it? Come in here." He looked down at the ground, clearing his throat, and for the first time he was acting shy. "Come on."

He looked over at her, taking a deep breath, then came into the room with his arms behind his back, but nothing could hide the beauty of the Gibson Hummingbird guitar that was peeking out from behind his legs. Her eyes lit up as he sat down, placing the beautiful guitar across his lap. He tapped his fingers against the base before looking up at her.

"You have to promise you won't tell anyone I did this, because I swear I'm like the biggest girl in the world for this, but when I heard this song after dating you, I had to learn it...for you," Elli took in a breath, covering her mouth as her eyes became bright with excitement, he gonna play for her! "And then I started singing along with it, and knew I had to do both because hopefully it would express how I feel, but you can't tell anyone!"

"I won't!" she gushed through her hands that still covered her mouth.

"Especially not Grace, I swear you tell her, I'll...I'll call your daddy and tell him you've been sleeping with me, and you're naughty girl!"

Elli giggled uncontrollably, as he grinned bashfully. She was falling for this guy. She knew it now, it was happening and damn it she was gonna let it! Because he was wonderful, he was gonna sing to her! He shook his head, then moved his hands to the strings of the guitar, he stayed there for a moment, not moving his fingers. Shea looked up at her, and she smiled, hoping to encourage him to go ahead. He didn't smile back but he looked down at the guitar and slowly started moving his fingers against the cords.

Elli was so impressed to see his large hands move so easily over each cord, creating the most beautiful melody, but then he started to sing, "Oh, her eyes, her eyes, make the stars look like they're not shining," she recognized the song immediately, and she couldn't help the little gasp or the 'Oh Shea' that left her lips. Bless his heart he wasn't the best singer, but it didn't matter, he was singing to her. A song that every girl wants sang to them, because being told that 'you're amazing, just the way you are,' would making any girl melt into a puddle of goo.

She couldn't believe this was happening. Things like this didn't happen in real life, only in books, and movies, but there he was, playing the most romantic song in the world to her. He wouldn't look at her as he sung, but a small smile would cross his beautiful mouth when he hit a note he knew he couldn't, or when the lyrics really didn't apply to her, because hello, her hair didn't lay flat.

He came to the end of the song, and stopped, moving the guitar off his lap, he looked up at her, and said, "Okay now really, don't laugh." He had the sweetest, most adorable sheepish grin on his face as he took her hands in his, looking deep in her eyes as he sung the chorus again.

That's when Elli started to cry.

The tears came quick, rolling down her cheeks, onto their hands. He stopped singing, laughing nervously as he moved his hand up to her cheek, catching some of her tears. "Elli, don't cry!"

"I'm sorry," she said sniffing as she tried to stop crying, "You're like a dream Shea, no one does that anymore."

"Sure they do, come here." She went into his arms willing, rubbing her nose against his shirt, taking in his heavenly scent. "I meant every word Elli, you're amazing."

How in the world did she get so lucky?

And why couldn't she believe him?

Elli was getting stronger, and Shea hoped embarrassing his self for her was helping with her recovery. When he had first heard 'Just the way you are' he was convinced it was for guys that needed to get laid, but then he met Elli and every single word in the song describe what he was feeling for her, what he thought, so he had to learn the cords, then he started singing as he played. Shea knew he wasn't the best singer, but it seemed Elli loved it, hell she even started crying. Good tears, making his embarrassment worth it.

Since he hadn't left in four days, he hadn't been working out, which was the longest he had ever went without working out. He tried to get Adler to run with him the other day, but the damn dog made it to the mailbox then just laid down, it was as if he was saying 'I'll be here when you get back'. Damn lazy dog. So while Elli slept after lunch, Shea went into the living room, looking for the P90x DVD set she had mention having. He looked through the racks, but it wasn't there, so he opened the drawers of the TV stand, seeing if they were in there.

They weren't but there was a drawer full of DVDs, on was marked 'Elli in: Funny Girl' and then a lot of other musicals. He pulled them all out, forgetting about his workout and fumbling with the DVD case to get the DVD out. He put the disc in, then slowly back up, sitting on the couch as the DVD started. The DVD started with a title screen and then went into the movie. It must have been one of her high school plays because the stage was big but not Broadway big. The curtains opened but the lights didn't come on the four girls that sat at a table. The spot line came down on a girl sitting in the front row in a leopard outfit, when the camera zoomed in and Shea saw that it was Elli, he smiled. She was a baby. A girl came out on the stage and the show started.

It was amazing, Elli was captivating, and that's not because he knew her and loved her so much, it was because she was absolutely amazing. Her voice was like angelic, it was just as her dad had said, it was like angels singing. When she would open her mouth everyone looked at her, even the people on stage. It was breathtaking.

So breathtaking, that when Elli came shuffling into the room, Shea didn't even look up at her. He kept watching the DVD as she came over and cuddled up on the couch with him. No one said anything as the DVD went black, then the spotlight came back on Elli in the middle of the stage in a black dress.

"This is my favorite part," she said beside him. On the DVD, Elli started singing again, the song was about the man she had lost Shea guessed, but he didn't care, Elli was compelling. She killed the performance, you believed she had just lost the love of her life, you believed she was hurting, but you didn't care, all you wanted was more of her voice, more of her.

The show ended with her standing there, no music playing, just big, shiny tears falling down her cheeks. Shea wanted to get up and clap and scream like the people were doing in the video, but instead he wrapped his arms around Elli, holding her close to him as the credits ran.

"I trained for a months to do that song, it was so hard."

"It was amazing, your fascinating Elli, truly."

Elli shook her head against his, turning her head up to look at him, "I was, not no more. I couldn't sing that song if my life depended on it."

"Sure you could, and you still are Elli. You fascinate me, every day."

A dazzling smile came across her face causing his heart to pound, and his skin to tingle. This was the moment, the moment for her to say it. It was all over her face, she loved him, she had too, he saw it in her eyes.

"I never loved myself until I met you," she said before snuggling closer to him, rubbing her nose against his neck.

She didn't love him, but she loved herself.

Great.

Now when the hell was she gonna love him!

Chapter 25

Elli opened her eyes slowly, she felt like someone was staring at her, and not to her surprise someone was.

Shea.

He gave her a cheeky grin, kissing her lips loudly. "Happy birthday, baby."

"Mmm…thanks," she said as she stretched her arms above her head, "What time is it?"

"Seven, we need to get back to Nashville."

"Why?" she asked rolling to her side to cuddle against his naked chest, "Why on earth would we leave this warm bed?"

Shea chuckled, "Baby, it's your birthday; things are planned for today you know."

"Like?"

He smacked her butt playfully, pushing her out of bed. "Not telling! Now get up, Harper will be at the condo by nine to pick you up."

Elli moaned as Shea continued to push her out of bed, "Fine, fine, I'm going," she complained as she threw the blankets off her and headed for the shower. "You're mean," she spat back at him as he just laughed.

"I bet you won't be saying that later!" he countered as she went into the bathroom. A grin covered her face, he was probably right. She was so excited for today, she could hardly contain it. It was weird for her to be excited about her birthday, but she was. Another thing Shea had made happen.

The man was a God send. He made her feel so good about herself, made her happy, made her excited about things that before she would never be excited for. He had taken care of her all week, making sure she recovered quickly, which she had. She had never bounced back from being sick so quickly, and when she said that to Shea, he laughed saying, "My mom always said that a lot of love will chase any sickness away."

Mrs. Adler was completely right.

Elli took off her t-shirt and hopped into the shower, letting the hot water warm her body. She had been so happy staying at her house with Shea and was a little sad that they had to return to Nashville. It seemed that time stood still when she was in her house, that the outside world didn't exist, or maybe that was the sickness because God knew she couldn't do anything but lay in bed. Elli didn't even know what was going on with the studio, she was sure it was okay, but she had no clue what the schedule or anything looked like.

After washing up, Elli got out and brushed her hair out before going back into the bedroom. Shea must have been out with Alder because he wasn't in bed. Elli went to her closet, looking through her clothes for something to wear. She decided on a pair of worn wranglers and a Toy Story t-shirt that she had gotten when she went to Toy Story on Ice with the kids. She went back into her bathroom, getting ready for the day. She didn't know if she should do her hair, so she just dried it, and put it up. After putting on some light makeup, she went to go pick some shoes. After taking twenty minutes to decide on boots or pumps, she went with her black cowboy boots that had red hearts all over them. They were her favorite, and her most broken in boots.

Elli made her way down the hall, through her living room to the kitchen, where Shea stood drinking his coffee. A grin went over his face as she wrapped her arms around his waist, placing her cheek in the middle of his chest. He was dressed in jeans and a sweater, with his trusty chucks. He was ready to go apparently.

"Ready babe? Adler's already in the car."

"Yup, you sure are in a hurry to leave my house," she teased as she let him go, putting on her jacket that hung on the peg by the hall, "You don't like my house?"

He shook his head, putting on his jacket as he stood in front of her. "Of course I do, but we need to get back. Like I said Harper is coming."

She nodded as she locked up, heading towards her truck as he went to his. When she climbed into her truck she saw that Adler wasn't there. She looked in the rearview mirror and there sat her dog, in the passenger side of Shea's car.

Damn dog.

Harper was already waiting when Elli pulled up. It was no surprise that Shea beat her home, he drove like a bat out of hell, so she wasn't even surprised when she pulled up to see Harper and Shea talking beside the truck. Elli got out the truck, locking it as she walked towards the two most important people in her life right now. Harper smiled over at Elli, wrapping her arm around her shoulders.

"Happy birthday!"

"Why thank you very much," Elli said with a grin, "What brings you by?"

"Part of the surprise of today, come on! Say bye to your boy toy, let's roll!"

Elli shook her head as she giggled, wrapping her arms around Shea. "When will I see you, Mr. Secretive?"

Shea laughed as he kissed her cheek, "Later on tonight, have fun."

"Doing what?"

"Shut up, stop trying to ruin the surprise," he said before leaning down to capture her lips with his. He kissed her long and lavishly before pulling away and smiling down at her. "See you tonight."

Elli narrowed her eyes at him, pouting her lips, "Bye."

She listened to his laughter all the way to Harper's Honda. They both waved at Shea as Harper backed up, heading south on West End. "You look great babe, real good."

"Thanks Harper, I feel a lot better." Elli answered as she looked out the window. As much as she was excited for the surprise, she hated not knowing.

"Shea took good care of you?"

"He did," Elli said beaming, "He bathed me Harp, like actually stood in the shower and held me in his arms to wash me; he's amazing."

Harper nodded, "Hell yeah he is, that's great. I was hoping you wouldn't be mad I called him."

"No I wasn't. I was actually glad, I didn't like that he saw me so sick, but I needed help. Lord knows you can't handle it."

Harper shook her head, a look of horror on her face, "It scares the living shit out of me when you get like that. I'm glad Shea handled it well though."

"Me too," Elli agreed as they pulled into Escape Day Spa and Salon.

Elli had never been there, and wondered why they were there now. Harper got out, leaving Elli to scramble to get out of the car. She only took a step before Jodi, Reese, Piper, and Trice jumped out from behind a car, yelling, "Surprise!"

"Ah! Gosh! Y'all scared the living crap out of me!" Elli exclaimed with her hand over her heart, "What in the hell are y'all doing here?"

"Spa day!" Trice exclaimed with a flip of his hand towards the Spa.

"We're getting out nails, hair, eye brows, everything done!" Piper gushed, basically bouncing on the heels on her feet.

"What? Really?" Elli asked.

"Yup," Harper said, taking Elli's arm in hers and walking towards the spa, "Shea's first gift."

Elli looked over at Harper surprised, "He did this?"

"Of course he did silly, we ain't got the cash too," Jodi laughed as everyone joined in.

"Wow, I'll have to call him," Elli said completely stunned.

"Not now you won't! Let's go!" Harper said pulling her towards the massive building.

That man and his surprises.

If this was the first of his gifts, a spa day with her closest friends at one of the most expensive spas in Nashville, no telling what else he had planned.

And Elli couldn't wait to find out.

Shea parked his truck behind Grace's van in the drive of the Belmont Mansion, and headed up the stairs to the front door of the mansion as he admired the beauty of the gazebo that stood off to the side. He was surprised Grace was able to get this place, considering how popular it was, but of course she came through. The mansion was beautiful with its light tan bricks, green shutters and white trim. The windows that lined the front of the mansion were floor and ceiling and so clear, like they had just been cleaned, which they probably had if Grace had anything to do with it. Shea had to past through two huge columns to get to the large, dark cherry colored door.

When he walked in, workers were setting up the million of candles that Shea said had to be there. One of the main things in the Pride and Prejudice movie was the candles. They were the only thing lighting the ball room in the movie, and Shea wanted Elli, along with the 300 guest that would be joining them, to feel like they walked into the movie.

Shea walked through the main ballroom to find Grace directing what looked like the food people in the kitchen. Grace looked worn out, and it made him nervous. Maybe this party was too much for her; maybe he should have hired someone else.

She would have killed him if he did.

Grace must have heard him come up because she turned, giving him a welcomed smile before turning back to the workers and yelling some more.

Once the guys did whatever the hell she was asking for, she came over to Shea, wrapping her arms around his one. "So what do you think so far?"

"Amazing, as always."

He looked around the ball room, taking in the way his sister had basically transformed the mansion into the Neitherfield ball room. It was so impressive. The windows were done with gold drapes; gold swirls were put on the walls, along with pictures of people from the 19th century. There were candelabras that hung in various places along the walls; each one had tall white candles in them. Hundreds of floor brass candle stick holders, stood tall with the tall white pillars in them. There were vintage couches and chairs throughout the whole ballroom, along with a very large, beautiful, wooden piano that sat in the corner.

Shea followed Grace into the dining room, and smiled at the result his sister had given him. Each table had a large crystal vase in the middle of it; each one was filled with large white candle and pretty gold wires that held crystals at the end of each of them along with white feathers. The place settings were gold with black napkins; the table clothes were white with gold swirls on them. Grace pointed up to the ceilings so Shea looked up, taking in the beauty of the nine chandeliers that graced the ceilings.

"You wouldn't believe the deposit I had to put down, plus we can't have candles burning all night; they start leaving snoot on the ceiling, so I got fake candles, but I don't think you can tell."

Shea shook his head, he couldn't tell the difference, he thought they were real, "You did great Grace, its perfect. Just like the movie."

"Good, I thought so, I'm happy with the result."

"Me too," he said wrapping his arm around her shoulders, "Good job, sis."

She smiled up at him, smacking his side. "Thanks."

They did another run through of the house, and Shea wanted to buy his sister the world. She had out done herself once again. God, he loved her.

"So your suit is upstairs, along with your socks."

"I told you I didn't want the socks," Shea complained, as Grace smiled.

"It completes the ambience," she said sweetly.

"I'll look like a dweeb."

"A hot dweeb, plus Elli will love it!"

Shea shrugged his shoulders, Grace was probably right.

"So what's up? I haven't seen you at all this past week." Grace said as they walked past the amazing staircase, that later Elli and Shea would come down.

"Elli got sick; I've been staying at her house."

"Is she okay?" Grace asked concern coming over her face.

"She's fine now, it was scary though. She couldn't walk, eat, nothing. She just slept, a lot."

"Oh no, that's crazy. What happened?"

"She says it happens sometimes, they changed her meds and everything. She has seemed good the last two days."

"Well good. Gosh, that's crazy. You should have called me, I would have came and helped."

"I had it under control," Shea said with a grin, "Oh by the way; I told her I love her."

Grace whipped her head over from where she was fixing a drape, "Say what? When?"

"Before we had dinner with mom and dad."

"Wow, what did she say?" She put her hands up, stopping him from answering, "Let me guess, 'Oh Shea, I love you too!'" Grace said in just about the worst country accent Shea had ever heard, and he thought he was bad at it.

"Actually no, she didn't say anything." Grace stopped laughing and looked over at Shea, surprised.

"Huh?"

"Yeah, she apparently doesn't love me and its driving me nuts."

"Well Shea not everyone falls in love at the same time, give her a minute."

"I know but I just want her to love me, I mean I don't know what else to do. I've completely changed for this girl and it just doesn't seem to be enough."

"You're acting like a chick, Shea. Yeah, you've changed and it's great, believe me, I'm the first one to say so, but gosh, let her be. It's not like she doesn't have feelings for you, it's obvious she does."

"I know that Grace, but I want to hear her say it. To me."

Grace scrunched up her face, shaking her head, "You're turning into a sissy."

"I am not!"

"You are! What are you going to do next, write her a poem? Haha, or maybe serenade her." Grace bent over; laughing her ass off. Shea prayed Elli would never say anything about him singing to her, because Grace would make his life a living hell if she ever found out.

Maybe he was turning into a sissy.

"Shut up!"

"No really, like could you imagine it?! Haha, you're standing there with a guitar singing some sappy Backstreet Boy song or something." She was actually slapping her leg as she filled the ballroom with her laughter.

Shea didn't think she was funny.

"You suck," Shea said crossing his arms as his sister, his twin, laughed at his expense. When she finally calmed herself she looked up at him.

"Oh shut up, you know its wicked funny," she giggled.

"I'm not laughing."

"Party pooper, anyways, like I said, give her time, I didn't tell James I loved him till Ryan was born, that was almost a year into our relationship. You've jumped the gun, telling her at three months, I know this is your first time, but damn Shea, give her some time."

Shea shoulders slump and he let out a frustrated sigh, "Is it too much to ask for, just to know I'm loved?"

"Aw, brother, I love you." Grace said batting her eyes at him before bursting out in a fit of giggles.

"Oh God," Shea said rolling his eyes as he started for the door, "I'll see you tonight, good job in here."

"Shea I love you, I do, so much! I love you! Bye!"

Damn twin.

Mud baths, messages, facials, oh my!

"This is the life," Elli basically moaned as she leaned back into her puffy chair, having her feet done. She held a glass of champagne in one hand and a chocolate covered strawberry in the other. "I will have to make sure to thank Shea extra long tonight."

Everyone giggled as they sat back enjoying their pedicures.

"Hell I might have to help," Reese said as one of the workers stood behind her chair, rubbing her shoulders. That earned her a round of giggles as everyone just basked in the treatments they were getting.

"In your dreams," Elli teased back, Reese laughed as she nodded her head.

"Hell yes in my dreams, that dude is sex on legs. Jeez, he's so pretty."

"He really is," Piper gushed.

"Hey you skinny hoes, back off my man!" Elli laughed, Reese and Piper giggled along, and Elli couldn't think the last time she felt so relax and happy.

Being with her friends, getting pampered was the greatest start to her birthday, and the way everyone was talking, tonight was gonna be even better.

After getting their feet and hands down, Elli had gotten French tip because when she said her usual purple, Harper flipped saying 'Get something classy for once!', so she got the French tip, they headed up to the hair salon. Elli sat in the chair as a girl named Andee, starting doing her hair. After getting it trimmed and washed up real good, Harper came over, smiling down at Elli.

"Okay, so we are covering the mirror."

"Huh?" Elli asked as two other salon workers came over covering the mirror with a black sheet, as everyone grinned over at Elli.

"You can't see what she does."

"Why?" Elli complained.

"It's part of the surprise so shut up."

Harper walked away sitting back in her chair, leaving Elli frustrated. She hated not knowing what she looked like, what if this chick jacked her hair up, or made her makeup look crazy. It was driving her crazy as she sat, letting the Andee girl do whatever she wanted with her hair. After about an hour and a half, Andee was finally done with Elli's hair and makeup.

Elli stood up as everyone came over towards her with smiles on their faces. Everyone, well expect Trice, had intricate up dos, with flowers or feathers in their hair. Everyone looked so classic, so beautiful.

"This isn't fair! I wanna know what I look like!"

Everyone laughed as Harper came towards her a blindfold in her hand. "Oh come on!" she complained as Harper was careful to tie it over her eyes.

"Don't ruin it, Shea's worked hard okay?" Harper whispered in her ear as the world went black around her.

Damn it, she was right.

Elli had no clue where she was; everyone was talking and moving around her when they arrived at wherever they were at as Elli stood there confused and frustrated.

She wanted the damn blindfold off.

She wanted to see Shea.

Her day had been amazing, except for the blindfold business, and she wanted to thank him.

"Are we getting her dressed now?" Harper asked as Elli was sat on a couch, maybe, hell it might have been a chair.

"Yeah, go ahead. Everyone is starting to arrive." Grace said.

"Grace?" Elli asked.

"Yeah, happy birthday!"

"Thanks, what are you doing here?"

"Um, I don't know. You don't hear me."

Everyone started laughing except Elli, she didn't think this was funny; gosh, she hated secrets. Someone started pulling at her clothes, and then she felt someone taking off her bra.

"Hey!"

"It's me El, shush," Harper said putting another bra on her; Harper directed Elli into what she guessed was a dress. The satin was cool against Elli's skin and she was dying to know what it looked like, what was going on, and when the hell she could take the damn blind fold off! Harper zipped her up and tied something, then Elli didn't feel anything, but she heard everyone's intake of breaths and their 'awes'.

"Okay, when you hear the door shut, take off the blind fold," Harper said. Elli just stood there waiting, everyone wished her luck, and then finally, the door shut.   Elli practically ripped the blindfold from her head, when her eyes adjusted she was looking at herself if a full length brass mirror.

"Oh my god," she muttered as her hand came up over her mouth. She was wearing the dress from the shop that Grace had her try on. Her hair was done up in pin curls with pearls holding in each curl. Her makeup was done so soft, that it was hard to tell she even had any one. The dress, oh it was masterpiece, beautiful, stunning; Elli could go on for days describing the beauty of it.

She looked like Elizabeth Bennet, and Elli had a feeling that when she walked out the door, she would be stepping into the Nethierfield ball. A nervous giggle escaped her lips as she looked back the large white door.

With every step she took to the door, she got more and more excited as questions filled her head.

Would it be just like the movie?

Would everyone be there?

Where was she?

And the biggest one, would Mr. Darcy be there?

Well not the real Mr. Darcy but Shea as Mr. Darcy.

Elli opened the door and took a step out, walking down the hall, taking in the exquisiteness of the place that she had no clue she was at. The walls were covered with beautiful gold paper that had white swirls on them. Vintage furniture was everywhere, along with large floor candle stick holders. It was beautiful.

When Elli came to the end of the hall, coming to some stairs that led down, her last question was answered.

Because there stood Shea, smiling up at her, in a black waistcoat with a white under coat, the cravat that covered his neck to his chin was white, the pants that came down to below his knees were black and bless his heart, to complete the outfit he wore sheer socks.

Elli couldn't help but laugh when she saw he didn't have the traditional shoes of the 19th century, but his chucks.

"My Mr. Darcy, Adler style huh?"

"Oh yeah, and Grace is livid about it," he said taking her hand as she made it to the last step.

"I bet, even though I love it. It's totally you."

He gave her a sheepish grin, "I felt like a sissy in those princess shoes."

Elli giggled as she pressed her lips against his, when they parted she smiled as she looked up into his eyes, running her hand down his cheek, "Thank you Shea."

"Oh you haven't seen nothing yet, come on."

He took her hand, leading her down the long staircase. When they reached the bottom, Elli heard people talking and laughing as Shea placed his hand on the small of her back, leading her to a pair of French doors.

"Ready?"

"Sure am," she gushed as he pushed open the door, everyone turned looking back at the door, before a chorus of 'Happy Birthday' rang through the filled ballroom. Elli's face lit up, seeing all her friends, Shea's friends, and her daddy, dressed in her favorite era. The ballroom was spectacular, it looked like Elli had step onto the set of Pride and Prejudice, with the gold drapes and candles that covered every square inch of the beautiful ballroom.

As Shea lead her through the room to greet everyone, Elli took in every detail. She wanted to remember this night for the rest of her life, so she remembered the candelabras that hung on the walls, the way the gold swirls twisted so finely on the walls, and how the violists that sat in the corner by the piano, looked exactly like the ones in the movie, but most of all she took in how gorgeous Shea was.

It wasn't any surprise that Shea would look good even in the 19th century. Some of the other guys that also had dressed up looked dorky in their dress coats, but not Shea. He looked regal, established, perfect, and he had done all this for her. He slid his hand into her, leading her to the middle of the dance floor. He stood her on one side, as Harper, Jodi, Reese, and Piper came to join her, then he went to the other with Jakob, Derrick, and two guys Elli didn't know.

When 'A Postcard to Henry Purcell' started Elli's mouth dropped. "No y'all didn't."

"Oh yes we did, now go!" Harper exclaimed basically pushing Elli to go.

Of course Elli knew the dance well, she had watched the movie so many times that she could do it in her sleep. She wouldn't admit it to anyone but she used to make Adler be Mr. Darcy, and carry the overweight pup through the living room as they watched the movie.

What surprised Elli the most was how perfect Shea knew the dance. He moved with ease around her, taking her hand when needed, while keeping in time.

"I love this dance." Elli said just for shit and giggles since it was the first line that Elizabeth Bennet said in the movie, but when Shea said, "Yes, it's most invigorating." Elli couldn't breathe. On they went, going back and forth the way Elizabeth and Mr. Darcy did in the movie. Shea was astonishing, and surprised her every day.

"You memorized the dance and the script?" she asked with a cheeky grin as they moved around each other.

"I did."

"Why?"

"Because I love you."

It was that simple.

The song ended just as the words left Shea's mouth, everyone awed as Elli turned deep red at being caught at what should have been a private moment between them. Elli came to him, wrapping her arms around him as some soft music started again. Shea wrapped his arms around her, taking her close into his arms, nuzzling his nose into her neck. She had taken his breath away with her beauty. Of course she was the most beautiful person on earth to him, but tonight she was picturesque. He couldn't take his eyes off her.

They held each other as the song went into another one, and then another before they parted, smiling at each other. "Are you hungry?" he asked.

"Kinda."

"There's a buffet."

"Let's go then."

He nodded, taking her hand in his, leading her through the dancing couples. When they reached the other ballroom, Elli looked up at him, "Where are we? The Belmont?"

"Yup," he said with a grin.

"I thought so."

"There are your parents," Shea said with he spotted Michael and Olivia.

"Why in the good Lord's name did you invite my mother?" Elli asked in horror as she looked up at him.

"I wanted your whole family here, to share you special night." He said with a shrugged as Michael and Olivia made their way over.

"Daddy," Elli grinned, kissing his cheek, "Mother." Elli didn't move to her though. She watched as Olivia put an awkward kiss on her cheek, and then smiled over at Shea.

"This beautiful Shea, you outdid yourself with this."

"Thank you, but it's my sister's work. I just came up with the idea," Shea said as Elli looked up at him, smiling.

"I'll have to thank her too," Elli said, before Michael took Elli's hands in his.

"Darlin', you look striking tonight."

"Aw thanks daddy," Elli gushed as red dusted her beautiful cheeks.

"You do sweetheart, just beautiful." Everyone looked over at Olivia in surprised. Shea didn't think anyone was more surprised than Elli was; her mouth was actually hanging open a little.

"Thank you, mother," Elli said, Shea could see the surprise all over her face, and loved the smiled that formed afterwards.

Shea and Elli wished them a good night, and then made their way to the buffet, making plates before sitting down with their friends. They enjoyed the amazing food Grace had ordered, and the conversation their friends provided them with. After eating, they made their way through the crowd, greeting more of their friends and for Shea to introduce Elli to some of his friend's she hadn't met yet.

"So this is Eleanor Fisher, damn Shea, she's hotter than you lead on," Damon Thompson, Shea's agent said.

"That she is," Shea agreed as Elli grinned up at both men.

"It's wonderful to meet you, thank you for coming." Elli gushed as Damon shook her hand.

"It's my pleasure. I love parties but when Grace said Shea would be wearing some girlie socks, I had to be here. Plus I wanted to meet you." Shea narrowed his eyes at his agent, while Damon laughed.

"You know I can replace you," Shea informed him.

"You could but you won't, we've known each other since we were kids, I'm not going anywhere, you and I both know that, brother." Damon said with a grin, before turning back to Elli, "Like I said, you are more beautiful than he let on, so when you're tired of him, give me a call." Damon left with a wink, and Shea's blood boiled.

"I don't know why I keep that guy," Shea said glaring at Damon's back as he flirted with one of Harper's sisters.

"Cause you love him, come on, I wanna dance!"

"Alright," Shea agreed as she drugged him to the floor as Duffy sung about syrup and honey. Like always, their bodies move with such ease, such skill. The sexy music made Shea want to be closer to Elli, in the naked sense, but that wouldn't be happening till later on that night.

They danced all through the night, only to stop to greet someone, or to get a glass of wine. They were standing with Jakob and Harper when Grace took a mic, smiling out at the crowd. "I think it's time for everyone to join in to sing to the birthday girl!" Unfortunately Grace kept the mic as she sang 'Happy Birthday'. Shea had always known he wasn't the best singer, but Grace was worst and now everyone knew it. Shea didn't think Elli cared though; she smiled and blushed as the three tiers, red velvet cake with white butter cream icing was wheeled out. The cake was topped with a sparkling 28, and twenty eight candles adorn the cake in various spots. When everyone was done singing, Elli blew out all her candles with a 'yeehaw' for good measure at the end.

Shea was rewarded with a dazzling grin as Elli wrapped her arms around his neck, kissing him deeply. When they parted, she was smiling so big at him that it was hard for him to catch his breath. How he could love someone so much, and so whole heartily would always be a mystery to him, but he did and was convinced he would for the rest of his life.

As 'Make you Feel my Love' filled the ballroom, Shea pulled Elli to the middle of the floor, taking her face in his hands as she placed hers around his waist. He leaned his forehead against hers, as they dance together, looking into each other's eyes.

"This night is magical, Shea."

"It's not over yet baby, we still got the after party," he leaned closer, bringing his lips against hers, but not kissing her, "in my bed."

Her giggles intoxicated him as they danced, moving closer with each step as nothing was said. When she looked up at him, biting her bottom lip, he smiled. "Could we make it our bed?"

Shea actually stopped moving as he looked down at her, "What?"

"I mean, is the offer of moving in together still on the table?"

His heart actually skipped a beat as his beautiful girlfriend looked up at him with a nervous smile, "Oh baby that offer will forever be on the table for you. Do you really want too?" Elli smiled big, nodding her head. Shea let out a whoop of laughter before pressing his lips against hers hard, lifting her off the floor.

And he thought he couldn't love her more.

Chapter 26

There was a trail of clothing from the front door of the condo to the bedroom, but they didn't care. Shea lifted Elli naked body off the ground, bringing her mouth to his as she wrapped her legs around his waist, her moist center teasing his growing arousal. He basically kicked the bedroom open, trying to get her to the bed, since she had complained the island was cold and hard, plus Adler could see.

Like the dog knew what they were doing!

He fell on top of her, kissing down her jaw to her neck, she ran her nails up his back making his mind swirl with lust. He wanted her so damn bad; it had been weeks since he had her like this, he couldn't wait. His lips made their way from her neck back to her lips as his hand moved down the side of her body, to between her legs. She was dripping with excitement as he slid a finger inside of her; she filled his mouth with a throaty moan as he moved his finger around her aching nub, causing her to squirm underneath him. He moved his hand away, smacking her thighs open, so that she was fully exposed to him. Her eyes went wide when he filled her with one swift motion.

They both groaned in appreciation at being joined in the most fulfilling way. Shea sat up on the back of his hunches, gyrate in slow, insistent circles as Elli let out short little spurts of breaths, her body squeezing him as he pushed himself into her. He looked down at where their bodies were joined, watching as he moved in and out of her before looking up at Elli's face. She was pink with arousal, looking up at him with her lust filled green eyes. God, she was hot, and he wasn't going to last.

But she hadn't come yet.

He stopped, taking a hold of her hips flipping her over to her stomach, before entering her from behind. She got up on her knees, her face to the side, so he could only see her profile over her beautiful round ass. She let out a lustful cry as he continued to push himself into her with total abandonment. Shea couldn't help the smirk that crossed his lips, she loved it this way, and he knew it, he could feel it. As she groaned in blissful agony from her climax, he slammed into her harder, taking what he wanted. It was the longest, hottest release of his life when he came. He filled her to the hilt, gripping her hips as he groaned long and low.

When he was able to focus, he looked down at Elli's profile, she was grinning. He smacked her ass playfully, making her jump before saying, "What are you grinning at?"

"You make hot sex noises," she giggled. Shea laughed as he pulled out of her, moving off the bed towards the bathroom. He started the shower, before coming back into the room, admiring her naked body as she laid on her side, picking at her nails.

"Did you have fun tonight baby?"

A gorgeous grin crossed her face as her eyes lit up, "Best birthday ever, thank you again."

He nodded, feeling good about himself since that's what he wanted, for her to have the best day, she deserved it.

"Anything for you."

"You're too good to me," Elli said rolling out of bed and coming towards him.

"Never, I could be better."

"Really?" she asked raising an eye brow as she wrapped her arms around his middle, nuzzling her nose in the middle of his chest.

"Yeah, I know there are things that drive you crazy about me."

"Well, it does bother me the way you strip me down naked and have your way with me," she teased as she bit his pec softly. "Other than that, can't think of anything." He laughed as he gathered her closer to him.

"I'm messy."

"Ah, you're a dude."

"I can't cook worth shit."

"That's okay; I cook good enough for both of us."

He smiled, biting her jaw before moving his nose against hers.

"I leave you a lot."

"It's your job Shea, you're supposed to leave," she smiled, leaning against him more, "You always come home, and I'm here when you get back."

"For good now huh?"

She blushed, closing her eyes as they moved their noses against each other's, "As long as you want me."

"Good because I don't see you leaving....ever."

The next morning, Elli rolled over, snuggling closer to Shea for his warmth. He was like a heater when he slept. He gave off so much heat, it drove her crazy before but now, she couldn't thank the good Lord enough. She moved her freezing toes under the blanket and in between Shea's thighs. It only took a second for his eyes to go wide, moving away from her quickly.

"Elli!"

"I'm cold!" she yelled back, trying to move towards him as he continued to move away from her, "Come back!"

"No, your toes are freezing!"

"Please, I'm cold!"

"Stop!" he laughed as she kept trying to put her toes in between his thighs. When Shea fell out the bed with a loud oomph, Elli laughed so hard that she had to hold her belly because it hurt from laughing. He sat up, turning his head to glare at her. "I'm gonna get you one of these days." Elli continued to laugh as Shea got up, and headed into the bathroom, shaking his head. "Go cook me some breakfast woman!" he yelled from the bathroom.

"Go cook your own breakfast! I'm cold! In less you're gonna come warm me up, go on and make your own!" Elli yelled back.

Shea popped his head out, a devilish grin on his face, "Oh I'll warm you up baby, but not the way you're asking for."

Elli bit her bottom lip, giving him her best seductive look, "Who says that's not the way I want to be warmed up?"

Elli stood at the stove, cooking some French toast with a grin on her face. The man rocked her world, and she couldn't get enough. The night before was a dream, nothing like that would ever have happened to her if Shea hadn't come along. In a matter of four months, she had so many first that her mind spun at the thought. One first being that in the last six years Elli never felt beautiful, now she felt like the prettiest girl in the world, all because of him.

Elli was taking some sausage out of the fridge when her phone rang; she went over to it seeing it was Harper.

"Hey!"

"Hey, whatcha doin?"

"Cooking some breakfast."

"At 12?"

Elli glanced at the clock, "We got started late this morning," Elli said with a giggle.

Harper laughed than said, "I hear ya, what y'all got planned this afternoon?"

"I don't know yet, like I said we just got out of bed a little while ago, we haven't even talked about the rest of the day."

"Well Jakob and I were wondering if you guys would meet us at a house we're thinking about getting."

"A house?" Elli asked as she paused in front of the island, leaning against it. When did Harper want to get a house with Jakob? A condo, Elli totally understood that, but a house?

"Yeah, I told you we were looking for something."

"You said a condo, Harper."

"Hey, just cause you have commitment issues doesn't mean I do." Elli laughed.

"I don't have any commitment issues!"

"Yes you do, you won't even say you moved in when you practically already have!"

"Well for your information Harper Allen, I am admitting now. We are moving in together," Elli said as warmth filled her body.

She was living with Shea! Yes, they had not worked out all the details but damn it, she was admitting to it!

"Liar!"

Shea went into the kitchen, giving Elli a smile before grabbing the plate she had laid out for him.

"No really," Elli said before looking over at Shea as he sat down to eat, "Honey, ain't I moving in for real?"

"Ain't? I mean baby you can't throw in a few more syllables and say 'Aren't?" he said with a twinkle of mischief in his eyes. Elli was surprised Harper could breathe with how hard she was laughing, Elli actually had to pull the phone away from her ear cause Harper was so loud.

"I don't know why your laughing, you say ain't just as much as I do!"

"Oh I know, but it's funny when Shea makes fun of you."

"Shut up," she said before looking over at her chuckling boyfriend, "You too, and tell my best friend that we are living together!"

"We are." Shea said before digging into his food.

"See," Elli said as she sat down across from him with her plate.

"Fine, but it ain't real till you tell your papa and daddy though."

Elli thought that over, Harper was kinda right, not that she would tell her that, "Whatever, so as you were saying, y'all want us to come out a see this house?" Shea looked up confused, and Elli shrugged her shoulders.

"Yeah, it's in Belle Meade, I'll text you the address, we're going out there in about an hour or so, depends when Jakob gets done at the physical therapist."

Elli couldn't even talk, she was speechless. They were looking at a house in Belle Meade?

"Belle Meade?"

"Yeah, can y'all make it?"

"Y'all are looking at a house in Belle Meade, where Al Gore lives?"

Harper got quiet for a moment, "He lives there?"

"Oh my god, yeah we'll go."

"Great! I'll text you the address."

"Alright, bye."

"Bye"

"Where are we going?" Shea asked, he was freshly showered, and dressed all sexy looking with his black thermal, and ripped up grey jeans.

"Jakob and Harper are looking at a house in Belle Meade," Elli explained, "They want us to come and look at it."

"Why us?"

"We are their best friends? I don't know. I just can't believe they are looking at houses."

"Why? I told you Jakob wants the whole deal, house, marriage, kids, this is totally normal for Jakob."

"I know but it's not for Harper, it's weird."

"I guess, so when do we need to be there?"

"In an hour, I'm gonna go take a shower," Elli said getting up and putting her full plate in the sink.

"You didn't eat."

"I ain't hungry," she answered before heading down the hall.

She had lost her appetite when Harper said Belle Meade. How could Harper want to live there? After everything Elli went through in that neighborhood with Justin. Why would Harper want to live there, when she knew Elli would be coming over a lot to see her? Elli was sure Justin still lived in the house that Elli had lived in for a year; Justin loved that house and would never get rid of it. What if Harper's house was by Justin?

Elli stomach churned at the thought.

Elli had worried over nothing, Harper's prospected house was nowhere near Justin's, but they did have to pass it to get to Harpers. When Shea turned onto Justin's road, Elli stomach dropped, she had traveled down this road so many times, but this time she wouldn't be pulling into the circular driveway of the 2.5 million dollar, 3 story high, blue colonial. Nope, she would be driving right on by it, hell she might even flip it the bird.

She didn't, she just pointed and said, "That's Justin's house." Elli didn't expect Shea to slam on the breaks, looking out his window at the huge, beautiful house.

"You lived there?"

"I did," Elli said, looking out the window too, Justin's Rolls Royce wasn't there, so he must have been out.

"It's too nice for a douche bag," he said before driving off.

"That it is."

They drove a little more before Shea spoke again, "You know, I was thinking."

Elli looked over at him, "Yeah?"

"You've heard me sing, but I have yet to hear you sing and you sang on damn Broadway." Elli smiled shyly over at Shea, out of all the things he could be thinking, he was thinking that?

"You heard me sing at the karaoke bar."

"That wasn't real, you were drunk. I want to hear you really sing."

"Not gonna happen," she said with a grin.

"Why not?" he asked as the GPS told him to turn again.

"Because I don't sing in less I'm drunk in front of people."

"That's crazy; you were amazing in the movies we watched."

"I was younger and could actually sing then."

"I bet you're still amazing."

"To bad you won't ever find out."

"Oh I will," he challenged just as the GPS said that they had arrived at their destination. Shea pulled into the one level stone home with huge white windows, as Elli grinned at a waving Harper and Jakob. They looked so happy, so much like a couple, that it blew Elli's mind. Who would have thought that Harper Allen would be living the life that she was?

Elli sure never thought she would be.

"It's a great house, don't you think?" Shea asked as they drove back to the condo, they were going to go home to change since they were meeting Harper and Jakob for dinner. They were going out to celebrate since they put an offer on the house once Shea and Elli saw and liked it.

"I do, it's great."

"I thought so, they seem happy with it."

"Yeah, I've never seen Harper so excited about something."

"Yeah," Shea agreed, "there is a lot of house for sale over here."

"Yeah."

Shea looked over at Elli; she was looking out the window at the houses as the past by, "Did you want to get a house together?"

Elli looked over at him, "The condos fine don't you think?"

He shrugged his shoulders, "I guess, but you have a lot of stuff, you're piano isn't going to fit in the condo."

"I was thinking that I was just gonna bring my clothes over, and shoes."

Shea thought for a moment, before saying, "So you're not truly moving in?"

"Well yeah I am, just I'm leaving my stuff at my house."

"Why? Why don't we get a bigger place? I don't want you to sell your house because I was thinking we could live there when I retire."

"Retire?"

"It will happen," he said with a laugh as he turned onto the exit for Nashville. "I'm not going to play forever."

"I know, but I didn't think you were thinking that far ahead, or even including me in that equation." He looked over at her; she was biting her bottom lip, her face flushed. How could she think he wasn't including her in the equation?

"Of course I am."

"Oh," Elli said, a delighted smile on her face, "I don't know if I want people living in my house."

"Fine, it's paid off isn't it?"

"Yeah."

"Alright, so it's not like we'll have to worry about that mortgage payment and a new one, so why don't we look into getting something bigger? I think Grace knows a good realtor, or maybe we can use the one Jakob and Harper are using."

Elli was quite for a moment as Shea drove, he didn't know if he should take her silence as a good thing or not, but he didn't want to say anything, plus he didn't know what to say, he said his peace, all he could do was hope for the best.

"A house?" she finally asked.

"Yeah, I mean my condo is on the big side, the only thing to add is more bedrooms you know?"

"Yeah, but we aren't married, what if we split up? Who gets the house?"

Shea thought about it for a moment, "Well I doubt that will happen, but if it does, we can sell it, split the profit, or if you want it, you can have it, because if I'm not with you baby, I'm not staying in Nashville."

"You'd really leave?"

Shea shook his head, "I don't know baby, I don't like thinking about it. In my mind, we'll be together forever."

"I like the way you think," she said after a moment with a grin, he smiled back.

"So what do you say?"

"I say," she bit her lip again, taking his hand in hers, "yes."

The biggest, brightest smile crossed his face. Shea felt on top of the world, as if nothing or no one could touch him. They were going to buy a house together, could life get any better?

Elli had been wearing the same grin for the past two days, not only was she with the most amazing man in the world. One that plans amazing birthday parties and makes her scream something crazy in the bedroom, but she was moving in with him. Really moving in, they had gotten the number of the realtor from Harper and Shea called Grace for the number of the one she knew. Everything was in the works, and Elli couldn't be happier.

Only thing left to do was tell her daddy and Papa.

Lucky for her (not!), they were both at the home game the following night, so Elli made her way up to Papa's box decked out in her Adler gear. Shea had said he was gonna get her a jersey that said 'Adler's woman' on the back along with his number, but Elli said no. Call her superstitious but she had had the same jersey since Shea became her favorite player, she was scared if she changed it something would happen, or he would get traded, he of course laughed when she told him that, but she didn't care, she was happy with her jersey. She wasn't ever gonna wear anything else.

Elli entered Bryan's box, finding her father and uncle drinking it up as they talked hockey. When the door shut behind her, they turned with grins forming on their faces when they saw her.

She doubted they would be smiling when she left, but oh well.

"It's about damn time you came and sat with us!" Bryan said in his booming voice as he got up, hugging her tightly.

"I ain't staying up here to watch the game, I love my seats, these are too far up," she said as she kissed her daddy's cheek, "I came up to talk to y'all."

"What's up? You alright?" Michael asked, concern covering his face.

"I'm fine daddy, why don't we sit down?" she asked pointing towards the bar, they didn't move. Not that she expected them too.

"What's going on Eleanor?" Bryan asked.

"Um, well, Shea wanted to come up here too, but you know he's getting ready and all but, um," she stuttered.

"Eleanor spit it out already, what's going on?" Bryan asked, crossing his arms, "He knocked you up, didn't he?"

"God no! Never! I'm on the pill!" Michael and Bryan cringed, as Elli turned beet red. Shit, this was not going the way she wanted it too. "No, I'm not pregnant."

"Then what it is? I know that boy has enough sense to come to me first if he is trying to put a ring on your finger." Michael said, as Elli cringed. This was not gonna be good.

"No daddy, he didn't ask me to marry him, um, but we are moving in together." It was like everything stop as Michael and Bryan zeroed in on Elli, Michael's eyes narrowing as Bryan's face turned red.

"You're moving in with him?" Michael asked.

"And y'all aren't married?" Bryan added.

"Now, I moved in with Justin," Elli said in her defense, "and these ain't the olden days, these are modern times, people move in together before they are married all the time."

"I don't care about other people, I care about you!" Michael yelled, "And I don't want my little girl living with some man that she is not married too!"

"I lived with Justin for a year before we got engaged, and he was a dick. Shea is a good man, I care for him a lot, and he loves me. I'm moving in with him," she said with a more confidence then she felt, "I just thought I would let you know. Y'all can be mad at me, but I'm living my life, don't you want me to be happy? Cause Shea makes me happy."

Michael and Bryan just stood there staring at her like she grew two extra heads, Elli swallowed loudly, they were gonna freak, she knew it, but to her surprise, a smile came across Michael face, as Bryan shook his head.

"You're twenty seven years old Eleanor, who am I tell you what to do? If you want to live with Shea, live with him, but I'm not happy about it" Michael said, shrugging his shoulders.

"And if you come up pregnant before you're married, I swear Eleanor, we'll kill him."

Elli grinned, letting out the breath she was holding, "Won't happen."

Michael leaned over kissing her softly on her forehead, "Alright honey, go on down there, the boys are about to come out and warm up."

"Okay, thanks daddy, Papa, I love you both."

Bryan kissed her cheek, smiling. "Love you too darling."

Well that was easier than she thought it would be.

Elli felt like the world had been lifted off her shoulders as she watched Shea warm up. She couldn't wait to tell him that everything went fine with her daddy and uncle, he would be so happy since he was as nervous as she was when she told him she was gonna tell them. He flashed her a grin as he passed by, moving the puck back and forth with his stick. He was so skillful, so stinkin' hot! He rallied the guys, starting a drill as all the fans looked on, cheering the guys on with their signs and their chants.

God, she loved hockey.

They were playing the Vancouver Canucks, Elli wasn't a fan since the guys played dirty, but so did the Assassins, so it was bound to be a great game. When the warm up ended, Shea looked over at Elli before getting off the ice. She gave him her regular wave; he smiled in return, and then headed off the ice as the clock counted down till game time. Elli stood up, looking for the beer guy, when she found him; she ordered her beer and hot dog of the game.

As she ate, she looked around at all the fans since she didn't have anyone to talk to. She couldn't wait for Jakob to start playing again so Harper would be there. She only had a couple more weeks; she was just as excited as Shea and Jakob were about Jakob's return. Elli was ready to have her hockey buddy back. Mark had said when he was in town he would love to sit with Elli again, and of course she obliged, Harper would have to go sit up in Jakob's box or with her Papa when Mark was in town, since Elli would never go back on her word, and Elli was sure Harper wouldn't mind.

When the lights went out, Elli scooted to the edge of her seat, ready for the game to start. The guys came out as the ice girls danced, and the fans cheered. Elli was so engrossed in the game once it started, watching the different plays, not only watching Shea but the rest of the team too. They were incredible, and like Elli thought, the Canucks came ready for the fight. Elli noticed that one of the Canucks' guys, Ryan Kesler, was messing with Shea extra hard.

She wasn't even surprised when the gloves came off and Shea square up, laying a good solid punch into Kelser's nose before they both locked each other up, falling to the ice. Of course Shea got put in the box, right along with Kelser. He gave her a sheepish grin, and she just shook her head, but she couldn't be mad, he was playing the game. After a minute, Vancouver scored. Shea shook his head, and Elli knew he was just as pissed as she was. The guys hit the ice again when the penalty was over and Kesler was still getting cheap hits on Shea. Elli didn't know what the hell the guy's problem was, but with every cheap shot that the officials didn't see, Elli became more nervous. Something was bound to happen.

It was the third period, and Kesler was on Shea like white on rice. She was pretty sure, he was trying to get Shea to retaliate and get put in the box, but Shea wasn't having it. He wasn't even fooling with Kesler, ignoring him and Elli was pretty sure it was because Shea got his ass reamed for getting put in the box because Vancouver had scored. Vancouver was winning because of that goal, and the Assassins were digging hard, trying to score since there was only three minutes left.

Shea came back on the ice after a short break, and skated towards the blue line, waiting for the next play. Elli watched as he watched the puck, his eyes moving back and forth. When the puck came to him, he set up to send it over to Welch, but out of nowhere came Kesler, he threw his elbow up, hitting Shea square in the shoulder, clipping him hard to where Shea spun in a complete circle before hitting the ice, hard.

Elli stood up quickly, along with the rest of the Assassins fans in the stand. Shea was lying with his face facing the bench which was away from Elli, so she couldn't see his face.

And he wasn't moving.

At all.

"Get up, get up, get up, Shea," Elli slammed her hand against the glass as she tears came hot and fast down her face because he still wasn't moving, even with the trainers and everyone out there, he just laid there, "Get up! Shea! Get the fuck up!"

Chapter 27

"How you feeling, Mr. Adler?"

Shea looked up at the doctor; the pain he was feeling was horrendous. After being out cold for more than two minutes, he woke up hearing trainers asking him if he was okay. He told them he was, but obviously he wasn't since it felt like his arm was hanging on by a thread, and his head was pounding. He didn't remember much after the hit that Kelser put on him, but he did remember looking for Elli.

He couldn't find her though.

Shea thought about Ryan, praying that he hadn't seen anything, but if he had, he hoped that Grace had taken care of the situation. Shea knew Grace was in the waiting room, every time he got hurt, even if it was minor, Grace was waiting, but for the first time, Shea wasn't in a hurry to see her, he wanted Elli.

He was worried about her, and he hoped she hadn't seen the hit, but he knew she probably had. He didn't know what was worst, the pain he was feeling or the pain of knowing that Elli was probably worried out of her mind.

"I'm hurting, I've got only two questions for you doc," the doctor nodded as Shea moved awkwardly in the bed, trying not to move where he would hurt more. "How long will I be out?"

"You have a grade two acromioclavicular joint injury, no surgery is needed but with PT and rest, you should be on the ice in six weeks time."

Shea nodded his head, it didn't sound as bad as it felt. Six weeks though, that sucked. "Okay, is there anyone waiting for me?"

"I would say so, since I just got cussed out by some woman because I wasn't giving her the information she needed."

"My sister is a little hard to deal with," Shea said with a shake of his head.

"Oh no, your sister was very nice, it's your girlfriend that tore into me."

"Elli?"

"Yes," the doctor laughed, "Eleanor Fisher, and she can have my license if she wanted."

A slow smile came around Shea's face, damn woman and her temper. "I want to see her."

Elli was freaking the hell out. After basically being carried out the arena by one of her uncle's guys, screaming, she was brought to the hospital where she had been pacing for the last hour. She was so scared, so freaked out. Shea had woken up when they started moving him off the ice but Elli was already being moved out her seat, while everyone stared and talked. Elli knew this was gonna happen, ever since Jakob had gotten hurt, she had this feeling in her gut that something like this would happen to him. She didn't know how to handle the feelings she was feeling, except to cry and freak out.

Grace had came a little after her, and she was calm as a cucumber as Elli freak out. Elli guessed it was cause Elli was freaking out enough for the both of them, but it did bother her that Grace was fine while God knows what is happening to Shea. When the doctor came out, with no information at all, Elli cussed him up one side and down the other before she threatened him.

Not like she really could get his license taken away but damn it, she needed to know if Shea was gonna be okay! All he would say is, 'We are assessing the situation.'

How long did it take to assess? And why the hell was he out talking to them when he should be assessing!

Elli flung herself down beside Grace, Grace was still grinning from Elli's freak out earlier and it bugged Elli to pieces. Shouldn't she be in tears? Shea could be dying for all they knew!

"Grace, I have to say, I'm a little upset with you." Elli said, on the verge of tears.

"Why?" Grace said looking over at her, James sat on the other side of her; he showed up after the freak out from dropping the kids off.

"Shea is back there, and we don't know what's wrong, he could be dying or is dead or has no arm, we don't know!"

"Elli, I've done this many of times, if I do what you are doing I would be a basket case by now. So do me a favor, shut up."

Okay then.

Elli blinked a few times, and then looked towards the doors that would bring someone to tell her something about Shea. They sat for another hour, and the waiting was killing her. Harper had texted to see if they knew anything since her and Jakob were worried, and they couldn't come to the hospital because they were on their way to New York to see Jakob's parents for Christmas.

"Elli," Elli looked over at James, he was leaning on his knees, looking over at her as Grace was texting her mom, "What is your plans for Christmas?"

Elli knew what he was doing; he was trying to take her mind off everything. He was such a great guy, "Going over to my parent's house for the whole shin dig."

"That's nice. I'm off work for the next three weeks, so we are going up to Boston to spend it with Jenna and Mark."

Elli smiled, "That's nice, y'all well have a great time."

"We always do, the kids are so excited," he said. Elli saw out the corner of her eye, the door open and the doctor she had cussed out walking out with Bryan towards them. Elli stood up confused, why did Bryan get to see Shea before her!

"Is he okay?" Grace asked as Elli glared at the doctor, Bryan cut her a look and she stopped but she wanted it known that she was very angry.

"First let me introduce myself since I couldn't get two words out before getting yelled at last time," the doctor said. Everyone cut Elli a look, while she turned deep read.

Asshole.

"My name is George Hansen; I am the chief orthopedic surgeon here at Vanderbilt. Mr. Adler is going to be okay, it's a grade two acromioclavicular joint injury, and luckily he won't need surgery"

"In English please," Grace cooed with a dazzling smile. Doctor Hansen smiled back while James glared over at Grace. Elli would say that Doctor Hansen was hot, if he wasn't such an asshole.

"His right arm is separated from the joint," Both Grace and Elli took in a sharp breath, before they listen to him explain the injury and watch as he drew little pictures, "his arm is completely unstable right now, and will be for a couple weeks."

"How long will he be out?" Grace asked.

"Six weeks at most, the first two weeks I want him to rest, third week he'll start intense PT since he is pretty darn eager to get back on the ice. I just got done taping him up pretty good, he won't be moving that arm at all, so he might need help with getting dressed and taking a shower, it just depends on what he'll let you do."

Grace let out a small laugh, "Which is nothing; he is so damn hard headed."

We will see about that, Elli thought as the doctor went on, "I am more worried about the concussion than I am the grade two. He seems fine, but we need to watch him. I want him to come in after the holidays for a post visit; I have some paper work printed for the signs of a concussion, so you know when to bring him back."

"When can we see him," Elli and Grace said at the same time, they looked at each other before looking back at the doctor.

"Only one person can go back right now, and he wants Elli, he'll be released soon enough, so everyone will see him soon."

Elli glanced over at Grace, and wasn't sure about the expression on her face. It was somewhere between irritated and angry, maybe both. Elli got up slowly, looking down at Grace, but she wouldn't look at her.

"Um, Grace do you want to go? I can't wait till you come out," Elli said softly, Grace looked up at her, putting on a fake smile. Elli's heart actually hurt at the sight of it, for the first time Grace was mad at her, and Elli didn't like it one bit.

"No, Elli, he wants you, so you go ahead." Grace got up, gathering her things as Elli and James watched. "I guess call us when you guys get home," she said, then looked over at the doctor, "Thank you for everything."

Elli watched as James took Grace's hand as they headed towards the door. Elli didn't know what to say or do, so she let them go before walking back to Shea's room. When she pushed open the curtain, Shea had his eyes close, and was breathing evenly. Her heart filled with the sight of him, he was safe, a little beaten up, but safe. She walked towards the bed, taking his hand into hers, looking over his naked chest, and the tape that held his arm against it. He had dark red and black burses all over his shoulder and some down his bicep. Elli didn't even realize she was crying, until her tears fell on her forearms while she was moved her fingers over his hand.

When Shea opened his eyes, she tried to smile but it looked more like a grimace. "Hey beautiful," he said before moving his hand from hers and cupping her cheek, moving his thumb over her cheek, catching all her stray tears. "Come on Elli, I'm fine."

"You're hurt."

"I am, but I'll be fine. Don't cry; it makes it hurt more." She smiled at his grin, trying to stop the tears, but she had been so scared, so freaked out, that even knowing he was okay still didn't help, and tears came faster.

"I was so scared." A sob ripped from her, and Shea shook his head, pulling her with his one good arm up against his side, "I was scared I would never hear you laugh again, or see you smile, feel your lips against mine, I was just so freaking scared Shea. One minute you're fine, the next your face down on the ice."

"I know baby, I know. Calm down. I'm fine." He moved his hand smoothly up and down her back, as she cried against his chest. "It's okay baby."

Not once did Shea remind her that this stuff happens; he just held her. They stayed like that till Shea was released with a bunch of paperwork and lots of meds. Elli was a wreck trying to get him home, and even more of a wreck when she got him into the condo. She woke up at least nine times just to make sure he was okay. The next morning she was so tired that it was hard to keep her eyes open as she followed him around the condo. He moved freely, like nothing was wrong, and would get mad when Elli would try to do everything for him.

"Elli, honey, I'm fine. I can do this."

"I know, but I just want to help. I don't want you to strain," Elli said, pouring him a glass of tea.

"Fine," he said exasperated as he lowered himself onto the bar stool by the island. She laid his glass in front of him, and smiled, waiting for him to say or try to do something. She covered her mouth as she yawn loudly. "Baby, why don't you go take a nap, you're dead on your feet."

"No, I'm fine," she said quickly before moving towards the sink to do the dishes.

"Elli, I've been hurt before, I can't take care of myself."

Elli turned, sending him a pointed look, "Didn't I say that when I was sick?"

He smiled, moving his fingers through his messy hair, "Touché." Elli laughed before turning back to the sink, feeling pretty satisfied with herself.

"So I guess we're gonna have to wait on the whole looking for a house, huh?" she asked.

"Why would we need to wait, I'm gonna be home for 6 weeks with nothing to do, except be pissed off I'm not on the ice."

"Oh yeah, that's true. We'll get started after the holidays then."

"Sounds good to me," he said just as his phone rang, and Elli listened as he picked it up.

"Hey mom, yeah, I'm fine, no big deal. Yeah, I know that but my shoulder is okay. Mom, I'm fine. Yes, Elli is here, yes, she is taking care of me. I don't know yet mom, I just got hurt yesterday. I know that mom, Oh my god, yes mom. I will let you know in a few. Okay, yes, okay, I love you too." Shea hung up the phone and Elli just grinned down at the sink, he was so flustered and it was only day two of being hurt.

This was not going to be an easy recovery.

"Jesus, women drive me nuts," Shea said under his breath, between his mother, his sister and his girlfriend, he was going to go crazy. It was simple, yes he was hurt, but damn it, he could take care of his self! He didn't need someone taking care of him 24/7, he didn't need his mother calling to say she wanted him to come home so she can take care of him, and he definitely didn't need his sister calling cussing him out about not wanting to see her first.

Damn women.

Shea got up, and cringed a little as he moved to take his glass to the sink. Elli stood wearing one of his old buttoned up shirts, with only panties under it. He watched her for a moment, loving the way she moved and the way she pushed her hair off her shoulders. She was so hot that even with all the pain he was in; he still wanted to take her to bed.

He didn't know what she had planned for Christmas, since he wasn't supposed to be there but in Chicago, but he needed to ask. His mother wanted him home, even if it was only for Christmas, it would at least shut her up and leave him alone for the length of the injury. As he watched Elli, he wondered if she would come home with him. He hated being away from her and the fact that the studio was closed till the beginning of the New Year, he didn't see a reason why she wouldn't want to go home with him.

Except that she might want to spend time with her family for Christmas. After the birthday party, Elli had talked to her mother twice, both times were good, Elli actually hung up smiling. Shea didn't want to come between the reunion of mother and daughter, but he also wanted her to come home with him, show her around Boston. He didn't get to spend Thanksgiving with her, and he definitely wanted to spend her favorite holiday with her.

When Elli glanced up seeing he was watching her, she smiled.

"I know that look Shea Adler, you aren't getting any, any time soon."

A slow grin went over his face, she knew him so well. "Come home with me."

She looked up at him, confusion all over her face, "I am home."

"No, I mean come home to Boston with me for Christmas. My mom wants me to come home since I'm hurt, and I wanna go, but I don't want to leave you."

Elli blinked a few times before looking down at the sink, "I have Christmas with my family though."

"I know, and I know things are good right now with your family, but this is probably the only time we'll be able to go home for Christmas. I really want you to come spend some time with my family, get to know them."

Shea watched as she nodded, moving away from the sink towards the fridge. "I," she stopped moving in front of the island. She then leaned against it as she looked over at him, "Yeah, okay." Shea had a huge grin go across his face as Elli went on, "I'll have to call to have Adler boarded and I'll have to run to Clarksville to drop off the gifts I got my family. So can we leave tomorrow?"

"That's fine; I'll call my mom, and get us tickets while you do what you need to do."

"Okay," she came over to him, kissing him softly before walking towards the bedroom.

He had a feeling she wasn't happy though.

The next morning Shea boarded a plane with Elli after spending an hour trying to get dress. He learned quickly that he was going to look like a one armed man while he was hurt since he couldn't run around with no shirt in 30 degree weather. He was embarrassed by the way he looked, but what was he supposed to do, put a fake arm in the other sleeve? It didn't seem to bother Elli though; she just smiled, holding his other hand as they walk through the airport onto the plane. He hated that she had to put their carrions in the space above their seats, but again it wasn't like he could do anything, he was a one armed man.

Elli hadn't said much since their conversation in the kitchen. She took Adler to the boarding house before running back to Clarksville to drop off gifts for the family. When she came back, Shea could tell she had been crying but when he asked, she said everything was fine.

"I figured we could go shopping when we land, before heading to my mom's. I haven't bought anything for my family yet."

Elli nodded, "I already packed my gifts for them, but I don't mind going shopping again. We all know I love to shop."

"You already got my family gifts?"

"Yeah, like a month ago."

"What did you get?" he asked, as she smiled over at him.

"Stuff. Why?"

"Cause I didn't get squat! Plus I thought maybe we would do it together," he said with a shrug.

"You were supposed to be in Chicago, I was just gonna send the package up to Boston."

"Oh, well I guess that makes sense. Getting hurt has messed up a lot of people's plans."

Elli shrugged, "It's no big deal, I'm just glad you're okay."

"No, you're mad because you're not home with your family, I bet the only reason you're here is because you're worried about my arm, and you probably don't even want to go home with me." Elli cut him a look, surprised by his outburst. Hell, he was surprised by it. She narrowed her eyes, taking in a deep breath.

"Um for one, I'm not mad. Yeah, I'm gonna miss my family during the holidays but I realize that my life is changing, I can't worry about just me anymore, I have you now. Second, I do want to go home with you, I love your family and you know I do. Thirdly, if you don't lose your little attitude, I'm gonna kick your ass." She smiled sweetly before pulling out her book, and started reading. He couldn't help the scoff that escaped his mouth, but he wished he had because Elli looked back over at him, madder than hell. "Are you laughing at me?"

He shook his head, "Never."

"That's what I thought."

Shea smiled and the side of her mouth lifted a little but not much as he said, "I never thought I would be scared of something so small."

"I'm not small, you're just huge."

He laughed at that, causing her to smile, "God, I love you."

He was rewarded with a dazzling smile before she took his hand in hers, kissing his cheek and laying her head on his shoulder, holding her book against his leg. He leaned his head against hers, loving the feel of her hair against his cheek. Just loving her, all of her.

Even her sassy little temper.

Elli stood in the freezing cold, outside of General Edward Lawrence Logan international airport, while Shea yelled at the rental guy about the Prius he thought he was gonna give them to rent. Shea was livid, Elli wasn't sure if it was cause he was in pain, or if he really did hate the car that much. Elli thought it was cute, plus it wasn't like Shea was gonna be driving it.

"It's a chick car!" Shea yelled, they both looked over at Elli, and she shook her head, cuddling into her jacket.

"Sir, this is all we have in less you want a BMW which is almost $300 a day." Shea looked at the dude like he was the biggest idiot on earth.

"Give me the BMW, please," Shea said through gritted teeth. The guy nodded, and Shea walked towards Elli, beat red from either his angry or the cold.

"It's just a car, Shea."

"I am not riding in that girlie ass car, and that dude is being an ass, he knows who I am, he just doesn't want to act like it because I don't play for Boston. Asshole."

"Why does it matter who you play for?"

"You will learn quickly, that in less you play for Boston, you aren't shit around here."

"You're the leading defensive man in the league; I think that means a lot more than playing for Boston."

"No actually it doesn't," Shea answered as the guy earlier drove a red BMW towards them, parking it in front of him. He got out, and helped load their bags. Afterwards, he walked with Elli to the front of the car, opening the door for her.

"Let me ask you a question," Elli said with a grin, the younger man smiled, he was her age, cute even.

"Sure."

"You know who he is?"

"There is only one team worth anything in the NHL, and that's Boston, so I only acknowledge Boston players. And I definitely won't acknowledge a guy that is from Boston not playing for Boston."

Okay then.

After leaving the rental place, they headed towards Copley Place, which Shea said was a really great shopping mall. After going through Louis Vuitton, and blowing more money than needed, Shea went to Tiffany's to get his mom and sister something. Since Tiffany's made Elli blow money, she headed for Gucci.

She should have just gone to Tiffany's.

After dropping her first-born's college fund, she walked out, meeting Shea in the middle of the mall. He eyed her bags, and then smiled. "Got enough?"

"Don't ask." Elli eyed his little blue bag, and nodded towards the bag, "Anything for me?"

"Maybe," he said with a grin, as he took as many as her bags that he could with his one arm.

"Anyone ask what happen to your arm?"

"No, they just stare, but one of the girls in there actually acknowledged who I was and said she hoped I recovered well."

Elli raised an eye brow, "I'm impressed. Everyone I meet keeps asking me where the hell I'm from, then they raise their noses at me when I say Nashville, they then ask if there is even a hockey/football/baseball team there. These people are crazy."

Shea laughed, leaning into her since that was all he could really do since her hand was full before saying, "Let's go, my mom is waiting."

When Elli turned onto Winthrop Shore Dr, she took in the sight of the water running up against the shore. The water was such a beautiful bluish green, it crashed up against some rocks that lined a lighthouse. The lighthouse stood tall, majestic, and beautiful. Elli had never realized how much she loved the ocean till that moment. It was like she was instantly calm as she looked out at the water that was glistening under the sun.

"We used to live in this house in the heart of Boston, but when I made it into the NHL, I bought my parents this house since they love the ocean," Shea said as Elli turned where the GPS said to turn.

She ended up in the driveway of the most beautiful colonial home she had ever seen. The home stood tall, white siding with dark blue shutters around glamorous wide windows. The second floor was bigger than the first floor; it came out over the front door acting as a cover for the porch. The windows that lined the whole top floor were huge, and poised. On the porch was a small lighthouse that must have been a replica of the one that Elli was admiring earlier, along with it was two wooden beach chairs and an end table that held a large bouquet of yellow sunflowers. The house was breath taking.

"It's beautiful," Elli gasped as she looked through the windshield up at the house.

"Yeah, mom had to have it. They sold their last house and used that money to fix it up, they've done a lot," Shea said with a grin as he open the door and got out. Elli followed behind him, popping the trunk as Jenna came out on the porch.

"You guys are here!" Jenna gushed, clapping her hands together, "Mark, James, come help with their bags, Shea's arm could fall off, you know."

Shea rolled his eyes, and Elli just smiled, oh yeah, she was gonna have a hoot of a time.

Chapter 28

After being greeted with hugs from Mark and Jenna, and kisses from Ryan, Elli sat on the bottom step with Ryan, admiring the beauty of the white hardwood floors, Elli had always loved the look of them, thought they looked classic. She made a mental note to make sure to see if houses in Nashville had them, and if not if she could get em. As she admired the rest of the house Shea argued with Grace. Ever since he got hurt, he's had been extremely argumentative, and it was getting on Elli's nerves, not that Elli could really say anything, she cussed him out for calling her 'sunshine' for goodness sakes.

When Shea had asked which room was his and Elli's, Elli knew things were about to blow by the worried look that crossed Jenna's face. When she said that they would be sharing a room with Ryan and Amelia, Shea flipped. Elli didn't care, it wasn't like they would be having sex, since Elli was convinced he would break, but apparently he was irate about it.

"Grace put the kids in your room, before they have to see Unky Shea's magic stick!"

"SHEA RYAN!" Jenna complained.

"Oh please!" Grace said with a roll of her eyes. "Like it's magical!"

"Oh I can show you!" Shea said before sticking his tongue out at Grace like they were nine years old, while she made a crude hand motion with her hand. Elli guessed she was trying to say, Shea's stuff was limp.

Little does she know.

"Unky Shea knows magic!?" Ryan exclaimed beside a beat red Elli.

"No honey, he doesn't." Elli basically groaned.

"He said he has a magic stick though!"

"I know, ignore him," Elli said, patting the young child's hands.

"Shea, you guys can't even do it, so why do you need a room to yourself?!" Grace objected, but that seemed to make Shea madder.

"Grace Caroline!" Jenna shrieked.

"Now Grace, come on!" Mark added, "Don't rub that in your brother's face."

"Yes we can!" Shea countered, Ryan looked up at Elli.

"Do what?" The whole family turned to look at Ryan, and then they looked at Elli, waiting to see what she would say. All it did was make her to want to climb into a hole.

"Color honey, you know since Unky's arm is hurt," Ellis said as she turned even redder, could she be any more embarrassed?

"Oh yeah, why does he think he can do it then?" Ryan asked.

Elli shrugged her shoulders, "He probably expects me to do everything."

Ryan made a 'o' face as everyone snickered, "You have to do all the coloring? That's not fair!"

"Who you telling?" Ryan gave her a toothy grin, while everyone else tried not to laugh.

"I'm not sleeping in a room with my niece, nephew, and girlfriend, no way. I didn't make those kids, you did."

"You weren't supposed to be here," Grace countered back.

"Well I am here now, put the kids in the living room, or with mom and dad."

"Hey now, some of us can still color!" Mark said, Jenna smacked him on his chest while Grace and Shea both yelled, "Ew."

"Really Mark?" Jenna asked, he answered her by wiggling his eye brows, causing Grace and Shea to again, yell "Ew."

James and Elli, the normal ones she thought, both laughed.

"Grace, the kids can sleep in the loft upstairs, doesn't the couch still turn into a bed, Jenna?" James asked Jenna.

"Yes, thank God you're in this family James, you're the only man with some sense."

"Hey!" Shea and Mark complained, as Jenna waved them off, gathering Ryan up in her arms.

"Want to go make some cookies with Grandma?"

"Sure do! Wanna help Ms. Elli?" Ryan asked as Elli stood up.

"I gotta unpack, plus I think I still have some presents to wrap for a special little boy," Elli said before squeezing his nose. She was rewarded with a giggle and a smiled from Jenna before they headed to the kitchen.

"Come on Elli, I'll bring these bags up for you." James said.

"Thanks," Elli said before following behind him, carrying some of the suitcases while Shea followed up behind them. After getting everything settled in the spacious white room, Elli looked out the windows, looking out at the endlessness of the blue ocean. It was so beautiful.

"I never want to leave." Elli gasped as a sailboat came into view. It was damn near 30 degrees outside, what were them maniacs doing out there!

"It really is a pretty view from here. I love this room," Shea said before lying carefully down on the bed, Elli smiled down at him before crawling beside him, cuddling up to his side. She was used to his other side, but the other one would have to do.

"Do you feel better?"

"No, Grace pisses me off."

"Crabby butt," Elli teased as she intertwined their fingers, "First you blow up on me, then the car guy, and now your sister. Who's next?"

"Probably my mom, she'll start smothering me."

"Temper, temper."

Shea gave her a cheeky grin, kissing her nose, "That's why I play hockey, to let my frustration out."

"It's been three days Shea," she emphasized.

"Hey, I was supposed to play tonight."

"Ah, true."

Elli decided to let it go, she didn't want to argue with him, she wanted to cuddle. He ran his hand up her back, than back down, into the back of her jeans. He looked down at her with half lidded eyes as he splayed his fingers along her ass. Her eyes met his, before shaking her head.

"Shea Adler, remove your hand from my ass."

He looked stricken as he took his hand out her pants, "I never thought I would hear you say that."

Elli smiled as she rolled out the bed, "Believe me, I never thought I'd say it"

Elli threw herself onto the floor, pulling out the stuff she bought from Gucci to hang up. She didn't know how long she was gonna last not having sex with her man, it was gonna be a long six weeks, that's for sure.

Elli was in the middle of hanging all her new clothes when Mark came into the room. Shea was sleeping since he had just taken his afternoon dose of pain meds, Elli prayed that when he woke up he would be in a better mood.

"Hey Elli," Mark said as he leaned into the door, "Get dressed in something warm, I'm taking you and James out on the boat."

"The boat?" Elli asked, "It's freezing out."

"No big deal, come all, let's go fishing."

"People do that in the winter?"

"Sure, come on lets go before Shea wakes up."

Mark turned and Elli couldn't help but grin, he just assumed she was going, which she was, but still. Damn Adler men, so damn head strong. Elli got up, looking for some warm clothes. After putting on a pair of jeans, with a grey sweater, and her black cowboy boots, she threw her hair up in the fuzzy grey hat she bought at Gucci. Before leaving, Elli went over to the bed, placing a light kiss on Shea's head. Elli shut the door quietly, and headed downstairs.

"Ready Elli?" Mark asked once Elli hopped off the last step.

"Sure am," Elli said with a grin.

"Alright, off we go."

Elli had been on a lot of boats in her time, but she had to admit Mark Adler's boat was pretty. Really pretty. It was a massive 40 foot boat, it had a generous cockpit, with a forward and aft sun lounges, it had a large walk around along with a swimming station and the operating spot, where Mark stood in his captain gear, which consisted of a captain hat and Shea's jersey with the 'C' on the breast.

Mark sure was a sight to see.

Elli sat with a beer in hand, and a large fishing pole in the other. She looked out at the large blue ocean, and let out a lengthy sigh. Spending the afternoon with James and Mark turned out to be one of the best afternoons of her life. They talked about everything, it was as if Mark and James wanted to know everything about Elli, and she wanted to know everything about them. She loved learning about Shea's family, these were his people. When the subject of hockey came up, they talked for hours, only stopping when Mark or James would get a bite, and reel one in.

Elli learned quickly that ocean fishing was way different than river or lake fishing. These fish were big, massive even. After every catch, they would take a picture. Elli loved how much Mark loved James, it still blew her mind the way he treated James like a son. It was sweet, amazing really. Mark treated Elli the same way, wrapping his arm around her shoulders, giving her big grins, pinching her cheeks when she would say something funny, and Elli swore a hour didn't go by without him say, 'You are amazing Elli, anyone ever tell you that?'.

Coming to Boston was turning out to be a good idea. Not only was she with Shea, but she got to know his family better. Yes, her family was livid with her, but hey, she was with someone now. Her life didn't revolve around them anymore; it was about her and Shea now. The thought that her and Shea were about to embark on a new stage in their relationship filled Elli with such warmth that it was hard not to grin.

Shea was the kind of man one considered spending the rest of their life with. Elli could see her and Shea together for the rest of her life, having kids with greenish blue eyes, and long dark hair. Hopefully bone straight like Shea's and not the fuzzy mess she had. Shea would make a great dad; he loved Amelia and Ryan like they were his. He was a good man, the kind of man that held her when she cried, bathed her when she was sick, and planned the most amazing parties, just for her. He was a keeper.

The more Elli thought about it, the more she thought that if he did leave, get traded, or whatever, she would go. She would have to. After feeling like she almost lost him when he was laying face down on the ice, she felt she would do anything for him, go anywhere. Life without Shea wasn't even possible, she couldn't even fathom it.

She loved him.

Elli stood slowly, right as her reel started going nuts.

"Elli babe! You got something!" Mark yelled but Elli wasn't listening.

She loved Shea.

She loved him so much it hurt her chest.

No wait that was the pole hitting against her chest.

"Shit!" Elli yelled, dropping her beer, and taking the pole in her hands. Whatever was on the end of the line was huge, and strong. When the massive fish flung itself out the water, Elli let out a girlie scream, causing Mark and James to laugh.

"Oh hell, El, looks like a wolf fish to me!" Mark yelled, smacking Elli on the back like she was one of the guys.

"A what?! Shit it's strong!" Elli grunted as she reeled her little ass off. Why weren't these men trying to help her!?

"Massive strong fish, I got one last time I was here," James said as him and Mark made their way to the side, looking over the side as Elli continued to reel her ass off. After what seemed like an hour of reeling, Mark got out a hook looking stick, and pulled on the line, finally helping Elli to get the fish up. When Mark flung the fish over board, Elli let out a horrid scream.

"It has teeth!" Elli screamed jumping up on the chair she had been sitting on, receiving herself a round of laughter from James and Mark as they admired the fish.

"Damn Elli, you got a big one. We'll have to weigh it." Mark said, hooking the ugly blue fish in the mouth and holding it up. The damn thing was as big as she was, and Elli was on the big side.

"I say close to 30 pounds, it's a biggie," James said, leaning in closer to look at the fish's face.

"It's a beaut, good job Elli," Mark said before sending her a grin, "Damn good job."

"Okay for one, that damn thing is ugly as all get out, and for two, I just sat there."

Finally realizing, she loved Shea, not that she was gonna tell them that.

James and Mark laughed long and hard before Mark picked the fish up, motioning for Elli to come over, as James pulled out a camera. "Come on now Elli, come hold your beaut, so we can get a picture," Mark said, Elli shook her head.

"I ain't coming anywhere near that thing, it's got damn teeth!"

"Come on now!" Mark said more sternly, so Elli went, grabbing the pole slowly, before holding the fish up. It was almost as long as she was, and damn near the ugliest thing she had ever seen.

"Smile Elli!"

Yeah, right.

Shea had never laughed so hard in his life. The picture he held in his hand had him almost busting a gut as he laughed. His beautiful girlfriend stood on a boat holding a massive fish up, with a look of horror on her face. The fish was as big as she was, and Shea couldn't believe she got it out of the water all by herself. Grace and his mom stood beside him, laughing as hard as he was.

"Oh Elli, your face is priceless!" Jenna gushed, before kissing Elli's cheek and turning back to the stove.

"I tell you what, that damn thing was ugly as all get out!" Elli complained in her thick accent. With Shea being home around his Boston speaking family, Elli stuck out like a sore thumb.

"I can't believe you got it on the boat Elli, I'm impressed!" Grace said, before leaving Shea's side to go to James.

"I'm having the damn thing stuffed for her Christmas present, it will look good over you guys bed," Mark said with a grin just for Elli. Shea didn't think Elli thought he was funny though.

"He has teeth, Shea. Tell them they are crazy," Elli pleaded beside him, looking at her picture, shaking her head.

"Honey, you did good. You should be proud," he said, smiling down at her.

"Proud of that? He's ugly!"

"He's a beaut!" Mark complained as he came over looking at the picture, "Wicked pretty fish."

"You're nuts," Elli laughed as she took the cup of hot chocolate from Jenna,

"He sure is," Jenna said with a laugh, everyone laugh along, as Shea leaned into Elli, kissing her cheek softly.

Shea was a little upset when he found out that Elli had left with his dad and James, but then thought maybe it was good. Letting Elli bond with them was good, since he didn't see her going anywhere. He wanted her to love his family, he wanted them to love her, and it seemed to have worked too. Mark and James joked around with Elli, and she gave them just as much as they gave her. He loved when she had such a full smile on her face, and knowing that his family was the ones to put it there, made him just as ecstatic as if he had done it.

Shea life was basically complete, well it would be if he could play hockey and Elli loved him, but he was feeling pretty damn good at that moment standing in the kitchen with all the people the loved.

The next day, Shea and Elli went for a drive to Shea's old neighborhood. He showed her his old house, his old school, and then the place he learned to play hockey at. After seeing that the place was turning into a dump, Shea made a call to his accountant, telling them to make a donation to the rink. He'd be damn if the place he learned how to play man's greatest sport at was going to be ran into the ground.

Cold day in hell.

After leaving his home town, they headed into Boston for some shopping and to get some lunch. Shea was starting to notice that Elli had a spending problem. He never noticed it before, but then again he never really went shopping with her. When she saw something she liked, her eyes would light up like a Christmas tree, and she would gush as she explained the reason she needed that particular thing. She was crazy; Shea had never spent as much money on one item like she did on shoes. He had the best of everything too, but the girl sees a pair of thigh high boots and goes nuts and drops over two grand on them.

Shea stood beside her, shaking his head as she ran her little black card.

"What?" she asked, smiling at the lady when she handed her, her bag.

"Two grand on a pair of boots?"

"Shea, they're Gucci."

"Okay?"

"I bought you some shirts too; the boots were only fifteen hundred."

"Only? And why are you buying me stuff?" Shea said with an annoyed look on his face, he didn't like her spending her money on him. He was supposed to spend all his money on her.

"Cause I want too crabby pants, now come on, there are so many stores I want to hit!"

"I bet, are we gonna be here all day?"

Elli smiled sweetly at him, before running her hand down his chest, over his limp arm that was tapped to his chest, "I think they have an Intimacy here. "

"What's that?"

"A lingerie store."

It took Shea two second to comprehend what she was saying, and another second to grab her hand before saying, "Lead the way."

After dropping more money than Shea needed too, they headed home. When they arrived back at the house, they sat down for dinner with his family. Afterwards, Elli helped with the dishes. When she was done she met Shea up in the room, where he laid on the bed as she went through all her treasures that she bought that day. She had promised to model some of the things for him, so when she got up, locking the door and stripping, he took in his fill.

He loved how she wasn't shy around him anymore; she was starting to trust him more, which was great. He knew in his heart that she was starting to fall in love with him, she had to be, or he was going to go bat shit crazy. It was that simple.

Shea watched as she slid the grey lace panties and bra set on, that she had gotten at Intimacy, his mouth watered as she slid some knee high grey socks up her legs, before putting on the ridiculous priced boots that she had to have on. They were suede, and had a sexy little heel on them, but still fifteen hundred dollars!?

When she stood up, placing her hands on her hips and looking over at him, with her hair falling down her shoulders over the top of her breast, Shea took in a breath, gawking over the beauty of her body.

Okay, maybe the boots were worth fifteen hundred dollars, because they sure made her ass look amazing.

"Why don't you bring that sexy ass over here, let me play a little," he asked as she moved around the room, testing out the boots he guessed.

"No way, I said I would model for you, not let you touch me."

"Don't make me get up," he warned, but all she did was giggle.

"Don't make me tell your momma."

"Okay, that's just dirty."

Elli smiled sweetly before changing into another lingerie set she had gotten, by the end of her little fashion show, Shea was as hard as a rock, and Elli wasn't going to help him out at all. All she did was grin, as she left the room to go join his mom downstairs.

"Evil woman!" he yelled as the door shut.

Elli opened it back, smiling over at him before saying, "And you love me just the same."

Elli shut the door, and he groaned. It was going to be the longest recovery ever and Shea wasn't sure he was gonna make it. If he had to deal with the nagging of his mother, sister, and girlfriend, he should at least be getting laid while suffering.

Was that too much to ask for?

Shea decided it wasn't too much, so he got out of bed carefully and marched his ass down stairs. When he entered the kitchen, Elli and his mom sat at the table, looking at some photo albums of course of him, probably naked.

"Okay, this isn't going to work!" Elli and his mom looked up at him; Elli narrowed her eyes, as Jenna just smiled.

"What honey? I was just showing her some pictures of you in college." Jenna said sweetly, but he wasn't going to let her distract him.

"That's fine! But if I'm gonna be nagged by all you women, I need some kind of release!" Shea complained, causing Elli to turned deep red as her eyes widen.

"Shea!" Elli yelled, as Jenna looked over at her confused, when his mother caught on she high tailed it out of the kitchen with a quick goodnight. "Shea, really? I was spending some time with your momma! You couldn't wait till I came back up there?"

"No, I couldn't. I'm mad as hell, I want you."

"Shea, you're being loud!"

"Damn right! I'm pissed off! I want sex."

"Shea! Jesus!"

Elli stormed by him, when he went to grab her, he tried using the arm that was tapped to his chest, and pain ripped through his body. He almost threw up from the pain, what the hell was he thinking. Elli must have heard him make his sound of distress because she was at his side in a second as he put his hand down, leaning against the counter.

"What happen, are you okay?"

"I tried to grab you with the wrong arm."

"I mean shit Shea, this is why you ain't getting any, not for a while at least," she said, running her hand up and down his back, he leaned his head down laying it against the cool of the counter.

Shit, that had hurt. Maybe she was right.

"Okay."

"Okay now, come on. Let's go upstairs."

He nodded before following her up the stairs, once inside the room, she helped him get undressed. Shea watched as she carefully removed his shirt, making sure not to touch his arm. "It's just hard being so close to you, and not being able to throw you against the wall and have my way with you."

"Oh hush," she giggled as she undid his pants, lowering them down to the ground, her face passing by his growing erection.

"No really Elli, I want you all the time, so fucking bad." Elli looked up at him from her knees, and smiled.

"So fucking bad, huh?"

"You have no idea."

Her eyes lowered a little, becoming half lidded before she pulled his boxers down, releasing his engorged flesh. "I think I do, cause I feel the same way." That was the last thing said before she took him whole in her mouth. He leaned back against the wall, thanking God for giving Elli her hot little mouth, and the things she could do with it.

Pure bliss, he thought as he tangled his fingers into her hair, pure damn bliss.

Elli was having the best time with Shea and his family. Christmas was amazing, of course she had missed her family something crazy, and called them all Christmas morning, but being with Shea and the rest of the Adler clan made it okay. Everyone loved the gifts Elli had gotten them, and Elli loved the gifts they had gotten her. She felt so much a part of the family it was mind blowing. When she opened her gift from Shea, she smiled big as she held the diamond incrusted six in her hand. When she pulled the charm necklace he had given her so long ago out of her shirt, he smiled.

"What? I always wear it," she said with a grin as she slid the charm beside the hockey stick.

Elli had to admit though, the best part of Christmas morning was when Mark brought out her wolf fish, stuffed and mounted on a cherry finished board, with her name and the date underneath the fish. It almost brought Elli to tears, because she would forever have that moment on her wall, the moment she fell in love with his family.

And realized she loved Shea.

It was crazy how she came up there not loving anyone, or so she thought, and when she would go home in the next couple days, she would not only love Shea with all her heart, but she loved his family. She loved Jenna and her quirky sense of humor and how she babied everyone. She loved how Mark would laugh so hard he would cry when he would tell a story. How James would pick on Shea and Grace, calling them dorks and weirdoes when they would go into Shea and Grace mode. She loved Grace, because she was so strong, and loved everyone so much, Elli knew in her heart that Grace might be a tad bit jealous of her but she loved her. Ryan and Amelia were doll babies, Elli loved them at first glance, and she knew that a long time ago. Then there was Shea, her hunky hockey player who rocked her world. How could she not love all these people with everything inside of her? If anything, God forbid, ever happen between her and Shea, Elli would be forever broken. These people were part of her heart now, and probably would be for forever.

After cleaning up after Christmas dinner, Elli sat with Grace and Jenna, looking through the Adler family album while James and Mark sat in the living room with the kids, and Shea was laying down cause his arm was hurting. When Jenna turned the page of the Shea's book, Elli stopped her. The pictures that filled the page were of Shea and some red head.

"Alyson Jacobs," Grace said with a shake of her head, "Shea was obsessed with her, it was sad really."

Elli giggled as she took in the beauty of the red head, with light blue eyes and freckles covering her cheeks, while Shea looked gorgeous in all of his eighteen year old glory.

"Oh Elli, he really was, and damn that girl but she broke my baby's heart in a thousand different pieces." Jenna said with a shake of her head, "I heard though that she married a stock broker that cheats on her every chance he gets, so she got what was coming to her."

Elli and Grace laughed as Jenna just smiled, "Shea met up with her back in Philly, used her like the trash she was then dumped her. I was surprised with the way handled her the second time though, I was for sure we would have another episode like the time before." Grace said, looking closer at the picture as Jenna just shook her head.

"Little hussy."

Elli looked over at Grace, "Episode?"

"Oh yeah, it was bad. I was in love with the Backstreet Boys, hell I still am, but anyways," she took a sip of her coke, or as she called it pop, and continued with her story, "I listened to their music nonstop, and well when Alyson broke up with Shea, I went into the room to check on him and he was laying on the floor, bawling his eyes out, singing all the sad love songs by them. I didn't know what to do so I ran for my mom, and she went in there doing her mom thing, it was crazy."

Elli wanted to laugh so hard. Shea? Crying over some female? Please. Elli contained her laughter since Jenna and Grace were just shaking their heads. Jenna looked across the table at Elli, a small smile on her face.

"The thing is Elli, Shea is emotion, extremely. All these different women he has been through was because the first and only time he ever loved someone, he was found in a ball on the floor crying his eyes out, so it didn't surprise me the line of women that I have seen him go through," she paused for a moment, taking a sip of her coffee, "With Grace it was totally different, she never loved guys or had that puppy love, when she came up pregnant, I was totally shocked, not that I didn't think she was having sex, but to be so careless with a man, she must have cared for him."

"Yeah, I knew James was different, but even so, I didn't tell him I loved him till after I had Ryan. I swear I have never seen a man leave so quickly to get a ring, it was crazy." Grace said with a grin.

"It always has blown my mind how in sync they are about everything else but love. People used to think they were the same, but I knew differently. Shea could fall in love if he let his self while Grace had to be pushed into it."

"I wasn't pushed."

"Grace Caroline, you had a child before you even admitted to it." Jenna pointed out.

"Okay maybe it was a little push," Grace agreed with a nod, "But like she said Elli, Shea hasn't loved anyone but Alyson, that's why it's hard for me. I've always been the other half of him, and then you come along."

"I could never replace you Grace, you know that." Elli said sincerely, Grace smiled, taking her hand in hers.

"I know that, but you have his heart, he will always love me, we chilled in the same space for nine months and we were inseparable growing up, but I can't even compete with the love he feels for you. We all see it." Elli watched as the tears welled up in Grace's eyes. "It's taken a lot for me to accept the change, but change is good, and if I have to give my brother away to anyone, it would be you."

Elli and Grace stared into each other's eyes, complete understanding passing through them before they were irrupted by Jenna bawling.

"Oh my God mom! You are so damn emotional! That's where Shea gets it; I'm like dad, thank God!" Grace said with a grin for Elli before standing up and leaving the kitchen.

"Grace! Shut your mouth, I swear she should have been the guy, while Shea should have been the girl." Jenna said as she dried her tears.

Thank God that didn't happen. Elli loved Shea the way he was, didn't want him to change at all.

When Elli reached the bedroom, Shea was laying on his back, watching TV. He smiled at her, turning it down as she crawled into bed beside him. "Why didn't you come down if you were awake?"

Shea smiled, wrapping his arm around her, "I didn't want to interrupt your time with my mom and sister."

"Oh, I'm glad, I learned a lot about you."

He laughed, "Should I be scared?"

"I don't know. Does the fact that they told me about Alyson Jacobs scare you?"

When Shea's face went white, Elli had to bite her lip from laughing, "What did they say?"

Elli couldn't help it, she had too, so she smiled before saying, "Nothing much, but Shea,"

"Yeah?" he asked wearily as she smirked up at him.

"I'll never break your heart, I'll never make you cry," she continued to sing the chorus of the well known Backstreet Boys song as Shea turned beet red with embarrassment.

"Grace, I swear I'm going to kill you!" Shea yelled, when Elli heard Grace giggle, she smiled.

"Leave her alone," Elli said nuzzling her nose against his jaw.

"I can't believe they told you about that."

"It was good to know, you know about all my stuff."

"Whatever."

Shea turned the TV back on, watching the highlights from the Assassins game. They guys had won, which was great. The guys were having a great season, and Elli couldn't wait to see Shea out there again. They finished watching all the highlights before turning off the TV and getting ready for bed. They would be leaving in the next couple days, which saddened Elli but she was ready to get back, start looking for houses and she needed to go to the office. She hadn't been in weeks.

With the lights off, cuddle up against Shea, Elli felt complete. Shea moved his hand along her hip, up her back to her hair, where he moved his fingers through her hair. Elli sat up slowly, to look down at him. With only the moon as the light, she slowly blinked as she brought her hand up to his face. Shea gave her a small smile, squeezing her hip in his hand.

"I'm so glad I met you, Shea."

His smiled remained as he said, "I'm glad I met you too, baby."

She smiled shyly, moving her thumb up and down his cheek; he leaned into her hand closing his eyes as she continued to move her fingers along his exquisite jaw.

"Shea."

"Yeah?" he asked opening his eyes; she took a deep breath, swallowing hard as her eyes watered with tears.

"I love you."

His eyes went wide before a slow grin went across his face.

"You do?"

"I do, so much."

His hand came up here back, along her neck bring her down for a long lengthy kiss, when they parted he was smiling so big, that it took Elli's breath away.

"Say it again."

She giggled before doing as he asked, with a breathless sigh, she said, "I love you."

"Oh baby, I love you, more than you'll ever know."

Shea wrapped her up in his one arm, kissing her senseless. Nothing could ever top the way she felt at that moment, they were in love and nothing would ever come between them.

Chapter 29

Elli stood by the player's bench in the arena thinking what the hell was Shea doing? It had only been a week since he had gotten the tape taken off, and he thought it was a good idea to come out and shoot some pucks? Elli watched as he would swing the stick back then release, the crack of the stick filling the area as he made contact with the punk, shooting it straight into the net.

It was as if he hadn't been out of the game for three weeks, just three days. His accuracy was outstanding, his form, delectable. She was getting turned on watching him shoot a puck, yeah, he was something that's for sure, and she loved him more each day. That was probably why she was pissed as hell at him. What was he trying to do, mess his arm up again?

He put all of his weight behind his next shoot; Elli didn't even see the puck till it went in. She smiled, throwing her arms up in the air. "And he scores!!!!! The crowd goes wild!" she said in her best announcer voice, he looked over his shoulder, his look said it all, he knew he was caught.

"Hey baby, what are you doing here?" he asked, skating towards her, "Oh yeah, you had that promo with some of the guys today."

"I did, and to my surprise, I heard a rumor my boyfriend was down here shooting pucks, I knew they had to be crazy so I came to look for myself, and look what I see," she said with a shake of her head as he leaned against the boards, kissing her softly on the lips; she let him because of course she couldn't get enough of his kisses. "How many buckets?"

He looked sheepish as he looked behind him, "Four."

"Four? Are you kidding me?" she asked, since that meant he probably shot close to 500 pucks, "You're gonna be hurting tonight."

"Probably, but it's worth it, I'm known for my slap shot, I can't lose it because of an injury."

"I know Shea, but you need to get better."

"I'm fine."

He was such a liar, she could tell he was in pain, but he was pushing beyond it, "Oh well, do what you do I guess, but when you can't move tomorrow, don't come cryin' to me."

"I won't, I've been shooting since I got my tape off, I'm okay I swear."

Elli eyes filled with anger, he'd been shooting for a week! "You're a crazy fool Shea Adler."

He gave her a grin, "Oh and you love me."

"I do, damn it, that's why you worry the piss out of me."

"I'm fine babe, I gotta keep strong. Keep breaking the glass."

Elli smiled, "I'm pretty sure you can still break the glass Shea."

Shea was known for breaking the glass behind the goal when he would try to shoot, and totally miss. He did it a lot when he was a rookie; it had only happen a few times since.

"Wanna see?"

Elli laughed, "Doesn't Papa get angry about that?"

"Oh yeah, but he just yells and makes me pay a fee, no big deal."

Elli looked at him confused, "A fee?"

"Yeah, two grand," he said, looking around the rink.

"Oh my god! That's crazy! You need to stop doing that, not only can you hurt someone but you gotta pay a fee, that wasting money!"

"Okay, for one, it's not like I mean to do it. Two, no one can get hurt, the glass takes all the force, at most they'll get cut, no biggie, and third, it's just two grand, that's like two dollars to you."

"Hey! What does that mean?"

"It means that you dropped enough money to pay off a house while we were in Boston, you can't talk to me about wasting money."

Elli blinked a few time, cause there was no come back to that, he was completely right, "Shut up."

He laughed, pulling back and shooting the puck, hitting the back of the net hard. "Don't worry about me baby, I'm good."

"I'll always worry about you, you big lug. Now come here, give me a kiss. I gotta get back to the office," she said pulling him by the skin tight shirt he had on, placing her lips on his. He gave her a long, drugging kiss, before she pulled back. Not only was she having problems breathing but she could hardly walk away. His laughter followed her out the arena, hold on, wasn't she supposed to be mad at him? Not dizzy with his kisses?

Crap.

Shea was ready to stand in front of a leading scoring forward and take the puck he was shooting, in the head. They had been looking at houses for almost three weeks and Elli was driving him insane. When he would like one, she hated it, when she thought the house was okay, he hated it. They had looked at more than thirty houses and Elli only liked one, and Shea thought it was dog ugly. Who would have thought looking at houses was going to be so hard?

Shea sat with Elli, and Jill Mancina, their realtor, shaking his head. Jill had said she worked all week on the list of house she had found for them, and Elli didn't like any of them, Shea didn't even bother looking at the list, it would be a waste of time.

"Baby, maybe if we go see some of them, maybe you would like them in person," Shea suggested, Elli shook her head.

"I have a list of requirements I want, I don't understand why I can't have the house I want?" she complained, Shea rolled his eyes as she went into the list of things she wants, not that he hadn't heard them nine hundred times.

5 bedrooms, white hardwood floors, a big yard, and big porch.

"Ms. Fisher, the problem is the white hardwood floors, plus the porch. The houses made today have standard stuff in them, and country porches aren't really done anymore." Jill said desperately, Shea felt so bad for her.

"We can put white hardwood floors in baby, let's just fine something. I want a house."

Elli glanced over at Shea, before shaking her head. "I want my floors, there has to be a house in Nashville with them, after we exhausted all the options, then we'll go with what you said Shea. Thanks for meeting with us Jill. See ya next week; call us if you find anything." Elli stood up, gathering her things. Shea let out a frustrated breath, shaking hands with Jill before following Elli out.

When they got in the truck, Shea didn't start it, he looked over at Elli; she was on her phone doing something. "Elli, you're really starting to piss me off."

She looked up surprised, "Why?"

"Because we have spent almost four weeks on looking at different houses, you've liked one."

"And you didn't like it, what was I supposed to do?"

"Um pick another one! Are you doing this on purpose?"

She narrowed her eyes, turning so she was facing him, "What do you mean by that?"

"Are you not choosing a house because you don't really want to move in with me?"

"Really Shea? I've brought all my clothes and all my shoes to your condo. I want a house just as bad as you do! Do you think I like lining my damn shoes along the dining room wall! Hanging my clothes anywhere I can find a space for them! Be real."

"I am being real; I think you're subliminally doing this to us. You don't want to move in with me."

"Again are you crazy? I already have!"

"No you haven't, saying you don't want this house or that one keeps you from fully committing to me."

Elli just sat there, staring at him as if he was dumbest idiot on earth. "Take me to the office Shea."

"Fine," Shea spat out as he turned the truck on and drove off, towards the studio. The whole way over, she didn't say anything, just played on her phone. When they arrived to the studio, she gathered her things and got out, before shutting the door, she looked over at him.

"If you have to question my commitment to you, than why are you with me?" Before he could answer her, she slammed the door, sending him a glare as she marched her beautifully round ass inside. Her outfit was completely unpractical, it was 20 degrees out, but damn she was hot in them little grey wool shorts with them naughty thigh high suede boots. He should be mad, not getting hot.

Damn woman drove him insane!

When Elli got home that night, Shea was sitting on the couch watching TV. Even thought they had fought earlier that day, and hadn't talked, Shea was bursting with the news he received that afternoon. But when Elli didn't so much as look at him as she passed by, he knew he was in the dog house. He was just so frustrated. He wanted a house, with her. He was tired of his little condo, not only did it hold all the memories of all the females that he brought through there, but it wasn't a home, he wanted a home with Elli. He wanted to start a new life with her, just them. And Adler, of course.

He watched as she passed by, her heels clicking on the hardwood as she walked towards the kitchen, cooing at Adler. "Hello baby boy, how are you today, are you hungry?"

"I just fed him," Shea said, but she ignored him, leaning against the island, unzipping her boots. His mouth watered at the sight of her inner thigh, he wanted so bad to be the one to unzip them boots, just to feel her skin under his fingers. God, he was hard just watching her, but it wasn't as if he could go over there and have his way with her, she was pissed off, and he didn't think he was wrong, so he would not be apologizing.

Shea tried to watch TV, but his eyes kept drifting to Elli, moving around the kitchen, getting stuff out to cook. He usually helped cook, but since she was ignoring him, he wasn't moving. When she bent down to get a pot out of the compartment under the island, Shea's head feel to the side as his mouth parted, his breathing picking up. His heart was hammering against his chest as he imagine all the different ways he could get those grey knee high socks off with his mouth.

He found himself getting up, and going over to her, wrapping his arms around her middle, pressing his hard length against her butt. She tensed up, smacking at his hands.

"Excuse me," she sneered as she tried to move away, but he wasn't letting her go.

"I'm sorry," he whispered against her neck as he nuzzled his nose into the mass of curls that hung along her shoulders, "You're right, I'm an idiot for questioning your commitment to me. I'm just ready to be in a house, for us to start a new chapter in our life."

God, he was a wuss.

All the tension left her body, and she leaned against him, wiggling that naughty little butt against his length before turning in his arms to look up at him.

"I'm sorry too, I want us to find the perfect house, because I don't plan on ever leaving it," she said looking up at him.

"Baby, any house will be perfect as long as your there." She bit her lip, running her hands down his arms, then around to his ass, putting her hands in his pockets.

"I love you Shea," she said, kissing his chin, he smiled.

"I love you too." He slid his hands down to her ass, lifting her up onto the island before capturing her mouth in delicious need. Her hands came up his biceps, to his shoulders, before going around his neck as he moved in between her legs. She scooted to the edge of the counter, her hot center, warming his. When she pulled back, he tried to reclaim her mouth, but she just laughed.

"Shea, come on, I gotta cook," she said trying to get away.

"I'm only hungry for one thing baby," he said against her collarbone as he nip and nibbled.

"Well that one thing ain't gonna happen until you have clearance, mister."

He pulled back grinning hard at her, "I have clearance. Today was my appointment, I play tomorrow night."

Her eyes lit up, "It hasn't been six weeks yet!"

"I'm ready to play," he said shrugging his shoulders, "On the ice, and with you, so hush, come here." Of course, she went willingly. It was easy to assume that there would be no cooking that night.

Elli had missed the arena so much. Sitting beside Harper, a beer and hot dog in hand, being decked out in her Adler gear, it was hard to contain her excitement. She was ready for some hockey.

"It's so great for both guys to be back," Harper gushed as she took a hearty drink of her beer. Jakob had came back two weeks earlier, and apparently missed Shea something crazy, which Elli thought was so cute.

"I know, I have missed watching the games live, so much," Elli gushed as she took a bite of her hot dog, looking around the arena. She tried not to think about the last time she sat in her seats, since every time she did her heart hurt. Shea was healthy; he had proved that the night before. Everything was fine.

"So we are completely moved in, and the home decorator is coming tomorrow to meet with me and Jakob, so Jakob can look over everything and approve everything I've picked out."

Elli smiled over her, "You think he will?"

Harper giggled, "Oh course, he wants to continue getting laid, Elli. Be realistic here."

"Duh," Elli laughed, Harper joined in, a big grin on her face. Every time Elli saw her; she was always smile or giggling. It was weird, but hey Harper was happy, what more could Elli ask for? "We still haven't found anything, nothing is appealing to me."

"It takes time El, I mean I looked at a thousand houses it seemed, until I found the one, and it still didn't feel like the one till y'all came to look at it," Harper said, sounding all older and wiser. Elli didn't let it bother her, she just nodded.

"I know but Shea is getting impatient. He said I'm subliminally not picking a house."

"Is he right?"

"Really Harper?"

"I'm just asking, y'all have looked at a lot of house, your damn list of requirements is a mile long!"

"Its four things I want!"

"Still lower your standards, Shea was hoping to be in something before he had to leave again for the road. He's leaving for three weeks next week, and y'all don't have any prospects. I don't blame him for being angry for you."

"Whatever, whose side are you on anyway?" Elli glared at Harper before looking out at the ice. Was she being too picky? Was she subliminally not picking something because she truly didn't want to commit to Shea?

No.

She loved him, wanted to be with him, but like she said, she just wanted the perfect house for them, and damn it she would find it!

Shea sat on the bench in front of his locker, lacing up his skates. It had been a long five weeks, a good five weeks but long. He was ready to get out of the ice, even though he knew Coach wouldn't play him like he had before. It was gonna be at least two weeks before he was staying on the ice for his normal forty minutes, but hey just being able to play was enough. Knowing Elli was in the stands made it even better for him.

Jakob sat beside Shea a grin on his face as he strapped his elbow pads on.

"Ready?"

"More than ready," Shea said, making sure his skates were extra tight.

"Good, let's do this."

"Hell yeah."

After they were done, they headed for the ice, ready for the warm up. Shea was ready to hear the roar of the crowd. After all the blog sites announced his return a week early, fans went nuts, posting great, encouraging comments for him. It was great, and he was ready to show his fans that he was ready to win for them.

Shea's heart race when he heard the roar of the crowd, the JumboTron must have been showing them walking down the hall. Shea closed his eyes, thanking the Lord above for all the blessing he had been receiving, he then asked for Him to protect him on the ice. Shea took a deep breath before walking through the opening that led to the bench, onto the ice. When he hit the ice, the crowd went nuts. Fans held their signs up, wishing him luck and welcoming him back. Shea was convinced Nashville had the best set of fans. He skated around the rink once, even along the visitor's side, holding his stick up as a thank you to his fans before he saw the most important sign.

I'm so proud of you.

I love you so much.

It was Elli's, and as she held it, she had the brightest smile on her face. He smiled back at her since he couldn't kiss her like he wanted. Just knowing that she loved him and she was proud of him made him feel like it was going to be the best damn game of his life.

After being on the road for three weeks with only a day break, Shea was glad to be home for a week. Elli and Shea had been blissfully in love ever since Christmas and Shea couldn't ask for more. Well a house would be nice, but he was just happy he had Elli. They were coming up on six months of being together and Shea couldn't believe that he had been in with one woman for that long. Never had he thought he would be living with a woman, looking for a house, and telling her he loved her every chance he got. It still blew his mind.

Luckily Shea was home when they got the call. He was lying in bed, cuddled up beside Elli when Jill called.

"Shea, I found it, I freaking found it!"

Shea sat up, causing Elli to fall off his chest. She woke up in a stir, "Jesus, Shea," she complained, moving her hair out of her face.

"It's Jill, babe," he said before answering Jill, "What do you mean you found it?"

"I found Elli's dream home, I've been sitting on it for a week, trying to see if it was the right house. Oh Shea it is," Jill said dreamily, Shea got excited, putting the phone on speaker phone so Elli could hear.

"Tell me," Shea said, so excited he couldn't see straight. Jill knew Elli by now, ever since they met in her office when Elli hated every house she had shown them, Jill hadn't called with any, she only called to say that she was still looking, so Shea knew this had to be it.

"Okay, well its over in Brentwood, it just came on the market last week, it has the porch she wants, 6 bedrooms, four and half baths, 7,364 square feet, on a 2 Acre Lot, it's beautiful Shea, simply beautiful."

It sounded good to him, but anything sounded good at this point. Elli's stuff was everywhere; the condo was too small for all their stuff.

"Does it have the white hardwood floors?" Elli asked.

Damn it, he forgot it had to have that.

"Yes! Didn't I say that?! Goodness me, I'm so stinkin excited that it totally slipped my mind. I wasn't even gonna go look at it until one of my colleagues said 'What the hell, white floors, no one wants that!' I almost fell out of my chair trying to get the listing from the guy. Oh Lord, I'm so excited."

"When can we see it?" Shea asked.

"As soon as y'all want!"

"An hour?" he asked, Elli was already out the bed, going to the bathroom.

"Yes sir! See ya there, I'll text you the address."

"Awesome." Shea got out of bed, ready to say bye, but Jill kept talking.

"Do you want to know the price? I think we can get it at ten thousand less."

"Jill, at this point I don't care about the price, I just want a house."

He hung up to Jill's laugher, this was it. It had to be.

This was it; this was the house of Elli's dreams. Beautiful white hardwood floors, all the rooms were white, but of course Elli would change that, she would hire the gal Harper was using. The rooms were big, spacious, the windows, oh God, they were to die for. Huge and clear, the trim along with windows had pretty little designs in them. The bathrooms all had the same shower as Shea's condo; only the master bathroom had a spa bathtub. There was beautiful entry ways to each room, the kitchen; spectacular.

And the porch was every country girls dream.

It wrapped around the whole house, with big pillars holding up the second story. The back patio was done in cobblestones that lead to the huge in ground pool. The whole property was gated in by a tall white picket fence.

This was it.

This was Elli and Shea's house.

"I have to have it," Elli said up to Shea as they stood on the cobblestone walkway that when Elli got a chance would be surrounded by tulips.

He nodded, looking up at the beauty of the red brick home. It was perfect, there was a four car garage at the bottom, and there was a man cave for goodness sakes! This had to be their home.

"I love it," Shea said, causing Elli to grin ear to ear.

"Me too."

"We'll need to have everyone come see it, see what they think," Shea said, Elli nodded in complete agreement.

"But if they don't like it, is it bad that I really don't care? Cause I want this house Shea."

Shea laughed, nodded his head, "I couldn't agree more with you," He looked down at her, as she grinned up at him. He turned wrapping her up in his arms, kissing her with such care. When they parted he picked her up, spinning her around as she giggled.

"We found our house!" Elli yelled with her arms up in the air, making Shea laugh.

"Thank god!" Jill yelled causing everyone to laugh.

"Shea, it's beautiful," Grace said, as she stood in front of her stove, cooking some lunch for him and the kids.

"We think so," Shea grinned as he colored with Ryan, "Hey bud, when me and Ms. Elli get our house, you wanna come stay the night?"

"I sure do! Can I have my own room!?"

"I don't see why not, a hockey room for sure," Shea gushed, kissing Ryan's head before looking over at a smiling Grace.

"I've never seen you this happy Shea," she pointed out as she laid a grill cheese in front of Amelia, then Ryan, before giving one to Shea.

"I've never been this happy. I'm with the most amazing woman in the world, we're buying a house, the hockey season is looking like another cup winning one, my family is healthy, and good. Why wouldn't I be happy?"

"I love how Elli beat out everything else on why you're happy," Grace said with a chuckle as she sat down with her own sandwich.

"Jeez Grace, why are you always so jealous all the time."

"Shut up, I am not jealous."

"Yes you are,"

"Whatever," Grace laughed before taking a bite of her sandwich, and then she said, "I'm happy for you."

"Good, cause I'm always happy for you."

They shared a smile, before going back to eating.

"I think it's time, Grace," Shea said after a moment, Grace looked up, nodding her head.

"I thought that was the reason you came over," she said with a grin, "and Shea, I couldn't agree more. It's early, but yeah, I couldn't agree more."

Gosh, he loved his twin.

Shea hated lying to Elli, but she was so damn nosy, he had no choice but to say he had a meeting with his agent and that's why he was gonna be gone all day. Of course she was upset since she wanted to go look at paint and other house things, since their offer on the house was accepted and they would be signing the paperwork later that week. Hopefully they would be moved in by the end of the month when Shea would be on a small break before heading out for another couple weeks on the road. Playoffs were coming up quick, and the Assassins were kicking some major hockey ass. They were number one in their division right now, and things were looking great for another cup year.

Things were going good, great even. All he could do was hope that the next hour would go as great as his life had the past six months.

Shea pulled up to the security house as Mr. Harris walked towards the car, his hand on his trusty gun once more. Shea rolled down the window, smiling when the old man noticed who he was.

"Mr. Adler! How are you, is Elli with ya?" he asked, looking into the car.

"No sir, I'm on my own today, I have a meeting with the Fishers."

"Oh I think I do have a memo that you were coming by, go on up son. It was nice seeing you," he said with a wrinkled grin as he pushed a button for the gates to open up. Shea nodded, and waved before driving through the gate.

Shea pulled in by the large fountain before getting out his truck, and making his way up the stairs to the front door of the large plantation home. Shea ranged the doorbell, and after a minute or so, Mrs. Harris opened the door with a grin.

"Well hey there, Mr. Adler. Come on in, Mr. Fisher is waiting in the study for you."

"Thanks Mrs. Harris," Shea said with a nod, before following her through the many rooms, to Michael Fisher's study. Michael stood with a large smile on his face when Shea walked into the room. Shea couldn't return the smile because he felt as if he was going to throw up, his nerves were on edge, and he felt like he might faint. Walking through the house he was fine, but standing in front of Michael Fisher, Shea wasn't sure he was going to make it.

"Shea, so great to see you, I'm been wondering all day what you need to speak with me about," he said, shaking hands with Shea, Shea went through the motions but he was sure he wouldn't remember doing them later. "Have a seat son." Shea fell into the chair that sat across from the chair that Michael sat down into.

"Thanks for seeing me," Shea all but mumbled out, he cleared his throat, embarrassed by his actions and his intense nervousness. Shea had went through this billions of times on the way over there, he knew what he wanted to say, what the hell was wrong with him?

"Anytime, so what brings ya by? Everything alright? You're sweatin' something crazy there son," Michael said with a laugh, Shea couldn't laugh but he did wiped his dripping wet forehead with the back of his hand. He was sweating like he was playing in the Stanley Cup finals and he was about the make the goal winning shot.

Damn it, he had to get it together!

"Um, well, I came by because, I um," Shea was interrupted by Michael's laughter.

"Jesus Shea, what's wrong with you?"

Shea looked up, taking a deep breath in before saying, "I want to marry Elli."

Chapter 30

Shea eyes went wide when Olivia and Victoria busted into the room, their hands over their mouths.

"Well then," Michael said with a grin.

"I'm sorry. I had this whole big speech ready for you on the reasons I want to marry her, but I have forgotten all of it. All I know is that I love her, very much, and I need your approval before I ask her, because if I know anything, it's that Elli is a down home old fashioned girl, and she would want your blessing."

Michael nodded, "You're right on that one."

"You want to marry Eleanor?" Olivia asked, "It's only been what a couple months."

"We've been together six months, almost seven, but I mean when you know you know? And I know. I want to be with Elli for the rest of my life, I love her."

Olivia looked Shea over, as Victoria stood beside her mother with a look of contempt on her face. He would never understand these people. "I never noticed your arms before Shea," Olivia said, Shea looked down at his arms, then back up at her. "Last time, you were dressed up I guess."

Okay, what the hell did that mean? Yeah, they were all wearing their nice clothing while Shea was wearing a tee and jeans, but still what the hell was she trying to say!

"Yes, last time I came for dinner. Today, I just came to talk, so I didn't think I needed to be dressed up."

"Shea, ignore her. Back to the situation on hand," Michael said with a wave of his hand towards Olivia and Victoria. "Wanna marry my daughter, huh?"

"Yes sir," Shea said, focusing on Michael and not the two women that were looking at him as if he was a bum off the street while they whispered something to each other.

"I like you Shea, a lot. You're a good man, and my Eleanor has never been so happy till you came along, so my answer is yes. Absolutely, you have my blessing."

A relieved sigh left Shea's mouth, as he grinned, "Thank you, so much. I haven't asked her or anything, I haven't even bought the ring."

"Oh! Well you should take Victoria with you Shea!" Olivia gushed coming towards Michael's chair, leaning against him, "Victoria knows what Elli likes, and plus what Justin had gotten her, so you don't pick anything like it since Elli hated that ring."

Victoria nodded, coming up beside Shea, "Yeah Shea, I'm great at shopping and I know what my baby sister likes."

"Um, well."

Shea kind of wanted to go by his self and get the ring. He had planned on asking Elli the day they signed for the house. They were supposed to sign the papers on Valentines' Day, him and Elli had laughed saying that would be their gift to each other, but Shea wanted to ask her when they went back to the house after signing the papers. Grace said she would have the living room filled with candles, and Jill had already agreed to give Grace the key early so she could go do it for him.

What he didn't plan on was going shopping with Victoria for Elli's ring, but the way Olivia and Victoria were looking at him before he thought he might need too, just to make sure things were okay between them all.

"It will be fun!" Victoria said again, while Olivia nodded.

"Be good for y'all to get to know each other too, since you and Eleanor have been spending a lot of time with Noah and Liam," Michael said, Shea nodded, he and Elli had been over at her brothers' house a lot lately, but that was to see the kids.

"It will be your decision Shea, I'll just suggest what I think Elli would like," Victoria added.

"Yeah, that would be fine." Shea said, even though he felt like it was the worst idea ever.

"Great!" Olivia and Victoria gushed, with big grins. Evil grins, Shea noticed, yeah there would be no trusting those two.

"Good," Michael said, with a nod, standing up and pulling Shea into a back slapping hug, when he pulled back, Shea saw tears in his eyes, and Shea actually became nervous again. What if he changed his mind? "Only one thing left to do my boy,"

"Which would be?" Shea asked.

"Go ask Bryan, you know Eleanor would want his approval too."

Fuck.

Elli didn't think she could be any happier, not only was she getting the house of her dreams in five days time, but she was doing so much more promotion work with the Assassins', that she was wearing a permanent grin on her face. She was working with Melody Yates again, this time on a wine charity event at the arena. After working all morning on the shots she needed, the people Elli had to take pictures of, Elli walked out towards the back entrance of the arena.

A small flutter went through her as she walked towards the back door, it was the same door she went through the day she met Shea. That day would forever hold the most amazing memory of her life. Who would have known that that was the day she was gonna find the man of her dreams, the same man she would love, and being moving into the house of her dreams with. It was almost unbelievable how happy Elli was.

Elli was about to reach the door, the heels of her boots clicking against concrete floor, when the door open, and the same man she had been thinking about came through it. He wasn't looking and ran right into her, catching her before she fell over.

"Crap, I'm so-," when Shea saw it was her, he grinned, "I am not sorry I ran into you, Ms. Fisher," he said before he kissed her lavishly, Elli's heart swelled at the feeling of it. God, she loved him.

"Well that's one hell of a hello, what are you doing here?"

"I have a meeting with Bryan," he said as he let her go, still holding her hand in his. His eyes were the brightest blue, his smile almost match the brightness of his eyes, he was happy about something.

"What about?"

"Business crap, I'll see you for dinner?"

"Yeah, I'm on my way to the studio." He nodded, kissing her cheek before moving around her.

"Okay baby, I'll call you, love you."

"Love you too," she said as she watched him walk away, he was up to something and Elli hated not knowing what. She would find out when she got home later, sexual incentives always worked on Shea.

Always, she thought with a grin.

When Elli arrived at the studio, things were crazy. They had a full waiting room, and only two photographers, Harper included. They had been so busy the past couple weeks, which had been wonderful since Shea was traveling a lot. It was sad to say, but Elli actually couldn't wait for hockey to be over. She and Shea had discussed going somewhere tropical as a vacation when the season was over. Shea had said he was gonna take his cup with them, but Elli was pretty sure he wouldn't be able to do that.

Only three months left till she was in paradise with Shea. Three long months.

Elli didn't waste no time, she threw her purse behind the desk and jumped right in, working her butt off to get everyone done and out; making sure they were happy. It was going to be a long day; the only thing that kept her smiling was that she would see Shea when she got home.

"Are you sure Shea?" Bryan Fisher asked, as he leaned back in his chair, "It's a big step."

"Yes, I've never been so sure about anything in my life, sir."

"Well then, you have my blessing." Shea smiled big, nodding his head. That was actually easier than he thought. "So I guess I won't have to pay you much for another five years huh?"

"I don't know about that, we're buying a new house, and Elli likes to shop."

"Well darn," Bryan said with a grin as he stood up, Shea did the same, "I was hoping I would be able to get you for cheap since your contract is about up. Guess I'll have to pay you full price, even though I'm letting you marry my Eleanor."

Shea laughed, "We'll see if we can cut a deal."

Bryan let out a gut busting laugh, and nodded his head before sticking his hand out for Shea's, "Welcome to the family son, that is if she'll say yes."

"Oh she'll say yes."

He hoped.

Shea sat beside Victoria in the gallery of Tiffany's, wishing like hell he didn't agree to have her come with him. Everything she picked was disgusting, gaudy, and Shea knew Elli would hate it. The girl had expensive taste, something he knew Elli had too, but Jesus, not only did he know Elli wouldn't want a ten carat diamond ring, but really, what the hell would she do when she couldn't pick her hand up to take a picture! The damn thing had to weigh ten pounds and Elli's hands where so small and cute, he was sure she wouldn't be able to pick up her hand!

Shea stood up, and the cute little girl behind the counter looked worried. She probably saw her big sale walking out the door. Victoria had no problem announcing who he was and what he did, so the girl knew he was shopping big.

The more time he spent with Victoria, the more he disliked her. No wonder Elli really didn't like her, she was mean as hell, and he was pretty sure she was trying to sabotage his ring selection.

"I'm going to look around," he said, as the girl and Victoria looked around.

"Okay, let me know if you see something," the girl said, Shea nodded and started towards the back of the store. He was looking in the cases, and wondering if he could get out of there without Victoria noticing even though that would be wrong since he drove her there from the condo, when someone called his name.

"Shea! How ya doing!?"

Shea looked over at the sweet looking blondish brown hair girl that was smiling at him. She looked a lot like Harper, and that's when it clicked, it was Harper's littler sister, but he couldn't remember her name to save his life.

"Hey," he said, raking his brain for her name, she giggled at him as he walked over to her.

"Its Piper, I don't think we really talked all that much at the party," she said with a grin, he smiled back; she was a cute little thing, so different from Harper's crazy ass.

"Piper, how could I forget, how are you doing?"

She smiled in delight, "Good, working my butt off since I took the semester off from school."

"Cool, you like it here?"

"I do; its good work."

"Good," Shea nodded, looking at the case that she stood behind. It was full of different colored stones, when he saw the pink one, he smiled. Elli would love them. "These are pretty."

"Yeah, they are amazing, my favorite is the pink diamonds, they are so pretty."

"They are diamonds?"

"Yeah, you should see em in a platinum setting, pure magic on your finger! They are awesome! You ain't ever heard of pink diamonds?"

Wow, once she got talking, she was Harper all over.

"No, I haven't, I thought diamonds came in one color," he said, feeling pretty stupid.

"Oh no, what are you looking to get?"

Shea smiled shyly, "An engagement ring."

Piper's face lit up, before she started bouncing up and down, "For Elli!" she gushed.

"Yes, but don't tell anyone, okay!"

"I won't! Oh my god! This is awesome! Oh goodness! Come on over here, come look at these amazin' pink engagement rings." Piper basically screamed as she drugged Shea across the store to a case that held the most sparking rings he had ever seen. He sat in the chair in front of the case as Piper brought out each display. "Ain't they pretty!"

"They are," he said breathlessly as he looked at each ring.

"What are you doing?" Shea looked up as Victoria sat down beside him. Piper made a face at Victoria then looked back down at Shea.

"Isn't that Elli's sister?"

"Yeah, she came to help."

"Why?"

"Because I can, I don't think Elli would like pink rings, their kind of childish, don't you think?" Victoria asked.

"Um no, they are actually very classic looking," Piper said, pointing down at a large pink diamond that was surrounded by little white ones. "See the cut, the elegance? A girl would die to have this on their finger, I know I would."

"Yeah, I guess it's pretty, but a white diamond is so beautiful, distinguished." Victoria countered.

"Yeah, but it's played out, a pink diamond is new, thrilling. Elli has amazing style, and this would add to her amazing style. All women will want to be like Elli because she has an engagement ring that no one else has. Not too many people buy these, they are crazy expensive."

Piper was right, and when she brought out another display, Shea found the ring.

"That's it," Shea said pointing to the elegant ring, Elli would love it.

"Oh yes, the cushion-cut fancy deep pink diamond with round brilliant white diamonds, in platinum ring setting, I know it's amazing, its two carats, with a clarity of VS2." Piper gushed, sounding like a ring magazine or better yet, a great seller because she had Shea sold. The pink princess cut diamond stood out with the hundreds of little round diamonds around it, the band was covered in them. It was beautiful; Elli would flip when she saw it. When Piper handed it to him, he held it in his hand and he was sure it wouldn't be too heavy for Elli's pretty hand. It was perfect.

"I'll take it."

"Seriously?"

"Shea! It's almost a million dollars!" Victoria complained as Piper still looked shocked.

"Yeah, Elli would love it; do you have a wedding band to match?"

"You want to buy that too?" Piper asked.

"Yeah," Shea said with a grin, "I want it all, she's going to love it."

Shea was on cloud nine as he drove back with his little packaged of two of the most gorgeous rings that his future bride would wear.

He hoped.

Shea chuckled to his self as he turned onto the road that led to his condo. "What are you laughing at?" Victoria asked, "Are you delirious because of how much money you spent on a two rings?"

"No, Elli is worth every penny. I'm laughing because I'm actually scared she might say no."

Victoria didn't say anything which surprised Shea, since she had an opinion on everything. He noticed though, that she didn't say much since he said he wanted the rings. It was weird.

When they pulled into the spot beside her car, Victoria got out as Shea hide the ring under his seat, before locking the doors. Elli was a snoop and he refused to bring the rings in the house, she would find them within an hour. Victoria stood at the end of the truck, looking as pristine as Elli always did; just Victoria didn't have the light in her eyes that Elli always had. Victoria was a very beautiful girl, but she wasn't his Elli.

"Thanks for going with me Victoria," Shea said as she came to stand in front of her. She smiled sweetly, putting her hand on his bicep.

"I had a wonderful time, Elli will love the rings."

"Yeah, she will," he said trying to shake her hand off.

"Well come here and give your future sister in law a hug, cause Elli would be crazy to say no," Victoria said before she threw herself into his arms, he caught her, even though he really didn't want to. When she pulled back some, she looked up at him before whispering, "She doesn't deserve you," Shea had no time to react, she pressed her mouth against his, and before he could pull back, she did slapping his face hard.

"Oh my god! You're with my sister, you pig!"

Shea looked down at her shocked as she moved away from him, "You crazy bi-"

"Are you fucking kidding me right now?"

Shea looked over; feeling like his stomach hit the ground, before meeting eyes with a very angry Elli.

Shit.

Elli only saw rage as she stomped her way past Shea and Victoria, and up the stairs to the condo. Shea kept calling her name and she kept ignoring him as she entered the condo; also ignoring Adler as she headed to the kitchen. When she found the black trash bags from under the sink, she made her way to the dining room, throwing each shoe in the bag with more force than needed.

How could he do this to her? It was her sister, the one person that if she could beat the crap out of she would. Elli hated Victoria, it didn't matter how nice Victoria had been to her lately, Elli knew it was all a crock of shit! Elli felt the tears that threaten to run down her face, but she pushed them back. There would be no way she would cry in front of Shea. He didn't deserve it.

Seeing them together made Elli physically want to puke. Shea in all his beautiful glory with a fucking hag! What was he thinking? Elli thought he was over them Barbie dolls! She shook her head as she threw each shoe in the bag, how could he do this to her?

She heard him coming into the house and was surprised it took so long, he was probably trying to suck up to her sister, so Victoria would meet him later.

Douche bag.

"Elli, please, stop, what are you doing?"

"Get the fuck away from me Shea Adler," Elli yelled as she walked by him, placing the bag of her shoes by the wall, before she headed into the bedroom.

"Elli, she kissed me, I swear."

"Yeah I bet! It's funny how all these females kiss you but you never kiss them," Elli yelled, throwing clothes in the plastic bags she had grab on her way to his room. "I don't believe you, you're a liar just like Justin."

"Don't compare him to me!" Shea yelled, "I love you, I would never hurt you and you know that, why are you doing this? Why won't you believe me?"

"Because YOU KISSED MY MOTHER FUCKING SISTER! My sister! My worst enemy, I can't ever look at you!"

"I didn't kiss her! She fucking kissed me!"

"Whatever, your lips touched hers, you had her in your arms, oh my god, why am I even explaining myself," she said as she moved around him, picking up more of her shoes, and throwing them in bags.

"Elli please, I swear to you, I don't want her, I want you, please," Shea went around, bending down to her level, trying to get her to look at him. She didn't know why he was trying to get in her face, didn't he know that she was libel to knock him the hell out! "Elli I would never do anything to cause you to leave me, I love you baby, please, stop, let's talk."

"There is nothing to talk about Shea, you are a liar, an asshole, and I don't want nothing to do with you."

"You don't mean that, stop for a minute," he said trying to stop her but she went by him, packing more things.

"Leave me alone, Shea."

"No, please Elli, I'll do anything."

"There is nothing you can do to get that fucking image out of my head, get away from me,"

"Let me try, listen to me!" he yelled, but she ignored him, continuing to pack.

"You know I should have known no man is like you. Now I know it was all an act, you were probably trying to insure you have a way to my money huh? Being with me gave you a one way ticket to the Assassins, God you disgust me!"

"Now you know that is not true! I don't want the Assassins; I told you I wanted to teach kids!"

"Yeah I bet that was a lie too, you're full of it. You just want my money, my team, my everything, but let me tell you something you asshole you ain't gonna get it from me, and you sure ain't gonna get it from Victoria. She don't have shit!" Elli sneered as she threw shirt after shirt into her suitcase.

"I don't want your money, I have my own! I want you, and you're fucking crazy to think differently!"

"Yeah, crazy to ever fall for your bullshit! You are just like every other asshole in the world, hell you and Justin could be best friends."

"Well you stop comparing me to him and get your head out of your ass! You've been making me pay for his mistake for months, I looked past it, dealt with your craziness, loved you, but you can't even listen to me for a minute!" Elli sent him a look of death before he went on, "If you actually calmed down and listen to me, you would find that I didn't kiss your sister, she kissed me, and before I could even do anything about it, she slapped me! Making it look like I kissed her, she played me!"

"Why were you with her anyways? No, don't tell me I don't care!"

"She went to help me with something; I didn't know she was planning this!"

"Whatever, you're a liar; I don't give a shit what you have to say!"

"Stop, you are freaking out on me! Calm down! Give me a chance to explain!"

"Fuck you! Get away from me!"

Elli stormed past him but he grab her by her arm, causing her to jerk to a stop, "Elli, please-"

The crack of Elli's hand against his face stopped any words from forming. Hell, it stopped everything. Elli just stood there staring up at him as traitorous tears rolled down her cheeks. She had never thought she would ever bring her hand against Shea's face, Justin's yes; he was a complete ass but not Shea. She loved him so much, and she felt like he had taken her heart and hit it with his hockey stick, shattering it in a million pieces.

He took a deep breath, moving his hand up to his red cheek as he looked down at Elli. "Don't touch me," she cried as she walked past him, moving around the room, grabbing more things, her iPod, her picture frames of the kids, everything. He could keep the ones of them, at that moment she wanted to forget everything that ever happened between them. She cleaned out the bathroom and when she came out, he was sitting on the bed, watching her. When she saw the tears rolling down his cheeks, she almost broke, but instead she moved to the closet grabbing her suitcases full of her clothes and taking them downstairs, after three trips, she only had a few more bags to grab. She couldn't make the same mistakes she made with Justin, she just couldn't. When Elli went back into his room, he stood there with the most awful look on his face.

"Elli, the things you have said, they aren't true and you know it, you're making the biggest mistake of your life right now."

"The only mistake I ever made was falling in love with you."

It was like she had hit him again, the way he jerked back as the tears made their way down his beautifully sculpted face. It made her sick that she thought he was beautiful, gorgeous, but that was what he was; a playboy. He would never change.

"If you walk out that fucking door without talking this over with me first, we're done."

She bent down, picking up the bags that she had left before looking up at him with all the anger and hurt in the world in her eyes, "No Shea, we were done when you kissed my mother fucking sister."

With that, she was gone, and even though it hurt so much she couldn't breathe, she knew she would never see him again.

Chapter 31

Elli missed the way Shea slept.

It was one of the main things she missed. As the tears threaten to come down her cheeks all she could do was think about the many mornings she would wake up, and stare at him. His long eye lashes would touch the top of his cheeks, his lips would be parted some, and his breathing would be so even that Elli could only think that he was dreaming about something good. When she would get bored, she would run her finger down from his nose, across his top lip to his bottom, and giggle when he would pursed his lips. He would always wake up, glaring at her, but he wasn't really mad. He would wrap her up in his arms, kissing her long and hard before letting her go.

He loved her.

That was what Elli was thinking about as she stood in the middle of Starbucks, a block over from the arena where she was working that day. Out of all the things she could be thinking about, she was thinking of Shea. She should be thinking about the paperwork that was accumulating at the studio and in her office at the Assassins' headquarters, but nope, she was thinking about her ex boyfriend.

Like always.

When her phone rang, she rolled her eyes, hoping it wasn't the same person that clouded her brain. It wasn't, it was her mother.

"Hello?"

"Hello darling, are you coming to dinner with me and Victoria today?"

"I don't know Mother, I'm not really feeling it, I still don't want to be around Victoria."

"Oh come on, you've been weird ever since that womanizing ex boyfriend of yours kissed her. Get over him, it's been what two months? And Victoria has apologized profusely, even though she shouldn't have too, it was him for goodness sakes."

"I loved him," Elli said as the tears rushed to her eyes, but she wasn't going to let them fall, she was in the middle of a damn Starbucks for goodness sakes. She would wait till she got home.

"So, he was trash, tattoos everywhere, he didn't know how to dress, he wasn't good enough for you. You're lucky you found him out before y'all got married or something crazy."

"I just hate what he did to me, and coming onto my sister out of all people. It just blows my mind; he wasn't the guy I thought he was."

"Again, he was trash, so come on, let's go to the dinner. At the club! You can stay at the house tonight instead of that crummy house of yours."

Elli rolled her eyes before saying, "I'll call you this afternoon."

"You better sweetheart, bye."

"Bye." Elli hung up the phone, when her mother's call went off and the picture of Shea laying in the snow making a snow angel came up, it felt like she was being punch in the chest. It happen every time she looked at it, with that happening it would only be smart to take the picture off, but ever since Shea sent it to her the day of the first snow fall with the caption saying:

I miss you like the snow misses an angel.

Elli was unable to do it; she set it to her wallpaper and put herself through the torture every time she turned her phone on. She missed him so much, but her pride kept her from returning the nonstop calls the first month, and the random texts she still got from him. She couldn't do it. He broke her heart, and no matter how much she missed him, she couldn't bring herself to talk to him. She wouldn't go through what she went through with Justin.

She wouldn't, couldn't.

"That's a cool picture, your boyfriend?" Elli jumped in surprised, turning to a very tall, very handsome man. Elli looked down at her phone, then back up at the stranger.

"Um, no, just some guy. It is a good picture."

"Well you have impeccable taste in photography," he said with a sly grin, "My name is Joseph Rinehart." He held out his hand, and Elli took it in hers.

"Elli Fisher, nice to meet you." He continued to grin at her.

"The pleasure is all mine, Ms. Fisher. Do you work around here?"

"I do, I own Time Standing Still studio on West End, but today I'm working over at Assassins' headquarters."

"Hard working woman, would you have time to date?" he said with a suggesting grin, "Me, if you're wondering."

Shit, Elli didn't see that coming, she thought the guy wanted to talk about photography as they waited in line. And he had a damn wedding ring on! With disgust, her smile fell, and she turned back around.

Being hit on was not what she wanted at the moment. The guy said something, but Elli wasn't listening as she put her headphones in, turning on her iPod. The way guys openly hit on Elli ever since she and Shea had broken up, never cease to amaze her. Yeah, she had lost twenty pounds since the breakup and she was wearing a single digit number, something that hadn't happen since she gotten sick, but still, dudes need to back up.

It wasn't like Elli wanted to lose the weight, but she had gotten sick twice since the break up, and she just wasn't hungry. Plus, anything she ate reminded her of Shea and she would basically want to throw up, so eating really didn't happen much. Once she got to the Starbucks counter, her heart broke all over again as she ordered her regular drink. It was really sad that after two months, ordering the same coffee that she knew Shea drank still hurt. Shouldn't she be over him by now?

When she passed by the guy that had hit on her, he gave her a dirty look, not that Elli cared much. Elli made her way into the newly spring day, the warmth of the sun warmed her face bringing on a small smile, even though she knew it would be cold as all get out the next day.

Gotta love Tennessee weather, people always say, 'If you don't like the weather just wait, it'll change by tomorrow.'

Elli made her way up the block, then onto the next before reaching the arena. After riding the elevator up to the business part, she stepped off going towards her office that was right beside Bryan's. Her assistant Janet stood with a big welcoming grin on her face. Elli liked Janet, she was a good hardworking girl, and always tried to make Elli happy.

Even though, lately there was no making Elli happy, she was depressed. She probably needed medication for it.

"Hey Ms. Fisher! You had two new calls, one from your mother and the other from your daddy, Mr. Fisher also came to see you but I informed him you were out and he said to tell you that he would talk to you at the game tomorrow night. You have two new faxes, and six new emails." Janet said in a hurry, Elli had learned to listen closely when Janet talked, not only was her accent thick, but the girl spoke so damn fast, it made Elli's head spin.

"Thanks so much Janet, here's your lemonade since you don't like coffee, which still makes me wonder if I should keep you as an assistant," Elli said with a small smile, Janet grinned and handed her the faxes before taking her drink.

"Coffee is gross; I'll stick to lemonade and mountain dew, thank you."

With that she turned on her heels, making her way to her desk. Elli smiled, closing the door behind her as she walked to her desk, laying her things down as she made her way to it. Everything from her office at Time Standing Still had been moved here since Harper had taken her office and Alice took Harper's. With Harper running the studio now, Elli didn't feel it was right to have all her things there. She still took pictures for her regular customers, but the new ones went through Harper.

Elli missed her regular work at the studio, but was excited for the new possibilities the Assassins headquarters held. She was a co-owner of the Nashville Assassins at the age of twenty eight years old, what else could she ask for?

Oh there was a list, but Elli couldn't think of that right now.

She laid the faxes on her desk, before pulling up her emails. They were all from customers at the studio, so she answered them quickly saying she would get back to them when she was at the studio, which would be the next day. She had deliberately ignored the faxes, because she had a feeling one of them held the same bad news the ones before had said. She picked it up, and her heart fell at the words.

Ms. Fisher,

I'm sorry, but the house you and Mr. Adler wanted has already been sold. I don't know why you send me a fax every week asking if the house has came back on the market, because I'm pretty sure the people that bought it, bought it to live in it. I'm sorry, but I will no longer be answering your faxes.

Have a nice day,

Jill Mancina

Bitch.

Elli never did like that woman, she thought as she shredded the fax before reading the other one, that one was only the confirmation of someone buying her seats for the game that night. When she turned back to her desk, she looked at her laptop screen, dazing out into space. So much had changed in the months since breaking up with Shea.

Elli hated change.

When a tear fell on her hand, she looked down at it, hating it for falling. How could she be so weak? Her mother was right; it had been two damn months! It was time to get over him!

Elli wiped her face, picking her phone off the desk, pushing the unlock button so her wallpaper would come on, and Shea's beautiful face would be looking up at her. His eyes were so dull, even though they should have been the brightest thing in the picture.

She would try to get over him tomorrow; today she would stare at his picture.

Again.

Getting over Shea day, didn't really start out the way she hoped it would. She was still living out some of the plastic bags that lined the floor of her living room, and when she was looking for one of her belts, she found a pair of Shea's boxers. As she held them in her hands all she could do was imagine him wearing them, running through the apartment trying to pack before leaving for a road trip. It didn't matter how hard she tried to throw them down and walk away, instead she held them close to her chest as the tears ran down her cheeks.

She had spent the morning bawling her eyes out.

When she finally got herself under control and dressed, she made her way through the house. Going through the motions of her mornings; feeding Adler, cleaning up the mess from the night before, and eating a banana. Adler was just as depressed as she was, he would look at her like 'Hey, where's Shea? I miss him.' Elli found herself answering him sometimes too, saying 'He kissed our sworn enemy, he's dead to us.'

Even though, God and everyone knew that wasn't true. Shea would never been dead to her, no matter how hard she tried; she couldn't get him out of her head. There wasn't a day that past where she didn't think about him, miss him.

After cleaning up and making sure Adler was good for the day, she made her way downstairs to her truck to leave for the studio. Hoping the day would get better.

Elli was working on scheduling some of her regular clients when Harper walked in. She held a coffee for Elli and one for herself as she sat down in the chairs in front of her desk. Elli smiled, hanging up the phone and taking the coffee from her. "It's good seeing you behind your desk again, Elli. I didn't realize how much I missed seeing you there."

Elli smiled, rolling her eyes, "It's your desk Harp, thanks for letting me use it. I'm almost done."

"Take your time," Harper said taking a sip of her coffee, "So how are things over at the headquarters?"

"Good, doing a lot of paperwork, trades and junk like that. Jakob came in to sign his contract last week that was probably the highlight of my week."

Harper nodded, "Yeah, he said he saw you, he also said you looked tired, which you do."

Elli looked up at her. Harper wasn't there to visit, she was there to talk. Shit. "Um, well I haven't been sleeping much."

Not like she could if she tried. Her DVD didn't put her to sleep no more, Shea ruined that for her.

"Why not?"

"Harper you know damn well why not, so just let it go. I'm okay."

"You don't look okay Elli."

"I'm fine."

"Why do you lie to me? I've been your best friend since we were five; I know you're not okay."

"I'm fine," Elli said a little sharper than she meant too. Harper glared over at her, and Elli just shrugged her shoulders, "I'll be okay, it's just gonna take some time."

"I don't know why y'all are doing this to yourselves, it's not healthy. You can't sleep or eat for that matter and Shea drinks his self to a stupor!"

Elli's head shot up, "What?"

"Shit, I wasn't supposed to tell you that," Harper said her face turning red with guilt.

"Well, you might as well go on with it."

"Jakob has had to go get Shea a couple nights a week when they are home from the bar; Jakob says its kinda scaring him."

"Shea's drinking?"

"Yeah, a lot apparently."

"Wow," Elli was shocked; Shea took such care of his body. No wonder he was a little slower lately, Elli was probably the only one to notice, but he was lagging, and the drinking was the answer to that.

"Yeah, so here's my thing, why don't you just call him, try to work something out. It's obvious y'all aren't doing good apart."

Elli took a deep breath, shaking her head. "I don't want him back; I don't want to talk to him. I'm fine. I'm getting over him."

"You're such a liar Elli!" Harper stood up, slamming her coffee cup on the desk, causing Elli to scoot back some. Harper was kinda crazy sometimes, and just in case she started swinging, Elli wanted to be able to dodge them.

"I'm your best friend Elli, and I have seen you a total of two times out of work, when you are here, you don't even talk, you just lock yourself up in a office and do paperwork. I can't even talk to you because I'm scared I might say something to upset you, or piss you off." She reached into her pocket, pulling out something shinning. When she slid it on her ring finger, Elli knew it was an engagement ring. "I'm engaged, have been for a month, and I couldn't find a way to tell you. How is that fair Elli? We are best friend, aren't we supposed to be able to tell each other things without worrying about the others stability, cause now that I told you, I'm worried you might go home and kill yourself."

Elli shook her head, standing up and coming around the desk, "I'm not going to kill myself Harp, have a little more faith in me, but I am going to knock you senseless for not telling me!" Elli took Harper's hand in her, taking in the beautiful of the ring that Jakob had probably spent months picking out. It was gorgeous, but not as gorgeous as Harper. "It's beautiful."

"Thanks, it's a little earlier than planned, but, um." Harper looked down at the ground, then back up at Elli, "But I'm pregnant, and we wanted to be engaged before we tell our families."

She was pregnant! Oh, come on!

"Wow, gosh Harper! This is crazy," Elli gushed, trying to keep the tears at bay, she couldn't cry or it would prove Harper right, that Elli was a basket case and Alder should probably hide the knifes before Elli got home. Harper was pregnant and gonna be married before her! What the hell!

"Yeah, you've hid yourself from everything El, like I'm pregnant and Jodi and Derrick are having a boy, and Trice and Walter are adopting a baby, and you don't know any of that because you won't return anyone's calls, and when you're around me, you shut down, only talking about business."

Shit, all that stuff happen in two months!

"This has got to stop Elli. You've lost so much weight, you aren't sleeping, and you're a mess."

"I'm fine."

"You say your fine one more time Eleanor Ray Fisher, I will knock you stupid. I know you're not fine."

"Harper, you're being dramatic, I've closed off some, so what? I'm okay."

"If you were really okay Elli, then why are there two boxes full of home decorating magazines in the lobby that you have yet to take home."

For the first time, Elli actually wanted to physically hurt her best friend. How dare her bring up them boxes! She knew how Elli couldn't even look at them with feeling like her heart was breaking all over again. The day they came in, Elli cried for hours beside them, it was also the day she decided to start working over at the headquarters full time.

"I have no use for them."

"Well you are taking them home today; Jakob already loaded them in the back of your truck."

It took everything out of Elli to say, "That's fine."

"I bet it is. You listen to me Eleanor Fisher, you are done. You have two choices, straighten up, get back to your life, or stop being friends with me. I can't take it; I can't take the worry, the hurt every time I see you. I want my best friend back."

Elli looked at her like she was crazy, "You're gonna give up our friendship because I'm trying to get over my ex?"

"Elli if you were actually trying to get over Shea, I wouldn't threaten you, but look, I can't even say his name without you looking like I slapped you!"

Elli didn't even realize she had made face, so she looked down at the ground as Harper went on, "You are not trying to get over him, you are torturing yourself, when all you have to do is call him, talk to him and I'm pretty damn sure he will want to see you. He misses you, he needs you."

"I don't miss him," Elli lied, and Harper knew it. Harper shook her head, as tears came to her eyes. When they fell over her cheeks, Elli couldn't help but start crying too.

"I'm done," Harper cried, "You heard me, get your shit together or I can't be your friend."

"And how do you suggest I do that Harper, please tell me."

"You can't get over him because you're not meant to. You are meant to be with him for the rest of your life, I've talked to him, and I believe that he didn't kiss Victoria, and you of all people should believe him. Victoria is vicious, you know that!"

"You didn't see them together."

"And yet you still won't confront Victoria about it, why is that?"

"Because I hate her."

"No, it's because when you do, you'll know she's a fucking liar, and then you will look like an idiot for making yourself and Shea suffer. You are making him pay for Justin's mistakes. You want to be lonely. You're pathetic."

Elli narrowed her eyes, not believing what was coming out of Harper's mouth, "I mean shit Harp, don't hold back!"

"Oh I won't, this is two months of anger that you're getting. I've had it!"

"So you've made perfectly clear," Elli answered.

"There is a ball tomorrow, Shea is going. I want you to go. Maybe seeing him will help, because God knows when y'all are in the same room, people have to wear sunglasses the sparks are so bright."

"I'm not going," Elli argued.

"Okay, but you better hope the next time I see you, you better look better, or we're done."

"You don't mean that." Elli said with a shake of her head.

"Try me Elli, just fucking try me." With that Harper left the room as a jagged sob left her body. Elli fell into the chair that was beside her, and decided that her day wasn't gonna get any better as the tears fell down her cheeks.

"Jesus baby girl, every time I see you I wonder if it's even you." Bryan said as Elli entered his box, "You're getting skinner by the day, I swear to it."

"Is that complement?" Elli asked, wrapping her arms around her papa, kissing him on his cheek.

"No baby girl, it's not. You are scaring me."

"I'm fine." Elli said for the umpteenth time that day. She walked past him, going to the bar for a beer. Once she had one, she looked down at the ice, watching the guys warming up. Elli knew she could probably pick Shea out of a crowd of a million, and hated the way her eyes drifted right to him as he lined up his shot before shooting the puck in the net.

"Honey, aren't you cold? I should go get you a new jersey." Bryan said as he came to stand beside her, Elli shook her head. It would be a cold day in hell before she would ever wear another Assassins' jersey with someone else's name and number on the back.

"I don't want another jersey."

"I can have it say your name, darlin'."

Elli looked up at him, "That's not the reason I don't want another jersey, I'm fine."

"So you say; I know you're not darlin'."

"I am," Elli emphasized. Bryan let out a frustrated breath as Elli continued to watch the guys.

"Who did you sell your seats to tonight?"

"I don't know; someone on StubHub."

Bryan nodded, "You know if you don't want them anymore, I can give them to someone else."

Elli shook her head, "I do want them, I just wanted to sit with you for a while."

"Gracious me, you're lyin' your tail off," Bryan said with a laugh, Elli looked up at him.

"I am not."

"Well I don't want you to sit up here anymore, you depress me," he gave her a cheeky grin as he grabbed a hot dog off the buffet.

"Fine, I'll sit down in my seats next game."

"Sure you will."

"I will! And how am I depressing you!"

"You're a walking zombie darlin', it's sad how much your hurtin' and won't try to make it better or get the hell over him. Do you think he's okay? Cause I sure don't."

"I ain't no zombie, I'm fine!"

"So I've heard," he said with a shake of his head.

"And why don't you think he's okay?"

"Because he isn't! I saw him the other day and he's a mess, he couldn't even look me in the eye Elli; he probably thinks I think he is the sorriest piece of shit, especially after-" Bryan stopped, and Elli cut him a look.

"Especially after what?"

Bryan took a bit out of his hot dog, holding up a finger for Elli to wait. She knew he was buying himself some time, and it drove Elli crazy! He took more time than needed to swallow before saying, "I'm sure he knows you told me what happened."

"So? You do think that, don't you?"

Bryan looked deep into Elli's eyes, "Honey, if I believed he did what you said he did, do you really think he would still be on my team?"

Elli's heart came up into her throat, "But I thought you kept him because I asked you not to trade him!"

"No baby girl, I'm hoping, praying really that you'll come to your senses, but honey I don't know how much time you have to do that."

"What?"

"He hasn't signed his contract, he's a free agent, and I heard he has offers. He could leave at anytime."

"Oh," Elli said as her world crashed around her. Why it felt like her chest was seizing up, really didn't make sense to her, shouldn't she be happy he might be leaving? Maybe then she could get over him. "If he leaves he leave, I don't care either way." Elli made herself say as the arena went dark. With that the conversation was over, and Elli was glad.

Because if they kept talking, she was sure that her Papa would see right through her.

Which he probably already did.

Elli was finally hanging up all her clothes from the many bags that she had drugged in from her living the next afternoon when the text came.

Are you going?

It was from Harper.

Elli wiped her face, clearing the tears away. She had been hanging the clothes that she had bought when they were in Boston, and each outfit that Shea had picked out, brought a whole new round of tears.

She ignored the text, and continued to hang the clothes she would probably never wear in her closest as she listen to her 'break up' playlist she had made. It consisted of a bunch of disgusting, sad ass country music, that wasn't helping Elli's notion to move on at all. When her phone went off again, Elli rolled her eyes picking it up.

Come on Elli, please.

She continued to ignore the text, if Harper wanted to give up their friendship because Elli wasn't over Shea yet, and didn't plan on making amends with him, well forget her then. As she unzipped the dress bag that held three of the most gorgeous Gucci dresses money could buy, Elli's stomach heaved. Shea had loved all of them, saying she should wear them when they went on their vacation that summer. She ran her hand through her hair, God she missed him and just the thought that he might be leaving hurt her even more than she expected. He had told her so long ago, that if they weren't together then he would have no reason to stay in Nashville. Which he didn't. Elli was nothing important; she hadn't heard from him in weeks, not that she would have answered anyways, but still. He was probably over her, moved on.

But what if he wasn't.

Elli glanced down at the phone, watching it blink and beep, waiting for her to answer it.

What if he wasn't over her, and was just waiting for her to make a move, to come back to him. What if Harper was right? What if Papa was right? Could she really truly get over him if he left without her knowing if he still loved her? If he still wanted to be with her? Why did it matter though? She made her bed, she broke up with him, didn't give him the time of day, even though deep in her heart, she still felt he would never hurt her.

She slammed her hands against her head, wishing she wasn't such a basket case. What the hell was she supposed to do? Her phone beeped again, and she glanced down at the message from Harper.

I know you still love him. Please, come.

She couldn't believe it, but she picked up the phone.

Okay, When and where?

After hitting send, she could actually breathe. She was done trying to act like she was okay, that everything was fine. Because it wasn't, and until she knew what he felt, she would never be able to get over him.

Chapter 32

Beep.

Shea, this is crazy! I haven't seen from you in two months! Two fucking months! I am over it! I don't know where the hell you're staying but let me tell you this, you have thirty minutes before I call mom and tell her the truth, that your fucking MIA!!!!!!!

Beep.

Shea, its Jill Mancina. I had another fax about buying your house. I know you said before that it wasn't for sale, but are you even living in it? I mean I'm just looking out for your best interest but don't you think a house that beautiful should be lived in? Please call me back.

Beep.

Adler, Damon Thompson, you know the agent of yours that you won't return calls too. Just wanted to let you know that New York wants you, so does Boston, at double the rate Nashville is paying you. We gotta sign something buddy, I don't know what you're thinking but it would be nice if you called me. Soon. Please.

Beep.

Unky Shea? Its Ryan, I was calling because I haven't seen you in a really long time, and I miss you, a lot. The only time I see you is on TV and at the games, and you don't even come see us in the box. Mommy says I can't say much because it's your phone mail but I love you Unky.

Beep.

Shea? Its Jakob, do I need to come get you? Call me please, don't be driving dude. I know you're drunk. Don't do anything stupid, please.

Beep.

Okay, having Ryan call you was kind of a low blow, but I'm desperate Shea, I'm worry about you, and I love you so much, please just call me. The emails saying your okay, aren't working for me. I'm hurting and I'm your twin, please. Call me. If not for me, for Ryan and Amelia. Ryan is having surgery in a couple day- okay that was low, it's not like its life threatening, just some tonsils, but please, call me. We all miss you.

Shea deleted all the messages, shutting off his phone since the blonde beside him needed more attention than the people that left him messages. Yeah, Ryan's message hurt, but Shea wasn't going to think of that. He was gonna take home, Sarah, no wait, Julie, Jackie, no, Savannah! That was her name.

"Shea, do I need to call Jakob?" Ramsey asked, Shea shook his head as Savannah kissed down his neck, running her hand down his thigh.

"No Ram, I'm good. Savannah here is going to take me home, right ba-girl."

Shea was drunk, extremely drunk, but even in his drunken state, there was no way he would call Savannah baby. Baby was….was *her*.

Savannah grinned up at him, "Oh yeah I am."

So off they went, drunkenly walking to her car. A sexy little crossfire, something a girl should be driving, instead of that damn truck *she* had. Savannah drove like a mad man, and Shea wished he had known that before he got in the car with her, but how was he supposed to do that when he had just met her.

When they finally arrived at his condo, she was wrapped around him like a straight jacket as he walked through the condo with her mouth glued to his neck. She ripped off his clothes, biting and sucking all over his chest as he laid her down on the bed.

"Wow, your pretty beaten up huh?" she asked looking over his chest, she had that same look the others had, the 'oh well, at least his face is hot' look.

"I do play hockey for a living." She grinned seductively as she ran her tongue up from his belly button to the middle of his chest.

"What's this?" she asked breathlessly as she held the pink diamond engagement ring that hung around his neck in her fingers. "It's pretty."

"It's my reminder to never fall in love again," he said before pulling it out of her fingers, so he could continue to kiss down her throat.

"Wow, that's intense."

"Yeah, it is," he answered back, as she ripped her shirt off, her large full breast there for his taking.

"So I'm guessing this is a onetime thing, huh?"

"Yeah," he said with an empty chuckle as he ignored her breast, kissing down her stomach, before pulling down her jeans and panties with one jerk. When he looked at her warm center, he saw that she wasn't a true blonde. What a disappointment. He fell back on his hunches, running his hands through his hair as she looked up at him.

What was he doing?

"Get out."

"Huh?" she asked looking up at him. He picked up her clothes, throwing them down on her chest as he got off the bed.

"Go, leave, I don't want you."

She gave him a maddening look as she hurried to get her clothes on, obviously embarrassed. As she parted, she screamed, "You probably wouldn't be good, anyway!"

He shook his head as she marched her skinny little, fake blonde ass through his condo. When the door slammed, he let out the breath he was holding.

That was the seventh girl that week that he had kicked out. There was something wrong with a man when he couldn't even sleep with a willing female. Something seriously wrong. Or maybe it was the voicemails he had gotten earlier, maybe that was what was fucking with him.

Who was he kidding?

He missed *her*.

He moved his finger over the ring that hung around his neck, something he did often when he was thinking of *her*. He knew wearing the ring around his neck was a little masochistic of him, but ever since he found it, while cleaning his truck out a week after she had left, he had put it on his chain. Wearing it as a reminder, because he never wanted to feel this way again. He never wanted to feel like his world was crashing around him and there was no one to hold it together. Not his mother, Jakob, not even Grace could help him at this point. The alcohol he consumed every night, didn't even help but it did numb the pain, and really that's all he could ask for at this point.

Shea was still so mad. Mad because she didn't believe him, mad because she wouldn't answer his calls, his pleads, his flowers, his gifts, nothing! She ignored him, making him feel like he was worthless. He gave her everything, he was totally devoted to her, didn't cheat, nothing, he loved only her, and this was the way she repaid him? By continuing to break his heart day after day because she wasn't with him.

Because she didn't loved him no more.

Shea didn't know what was more pathetic, the fact that he was alone and couldn't even fuck a simple female or that he didn't want anyone but her, because there was no way he could replace her.

No matter how hard he tried.

Their whole breakup still blew his mind, it had been ten weeks since it happen, and still every day he would replay the whole fight, still not understanding how she didn't realize that he had been played. Wondering why she threw all those things in his face, making shit up, knowing damn well she was wrong for it. He would never be with someone because of their money, didn't he tell her that so many times before.

Maybe not, maybe that's why she left him because he didn't tell her enough how much he loved her and only her. How her eyes would light up his day, how her kisses would stun him for weeks. How waking up beside her would start his day off right. How after talking to her, he wore a permanent grin for the rest of the day. How her smile made him believe that life was worth living. How he needed her kisses like he needed to breathe. Maybe he didn't tell her enough that she was the one.

What had he done wrong?

Why didn't she believe him?

He had once thought their love could overcome anything. Boy how wrong he was, he thought as he crumbled down onto the hardwood of his bedroom, holding on to the ring she was supposed to wear. Holding on to the dream he thought he had with her.

God, he was pathetic.

When Shea opened his eyes, he was staring at a pair of the same shoes *she* always wore. He followed the legs up, seeing that the shoes didn't belong to *her* but to his sister. A very angry sister. When she reared back and kicked him hard in the stomach, Shea let out a horrid gasp, clutching his stomach since she knocked the wind out of him.

"You stupid piece of shit, how dare you!" she screamed as she rear back to kick him again but he got a hold of her ankle before she made contact, pushing her back, so she landed on her ass, as he tried to get away.

"Crazy bitch! Who kicks their family!?" Shea said, getting up, and stumbling to the bathroom to promptly puke. As he expelled the contents from the night before, Grace stood above him, screaming at him.

"Who fucking doesn't call their only sister, their fucking twin for two months! Who puts a five year old boy through the pain of missing their favorite person! Who Shea! Oh yeah! You! So yes, I kick my family when they are fucking stupid!"

"Oh God, please shut up!" Shea said before continuing to puke, but that didn't stop Grace.

"Hell no I won't shut up! Do you know who I had to hear that you guys had broken up!? Elli, I called her because I couldn't get a hold of you. She couldn't even get out that you guys weren't together anymore she was crying so bad! What the hell did you do!"

"I'm going to puke on your shoes, if you don't fucking leave me alone," he warned, looking up at her as he wiped his mouth. She was enraged, ready to kill him probably.

"You puke on my Gucci shoes that Elli got for me and I will kick you in the fucking mouth."

Maybe he should take his chances puking on them since *she* did get then for her.

"Please Grace, leave me the hell alone."

"No, not tell you answer me."

"If you haven't noticed, I'm puking my brains out, and not really in the mood to talk."

Grace let out a shrilling laugh, sending chills down his spine.

"Oh I wonder why that is, oh let me guess because you're a drunk now! Oh yeah, I had to call Damon to get that information, then Jakob informed me that he has been taking care of you when you need a ride home, because you knew better than to call me!"

Shea rolled his eyes, crossing his legs as he sat on the cool tile.

"Where the hell have you been? I have staked out this condo for weeks and you haven't been here, why are you here today?"

"I've been staying at the house; I was here because I brought someone home last night."

He would never bring a woman that was not *her* in the house he had bought for them to live the rest of their lives in.

Never.

"Are you serious? Oh my God, what is wrong with you?"

"I'm heartbroken Grace, what do you want me to say?"

Grace just looked down at him, when the tears rushed down her cheeks; he had to look away because his own tears threaten to fall. Grace fell onto the floor beside him, wrapping her arms around him, pulling him into her lap like he was Ryan and she was gonna make it all better. Even though they both knew she couldn't.

"What happened Shea? Tell me."

The tears came hot and fast, falling down his cheeks as he explained the biggest failure of his life to the only person that got him.

Well the person other than *her*.

Shea sipped on his coffee while not making eye contact with Grace as they sat in the little country café outside of Nashville. He was still embarrassed with how he broke down in front of her. He hated crying, he felt so weak, so pathetic, but a day didn't pass without him shedding some tears over *her*. Grace didn't say anything as she picked at her BLT that she had order, while he opted only for the cup of coffee. His stomach was still a little upset.

Grace looked up at him, and gave him a small smile before saying, "So you haven't tried to go see her, like before?"

"Yeah, I did. Went to her house and she basically ignored me as she got into her truck and drove off."

"Maybe she didn't see you," Grace suggested.

"Wouldn't you see me if I was parked in front of the house, standing beside the truck with roses in my hand?"

She shrugged, "Yeah I would, but I love you."

"Are you saying Elli didn't? That our six months together was a lie?"

"No, that's that what I meant. Its just-"

"Don't," he said putting his hand up to stop her, "Don't try to explain yourself."

"I'm sorry Shea; I don't know what to say."

Shea nodded, sipping his coffee. He didn't know what to say either; he didn't know what to do. Sometimes he felt like going on wasn't worth it, because he knew he would never be happy again. *She* made him happy, and there was basically nothing he could do to get her back. God knew he had tried.

"Have you not run into her? Don't you see her at the games?"

Shea shook his head, "She doesn't come to the games anymore, and no I haven't run into her. Even with her working for the Assassins full time now, I still don't see her. I actually asked Melody one time where she was since she was doing the promotional shoots for one of the events that was happening. Melody said that she had said not to schedule her at the same time as me."

"Wow, Shea. It's crazy, I just don't understand. Doesn't she know you? You would never hurt her."

"I guess she didn't. I don't know."

They sat for a moment, not speaking as they collected their thoughts. Shea knew she wanted to scream at him some more, but seeing how bad he was hurting was keeping her from doing it. He also knew that he should apologize for his actions the last couple months, but he couldn't. What other way would he have dealt with the pain? Go around acting like he was fine, that nothing was wrong? He couldn't do that, he never hid his feelings. People knew when he was mad, hurt, or happy, so why would he apologize for the way he had been? He wouldn't.

"Do you want me to call her?"

"No," he said with a shake of his head, "Don't."

"Okay."

"What's done is done, she obviously doesn't want me."

"I just don't think it's done."

"Grace, what else needs to happen for you to know it's over?"

Grace sat for a moment; he understood she was trying to get her line of thoughts straight. She may not be as emotional as he was, but when he was hurting she was too. Shea could tell Grace was confused, not knowing what to say when she looked at him. They had never been here; never at rock bottom when it came to someone he loved. Never at the point to where if Shea didn't change the way he had been living the past two months, he might lose everything.

When Grace looked up at him and he saw the tears in her eyes again, he felt as if Grace had kicked him in the gut again.

"I think it will be done when you decide on where you are playing next year."

He nodded, "Yeah, you are right."

"Because as long as you stay here there's always the chance you'll see Elli."

"I know."

"Do you want to leave?"

Shea looked up at her, looking deep into her eyes. Shea could see that she did not want him to go, and he knew that, he knew that if he ever tried to leave, Grace might uproot the whole family to come, but could he stay there? Could he stay in the place that with every turn, everything reminded him of *her*.

"I don't want to leave you," Shea answered since he didn't want to hurt her, plus it was the truth.

"But you do want to leave." Grace added for him, they shared a long emotional look before a single tear went down Grace's cheek, making it hard for him to breathe.

"I don't know."

When Shea entered the Assassins locker room, eyes followed him as he made it to his locker. He glanced at his name plate with his picture on it before sitting down on the bench in front of his locker. When he looked up, everyone's eyes moved away, he guessed it was because they didn't want to make eye contact with him. It wasn't like he didn't know why, he knew. Shea was aware that the team didn't like him much anymore that they continued to wonder why Shea was still the captain after not showing up to practice, or promotional shoots. Or why he was still captain when he didn't even rally the guys anymore, it was Jakob that did that.

Jakob had done a lot since the break up. Between cleaning up his puke, carrying him home from bars, and trying his best to clean up the mess *she* had left, Shea couldn't ask for a better best friend. He was a good man, someone that Shea would forever keep in his heart when he left Nashville, not that he had made that decision or anything. He would need to make the decision soon though, between Damon and Bryan Fisher, he was running out of time. They wanted answers, answers he didn't have.

When Jakob walked into the locker room, Shea's team mates greeted him like he was the captain, not that it bothered Shea much. He probably did deserve the title more than Shea did. Jakob wasn't a future mental patient, he was doing great. With a ring on Harper's finger and a baby in her belly, Jakob was on cloud nine, while Shea was trying to find someplace to crawl to and die. Jakob's happiness actually made Shea sick. He was so jealous of Jakob that he was disgusted with his self. He should be happy for his best friend, not wish the man was down in the dumps like him.

But hey, misery loves company.

"I see you made it," Jakob said under his breath as he sat down beside Shea, slipping off his shoes.

"Yeah, I was with Grace this morning."

"Good. I'm glad, and will excuse the fact that you weren't at practice."

"Thank you captain," Shea said sarcastically, receiving a glare from Jakob. They didn't say much else to each other as they started to suit up.

"Are you going to make it tonight?"

Shea looked over at Jakob, with his eye brows raised. "What?"

"The last time we played here, you had that-"

"I'm fine Jake, I've prepared myself," Shea said irrupting Jakob from telling the whole locker room his business.

The last home game they played, Shea hadn't prepared his self for the pain that came. When he skated out and saw that *she* wasn't there in her regular seats again, Shea had to leave the ice because he couldn't keep it together. The first time she wasn't there he wrote it off as her needing time to heal, even the second and third time and even the seventh, he thought nothing about it, but the last time he went out and she wasn't there. He lost it. Why it took eight times for him to realize that she wasn't going to be sitting there was way above his comprehension, but it hurt him bad.

"Okay good." Jakob said, with a nod of his head as he started to lace up his skates, "Have you talked to Damon? He called me again today."

"No, I'll call him tomorrow."

"Have you made a decision yet?"

Shea shook his head, "No."

"Well if it's worth anything, I vote you stay here. Just saying," Shea smiled weakly over at him, and Jakob returned the smile with a bigger one, "I don't want to play without you, and I can't leave. Harper would flip."

"I know."

"You know with her running the studio and with the house," Jakob continued. Shea didn't want to seem rude but hearing about Jakob's perfect life was not what he wanted at the moment.

"I know dude," Jakob looked over at Shea nodding before going back to lacing his skates, "I don't know what I'm doing."

"Okay."

They were silent again as they continued to suit up. All Shea could think about was if he was really ready to skate out on that ice, knowing he would not see *her*. He wished like hell, he would go out on the ice and she would be sitting there, grinning. With her hot dog and beer, a number six on her cheek, and his jersey on her beautiful body. God, how he wished for that. How if he could, he would go back in time. Not take Victoria with him to get *her* engagement ring, go alone, because he knew that if he had left that crazy bitch at home, he would be engaged right now, living in their house together, being happy.

But that was all a dream, this was his realty.

"Are you still going to the event tomorrow?" Jakob asked knocking him out of his dream land and back to real life.

"Yeah, I gotta get back to the way I was, starting with practice in the morning and the event tomorrow night," Shea answered with a nod, Jakob smirked over at him.

"Good, I feel good about tomorrow."

Shea didn't know what the hell there was to feel good about but whatever; Jakob was a weird dude sometimes.

When Shea was fully dressed, he got up, and headed towards the hall that would lead to the entrance to the ice. He grabbed his stick, and with every step the roar of the crowd got louder. This is what he loved; hockey is what always loved him. He was good at it, he loved it. Why couldn't it be enough? When he stepped on the ice, his eyes immediately went to her seats. Two older guys sat there, both pointing at the opposite team, and for the love of hockey they didn't even have Assassins' jerseys on, but Duck ones.

Shea was sure that the tightness in his chest was from the fact that she had sold her tickets to Duck fans, and not because she wasn't sitting there.

Who was he kidding?

When Shea's phone alarm when off the next afternoon, he rolled over, turning it off. He moved to his back, looking up at the vaulted ceilings of the room that they would never share. He figured the nap would do him some good after the vagarious practiced he had that morning, but he probably needed to sleep for the nap to help. With a huff, he got off the blown up mattress and headed into the bathroom to take a shower. He really needed to bring his things over from the condo, the damn blow up mattress was doing hell on his back, and he missed sleeping in his bed.

As Shea washed his body, he knew he wouldn't be able to bring that bed over to the house to sleep in, because of the same reason he couldn't sleep with a female in that bed. She had slept in that bed with him for months, they made loved in that bed. Even after kicking the females out of the condo, he always slept on the floor or on the couch. The bed held to many memories, and he couldn't do it. So Shea decided he needed to go shopping for a new bed the next day.

After doing his hair, he looked himself over. His playoff beard was growing in nicely; it was probably the only thing that was doing good in his life. Last year he placed fifth on the list for best beard, he was hoping for first this year. Hey, he didn't have much to look forward to in life right now. After putting on his suit, and tying up his chucks he was ready to go. Even though he'd rather stay home, he knew he had to go.

So he went.

Walking into the Ronald McDonald House event wasn't easy. It wasn't that Shea didn't love the program, he did, but he didn't want to be there. He didn't want to suck up to the big heads, he didn't want to see his team mates that didn't like him much, and he definitely didn't want to see Bryan Fisher, seeing him always made Shea want to break out in hives. Shea knew Bryan could see that he was hurting by just looking in his eyes. Shea hated that, he hated people knowing he was weak, but he just couldn't put on the 'everything is fine' act.

Shea wanted to drop off his donation and leave, but he couldn't. He had to put on a smile, act like life was grand, and he had to entertain his date. Some country singer Damon had hooked him up with, Audrey Lynn. She was nice, Shea guessed. Quiet, sweet, but not what he wanted. The big blonde hair, deep brown eyes, huge breast and small waist was not his thing anymore. No matter how hard he tried.

Audrey hung on Shea's arm in her long yellow gown, that accentuate her breast, with a grin so large, that he was blinded by her perfect white teeth. Audrey's teeth made Shea miss *her* teeth, the way the front one bent into the other one always drove him mad. It was crazy how he missed even the simplest things about *her*. When Shea saw Jakob, he put on a smile, but it promptly fell when he saw the look of horror on Jakob's face.

"Jake, are you okay?"

"I didn't know you were bringing someone," Jakob said looking at Audrey before looking behind him.

"Yeah, this is Audrey Lynn, Audrey my best friend Jakob." Audrey smiled, shaking his hand as Jakob looked around.

"Nice to meet you," Jakob mumbled before stopping and looking off to the side. Shea followed his gaze, and when his eyes met with the same green eyes he had been missing the past two months, he took in a sharp breath.

"Elli."

Elli stood in a long shinny purple gown that had rhinestones lining the low dipped front; it was the dress she bought in Boston. He had picked it out for her. Her beautiful green eyes were wide, filling with tears as seconds turned into minutes while they stood with their gazes locked. He couldn't look away though; she had lost weight, a lot of it. As he took in every single detail of her, the dark circles under her eyes, the sullen look on her face, she looked as bad as he did, but he still thought she was beautiful. Shea wondered if she was here to see him. Was this his chance?

Shea took a step towards her, but she shook her head before turning and taking off towards the exit.

"Elli! Wait!" Shea called as he tried to get by the hundreds of people that stood in his way. Shea received dirty looks as he pushed and moved past people, almost knocking over a waiter that held a platter of champagne, but he didn't care. He had to get to her. When he made it outside the arena, Elli was gone. He took out his phone, pushing on her icon, before putting it up to his ear. It surprised the hell out of him when her voice ranged through the phone.

"What Shea?"

"Elli, come on talk to me," he said pinching the bridge of his nose, "Let's meet up, talk."

"No Shea, I came here thinking that maybe I was wrong, maybe I needed to see you to prove to myself that we can work it out, because I'm not over you but God I was wrong!"

"Baby, you aren't wrong, we need to talk, please, come back."

"No, I'm done Shea, you've moved on, now I need too," she yelled into the phone, when he heard her take in a shaky breath, he knew she was crying. "You've moved on, while I've been a mess for the last two months, but no more."

"Elli I haven't-"

"No, I'm done. Don't you ever call me again, if you see me, act like you don't, cause you are dead to me Shea Adler. Dead."

When the line went dead, Shea let out a frustrated yell, throwing the phone into the street before sliding down the wall till he was sitting; his legs sprawled out in front of him. Shea cradled his face in his hands, listening to the traffic drive by while quiet sobs ripped through his body.

Why wouldn't she listen to him?

Why couldn't he catch a break when it came to Elli?

All Shea could do was ask *why?*

Chapter 33

When Elli arrived home, she stomped through her house, ripping off one of the most expensive dress she had ever bought, throwing it against the wall before throwing on a tee and going back into the foyer of her house. She had been torturing herself, leaving picture of that asshole up on her walls so that every time she passed by them, he would be fucking grinning at her! Elli's heart would break a little more each time she passed the picture because she couldn't put her pride aside and go to him! Go and tell him that she loved him more than she needed to breathe.

But no more!

Elli ripped down every single picture of Shea, placing each one by the door. Taking down the signed jersey was probably the hardest, and heaviest, but she did it. Even through the tears that fell down her cheeks, she continued to de-Shea her house. She had too. If she was gonna move on like he had, she was going to have to get rid of anything the reminded her of him. When she was done, a mound of things sat beside her door, staring back at her.

Elli closed her eyes, letting the tears leak out her eyes and down her cheeks as horrid sobs raked through her body. Elli never thought de-Shea-ing her house was gonna hurt so bad, but it had to happen.

It had too.

When Elli woke up the next morning, she went through her usual morning routine. As she walked through her house, Adler bounced beside her, ready to go out. When she reached the foyer and saw the mound of things she had piled up the night before, it was as if her legs gave out from underneath her, and she crumbled onto the ground, bawling as she stared at Shea's beautiful face that was staring back at her.

Adler came over to her nudging his way into her lap. Elli needed the comfort, so she wrapped her arms around her oversized pup, crying into his thick fur. Elli let the tears fall, soaking her poor dog's fur, not that she thought he minded. He would probably cry if he could, Elli knew he missed Shea, probably as much as she did. When she was done crying, she stood up, letting Adler out before sitting on the waiting chair that sat in front of the front windows. Her eyes moved along all the things that piled up so high against the wall, and felt like things wouldn't get better till they were gone, but she couldn't just throw them away.

It took about two seconds before Elli knew what to do with them. All she had to do was have the balls to go give them to him.

"Elli, it was so good to hear from you," Grace said as she held the door open, letting Elli in. Seeing Grace hurt as much as it did seeing Shea the night before, Grace looked so much like Shea that it was almost as if she was staring into Shea's eyes. She remember when she thought her life wouldn't go on without seeing Shea's family, that how it would kill her not being able to see them when she wanted and it had. She had missed Grace, James, Ryan and Amelia like she had missed Shea. There was a point in time when she felt that they were her family too, but that was ten weeks ago.

Now she was just another one of Shea's ex's, a notch in his bed post, a total loser.

When her eyes started to water up, Elli took in a deep breath, looking down at her heels.

"Yeah, um, every things in the truck," Elli said, mindlessly messing with the bottom of her shirt, she couldn't look Grace in the eyes, it hurt too much.

"James will get everything, come into the kitchen with me for a bit, we'll have some tea while he unloads."

"Oh well, it shouldn't take long," Elli said as Grace started walking towards the kitchen. Grace stopped, looking over her shoulder at Elli. Elli wasn't sure but she swore that she saw tears in Grace's eyes.

"Are you really going to run out on me Elli? I haven't seen you in months." Grace was guilt tripping Elli, and she knew it, but she followed Grace anyways into her spacious kitchen. What would it hurt to catch up for a minute or so?

When Elli saw Ryan, her heart got caught in her throat. She hoped he would have been at school, but nope, there he was grinning at her. Ryan popped up, running towards her, wrapping his small little arms around her waist, almost doing Elli in. Elli bent down some, taking the boy in her arms, hugging him tightly.

"Ms. Elli, I've missed you so much!"

"Oh Ryan, I've missed you buddy, what are you doing home?"

"They took my tonsils out! So I get to eat ice cream and lay around with mommy and daddy all day!" he said in his rambunctious five year old way. Elli had to smile at him; he was just so damn cute and she had missed him so.

"Oh my, are you alright?"

"I am! I'm strong just like my Unky, is he with you?"

The air rushed out of Elli, causing her to stop for a minute to try to breathe, he looked up at her with his innocent eyes, waiting for an answer. Elli slowly shook her head, "No sweetie, he's not."

Ryan's little face scrunched up as he looked up at her, "Have you seen him? I haven't seen him in so long, and I just want to see him."

Thankfully Grace swooped in, taking Ryan in her arms as she walked out the kitchen, cooing something about Shea coming to see Ryan soon. Why hadn't he been by to see Ryan? What the hell is wrong with him? Ryan needed him.

Selfish ass.

Ryan was a just a kid, a baby and knowing that Shea couldn't even come see him caused Elli to be so disgusted with him that angry tears threaten to fall down her cheeks.

When Elli realized she wasn't the only one in the room, she met eyes with James. He gave her a half grin as he walked towards her, wrapping her up in his arms.

"Hey."

"Hey James, how are you?"

"Good, better than you I'm guessing."

Elli nodded as the consent ache in her chest got worst. When Elli was in Boston she had bonded so much with James, and the fact that she hadn't seen or spoken to him in the last couple months made her just as big of a selfish ass as Shea was. Elli was more a bitch though, how could she intertwine herself with these people and then just complete forget about them. How dare she? They deserved better.

"I think my stuffed wolf fish is better than I am." James chuckled, his arm still around her shoulders.

"We miss you. You can still come see us you know?"

Elli nodded, feeling worst than she did two minutes ago, "I know," she said as she swallowed.

"Jenna and Mark are coming in next week; maybe we all can do dinner. Shea will be out of town if they win tomorrow."

"Which they will," Elli said as James nodded in agreement, "Give me a call, we'll see okay?"

"Okay," James said as Grace came back into the room.

"James, can you get everything out of Elli's truck?"

"Sure can," he said walking towards her, placing a kiss on her cheek before leaving the kitchen.

"Have a seat, Elli. I'll pour us some tea."

Elli did as she was asked, pulling out the large chair before settling in it. She watched as Grace moved through the kitchen, gathering the cups, sugar, and spoons before coming to the table, laying everything down for them. Nothing was said as they made their teas, they didn't even make eye contact.

Finally Elli couldn't take it no more and said, "How have you been?"

"Good, Amelia is finally sleeping through the night," they shared a smile since that was one of the first things they talked about so long ago, "Ryan is doing wonderful in school, James is working a lot and so am I."

"Good," Elli said, and she meant it. "Why hasn't Ryan seen Shea?" Elli blurted out, Grace shrugged her shoulders as she swirled her spoon in her cup.

"I'm not really sure, Shea's been taking time to his self I guess," Grace said before sharing a look with Elli that took Elli's breath away. What was she supposed to make of that? Time to his self? For what? "How are you doing, Elli?"

"That's a loaded question, Grace. You know that."

Grace smiled, taking a sip of her tea, "Elli there was a time when I was convinced you would be my sister, so yeah it may be a loaded question, but I want to know."

"For you or for him?"

"That's not fair, I care about you."

"Yeah but you care about Shea more, and that's fine." Elli said warming her hands from the cup she was holding, "I'm fine Grace, I'm starting a new chapter in my life, and I have to move on."

Sadness filled Grace's eyes, "Why Elli? He told me what happen; you honestly don't believe he kissed your sister do you?"

"It wasn't the first time Grace."

"What?"

"When I was in Tampa, a girl at the bar kissed him, and he didn't stop. He said it was cause the girl sucked his lips off and I believed him, but when I saw him with Victoria," Elli shook her head, "I still have nightmares about it. She swears up and down he kissed her from what my mother says, and he says she kissed him. So I just cut them both out of my life."

"And you okay with that?"

"Oh course not, I miss him every day, but what am I supposed to do?"

"Talk to him maybe?"

Elli shook her head, letting out an aggravated sigh, "I can't do what I did with the guy I was with before Shea, I always took him back, always accepted his apologies. I can't do it this time, no matter how hard it hurts."

"Elli, he loves you, so much."

"No, if he still loved me he wouldn't have been out with some woman last night."

Grace pinched the bridge of the nose, closing her eyes as she let out a long breath, "What woman?"

"I don't know some blonde. I went to the event last night knowing I would see him there; I was hoping that seeing him would-, hell I don't know what I was hoping it would do. I just wanted to see him," a tear leaked from her eye, rolling down her cheek, "I just missed him, and to be honest, I'm not over him, no matter how much I say that I am, no matter how many times I say I'm fine. I'm not." More tears ran down her cheeks, before Grace wrapped her arms around Elli, holding her close as they both sobbed.

They stayed liked that for a long time. Elli didn't realize how much she missed being hugged by someone again, even if it wasn't the arms she longed for, it still warmed her from head to toe. The only reason they parted, Elli thought, was because Grace's phone rang. Grace pulled back, grabbing her phone explaining that it might be the pharmacy about Ryan's meds. Elli knew by the look on Grace's face, that it was Shea.

"Hey, um, just having some tea, what are you doing? Oh, okay, yeah, um, he's awake, yeah. Sure, okay love you, bye."

Elli finished her tea before standing up and taking the cup to the sink, "He's on his way over?" Elli asked as she moved her fingers through her hair, pulling it up in the pony tail.

"Yeah," Grace said standing up, "Why don't you stay? James and I could leave with Ryan, and you know, maybe it will help."

Elli shook her head, "No Grace, he needs to spend time with Ryan, not see me," she said before walking up to Grace, enveloping her in a tight hug. "I'll come see you guys, I promise."

When she pulled back, Grace was still crying. "Good, but I wish you'd stay."

"I can't."

"Please."

"No, I can't. The faster I get over him the easier my life will be." Elli said as she made her way out the kitchen and down the hall to Ryan's room. He smiled up at her when she entered; he had on Elli's old jersey, along with the stick Shea had signed for her when he first got signed to the Assassins.

"I'm leaving buddy, I just wanted to say bye."

"Okay Ms. Elli, thanks for all my new stuff," he said before throwing his little arms around her neck, hugging her tightly. "Will I see you soon?"

"Sure darlin', maybe I'll come when Grandma and Grandpa get here."

"Awesome!" he said punching his fist in the air. Elli stood, and with a wave she left. Grace stood at the end of the hall and when Elli reached her, they hugged once more before walking towards the door.

"Are you sure you can't stay?" Grace asked again, hope filling her eyes.

"I'm sure," Elli said, walking down the steps, "But I'll be back."

"Okay, bye Elli."

"Bye Grace," Elli said with a wave, before getting into her truck and driving off. The new chapter in Elli's life might not include Shea, but it would include his family.

Elli swore to that.

When Elli got home, she cried, and cried before doing anything productive. There was a list of things she needed to do, but crying seemed like a better idea. Maybe she should have stayed, seen what Shea's reaction would have been. Would he of beg her for another chance? Would he ask why she was there? Or would he just take her in his arms, and kiss her senseless?

What would she have done if he had said or done any of them things?

The questions swarmed in her head as she turned on her laptop, checking her email. She deleted all the junk mail before coming to the one from her Papa.

Eleanor, you are not sitting with me tomorrow night, sit in your seats. I know the family will be up in the boxes, but I need pictures since this is the final game. When we win it we'll be going to the cup finals. Not that you don't know that, but still I better not see you anywhere but in your seats.

Love you.

Well shit.

"Was that Elli?" Shea asked when Grace answered the door. Grace stood there for a minute, before nodding her head. "What the hell was she doing here?" he asked as he came inside, still staring his twin down.

"She came to drop off some things to Ryan."

Shea's eye brows drew together, and his heart continued to hammer against his chest. He had missed her by a matter of seconds. She pulled out as he was pulling in. When he heard a pair of little feet running up the hall, he turned to see his special little guy with a biggest grin on his face and the biggest jersey on.

"Unky Shea!" he yelled running to him, jumping into his arms. Shea caught him eagerly, nuzzling his nose in Ryan's hair, taking in his scent, peanut butter and strawberries. When he pulled back grinning at Shea, Shea gave him a loud smacking kiss on the cheeks.

"How is my buddy doing?"

"Good, I've missed you so much. Where have you been?"

"Been busy Ryan, I'm sorry."

"It's okay, you see the new jersey Ms. Elli brought over, you should see all the things she bought me, they're awesome!"

Shea cut Grace a look, and of course she wasn't looking at him, "Ms. Elli came by to see you?"

"Yup, and she said when Grandma and Grandpa come next week, she'll come! Isn't that great?"

"Sure is bud," Shea said painfully as he put Ryan on his hip, walking with him towards his room.

"You should come too," Ryan gushed.

"Probably can't bud, got the finals next week."

"You should try."

"Yeah, I should," Shea agreed as they walked down the hall. When he saw all Elli's things from her foyer, he felt like the last nail to his coffin was nailed in. Elli wasn't kidding when she said she was done with him. Maybe he didn't fight hard enough, but he did everything short of breaking into her house and taping her to a chair to make her listen. He sent flowers for weeks, called at least three times a day, sent texts every hour it seemed. He fought, he tried, but what else could he of done?

After spending the afternoon with Ryan, Shea played dolls with Amelia. It hurt to see how much Amelia had changed in the last two months. Ryan was basically the same, a little taller, but not Amelia. She was taller, had longer hair, and she was talking so much more. How did so much change in two months, and how could he have missed it?

When he made his way back into the kitchen, Grace was sitting at the table. She had her hand under her chin, the other tangled in her long black hair as she leaned on her elbow. He watched her for a moment, she was so beautiful, and he was aware of what she was thinking.

"Amelia is talking a lot more," he said pulling out the chair that was across from her, and lowering himself into it. She looked up at him, nodding her head.

"She is, James says just like her mommy." Shea smiled, nodding his head. They all knew how much Grace liked to talk. "How are-"

"What did she say Grace?" Shea said cutting her off, he didn't mean too but he didn't think he could wait much longer to know. He felt like the biggest ass since the whole time he played with Ryan and Amelia, all he was thinking about was what Elli told Grace.

"What do you mean?" Grace asked innocently.

"Come on now, I know she said something."

"Just that she was doing okay."

"Liar, tell me what she said."

They shared a long intense look before Grace cracked, like Shea knew she would, "She said she went last night to see you because she missed you and that she isn't okay or fine, she just tried to act like she is. But when she saw you with some blonde, seeing that you moved on, she figured she needed too."

"Is that why she brought her stuff over?"

"She said she didn't want to give it to goodwill."

"Okay, so she brings it over here, knowing I'll see it?"

"I don't know what she was thinking Shea; she just wanted Ryan to have your things."

Shea was getting more pissed by the minute, "Pack it all up, Ryan can't have it."

"Shea! That's not right."

"No, I want her stuff because I've had enough. She is gonna listen to me, I don't want anyone else but her, I'm not over her, and she's gonna know it," he said as he stood, slamming the chair against the table.

"Where are you going?"

"Home."

"Home? I thought you were gonna go talk to her!" Grace said, following him from the kitchen to the door.

"I need to get my speech out right; I'll get her tomorrow before the game. I know she'll be there, from what Harper said she has been sitting with Bryan all this time."

"Oh," Grace said as he gave her a kiss on the cheek, "So you're going to do this in front of your boss?"

Shea nodded, "If I have too, but she will know tomorrow that I love her and I haven't given up on us."

Shea felt good the next morning, he worked out with Jakob, went to have lunch before going home for a nap, all with the confidence that by the end of the night not only would he be going to the Stanley Cup Finals, but he would have Elli back in his life. For good. He was done with all this nonsense, hell he was done with it two months ago, but she wasn't getting away anymore. He would tell her everything he felt, then he would kiss her. He knew that when their lips met everything would be okay. She would feel all the love he had been holding onto just for her. He just knew it.

The whole truck ride to the arena, he was ready, even after parking the car and going in the back way to the locker room. He was ready. When he enter the locker room, some of the team was getting ready, one being Phillip Anderson. Shea and Phillip had always butted heads, especially after him hitting on Elli when they were in Tampa but being in the mood he was, he smiled at Phillip, and when Phillip looked behind him, Shea guessed to see if anyone else was there, he said, "Ready for tonight Anderson?"

"Yeah Adler, you?"

"Always ready," Shea said confidently as he walked towards his locker, throwing off his clothes. As he dressed he kept telling himself that Elli wasn't over him, and that she missed him. That had to mean she still loved him. It took forever for her to say she loved him, so he knew that she wasn't over it. She couldn't be. After being fully dressed, he stood putting on his shoes. Members of the team were starting to fill up the locker room and Shea smiled and nodded towards each of them as he left the locker room heading for the elevator that took him up to the company boxes.

Shea walked with all the confidence in the world as he made him way to Bryan Fisher's box, but when he got closer, he became nervous, jerky even with every step. He saw the door to the box, and took a deep breath, before walking in unannounced. What he didn't expect was to have fourteen pairs of eyes gawking at him. Shea was expecting just Elli and Bryan, not the whole family. Shea took a deep breath, swallowing loudly as he moved from each face, trying to find Elli.

But she wasn't there.

"Adler, everything okay?"

Disappointment raked through Shea's body. Where was she?

"Yeah, um, is Elli here?" Shea found himself asking even though he knew the answer.

"No and if she was, you wouldn't be seeing her. What in God's name are you doing here anyways?" Olivia sneered, "You are not welcome anywhere near my family."

"Livi please," Michael said, moving in front of her, "Shea, son, she isn't here."

Which meant Shea wouldn't be able to see her till the end of the game, if he could even find her. Last time he went to her house, she wouldn't even answer the door.

Shea nodded slowly, "Well thank you, you guys enjoy the game."

Shea turned, going for towards the door when he met eyes with Victoria. Anger filled him as he stared her down, but she wouldn't look him in the eyes. "You have a lot of gall sitting up here Victoria."

"Don't you talk to her!" Olivia yelled as Victoria looked up at him.

"Do you know what I've been through? Do you know how much I ache for her and she won't even speak to me? You did this to me, and because of that I will always hate you."

Victoria had tears well up in her eyes as she looked up at him; she started shaking her head, her mouth trying to form words.

"Leave my daughter alone!" Olivia dug her nails into Shea's jersey pulling him back, he turned looking down at the Elli's mother, and held back the rage that was filling him as she screamed up at him, "You are a low life, nothing but a piece of crap! You would never deserve my daughter and the fact that y'all aren't together is not my baby's fault, it's your own! You're a playboy, the man that sleeps with anything that has legs."

"Olivia, stop!" Michael said, trying to pull Olivia back, but she kept screaming.

"You are nothing, even if Eleanor was here, what did you expect? For her to take you back? My daughter has more class than that, you thug! Get out of here, and never come back."

"Jesus woman, shut the hell up, Mike, please get this woman!" Bryan said standing in front of her, and looking up at Shea.

"Son, please just go."

Shea nodded, sending one more enraged look at Victoria before leaving.

Well that sure did blow Shea's confidence all to hell.

Olivia Fisher's words played over and over again as Shea made his way down to the locker room. Why did she think he was a thug? Or a piece of shit? He was a good guy, he always treated Elli with all the respect in the world, and he loved her. It was like he was a zombie, going through the motions of putting on his skates. How was he supposed to play game seven of the semifinals when he was just told he was a low life, no good, piece of shit, thug? Oh, and that would never get Elli back?

"Shea, I know that look. Get it together man."

"I got it, Jakob," he said, looking up at the ceiling before taking a deep breath. He followed his team mates down the hall to the entrance to the ice still in a daze as his confidence continued to break with every word Olivia Fisher said. This was not going to be his best game and he knew it, which was extremely bad since this was the damn finals! What he needed was to see Grace, she would know what to say, what to do. Or better yet, he needed Elli. Elli would make this all better.

When he stepped on the ice, like always his eyes went straight to Elli's seats. There were people sitting there, so he looked always but then jerked his head back, because it was Elli.

With some guy.

The rage from earlier filled Shea from the inside out. He knew that if his gloves weren't on, his nails would be biting into his palm, he was clenching his fist so hard. With every glance at her, his body tensed. When she would lean into the dude, he felt his nostrils flare as his temper rose with every lap he did of the ice. His face was hot, his heartbeat hammering, he wanted to beat the living fuck out of the guy. Tear him limb from limb; smash his face in the ice.

Oh Shea wanted kill him.

Elli was his damn girl…will be his damn girl.

Shea moved the puck back and forth with his stick, watching as Elli laughed, acting as if he wasn't ten fucking feet from her! He wasn't thinking straight, he didn't even feel his self set up, he just pulled back, and the only thing he heard was the crack of his stick.

And then the shattering of the glass.

When Elli stood with glass falling from her lap, she glared at him as if she was about to come on the ice and kick his ass.

But all he could do was think was, *Hey, at least I got her attention.*

Chapter 34

"Are you freaking crazy!? You could have killed me!" Elli screamed, shaking off the glass. She was wearing them naughty wool shorts that drove Shea crazy. Not only were they unpractical in a hockey rink, they were too hot. Elli was so pretty, skinny, but pretty. God, he had missed her.

"Do you really think I would do something that could hurt someone I love!" Shea yelled back, the guy that sat beside Elli, stood up also shaking off some glass. That guy he would kill, but not Elli. "Whats up with this guy!"

"Why does it matter to you, you crazy ass!"

"Damn right I'm a crazy ass, you're trying to make me jealous!"

"Oh please! Like I care if I make you jealous!"

"You know you do!"

Elli gave him a 'whatever' kind of look before saying, "You're acting like an idiot!"

"Damn right, love does this to a person!" she shook her head, throwing her arms up in the air.

"I ain't going around breaking glass!"

"No, but you aren't eating, why the hell are you so skinny!"

Elli's eye brows drew together before she yelled, "Why the hell you drinking so much!"

Touché.

"Yeah, that's what I thought; don't give in less you can take Shea Adler," she said as she put her hands on her skinny little hips defiantly, "Now, what in God's name made you break that glass! I know you did it on purpose!"

"You are right I did! I wanted to get your attention!"

"Well you freaking got it! What do you want!"

Shea paused.

When he had planned to do this it was supposed to be in front of Elli and Bryan, not the whole damn arena. People stood all around Elli with wide eyes, Shea swore that he could hear a pin drop if he was to drop one. Everyone was zoned in on him and Elli, and for the first time while wearing his hockey jersey, he felt self conscious.

"Um, well, you see-"

"For the love of God! The next time you wanna go breaking some glass, at least be ready to say what you were gonna say!"

"Will you shut up for a minute damn!" Shea yelled back at her, damn she was a feisty little thing. Elli shook her head and pushed the guy that stood beside her down into his seat as she went to go by him.

"Elli, wait!" She turned, with an exasperated look on her face.

"What Shea?" Elli said, he could tell she was pissed, but she brought this onto herself, if she would have listen to him a long time ago, then he wouldn't have to resort to damaging property to get her attention. So excuse him if he didn't give two shits if she was pissed, he had something to say, damn it.

"I love you!" Shea blurted out, even though that wasn't what he wanted to say, not yet at least. Everyone around them 'awed' at the same time and his eyes fell shut. Damn it, he had this all planned. He was ready for this, he knew what he wanted to say, why wasn't it coming back to him? "I just love you Elli, so much. I've missed you so much these past two months. I've tried so hard to get you to listen to me because I know you still love me Elli. I know. If you didn't you wouldn't have came to the ball last night-"

"Lot of good that did me, seeing you with your new girlfriend and all."

Some people around her gasp, while others said 'oooo', God, how Shea wished they could be doing this somewhere private.

"She isn't my girlfriend, her name is Audrey Lynn, Damon asked her to go with me since I didn't want to go alone."

Elli rolled her eyes, "Whatever."

"No not whatever, I can't be with anyone else, I've tried, I won't lie to you, you know that but I have tried to be with other women, and I can't."

"Is that supposed to make me feel better Shea? Knowing that you have been with other women?"

"I said I haven't! And you're with some dude right now!"

"He's my assistant you idiot! Come on! Unlike some people I don't even have the desire to be with anyone else!"

"I was trying to get over you! And it didn't work. I was meant to walk on this earth with only you, I was meant to give only you every piece of me. I don't want anyone but you, I love you. I had this whole speech baby, I did, but just looking into them beautiful green eyes that make me think of when we laid in the fresh green grass for lunch so long ago, I can't think of anything but the fact that I love you."

Elli shook her head, looking down at the floor before looking up at him, "Shea, I used to believe them things, because I had felt the same way you do, but you made a fool of me. When I saw you with Victoria, it felt like a knife going into my heart, you knew I'm self conscious, and seeing you kiss her, my sister, my extremely beautiful skinny sister! How am I supposed to move on from that?"

"I didn't kiss her! She kissed me, I don't want her. I want you." Elli rolled her eyes, looking towards the ice as he went on, "You know what, for five years you were with a ball less son of a bitch that was terrible to you, and you believe every single wrong thing he put in that pretty little head of yours, then you go six years believing them things, not trusting anyone and then I come along. I have done nothing but love you to the fullest of my abilities. I have never cheated on you, I have never lied to you, I have been completely and utterly devoted to you and only you." Elli looked over to him, looking deep in his eyes as he went on, "But you can't believe me when I say that your sister set me up. That I didn't want her then, and I don't want her now. I want you, and only you. I don't know how many times I gotta tell you, but baby believe me. Please."

Elli's eyes filled with tears as she looked down at him, he closed his eyes, willing his self not to fall to his knees and beg, because the way she was looking at him, it wasn't looking as if it was going to go the way Shea wanted it too. Which would be Elli leaping into his arms and them skating off the ice wrapped in each other arms.

"I saw you," Elli said so quietly Shea almost missed it.

"She set me up baby, I promise you. Ask anyone, I love you."

Elli blinked once, causing a large tear to run over her cheek. He begged her with his eyes for her to come to him, he just needed her lips to touch his, she would know then, she had too.

"If you don't want him honey, I'll take him," someone said, but Elli and Shea didn't look anywhere but at each other. When she took a step forward, his heart jump into his throat, she believed him!

But when she turned abruptly and took off up the stairs, he felt like Grace had kicked him all over again.

People were yelling at Elli to go back as she ran up the stairs into the lobby of the arena. Running in three inch heels was a feat, but Elli was bound and determined as she ran towards Papa's box. Of course she had forgotten her purse, but luckily the security guard that was guarding the floor of Papa's box was the same guy she had brought some brownies too the week before.

When Elli entered the box, her whole family looked towards her from where they all were basically leaning out the box, probably trying to see what was going on down on the ice.

"Eleanor what in God's name was Adler doing?" Papa asked as he came towards her.

"Darlin' are you okay?" Michael asked, following behind Bryan.

"Crazy fool of a man, could have killed my baby girl." Olivia said, as everyone came towards Elli, but she didn't want anything to do with any of them.

When her eyes fell on Victoria, who was sitting at the bar picking at the hot dog that was in front of her, rage filled Elli from the top of her head to the tip of her toes. Victoria looked up and her eyes went wide. It was the first time in months they had seen each other, and all the hurt and pain from the last two months came full force at Elli, and she was ready for the much needed confrontation that was about to happen between the two sisters. Every step Elli took, Victoria's eyes got wider as she moved out the chair, going behind it.

When Elli reach her, she pushed the bar stool away, going toe to toe with Victoria. Since Elli was wearing her boots she was as tall as Victoria, and as she looked into the eyes of the person she grew up with, loved even when she was terrible to her, she felt nothing but repulsion.

"Did you kiss Shea?"

Victoria didn't say anything, as she tried to look everywhere but at Elli, "Answer me!"

"Eleanor, that's enough," Olivia said.

"I, um, I," Victoria started, "I never meant to hurt you," she finally got out, and Elli couldn't control herself. She had always dreamed of hitting Victoria, and the feeling of her hand connecting to Victoria's face was so damn fulfilling that Elli wanted to do it again.

"Eleanor!" Olivia yelled.

"You stupid bitch! How could you! How could you do that to me!?"

Victoria's hand came up over where Elli had just made contact as her eyes filled with tears. "Answer me! Why!? Why did you do it!?"

"It wasn't me, I didn't want too-" Victoria started but Elli's mother interrupted her.

"Victoria Ann that is enough, if Eleanor is going to resort to hitting, then there is nothing left to be said, come here honey," Olivia said with her arms wide for Victoria, but Bryan stopped her.

"No, you answer her Victoria. Now." Bryan's booming voice filled the room, and Victoria looked at him before looking back into Elli's eyes.

"I didn't want to Elli, I didn't."

"What are you talking about!"

"She made me do it," Victoria said looking over Elli's shoulder to her mother, everyone took in a sharp breath as Elli turned slowly to see her mother with wide eyes as Victoria continued, "She said that Shea wasn't good enough for you when he came to the house to ask daddy if he could marry you and told me I had to break y'all up."

"He wanted to marry me?" Elli gasped out, as Victoria went on.

"I didn't want to do it, but she threatened to cut my cards off, and you know I need my credit cards Elli. I never wanted any of this to happen, I may be crazy jealous of you, but I would never take your man, you know that, but I had no choice."

"You did this?" Elli asked her mother; Olivia stood a little straight, running her hands down the front of her suit jacket before she looked up at Elli with a patronizing smile on her face.

"Oh darlin' I did this for you, he isn't good enough for you."

"Olivia!" Michael gasped.

"Are you kidding me?" Bryan yelled.

"Who are you to say who is good enough for me?" Elli said ignoring everyone, staring down the person that had betrayed her.

"Honey he's trash, tattoos up his arms, dresses like a thug, he is not the man for my daughter."

Elli just shook her head, "How dare you?"

"How dare me? Honey its simple, I did it for you," Elli felt like she was gonna puke. Her own mother? "It was the same thing with Justin. I knew he was cheating on you from the beginning, the way he would hit on Victoria so intently, but Victoria wanted nothing to do with him cause he had been with you, and I'd be damn before I let a Yates leave this family, so I told him about all the money you were getting and just to wait it out with you, that you'd give him everything he wanted. I did it for you, for your happiness."

"He ruined me," Elli said in a shaky voice, "I am better without him."

"Now that isn't true. He was a good man."

"He hit me!" Elli screamed, causing Olivia to jump as the tears ran down Elli's cheeks, Elli had never told anyone about that but Harper and Shea. Bryan stood up from his seat as Michael took a step forward. God help Justin Yates if her papa or daddy ever saw him again.

"I doubt that," Olivia dismissed with a wave of her hand.

"He did, and Shea loved me, he treated me good but you sabotaged that? Using my sister as your pawn?"

"You are blowing this out of portion honey, stop."

Everyone was quiet for a moment as Elli looked at her mother in disgust. She couldn't believe it, she couldn't comprehend it.

"You ruined my chance at happiness. How dare you?"

"Like I've said before, I did it for you."

"I'm twenty eight years old! I don't need you! I have been with trash and Shea is not trash! He made me feel like the most amazing person in the world! He loved me! Unlike you!"

"Oh now that's just uncalled for. You know I love you."

"No, you don't. If you did, you wouldn't have done what you did."

"I stand by my word Eleanor Ray, I did it for you."

Elli shook her head slowly, tears gushing down her face. "You deliberately tried to hurt me, and we are done."

Elli heard Victoria take in a sharp breath as her daddy moved in front of Elli, "I don't even know you anymore," he said, Elli watched as her mother's eyes went wide.

"Now Michael honey, she's overreacting."

"How could you do this to her?" Michael said with a shake of his head, "That's our baby girl."

"I did it for her."

Michael slowly shook his head as he looked down at her with one of the scariest looks Elli had ever seen, "Leave," he whispered.

The room went eerily quiet as Olivia and Michael stared each other down. "You don't mean that."

"If he doesn't I do, now go on Olivia." Bryan said, standing beside his brother. "You aren't welcomed here anymore."

Olivia looked around the room, and Elli knew she had to see that everyone was disgusted with her. Liam and Noah were shaking their heads with their arms around Adina and Lauran, while Michael and Bryan looked at her like she was the biggest piece of shit floating in the Red River. With Olivia being who she was, Elli watched as she tipped her chin up, before storming out the room slamming the door behind her.

When Michael turned facing Elli with the saddest look on his face. "I'm so sorry darling," he said before wrapping his arms around her, holding her close to him.

"He wanted to marry me?"

Elli felt him nod his head as he moved his hand up and down her back, "He did."

"What did you say?" Elli asked.

"Yes, of course."

Elli started to sob loudly into her father's chest. She cried for the betrayal her mother had done, she cried because Victoria had fallen to her mother's threats, and she cried because she missed Shea more than anything. How could she be so stupid? Shea was right, she was making him pay for the things Justin had done to her. She was always looking for a reason to doubt Shea, not believe his word, and again, he was right when he said that he had always been true to her, because even with all her insecurities she knew he would never hurt her. So why did she believe the lie her mother set up? Why didn't she believe him when he said that he had been played? God would only know, but now Elli was paying the price for her stupidity.

When Elli finally calmed down, her father let her go and she moved towards the chair that over looked the ice. The game had already started and Shea was on the ice, hitting people so hard that Elli was convinced he would either hurt his self, or owe her Papa more money when he broke another sheet of glass.

Elli had never met such an amazing man. Shea was sweet, caring, devoted, compassionate, funny, and passionate, Elli could go on for hours describing him, she loved him so much. When she was with him she felt complete, he made her love herself something that she hadn't down since she was in high school. Elli had given him her heart, her soul and thought she would be with him forever. She knew Shea loved her, but when she saw Victoria and him together, she lost it. She felt like everything he had ever said to her was a lie, and without thinking she threw away the most amazing man she would ever meet.

Elli didn't deserve him, because even after all this time he still wanted her back. He still loved her, but could she swallow her pride and admit she was wrong? Admit that she was wrong to doubt him? As she watched him skate around, shooting the puck every chance he got, she thought about their relationship. They had their up and downs, but more ups than downs. Elli smiled as she thought back to the little things that made their relationship so spectacular.

Their joking banter with each other. The dinners they cooked together. The bubble baths they would share. The arguing over what to watch because he had seen Pride and Prejudice a hundred times in six months and he was done with the damn movie. He had lived it with her with her party and just thinking of that brought a grin to her face. The waking up in the middle of the night just to make sure he was still there, because sometimes it felt like a dream. A dream she wanted. She wanted back her little things with him, she wanted it all back. Everything.

But how?

When the goal buzzer went off and the crowd started screaming, Elli eyes searched for Shea, when she found him, he wasn't grinning like his teammates; he stood by the bench with no emotion on his face. How was she ever going to apologize? Would be believe her? What if he never wanted anything to do with her? She walked away from him when he poured his heart and soul out to her, yeah it was to find Victoria and get to the bottom of the situation but still. Why would he even want her when all she did was ignore his feeling, not listen to his pleas, and not give him the benefit of the doubt. He was a good man, and all she did was walk away. Elli should have run to him, jumped into his arms while telling him that she still loved him, that she would always love him, that she would never doubt him again.

It was the truth, but would he believe her. She didn't believe him when she should have, so why would he? He had proved that he loved her many times over, but had she ever done that for him? It took her damn near four months just to admit she loved him, so when Elli walked away from him for the fourth time since they been together, she knew she had to of stomped his pride into the ground. Why did she deserve to even have a second chance with him, she wasn't good enough for him. She was selfish, whinny, insecure, he needed someone better.

Even if the thought made Elli's heart break since she wanted to be Shea's forever, she knew she wasn't good enough.

Midway through the third period, Bryan sat down beside Elli, handing her a beer.

"So will I be helping pay for a wedding?" Elli looked over at him, a small smile forming on her face.

"I don't know."

"I'm pretty sure all you gotta do is say you love him and he would marry you tomorrow, hell maybe tonight."

"I don't deserve someone so amazing; look at the crazy freaks I come from."

"Hey now, that's your mother side, your daddy's side ain't crazy." Elli scoffed at that, and smiled when Bryan finished, saying "You're perfect darling, Adler knows that."

"I have issues, I'm crazy, loud, I have a temper, I get sick, and I'll probably always gonna be a little fat. But Papa, even with all them things about me, he still loved me, and when he needed me to believe him, I didn't. When he basically begged me to take him back, I ignored him. Why do I deserve the perfection of a man like that, when I'm far from it?"

Bryan smiled, taking Elli's hand in his large old one, "You've changed Elli."

"No I haven't," she said with her face scrunched up.

"Oh yes, you used to walk this earth with no purpose after leaving New York, but when Shea came into your life, I saw you transform over night. Your eyes were brighter, you wore clothes that fit your body, and you glowed darlin'. You are a ray of sunshine when you are with him. These past couple mouths, you've been a damn storm cloud and I want my sunshine back, so damn it, go get it."

"But he deserves better than me."

"Like hell you say, let me tell you something. When Shea came to ask me for your hand, I said, 'Are you sure?' and you know he said, 'I've never been so sure of something in my whole life'. So obviously, you're perfect to him."

Elli smiled, loving that Shea had asked her Papa too, could he get any better? "I just don't know what to say to him."

"Who said you had to say anything? Just kiss him senseless, y'all seem good at that," Bryan said with a laugh, Elli smile brighten at just the thought of Shea's lips on hers.

"I don't know."

"Well you better figure it out Eleanor Ray, because there is two minutes left in this game and I'm pretty sure Shea won't be happy about going to the cup finals in less he knows you'll be cheering him on."

Elli glanced at the scoreboard, seeing that the guys were up by two and that like Papa had said only two minutes were left. Elli let out a frustrated sigh. She only had two minutes to figure out how she was gonna prove her love to Shea. Bryan stood up, putting his hand on Elli's shoulder.

"Go get your man, baby girl. Y'all deserve each other."

Elli smiled, like always Papa was right. As the seconds counted down, it was like a light bulb went off in Elli's head and she stood up quickly, causing the chair to fall behind her as she sought Papa out.

"I need a microphone."

The Ducks were playing hard, they wanted the chance at the cup just as bad as the Assassins did, but Shea wasn't gonna give it to them. He was mad, hurt, and heartbroken, so when Perry skated by and Shea demolished him into the boards, he didn't even feel the least bit bad. Since this would be his last year as an Assassin he was gonna win this game, and then he would win the cup again before going off to Boston or New York, or wherever. He didn't care as long as he didn't play in this rink ever again, since every time he past the board that held the glass he had broke for Elli, he felt like chips of his heart falling with every glance.

He had to get out of here.

When the final buzzer rung and the crowd went nuts, Shea closed his eyes taking the energy of the crowd. The place was deafening as people screamed, threw their rally towels on the ice, and blew horns, it was crazy. As Shea was wrapped up in a hug from his team mates all he could think about was Elli. Not that he had just won the semifinals in the NHL or that more than likely he would be holding the cup above his head in a week's time.

Nope, just Elli.

Shea was in the middle of the huddle when he heard it. The soft sound, words to a song he knew. A song that he had listen to so many time since watching Elli sing it on the DVD from the play she was in, 'My Man'. He quickly moved out of the huddle, it was easy since everyone started moving out of the way to see who was singing. When Shea saw Elli standing in the middle of the ice in them naughty shorts and thigh high boots, he was unable to breath, think or even move. He just watched, as the woman he loved more than anything on God's green earth sang to him.

Elli eyes was fixed on his as she belted out the notes like she was seventeen with no one but him in the room listening. Not the fourteen thousand that watched as aw struck as he was. Shea was sure that she was better now than she was when she was seventeen. Her voice was mature, beautiful. She was beautiful, and he would never love anyone but her. Shea whole body tingled as she hit the last note, her one hand raised in the air, her other holding the microphone out some as she sung her little heart out. When she took a deep breath, dropping the microphone to her side, opening her eyes to look at Shea, his whole body filled with warmth as he took in a shaky breath before skating towards her as the crowd continued to be boisterous.

When he reached her, Elli looked up at him, her eyes filling quickly with tears. She stood a couple inches away from him, as the tears started to drip down her face.

"You sang for me," Shea said when he could actually form words, she nodded slowly.

"I did," Elli said taking a deep breath. They stood for a good minute only looking into each other eyes as the crowd went nuts around them, but it didn't matter. All that matter was them two at that moment. This was the turning point, she had made the effort. She had said she would never sing for him, and here she was. Beautiful as ever, singing just for him, so there was only one thing to say.

"Elli, I love you baby, more than anything"

She nodded slowly again, and than just feel into him, her arms coming around his chest. Shea caught her holding her tight against him as he pressed his lips to her. The kiss felt like their first. It was intoxicating, the feel of the lips he had missed so much. When she pulled back some to say something, he shook his head before capturing her mouth in such urgency, because nothing beat kissing Elli, especially when he hadn't been able to in months. She came willing, giving him just as much passion as he gave her. When they parted, she looked deep into his eyes, her lips only millimeters from his.

"I love you so much" She said against his lips, his heart banged against his chest at the sound of the words he had missed so much, "So much" she added before joining their mouths again. Shea hands moved from her cheeks, down to her back of her legs, lifting her some so he could deepen the kiss more since he was so much taller than her with his skates on.

Elli pulled back, tears streaming down her face from her sparkling green eyes. "I don't want to be proud no more Shea, I love you, only you. I'm sorry. So sorry."

Shea shook his head, "No baby, don't be sorry. I'm sorry, I should have fought harder."

"No Shea, how much harder could you have fought? I was a complete and utter idiot and I'll own you the rest of my life, I'm so sorry."

Shea smiled, "It's in the past baby, let's start our future." He took a deep breath before pulling the chain out from his jersey, pulling it so it broke causing the silver chain that had been his constant companion to fall to the ice.

"Shea?"

When he held up a ring, looking down at her, the tears came faster down her face as what he was doing sank in, but he was ready.

Shea was ready for his forever with Elli.

"Marry me Elli."

Elli gasped as her hand came over her mouth, knowing what he was about to do and actually hearing him do it was two different things. As she looked into his eyes, he said, "Don't ever leave me again. Love only me, for the rest of our lives. Move into our house, make love to me every night, and make babies with me Elli. Please, because being with you made me a better man, and I could never love anyone the way I love you. So please, marry me."

"Oh Shea," she cried, looking at the beauty of the ring, the pink diamond was sparkling so bright it took her breath away. How did he know that she had dreamed for an untraditional ring especially after the horrid one Justin had given her, but this was not the time to think of Justin. Elli watched as he started to get nervous, which who could blame him, he was asking her to marry him in front of thousands of people during the Stanley Cup Playoffs and all she could do was gape at him.

"But our house was sold," she said sadly since it was the only thing she could get out, he smiled shaking his head.

"Yeah, to me. Do you think I would let something you love go to someone else?"

Elli's body tingled as she looked into his beautiful blue eyes, "So you aren't going anywhere?"

"Not as long as you want me."

"I want you for forever."

"Good, so what do you say?"

She thought for a moment, a small grin on her face. "How many babies we makin'?"

"At least three," he said with a grin, she thought that over for a moment, narrowing her eyes up at him.

"I don't know, three?" she said just to tease him.

"Damn it Elli, say you'll marry me!"

"Oh course! Yes!" Elli said with a giggle as Shea laughed, after letting out the gust of air he was holding. Shea slid the ring down her finger before picking her up kissing her laughing mouth hard. Elli was gonna marry Shea, they were gonna have babies, move into their house, love each other for forever. Her dreams would be her reality.

Elli's heart felt like it was gonna explode at all the love that was filling her as she looked into Shea's sparkling eyes. Elli smiled against his lips as they parted, moving her fingers up into his sweaty hair.

"There's gonna be a fee for that glass," she whispered against his lips. He smiled, biting her bottom lip before saying, "Best two grand I've ever spent."

Epilogue

"I can't find anything!" Elli yelled as she moved through her and Shea's spacious bedroom, tearing into the suitcases that still lay on the floor, three days after they had arrived home from their honey moon in the St. Luca Islands. She was looking for her grey wool hat and couldn't find it anywhere. Elli was running crazy late; she wanted to stop by the hospital to see Harper and new baby Allison before heading into the office since she had a meeting of her own with Shea later that afternoon.

"Baby, what are you looking for?" Shea asked as he came out the shower with a towel wrapped around his waist, his razor in one hand, Elli's mouth watered at the sight.

"My hat! The wool one," she said throwing clothes over her shoulder as she looked through the suitcases again. If she left that damn hat at the resort in the islands, she would cry. She loved that hat.

"Baby, it's in the truck."

Oh yeah.

When Shea's arms came around Elli waist she smiled, running her hands over his forearms before turning his arms looking up into his eyes. "Are you gonna go see Allison today?" he asked as he nibbled on her neck.

"I am," Elli said breathlessly before Shea ran his tongue right under her ear, taking her ear lobe into his mouth.

"How much time do you have?" he whispered in her ear while his hands came down over her ass, pressing her into his hard length. The man never quit...not that she would ask him too.

"Mmm, five minutes top."

Elli was on flat on her back before 'minutes' left her lips.

Forty five minutes later, Elli rushed through the house, fixing her clothes as she looked for her brief case. Elli couldn't say no to Shea if her life depended on it, not that she really wanted to say no.

Elli walked into the kitchen that they had painted while they were in St Luca, to get her coffee as she admired the color, a pale green. The people Shea had hired to do the home décor were doing such a wonderful job, Elli loved it. She loved their home.

Elli found her brief case and cut through the dining room to the living room, glancing up at the large portrait of Elli and Shea in front of the Belmont Mansion. Elli's gown was sparking, magnificent in the bright fall sun while Shea's black tux looked refined. Even with his damn chucks, Shea still looked dashing, and he was all hers.

For forever.

"Honey I'm going!" Elli yelled as she slid her feet into her heels. Shea came around the corner, only a pair of boxers on as he walked with a little pep to his step. The man drove her mad. He grinned as he wrapped her up in his arms, kissing her softly on his lips.

"Give Allison a kiss for me, and I'll see you at twelve right?"

"Yup, when are your momma and daddy gonna be here?"

"Four-ish I think? Grace is pissed they are staying with us and not her."

Elli laughed, her new sister in law became jealous so damn easily, "They haven't stay in the new house yet, Grace will be okay. Hell, invite her to stay too. Ryan would love to stay in his room."

Shea smiled, kissing the side of her mouth, "I will."

"Alright, love ya."

"Love you more. Have a good day."

"Will do," Elli said with a grin before she walked past the picture of her and Shea in front of the Cup the Assassins had won a week after they had gotten back together. What a great day it was, she sat in her seats at every home game and went to all the away games, cheering on her fiancé. It was one of the greatest feelings ever, watching her man hold that cup over his head. Elli couldn't ask for anything better than what she had, she was so happy, she walked around with a permanent grin on her face.

Elli got into her truck and drove around the circular driveway, going the way towards the hospital. After stopping to get flowers in the gift shop for Allison, Elli made her way up to the maternity wing. Since her and Shea had been there yesterday, Elli knew where to go. When she entered the room, Harper stood with sweet baby Allison in her arms, walking back and forth in front of the bed. Harper looked up at Elli with a freaked out expression on her face.

"I'm fu-screwed Elli."

Elli giggled, laying the flowers on the table beside the bed, and then heading to look at the bundle of pink in Harper's arms. Allison was red from where she had been crying, Elli could tell she was a little fussy.

"Why, what's wrong?"

"She's just like me and she's only a day old!"

"Harper, she is beautiful, perfect. She's probably just hungry."

"See that's where I say she's Jakob's baby, she eats all the damn time!"

They both looked down at Allison's beautiful little pink face, and Elli smiled as Harper just looked scared out of her mind.

"Aw, she's sweet."

"Whatever, you're just blinded by the cuteness."

"Probably," Elli agreed as she took the baby in her arms, loving the feel of something so sweet and perfect resting in her arms.

"Did you tell him yet?"

Elli laid her lips softly to Allison's forehead before shaking her head, "Not yet."

"But you will today right?"

"Yeah, when he signs the contract today, he'll see."

"Good," Harper said just as Jakob entered the room, decked out in his 'I'm a daddy' shirt.

"Elli! Where's Shea?"

Elli smiled as Jakob took Allison from her, kissing her head. "He's doing yard work or something, I don't know."

"Cool, he should have come. Ally misses her *Godfather*," Jakob said with a laugh as Elli and Harper shook their heads. The ongoing joke of Shea being the 'Godfather' was about to get on Elli's last nerve. She didn't know if it was the way they said it or just the fact that when Shea was in the room, he was the 'Godfather' not Shea. Elli couldn't really be mad though because bless their hearts they were just so excited to have Allison finally, and so was she.

Elli watched as Harper snuggled close to Jakob, both of them looking down at beautiful Allison, nothing but love in their eyes for their perfect bundle of perfection. Elli wanted that moment, she wanted her baby. Elli started to feel like she was interfering in a private moment, so she gathered her things.

"I hate to run guys, but I gotta get to the office."

Harper looked up, while Jakob was still memorized by the beauty of his daughter, "Oh no, don't go yet."

"I have too. I love you guys," Elli said hugging Harper tightly. She went over to Jakob, kissing his cheek before laying a soft one on Allison.

"She's beautiful huh?" Jakob asked, Elli grinned up at him.

"Most beautiful baby ever."

Jakob grinned big at Elli before walking with Allison to the little chair in the corner.

"Call me later, you know, afterwards," Harper said as she wobbled with her to the door.

"Will do, congratulations again Harp, she's gorgeous."

"Thanks, she gets that from me."

Elli left laughing, everything was so perfect.

 Or at least it would be after Elli's meeting with Shea.

"Mr. Adler, Mrs. Adler will see you now," Janet, Elli's assistant said. Shea rolled his eyes as he got up, walking into Elli's office. Why he had to wait to see his wife was beyond him, but whatever. Elli grinned up at him when he entered, and he couldn't help but grin back. She would forever be the most beautiful woman in the world to him. He loved her more with every day that passed, and he couldn't wait to spend the rest of his life with her.

They had only been married a week, but it felt like forever. The wedding was magical, the honeymoon perfect, now it was time to start their lives together. Grow old; raise their children when they finally decided to have some, and to just be together as man and wife. Shea knew when he set eyes on her so long ago that she was the one, and he just loved when he was right.

"Hey baby," he said, leaning over the desk to place a kiss on her lips, she smiled as they parted.

"Hey," she cooed as he sat back in the chair in front of her desk.

"Where's everyone at?" Shea asked, Bryan wasn't there, neither was Damon.

"I figured we could do this between us."

Shea's body filled with lust, something that always happen when his hot little wife was around, he gave her a seductive grin before saying, "Let's just skip it then, come over here, let me show you the benefits of signing and being married to this hockey player."

"Hush Shea! Janet might hear you!"

"When did we ever care about people hearing us?"

Elli turned deep red, "If you don't hush, I won't be showing you the benefits of having me as your wife and boss when I get home." Shea gave her an amused grin and nodded his head.

"Okay, so where's the contract? I need to get home, do some more yard work."

Elli smiled as she moved the file across the desk to him; he picked up a pen, signing the bottom without reading it and handing it back to his sexy little wife. He didn't care what it said, she could be paying him a hundred dollars a game and he would still play. As long as he stayed in Nashville, with her, he didn't care about the money. He had more than enough, and so did she, they would be more than comfortable for the rest of their lives.

When he looked up, Elli narrowed her eyes as she crossed her arms. "You didn't even read it."

"I trust you."

"That's not the point; you didn't look at the length of the contract or the reasoning."

"Huh?" he asked pulling the contract towards him, "What do you mean length?" He wasn't expecting a time length, he just assumed he would be indefinite, or until he wanted to retired. He read it over, it was the same information every other contract he had ever had had, but at the bottom, it said the length was only for a year. "A year?" he asked, than he changed the page over to the reason. It was in her handwriting, not typed in.

We're pregnant.

Shea actually felt like the world had came out from under his feet. His heart started to races as his fingers splayed against Elli's desk.

They were pregnant?

He started to feel light head as Elli just grinned at him.

"You're pregnant?"

She smiled, nodding her head. "I am, and since you said you want to retire when we had kids, I thought the contract should only be a year."

He wasn't listening to the last part she said, he was stuck on, 'I am'. "You're pregnant with a baby?"

She laughed, "No Shea, I'm pregnant with a hockey puck! Yes I'm pregnant with a baby, your baby."

A heavy feeling filled his stomach as he struggled to speak, "I'm gonna be a daddy?"

Elli nodded again, tears welling up in her eyes. "Yes, and I have a feeling you'll be the best."

A shaky, slow smile started to build as the surprise sank in, he was going to be a daddy. He stood, coming around the desk, pulling her up into his arms, before kissing her hard. When he pulled back and looked down at her as big wet tears streamed down her face. He felt like his was soon to follow, he had never been this happy.

A baby, their baby.

"We're having a baby."

"We are Shea, and I couldn't be happier."

Shea lifted her into his arms, kissing her lavishly. As they parted, Shea grinned against her lips. "Oh baby, I love you."

"Not as much as I love you."

Acknowledgments

There are some people in my life that I need to thank.

First, my husband, Michael. No one will ever love me the way you does. You are my Shea Adler. My heart races at even the sight of you even after fourteen years of being together. You have been nothing but supportive through this whole process and I wouldn't be the woman I am today without you. I love you baby, thank you for the support.

My children, Mikey and Alyssa, y'all are my heart and soul, and I love you both so much, even when y'all are fighting while I'm trying to write.

Nick, you're not my son, but I love you like one. Thank you for always being there, and for the support. I love you.

My mom, I wouldn't have started writing if you didn't introduce me to books at such a young age. You've always encouraged me to do the things I wanted to do, and for that I love you and I thank you from the bottom of my heart.

Noey, you've made fun of my porno for women but look at me now, I'm writing you telling you I love you in my acknowledgements....I know I can't believe it either!

Janet, what do I say to the person that I have cried, screamed, cried, and complained too when I thought I couldn't do this? You have been my rock through this writing process, and I truly love you. Thank you so much, and I swear one of my next books will be dedicated to you!

Susie, thank you from the bottom of my heart for all your help and love through this process, you have been so patient with me and I truly do love you! I always have and always well!

My girls, Jackie, Kristi, Tera, Althea, and Barbie Y'all are the very first people that read my book, and I will always love you guys. Thank you for the support, the criticism, and just being there for me. Y'all will always hold a special place in my heart.

My Booksie girls, y'all rock!!! I will always love you guys because y'all were the very first people other than my girls to read my book! Your comments made me keep writing when I felt like I couldn't do it. Your support has made me the writer I am today and I couldn't thank you enough. Thank you.

Printed in Great Britain
by Amazon.co.uk, Ltd.,
Marston Gate.